JACK HIGGINS

JACK HIGGINS

HELL IS ALWAYS TODAY

TOLL FOR THE BRAVE

THE VALHALLA EXCHANGE

INDEX

This edition published in 1995 by Index
Unit 1, A1/M1 Centre, Garrard Way, Kettering, NN16 8TD

1 3 5 7 9 10 8 6 4 2

ISBN 1-85868-073-5

Printed in Great Britain

Contents

Hell Is Always Today

Prologue

The police car turned the end of the street and pulled into the kerb beside the lamp. The driver kept the motor running, and grinned at his passenger.

'Rather you than me on a night like this, but I was forgetting. You love your work, don't you?'

Police Constable Henry Joseph Dwyer's reply was unprintable and he stood at the edge of the pavement, a strangely melancholy figure in the helmet and cape, listening to the sound of the car fade into the night. Rain fell steadily, drifting down through the yellow glow of the street lamp in a silver spray and he turned morosely and walked towards the end of the street.

It was just after ten and the night stretched before him, cold and damp. The city was lonely and for special reasons at that time, rather frightening even for an old hand like Joe Dwyer. Still, no point in worrying about that. Another ten months and he'd be out of it, but his hand still moved inside his cape to touch the small two-way radio in his breast pocket, the lifeline that could bring help when needed within a matter of minutes.

He paused on the corner and looked across the square towards the oasis of light that was the coffee stall on the other side. No harm in starting off with something warm inside him and he needed some cigarettes.

There was only one customer, a large, heavily built man

9

in an old trenchcoat and rain hat who was talking to Sam Harkness, the owner. As Dwyer approached, the man turned, calling goodnight over his shoulder and plunged into the rain head down so that he and the policeman collided.

'Steady on there,' Dwyer began and then recognised him. 'Oh, it's you, Mr. Faulkner. Nasty night, sir.'

Faulkner grinned. 'You can say that again. I only came out for some cigarettes. Hope they're paying you double time tonight.'

'That'll be the day, sir.'

Faulkner walked away and Dwyer approached the stall. 'He's in a hurry, isn't he?'

Harkness filled a mug with tea from the urn, spooned sugar into it and pushed it across. 'Wouldn't you be if you was on your way home to a warm bed on a night like this? Probably got some young bird lying there in her underwear waiting for him. They're all the same these artists.'

Dwyer grinned. 'You're only jealous. Let's have twenty of the usual. Must have something to get me through the night. How's business?'

Harkness passed the cigarettes across and changed the ten-shilling note that Dwyer gave him. 'Lucky if I make petrol money.'

'I'm not surprised. You won't get many people out on a night like this.'

Harkness nodded. 'It wouldn't be so bad if I still had the Toms, but they're all working from their flats at the moment with some muscle minding the door if they've got any sense. All frightened off by this Rainlover geezer.'

Dwyer lit a cigarette and cupped it inside his left hand. 'He doesn't worry you?'

Harkness shrugged. 'He isn't after the likes of me, that's

for certain, though how any woman in her right mind can go out at the moment on a night when it's raining beats me.' He picked up the evening paper. 'Look at this poor bitch he got in the park last night. Peggy Nolan. She's been on the game round here for years. Nice little Irish woman. Fifty if she was a day. Never harmed anyone in her life.' He put the paper down angrily. 'What about you blokes, anyway? When are you going to do something?'

The voice of the public, worried, frightened and looking for a scapegoat. Dwyer nipped his cigarette and slipped it back into the packet. 'We'll get him, Sam. He'll overreach himself. These nut-cases always do.'

Which didn't sound very convincing even to himself and Harkness laughed harshly. 'And how many more women are going to die before that happens, tell me that?'

His words echoed back to him flatly on the night air as Dwyer moved away into the night. Harkness watched him go, listening to the footsteps fade and there was only the silence and beyond the pool of light, the darkness seemed to move in towards him. He swallowed hard, fighting back the fear that rose inside, switched on the radio and lit a cigarette.

Joe Dwyer moved through the night at a measured pace, the only sound the echo of his own step between the tall Victorian terraces that pressed in on either side. Occasionally he paused to flash his lamp into a doorway and once he checked the side door of a house which was by day the offices of a grocery wholesaler.

These things he did efficiently because he was a good policeman, but more as a reflex action than anything else. He was cold and the rain trickled down his neck soaking

11

into his shirt and he still had seven hours to go, but he was also feeling rather depressed, mainly because of Harkness. The man was frightened of course, but who wasn't? The trouble was that people saw too much television. They were conditioned to expect their murders to be neatly solved in fifty-two minutes plus advertising time.

He flashed his lamp into the entry called Dob Court a few yards from the end of the street hardly bothering to pause, then froze. The beam rested on a black leather boot, travelled across stockinged legs, skirt rucked up wantonly, and came to rest on the face of a young woman. The head was turned sideways at an awkward angle in a puddle of water, eyes staring into eternity.

And he wasn't afraid, that was the strange thing. He took a quick step forward, dropping to one knee and touched her face gently with the back of his hand. It was still warm, which could only mean one thing on a night like this. . . .

He was unable to take his reasoning any further. There was the scrape of a foot on stone. As he started to rise, his helmet was knocked off and he was struck a violent blow on the back of the head. He cried out, falling across the body of the girl, and someone ran along the entry behind him and turned into the street.

He could feel blood, warm and sticky, mingling with the rain as it ran across his face and the darkness moved in on him. He fought it off, breathing deeply, his hand going inside his cape to the two-way radio in his breast pocket.

Even after he had made contact and knew that help was on its way, he held on to consciousness with all his strength, only letting go at the precise moment that the first police car turned the corner at the end of the street.

One

It had started to rain in the late evening, lightly at first, but increasing to a heavy, drenching downpour as darkness fell. A wind that, from the feel of it, came all the way from the North Sea, drove the rain before it across the roofs of the city to rattle against the enormous glass window that stood at one end of Bruno Faulkner's studio.

The studio was a great barn of a room which took up the entire top floor of a five storey Victorian wool merchant's town house, now converted into flats. Inside a fire burned in a strangely mediaeval fireplace giving the only light, and on a dais against the window four great shapes, Faulkner's latest commission, loomed menacingly.

There was a ring at the door bell and then another.

After a while, an inner door beyond the fireplace opened and Faulkner appeared in shirt and pants, a little dishevelled for he had been sleeping. He switched on the light and paused by the fire for a moment, mouth widening in a yawn. He was a large, rather fleshy man of thirty whose face carried the habitually arrogant expression of the sort of creative artist who believes that he exists by a kind of divine right. As the bell sounded again he frowned petulantly, moved to the door and opened it.

'All right, all right, I can hear you.' He smiled suddenly. 'Oh, it's you, Jack.'

The elegant young man who leaned against the wall

outside, a finger held firmly against the bell push, grinned. 'What kept you?'

Faulkner turned and Jack Morgan followed him inside and closed the door. He was about Faulkner's age, but looked younger and wore evening dress, a light overcoat with a velvet collar draped across his shoulders.

He examined Faulkner dispassionately as the other man helped himself to a cigarette from a silver box and lit it. 'You look bloody awful, Bruno.'

'I love you too,' Faulkner said and crossed to the fire.

Morgan looked down at the telephone which stood on a small coffee table. The receiver was off the hook and he replaced it casually. 'I thought so. I've been trying to get through for the past couple of hours.'

Faulkner shrugged. 'I've been working for two days non-stop. When I finished I took the phone off the hook and went to bed. What did you want? Something important?'

'It's Joanna's birthday, or had you forgotten? She sent me to get you.'

'Oh, my God, I had—completely. No chance that I've missed the party I suppose?'

'I'm afraid not. It's only eight o'clock.'

'Pity. I suppose she's collected the usual bunch of squares.' He frowned suddenly. 'I haven't even got her a present.'

Morgan produced a slim leather case from one pocket and threw it across. 'Pearl necklace . . . seventy-five quid. I got it at Humbert's and told them to put it on your account.'

'Bless you, Jack,' Faulkner said. 'The best fag I ever had.'

He walked towards the bedroom door and Morgan turned to examine the figures on the dais. They were life-

14

size, obviously feminine, but in the manner of Henry Moore's early work had no individual identity. They possessed a curious group menace that made him feel decidedly uneasy.

'I see you've added another figure,' he said. 'I thought you'd decided that three was enough?'

Faulkner shrugged. 'When I started five weeks ago I thought one would do and then it started to grow. The damned thing just won't stop.'

Morgan moved closer. 'It's magnificent, Bruno. The best thing you've ever done.'

Faulkner shook his head. 'I'm not sure. There's still something missing. A group's got to have balance . . . perfect balance. Maybe it needs another figure.'

'Surely not?'

'When it's right, I'll know. I'll feel it and it's not right yet. Still, that can wait. I'd better get dressed.'

He went into the bedroom and Morgan lit a cigarette and called to him, 'What do you think of the latest Rainlover affair?'

'Don't tell me he's chopped another one? How many is that—four?'

Morgan picked up a newspaper that was lying on a chair by the fire. 'Should be in the paper.' He leafed through it quickly and shook his head. 'No, this is no good. It's yesterday evening's and she wasn't found till nine o'clock.'

'Where did it happen?' Faulkner said as he emerged from the bedroom, pulling on a corduroy jacket over a polo neck sweater.

'Not far from Jubilee Park.' Morgan looked up and frowned. 'Aren't you dressing?'

'What do you call this?'

'You know what I mean.'

15

'Who for, that bunch of stuffed shirts? Not on your life. When Joanna and I got engaged she agreed to take me exactly as I am and this is me, son.' He picked up a trench-coat and draped it over his shoulders. 'I know one thing, I need a drink before I can face that lot.'

'There isn't time,' Morgan said flatly.

'Rubbish. We have to pass The King's Arms don't we? There's always time.'

'All right, all right,' Morgan said. 'I surrender, but just one. Remember that.'

Faulkner grinned, looking suddenly young and amiable and quite different. 'Scouts' honour. Now let's get moving.'

He switched off the light and they went out.

.   .   .   .

When Faulkner and Morgan entered the saloon bar of The King's Arms it was deserted except for the landlord, Harry Meadows, a genial bearded man in his mid-fifties, who leaned on the bar reading a newspaper. He glanced up, then folded the newspaper and put it down.

' 'Evening, Mr. Faulkner . . . Mr. Morgan.'

' 'Evening, Harry,' Faulkner said. 'Two double brandies.'

Morgan cut in quickly. 'Better make mine a single, Harry. I'm driving.'

Faulkner took out a cigarette and lit it as Meadows gave two glasses a wipe and filled them. 'Quiet tonight.'

'It's early yet,' Morgan said.

Meadows pushed the drinks across. 'I won't see many tonight, you mark my words.' He turned the newspaper towards them so that they could read the headline *Rain-lover strikes again*. 'Not with this bastard still on the

16

loose. Every time it rains he's at it. I'd like to know what the bloody police are supposed to be doing.'

Faulkner swallowed some of his brandy and looked down at the newspaper. 'The Rainlover—I wonder which bright boy dreamed that one up.'

'I bet his editor gave him a fifty pound bonus on the spot.'

'He's probably creeping out at night every time it rains and adding to the score personally, just to keep the story going.' Faulkner chuckled and emptied his glass.

Meadows shook his head. 'It gives me the shakes, I can tell you. I know one thing . . . you won't find many women on the streets tonight.'

Behind them the door swung open unexpectedly and a young woman came in. She was perhaps nineteen or twenty and well made with the sort of arrogant boldness about the features that many men like, but which soon turns to coarseness. She wore a black plastic mac, a red mini-skirt and knee-length leather boots. She looked them over coolly, unbuttoning her coat with one hand, then sauntered to the other end of the bar and hoisted herself on to a stool. When she crossed her legs, her skirt slid all the way up to her stocking tops. She took a cheap compact from her bag and started to repair the rain damage on her face.

'There's someone who doesn't give a damn for a start,' Faulkner observed.

Morgan grinned. 'Perhaps she doesn't read the papers. I wonder what the Rainlover would do to her?'

'I know what I'd like to do to her.'

Meadows shook his head. 'Her kind of custom I can do without.'

Faulkner was immediately interested. 'Is she on the game then?'

Meadows shrugged. 'What do you think?'

'What the hell, Harry, she needs bread like the rest of us. Live and let live.' Faulkner pushed his glass across. 'Give her a drink on me and I'll have a re-fill while you're at it.'

'As you say, Mr. Faulkner.'

He walked to the other end of the bar and spoke to the young woman who turned, glanced briefly at Faulkner, then nodded. Meadows poured her a large gin and tonic.

Faulkner watched her closely and Morgan tapped him on the shoulder. 'Come on now, Bruno. Don't start getting involved. We're late enough as it is.'

'You worry too much.'

The girl raised her glass and he toasted her back. She made an appealing, rather sexy picture sitting there on the high stool in her mod outfit and he laughed suddenly.

'What's so funny?' Morgan demanded.

'I was just thinking what a sensation there would be if we took her with us.'

'To Joanna's party? Sensation isn't the word.'

Faulkner grinned. 'I can see the look on Aunt Mary's weatherbeaten old face now—the mouth tightening like a dried prune. A delightful thought.'

'Forget it, Bruno,' Morgan said sharply. 'Even you couldn't get away with that.'

Faulkner glanced at him, the lazy smile disappearing at once. 'Oh, couldn't I?'

Morgan grabbed at his sleeve, but Faulkner pulled away sharply and moved along the bar to the girl. He didn't waste any time in preliminaries.

'All on your own then?'

The girl shrugged. 'I'm supposed to be waiting for somebody.' She had an accent that was a combination of Liverpool and Irish and not unpleasant.

'Anyone special?'

'My fiancé.'

Faulkner chuckled. 'Fiancés are only of secondary importance. I should know. I'm one myself.'

'Is that a fact?' the girl said.

Her handbag was lying on the bar, a large and ostentatious letter G in one corner bright against the shiny black plastic. Faulkner picked it up and looked at her enquiringly.

'G for . . .?'

'Grace.'

'How delightfully apt. Well, G for Grace, my friend and I are going on to a party. It occurred to me that you might like to come with us.'

'What kind of a party?'

Faulkner nodded towards Morgan. 'Let's put it this way. He's dressed for it, I'm not.'

The girl didn't even smile. 'Sounds like fun. All right, Harold can do without it tonight. He should have been here at seven-thirty anyway.'

'But you weren't here yourself at seven-thirty, were you?'

She frowned in some surprise. 'What's that got to do with it?'

'A girl after my own heart.' Faulkner took her by the elbow and moved towards Morgan who grinned wryly.

'I'm Jack and he's Bruno. He won't have told you that.'

She raised an eyebrow. 'How did you know?'

'Experience . . . mostly painful.'

'We can talk in the car,' Faulkner said. 'Now let's get moving.'

As they turned to the door, it opened and a young man entered, his hands pushed into the pockets of a hip-length tweed coat with a cheap fur collar. He had a narrow white face, long dark hair and a mouth that seemed to be twisted into an expression of perpetual sullenness.

He hesitated, frowning, then looked enquiringly at the girl. 'What gives?'

Grace shrugged. 'Sorry, Harold, you're too late. I've made other arrangements.'

She took a single step forward and he grabbed her arm. 'What's the bloody game?'

Faulkner pulled him away with ease. 'Hands off, sonny.'

Harold turned in blind rage and swung one wild punch that might have done some damage had it ever landed. Faulkner blocked the arm, then grabbed the young man's hand in an aikido grip and forced him to the ground, his face remaining perfectly calm.

'Down you go, there's a good dog.'

Grace started to laugh and Harry Meadows came round the bar fast. 'That's enough, Mr. Faulkner. That's enough.'

Faulkner released him and Harold scrambled to his feet, face twisted with pain, something close to tears in his eyes.

'Go on then, you cow,' he shouted. 'Get out of it. I never want to see you again.'

Grace shrugged. 'Suit yourself.'

Faulkner took her by the arm and they went out laughing. Morgan turned to Meadows, his face grave. 'I'm sorry about that.'

Meadows shook his head. 'He doesn't change, does he, Mr. Morgan? I don't want to see him in here again—okay?'

Morgan sighed helplessly, turned and went after the others and Meadows gave some attention to Harold who stood nursing his hand, face twisted with pain and hate.

'You know you did ask for it, lad, but he's a nasty piece

of work that one when he gets started. You're well out of it. Come on, I'll buy you a drink on the house.'

'Oh, stuff your drink, you stupid old bastard,' Harold said viciously and the door swung behind him as he plunged wildly into the night.

Two

Detective Sergeant Nicholas Miller was tired and it showed in his face as he went down the steps to the tiled entrance hall of the Marsden Wing of the General Infirmary. He paused to light a cigarette and the night sister watched him for a moment before emerging from her glass office. Like many middle-aged women she had a weakness for handsome young men. Miller intrigued her particularly for the dark blue Swedish trenchcoat and continental raincap gave him a strange foreign air which was hardly in keeping with his profession. Certainly anything less like the conventional idea of a policeman would have been hard to imagine.

'How did you find Mr. Grant tonight?' she asked as she came out of her office.

'Decidedly restless.' Miller's face was momentarily illuminated by a smile of great natural charm. 'And full of questions.'

Detective Superintendent Bruce Grant, head of the city's Central C.I.D., had been involved in a car accident earlier in the week and now languished in a hospital bed with a dislocated hip. Misfortune enough considering that Grant had been up to his ears in the most important case

21

of his career. Doubly unfortunate in that it now left in sole charge of the case Detective Chief Superintendent George Mallory of Scotland Yard's Murder Squad, the expert his superiors had insisted on calling in, in response to the growing public alarm as the Rainlover still continued at large.

'I'll tell you something about policemen, Sister,' Miller said. 'They don't like other people being brought in to handle things that have happened on their patch. To an old hand like Bruce Grant, the introduction of Scotland Yard men to a case he's been handling himself is a personal insult. Has Mallory been in today, by the way?'

'Oh yes, but just to see Inspector Craig. I don't think he called in on Superintendent Grant.'

'He wouldn't,' Miller said. 'There's no love lost there at all. Grant's one satisfaction is that Craig was in the car with him when the accident happened which leaves Mallory on his own in the midst of the heathen. How is Craig?'

'Poorly,' she said. 'A badly fractured skull.'

'Serves him right for coming North.'

'Now then, Sergeant, I was a Londoner myself twenty years ago.'

'And I bet you thought that north of High Barnet we rolled boulders on to travellers as they passed by.'

He grinned wickedly and the night sister said, 'It's a change to see you smile. They work you too hard. When did you last have a day off?'

'A day? You must be joking, but I'm free now till six a.m. As it happens, I've had an invitation to a party, but I'd break it for you.'

She was unable to keep her pleasure at the compliment from showing on her pleasant face and gave him a little push. 'Go on, get out of it. I'm a respectable married woman.'

22

'In that case I will. Don't do anything I would.' He smiled again and went out through the swing doors.

She stood there in the half-light, listening to the sound of the car engine dwindle into the distance, then turned with a sigh, went back into her office and picked up a book.

.   .   .

Nick Miller had met Joanna Hartmann only once at a dinner party at his brother's place. The circumstances had been slightly unusual in that he had been in bed in his flat over the garage block at the rear of the house when his brother had arrived to shake him back to reality with the demand that he get dressed at once and come to dinner. Miller, who had not slept for approximately thirty hours, had declined with extreme impoliteness until his brother indicated that he wished him to partner a national television idol who had the nation by the throat twice-weekly as the smartest lady barrister in the game. It seemed that her fiancé had failed to put in an appearance, which put a completely different complexion on the whole thing. Miller had got dressed in three minutes flat.

The evening had been interesting and instructive. Like most actresses, she had proved to be not only intelligent, but a good conversationalist and for her part she had been intrigued to discover that her host's handsome and elegant younger brother was a policeman.

A pleasant evening, but nothing more, for a considerable amount of her conversation had concerned her fiancé, Bruno Faulkner the sculptor, who had followed her north when she had signed to do her series for Northern Television and Nick Miller was not a man to waste his time up blind alleys.

23

Under the circumstances her invitation was something of a surprise, but it had certainly come at the right moment. A little life and laughter was just what he needed. Something to eat, a couple of stiff drinks and then home to bed or perhaps to someone else's? You never knew your luck where show people were concerned.

She had the top flat in Dereham Court, a new luxury block not far from his own home and he could hear cool music drifting from a half-open window as he parked the green Mini-Cooper and went up the steps into the hall.

She opened the door to him herself, a tall, elegant blonde in a superb black velvet trouser suit who looked startlingly like her public image. When she greeted him, he might have been the only person in the world.

'Why Nick, darling, I was beginning to think you weren't going to make it.'

He took off his coat and cap and handed them to the maid. 'I nearly didn't. First evening off for a fortnight.'

She nodded knowingly. 'I suppose you must be pretty busy at the moment.' She turned to the handsome greying man who hovered at her elbow, a glass in one hand. 'Nick's a detective, Frank. You'll know his brother, by the way. Jack Miller. He's a director of Northern Television. This is Frank Marlowe, my agent, Nick.'

Marlowe thawed perceptibly. 'Why, this is real nice,' he said with a faint American accent. 'Had lunch with your brother and a few people at the Midland only yesterday. Let me get you a drink.'

As he moved away, Joanna took Miller's arm and led him towards a white-haired old lady in a silver lamé gown who sat on a divan against the wall watching the world go by. She had the face of the sort of character actress you've seen a thousand times on film and television and yet can never put a name to. She turned out to be Mary

Beresford, Joanna's aunt, and Miller was introduced in full. He resisted an insane impulse to click his heels and kiss the hand that she held out to him, for the party was already turning out to be very different from what he had imagined.

That it was a very superior sort of soirée couldn't be denied, but on the whole, the guests were older rather than younger, the men in evening wear, the women exquisitely gowned. Certainly there were no swinging young birds from the television studios in evidence—a great disappointment. Cool music played softly, one or two couples were dancing and there was a low murmur of conversation.

'What about the Rainlover then, Sergeant Miller?' Mary Beresford demanded.

The way she said sergeant made him sound like a lavatory attendant and she'd used the voice she kept for grand dowager parts.

'What about him?' he said belligerently.

'When are you going to catch him?' She said it with all the patience of an infant teacher explaining the school rules to a rather backward child on his first day. 'After all, there are enough of you.'

'I know, Mrs. Beresford,' Miller said. 'We're pretty hot on parking tickets, but not so good on maniacs who walk the streets on wet nights murdering women.'

'There's no need to be rude, Sergeant,' she said frostily.

'Oh, but I'm not.' Behind him Joanna Hartmann moved in anxiously, Frank Marlowe at her shoulder. Miller leaned down and said, 'You see the difficulty about this kind of case is that the murderer could be anyone, Mrs. Beresford. Your own husband—your brother even.' He nodded around the room. 'Any one of the men here.' There was an expression of real alarm on her face, but he didn't

25

let go. 'What about Mr. Marlowe, for instance?'

He slipped an edge of authority into his voice and said to Marlowe, 'Would you care to account for your movements between the hours of eight and nine last night, sir? I must warn you, of course, that anything you say may be taken down and used in evidence.'

Mary Beresford gave a shocked gasp, Marlowe looked decidedly worried and at that precise moment the record on the stereogram came to an end.

Joanna Hartmann grabbed Miller's arm. 'Come and play the piano for us.' She pulled him away and called brightly over her shoulder to Marlowe who stood there, a drink in each hand, mouth gaping. 'He's marvellous. You'd swear it was Oscar Peterson.'

Miller was angry, damned angry, but not only at Mary Beresford. She couldn't help being the woman she was, but he was tired of the sort of vicious attack on the police that met him every time he picked up a newspaper, tired of cheap remarks and jibes about police inefficiency from members of the public who didn't seem to appreciate that every detective who could be spared had been working ninety to a hundred hours a week since the Rainlover had first killed, in an attempt to root him out. But how did you find one terrifyingly insane human being in a city of three-quarters of a million? A man with no record, who did not kill for gain, who did not even kill for sexual reasons. Someone who just killed out of some dark compulsion that even the psychiatrists hadn't been able to help them with.

The piano was the best, a Bechstein grand and he sat down, swallowed the double gin and tonic that Marlowe handed him and moved into a cool and complicated version of 'The Lady is a Tramp'. One or two people came across to stand at the piano watching, because they knew talent when they heard it and playing a good jazz piano was Miller's greatest love. He moved from one number into another. It was perhaps fifteen minutes later when he heard the door bell chime.

'Probably Jack and Bruno,' Joanna said to Marlowe. 'I'll get it.'

Miller had a clear view of the door as she crossed the room. He looked down at the keyboard again and as he slowed to the end of his number, Mary Beresford gave a shocked gasp.

When Miller turned, a spectacularly fleshy-looking young tart in black plastic mac, mini-skirt and knee-length leather boots stood at the top of the steps beside the maid who had apparently got to the door before Joanna. A couple of men moved into the room behind her. It was pretty obvious which was Bruno Faulkner from what Miller had heard, and it was just as obvious what the man was up to as he helped the girl off with her coat and looked quickly around the room, a look of eager expectancy on his face.

Strangely enough it was the girl Miller felt sorry for. She was pretty enough in her own way and very, very nubile with that touch of raw cynicism common to the sort of young woman who has slept around too often and too early. She tilted her chin in a kind of bravado as she looked about her, but she was going to be hurt, that much was obvious. Quite suddenly Miller knew with complete certainty that he didn't like Bruno Faulkner one little bit. He lit a cigarette and started to play—'Blue Moon'.

Of course Joanna Hartmann carried it all off superbly as he knew she would. She walked straight up to Faulkner, kissed him on the cheek and said, 'Hello, darling, what kept you?'

'I've been working, Joanna,' Faulkner told her. 'But I'll tell you about that later. First, I'd like you to meet Grace. I hope you don't mind us bringing her along.'

'Of course not.' She turned to Grace with her most charming smile. 'Hello, my dear.'

The girl stared at her open-mouthed. 'But you're Joanna Hartmann. I've seen you on the telly.' Her voice had dropped into a whisper. 'I saw your last film.'

'I hope you enjoyed it.' Joanna smiled sweetly at Morgan. 'Jack, be an angel. Get Grace a drink and introduce her to one or two people. See she enjoys herself.'

'Glad to, Joanna.' Morgan guided the girl away expertly, sat her in a chair by the piano. 'I'll get you a drink. Back in a jiffy.'

She sat there looking hopelessly out of place. The attitude of the other guests was what interested Miller most. Some of the women were amused in a rather condescending way, others quite obviously highly indignant at having to breathe the same air. Most of the men on the other hand glanced at her covertly with a sort of lascivious approval. Morgan seemed to be taking his time and she put a hand to her hair nervously and tilted her chin at an ageing white-haired lady who looked her over as if she were a lump of dirt.

Miller liked her for that. She was getting the worst kind of raw deal from people who ought to know better, but seldom did, and she was damned if she was going to let them grind her down. He caught her eye and grinned. 'Anything you'd like to hear?'

She crossed to the piano and one or two people who had been standing there moved away. 'What about "St. Louis Blues"?' she said. 'I like that.'

'My pleasure. What's your name?'

'Grace Packard.'

He moved into a solid, pushing arrangement of the great jazz classic that had her snapping her fingers. 'That's the greatest,' she cried, eyes shining. 'Do you do this for a living?'

He shook his head. 'Kicks, that's all. I couldn't stand the kind of life the pro musicians lead. One night stands till the early hours, tour after tour and all at the union rate. No icing on that kind of cake.'

'I suppose not. Do you come here often?'

'First time.'

'I thought so,' she grinned with a sort of gamin charm. 'A right bunch of zombies.'

Morgan arrived with a drink for her. She put it down on top of the piano and clutched at his arm. 'This place is like a morgue. Let's live it up a little.'

Morgan didn't seem unwilling and followed her on to the floor. As Miller came to the end of the number someone turned the stereogram on again, probably out of sheer bloody-mindedness. He wasn't particularly worried, got to his feet and moved to the bar. Joanna Hartmann and Faulkner were standing very close together no more than a yard from him and as he waited for the barman to mix him a large gin and tonic, he couldn't help but overhear their conversation.

'Always the lady, Joanna,' Faulkner said. 'Doesn't anything ever disturb your poise?'

'Poor Bruno, have I spoiled your little joke? Where did you pick her up, by the way?'

'The public bar of The King's Arms. I'd hoped she might enliven the proceedings. At least I've succeeded in annoying Frank from the look on his face. Thanks be for small mercies.'

Joanna shook her head and smiled. 'What am I going to do with you?'

'I could make several very pleasant suggestions. Variations on a theme, but all eminently worthwhile.'

Before she could reply, Mary Beresford approached and Faulkner louted low. 'Madam, all homage.'

There was real disgust on her face. 'You are really the most disgusting man I know. How dare you bring that dreadful creature here.'

'Now there's a deathless line if you like. Presumably from one of those Victorian melodramas you used to star in.' She flinched visibly and he turned and looked towards the girl who was dancing with Morgan. 'In any case what's so dreadful about a rather luscious young bird enjoying herself. But forgive me. I was forgetting how long it was since you were in that happy state, Aunt Mary.' The old woman turned and walked away and Faulkner held up a hand defensively. 'I know, I've done it again.'

'Couldn't you just ignore her?' Joanna asked.

'Sorry, but she very definitely brings out the worst in me. Have a Martini.'

As the barman mixed them, Joanna noticed Miller and smiled. 'Now here's someone I want you to meet, Bruno. Nick Miller. He's a policeman.'

Faulkner turned, examined Miller coolly and sighed. 'Dammit all, Joanna, there is a limit you know. I do draw the line at coppers. Where on earth did you find him?'

'Oh, I crawled out of the woodwork,' Miller said pleasantly, restraining a sudden impulse to put his right foot squarely between Faulkner's thighs.

Joanna looked worried and something moved in the big man's eyes, but at that moment the door chimes sounded. Miller glanced across, mainly out of curiosity. When the maid opened the door he saw Jack Brady standing in the

30

hall, his battered, Irish face infinitely preferable to any that he had so far met with that evening.

He put down his glass and said to Joanna. 'Looks as if I'm wanted.'

'Surely not,' she said in considerable relief.

Miller grinned and turned to Faulkner. 'I'd like to say it's been nice, but then you get used to meeting all sorts in my line of work.'

He moved through the crowd rapidly before the big man could reply, took his coat and cap from the maid and gave Brady a push into the hall. 'Let's get out of here.'

The door closed behind them as he pulled on his trench-coat. Detective Constable Jack Brady shook his head sadly. 'Free booze, too. I should be ashamed to take you away.'

'Not from that lot you shouldn't. What's up?'

'Gunner Doyle's on the loose.'

Miller paused, a frown of astonishment on his face. 'What did you say?'

'They moved him into the Infirmary from Manning-ham Gaol yesterday with suspected food poisoning. Missed him half an hour ago.'

'What's he served—two and a half years?'

'Out of a five stretch.'

'The daft bastard. He could have been out in another ten months with remission.' Miller sighed and shook his head. 'Come on then, Jack, let's see if we can find him.'

Three

Faulkner ordered his third Martini and Joanna said, 'Where have you been for the past two days?'

'Working,' he told her. 'Damned hard. When were you last at the studio?'

'Wednesday.'

'There were three figures in the group then. Now there are four.'

There was real concern in her voice and she put a hand on his arm. 'That's really too much, Bruno, even for you. You'll kill yourself.'

'Nonesense. When it's there, it's got to come out, Joanna. Nothing else matters. You're a creative artist yourself. You know what I mean.'

'Even so, when this commission is finished you're taking a long holiday.'

Frank Marlowe joined them and she said, 'I've just been telling Bruno it's time he took a holiday.'

'What an excellent idea. Why not the Bahamas? Six months ... at least.'

'I love you too.' Faulkner grinned and turned to Joanna. 'Coming with me?'

'I'd love to, but Frank's lined me up for the lead in Mannheim's new play. If there's agreement on terms we go into rehearsal next month.'

'But you've only just finished a film.' Bruno turned to Marlowe and demanded angrily, 'What's wrong with you? Can't you ever see beyond ten per cent of the gross?'

As Marlowe put down his glass, his hand was shaking slightly. 'Now look, I've taken just about as much as I intend to take from you.'

Joanna got in between them quickly. 'You're not being fair, Bruno. Frank is the best agent there is, everyone knows that. If a thing wasn't right for me he'd say so. This is too good a chance to miss and it's time I went back to the stage for a while. I've almost forgotten how to act properly.'

The door bell chimed again and the maid admitted another couple. 'It's Sam Hagerty and his wife,' Joanna said. 'I'll have to say hello. Try to get on, you two. I'll be back soon.'

She moved away through the crowd and Marlowe watched her go, his love showing plainly on his face.

Faulkner smiled gently. 'A lovely girl, wouldn't you say?'

Marlowe glared at him in a kind of helpless rage and Faulkner turned to the barman. 'Two brandies, please. Better make it a large one for my friend. He isn't feeling too well.'

.   .   .   .   .

Jack Morgan and Grace Packard were dancing to a slow cool blues. She glanced towards Faulkner who was still at the bar. 'He's a funny one, isn't he?'

'Who, Bruno?'

She nodded. 'Coming to a do like this in those old clothes. Bringing me. Have you known him long?'

'We were at school together.'

'What's he do for a living?'

'He's a sculptor.'

'I might have known it was something like that. Is he any good?'

'Some people would tell you he's the best there is.'

She nodded soberly. 'Maybe that explains him. I mean

when you're the best, you don't need to bother about what other people think, do you?'

'I wouldn't know.'

'Mind you, he looks a bit of a wild man to me. Look at the way he handled Harold at the pub.'

Morgan shrugged. 'He's just full of pleasant little tricks like that. Judo, aikido, karate—you name it, Bruno's got it.'

'Can he snap a brick in half with the edge of his hand? I saw a bloke do that once on the telly.'

'His favourite party trick.'

She pulled away from him abruptly and pushed through the crowd to Faulkner.

'Enjoying yourself?' he demanded.

'It's fabulous. I never thought it would be anything like this.'

Faulkner turned to Marlowe who stood at his side drinking morosely. 'There you are, Frank. Fairy tales do come true after all.'

'Jack says you can smash a brick with the edge of your hand,' Grace said.

'Only when I'm on my second bottle.'

'I saw it on television once, but I thought they'd faked it.'

Faulkner shook his head. 'It can be done right enough. Unfortunately I don't happen to have a brick on me right now.'

Marlowe seized his chance. 'Come now, Bruno,' he said, an edge of malice in his voice. 'You mustn't disappoint the little lady. We've heard a lot about your prowess at karate . . . a lot of talk, that is. As I remember a karate expert can snap a plank of wood as easily as a brick. Would this do?'

He indicated a hardwood chopping block on the bar

and Faulkner grinned. 'You've just made a bad mistake, Frank.'

He swept the board clean of fruit, balanced it across a couple of ashtrays and raised his voice theatrically. 'Give me room, good people. Give me room.'

Those near at hand crowded round and Mary Beresford pushed her way to the front followed by Joanna who looked decidedly uncertain about the whole thing.

'What on earth are you doing, Bruno?'

Faulkner ignored her. 'A little bit of hush, please.'

He gave a terrible cry and his right hand swung down, splintering the block, scattering several glasses. There was a sudden gasp followed by a general buzz of conversation. Grace cried out in delight and Mary Beresford pushed forward.

'When are you going to start acting your age?' she demanded, her accent slipping at least forty-five years. 'Smashing the place up like a stupid teenage lout.'

'And why don't you try minding your own business, you silly old cow?'

The rage in his voice, the violence in his eyes reduced the room to silence. Mary Beresford stared at him, her face very white, the visible expression one of unutterable shock.

'How dare you,' she whispered.

'Another of those deathless lines of yours.'

Marlowe grabbed at his arm. 'You can't talk to her like that.'

Faulkner lashed out sideways without even looking, catching him in the face. Marlowe staggered back, clutching at the bar, glasses flying in every direction.

In the general uproar which followed, Joanna moved forward angrily. 'I think you'd better leave, Bruno.'

Strangely, Faulkner seemed to have complete control of

himself. 'Must I?' He turned to Grace. 'Looks as though I'm not wanted. Are you coming or staying?' She hesitated and he shrugged. 'Suit yourself.'

He pushed his way through the crowd to the door. As he reached it, Grace arrived breathless. 'Changed your mind?' he enquired.

'Maybe I have.'

He helped her on with her plastic mac. 'How would you like to earn a fiver?'

She looked at him blankly. 'What did you say?'

'A fiver . . . just to pose for me for a couple of minutes.'

'Well, that's a new name for it.'

'Are you on?' he said calmly.

She smiled. 'Okay.'

'Let's go then.'

He opened the door and as Grace Packard went out into the hall, Joanna emerged from the crowd and paused at the bottom of the steps. Faulkner remembered her birthday present and took the leather case from his pocket. 'Here, I was forgetting.' He threw the case and as she caught it, called, 'Happy birthday.'

He went out, closing the door and Joanna opened the case and took out the pearls. She stood there looking at them, real pain on her face. For a moment she was obviously on the verge of tears, but then her aunt approached and she forced a brave smile.

'Time to eat, everybody. Shall we go into the other room?' She led the way, the pearls clutched tightly in her hand.

. . . .

In Faulkner's studio the fire had died down, but it still gave some sort of illumination and the statues waited there

36

in the half-light, dark and menacing. The key rattled in the lock, the door was flung open and Faulkner bustled in, pushing Grace in front of him.

'Better have a little light on the situation.'

He flicked the switch and took off his coat. Grace Packard looked round her approvingly. 'This is nice . . . and your own bar, too.'

She crossed to the bar, took off her mac and gloves, then moved towards the statues. 'Is this what you're working on at the moment?'

'Do you like it?'

'I'm not sure.' She seemed a trifle bewildered. 'They make me feel funny. I mean to say, they don't even look human.'

Faulkner chuckled. 'That's the general idea.' He nodded towards an old Victorian print screen which stood to one side of the statues. 'You can undress behind that.'

She stared at him blankly. 'Undress?'

'But of course,' he said. 'You're not much use to me with your clothes on. Now hurry up, there's a good girl. When you're ready, get up on the dais beside the others.'

'The others?'

'Beside the statues. I'm thinking of adding another. You can help me decide.'

She stood looking at him, hands on hips, her face quite different, cynical and knowing. 'What some people will do for kicks.'

She disappeared behind the screen and Faulkner poured himself a drink at the bar and switched on the hi-fi to a pleasant, big-band version of 'A Nightingale sang in Berkeley Square'. He walked to the fire, humming the tune, got down on one knee and started to add lumps of coal to the flames from a brass scuttle.

'Will this do?' Grace Packard said.

37

He turned, still on one knee. She had a fine body, firm and sensual, breasts pointed with desire, hands flat against her thighs.

'Well?' she said softly.

Faulkner stood up, still holding his drink, switched off the hi-fi, then moved to the bedroom door and turned off the light. The shapes stood out clearly in silhouette against the great window and Grace Packard merged with the whole, became like the rest of them, a dark shadow that had existence and form, but nothing more.

Faulkner's face in the firelight was quite expressionless. He switched on the light again. 'Okay . . . fine. You can get dressed.'

'Is that all?' she demanded in astonishment.

'I've seen what I wanted to see if that's what you mean.'

'How kinky can you get.'

She shook her head in disgust, vanished behind the screen and started to dress again. Faulkner put more coal on the fire. When he had finished, he returned to the bar to freshen his drink. She joined him a moment later carrying her boots.

'That was quick,' he told her.

She sat on one of the bar stools and started to pull on her boots. 'Not much to take off with this year's fashions. I can't get over it. You really did want me to pose.'

'If I'd wanted the other thing I'd have included it in our arrangement.' He took a ten-pound note from his wallet and stuffed it down the neck of her dress. 'I promised you a fiver. There's ten for luck.'

'You *must* be crazy.' She examined the note quickly, then lifted her skirt and slipped it into the top of her right stocking.

He was amused and showed it. 'Your personal bank?'

'As good as. You know, I can't make you out.'

'The secret of my irresistible attraction.'

'Is that a fact?'

He helped her on with her mac. 'Now I've got some work to do.'

She grabbed for her handbag as he propelled her to-wards the door. 'Heh, what is this? Don't say it's the end of a beautiful friendship.'

'Something like that. Now be a good girl and run along home. There's a taxi rank just round the corner.'

'That's all right. I haven't far to go.' She turned as he opened the door and smiled impishly. 'Sure you want me to leave?'

'Goodnight, Grace,' Faulkner said firmly.

He closed the door, turned and moved slowly to the centre of the room. There was a dull ache just to one side of the crown of his skull and as he touched the spot briefly, feeling the indentation of the scar, a slight nervous tic developed in the right cheek. He stood there examining the statues for a moment, then went to the cigarette box on the coffee table. It was empty. He cursed softly and quickly searched his pockets without success.

A search behind the bar proved equally fruitless and he pulled on his raincoat and hat quickly. As he passed the bar, he noticed a pair of gloves on the floor beside one of the stools and picked them up. The girl had obviously dropped them in the final hurried departure. Still, with any luck he would catch up with her before she reached the square. He stuffed them into his pocket and went out quickly.

Beyond, through the great window, the wind moaned in the night, driving the rain across the city in a dark curtain.

Four

When they carried Sean Doyle into the General Infirmary escape couldn't have been further from his mind. He was sweating buckets, had a temperature of 104 and his stomach seemed to bulge with pieces of broken glass that ground themselves into his flesh and organs ferociously.

He surfaced twenty-four hours later, weak and curiously light-headed, but free from pain. The room was in half-darkness, the only light a small lamp which stood on the bedside locker. One of the screws from the prison, an ex-Welsh Guardsman called Jones, nodded on a chair against the wall as per regulations.

Doyle moistened cracked lips and tried to whistle, but at that moment the door opened and a staff nurse entered, a towel over her arm. She was West Indian, dark and supple. To Doyle after two and a half years on the wrong side of the wall, the Queen of Sheba herself couldn't have looked more desirable.

As she moved across to the bed, he closed his eyes quickly. He was aware of her closeness, warm and perfumed with lilac, the rustle of her skirt as she turned and tip-toed across to Jones. Doyle watched her from beneath lowered eyelids as the Welshman came awake with a start.

'Here, what's going on?' he said in some alarm. 'Is the Gunner all right?'

She put out a hand to restrain him. 'He's still asleep. Would you like to go down to the canteen?'

'Well, I shouldn't really you know,' Jones told her in his high Welsh voice.

'You'll be all right, I'll stay,' she said. 'Nothing can pos-

40

sibly happen—he's still asleep. After what he's been through he must be as weak as a kitten.'

'All right then,' Jones whispered. 'A cup of tea and a smoke. I'll be back in ten minutes.'

As they moved to the door she said, 'Tell me, why do you call him the Gunner?'

Jones chuckled. 'Well, that's what he was you see. A gunner in the Royal Artillery. Then when he came out and went into the ring, that's what they called him. Gunner Doyle.'

'He was a prizefighter?'

'One of the best middleweights in the game.' Jones was unable to keep the enthusiasm from his voice for like most Welshman he was a fanatic where boxing was concerned. 'North of England champion. Might have been a contender if he could have left the skirts alone.'

'What was his crime?' she whispered, curiosity in her voice.

'Now there he did really manage to scale the heights as you might say.' Jones chuckled at his own wit. 'He was a cat burglar—one of the best in the game and it's a dying art, believe me. Climb anything he could.'

The door closed behind him and the staff nurse turned and looked across at the Gunner. He lowered his eyelids softly as she came across to the bed. He was acutely aware of her closeness, the perfume filled his nostrils, lilac, heavy and clinging, fresh after rain, his favourite flower. The stiff uniform dress rustled as she leaned across him to put the towel on the table on the other side.

The Gunner opened his eyes and took in everything. The softly rounded curves, the dress riding up her thighs as she leaned across, the black stockings shining in the lamplight. With a sudden fierce chuckle he cupped his right hand around her left leg and slid it up inside her

41

skirt to the band of warm flesh at the top of her stocking.

'By God, that's grand,' he said.

Her eyes were very round as she turned to look at him.
For a frozen moment she stared into his face, then jumped
backwards with a little cry. She stared at him in astonishment and the Gunner grinned.

'I once shared a cell at the Ville with a bloke who did
that to a big blonde who was standing in front of him in a
bus queue one day. Just for a laugh. They gave him a year
in the nick. Makes you wonder what the country's coming
to.'

She turned without a word and rushed out, the door
bouncing back against the wall before closing. It occurred
to the Gunner almost at once that she wasn't coming
back. Add that to the fact that Jones would be at least
fifteen minutes in the canteen and it left a situation that
was full of possibilities.

It also occurred to him that with full remission he had
only another ten months of his sentence to serve, but at
that sudden exciting moment, ten months stretched into
an infinity that had no end. He flung the bedclothes to one
side and swung his legs to the floor.

An athlete by profession all his life, the Gunner had
taken good care to keep himself in first-class physical trim
even in prison and this probably accounted for the fact
that apart from a moment of giddiness as he first stood up,
he felt no ill effects at all as he crossed to the locker against
the wall and opened it. There was an old dressing-gown
inside, but no slippers. He pulled it on quickly, opened the
door and peered out into the corridor.

It was anything but deserted. Two doctors stood no
more than ten yards away deep in conversation and a
couple of porters pushed a floor polisher between them,
its noiseless hum vibrating on the air. The Gunner turned

42

and walked the other way without hesitation. When he turned the corner at the far end he found himself in a cul-de-sac. There was a service elevator facing him and a door at the side of it opened on to a dark concrete stairway. The elevator was on its way up so he took the stairs, running down lightly, the concrete cold on his bare feet.

Ten floors down, he arrived at the basement, opened the door at the bottom and found himself in a small entrance hall. One door opened into a side courtyard, heavy rain slanting down through the lamp that was bracketed to the wall above the entrance. But he wouldn't last five minutes out there on a night like this without shoes and some decent clothes. He turned and opened the other door and immediately heard voices approaching. Without hesitation he plunged into the heavy rain, crossed the tiny courtyard and turned into the street keeping close to the wall.

.   .   .   .

'So you were only out of the room for fifteen minutes?' Brady said.

'As long as it took me to get down to the canteen, have a cup of tea and get back again.' Jones' face was white and drawn. 'The dirty bastard. Why did he have to do this to me? God knows what might happen. I could lose my pension.'

'You've only yourself to blame,' Miller said coldly. 'So don't start trying to put it on to Doyle. He saw his chance and took it. Nobody can blame him for that.'

He dismissed the prison officer with a nod and turned to the young staff nurse. 'You told Jones you'd stay in the room till he got back. Why did you leave?'

She struggled with the truth for a moment, but the

thought of recounting in detail what had happened to the two police officers was more than she could bear.

'I'd things to do,' she said. 'I thought it would be all right. He was asleep.'

'Or so it seemed. I understand you told the first officer you saw that there was only an old dressing-gown in the cupboard?'

'That's right.'

'But no shoes or slippers?'

'Definitely not.'

Miller nodded and went out into the corridor, Brady at his heels. 'All right, Jack, you're Doyle in a hurry in bare feet and a dressing-gown. What do you do?'

Brady glanced left along the quiet end of the corridor and led the way. He paused at the lift, frowned, then opened the door and peered down into the dark well of the concrete stairway.

'On a hunch I'd say he went this way. A lot safer than the lift.'

They went down quickly and at the bottom Miller pushed open the outside door and looked out into the rain. 'Not very likely. He'd need clothes.'

The other door led into a narrow corridor lined on one side with half a dozen green painted lockers. Each one was padlocked and carried an individual's name on a small white card. They were aware of the gentle hum of the oil-fired heating plant somewhere near at hand and in a small office at the end of the corridor, they found the chief technician.

Miller showed him his warrant card. 'Looking for the bloke that skipped out are you?' the man said.

'That's right. He'd need clothes. Anything missing down here?'

'Not a chance,' the chief technician shook his head. 'I

don't know if you noticed, but all the lads keep their lockers padlocked. That was on advice from one of your blokes after we had a lot of pinching last year. Too easy for people to get in through the side door.'

Miller thanked him and they went back along the corridor, and stood on the steps looking out at the driving rain.

'You're thinking he just walked out as he was?' Brady suggested.

Miller shrugged. 'He didn't have much time remember. One thing's certain—he couldn't afford to hang about.'

Brady shook his head. 'He wouldn't last long in his bare feet on a night like this. Bound to be spotted by someone sooner or later.'

'As I see it he has three possible choices,' Miller said. 'He can try to steal a car, but that's messy because he's got to nose his way round till he finds one that some idiot's forgotten to lock and in that rig-out of his, he's certain to be noticed.'

'He could always hang around some alley and wait his chance to mug the first bloke who went by.'

Miller nodded. 'My second choice, but it's still messy and there aren't many people around the back streets on a night like this. He could get pneumonia waiting. My own hunch is that he's making for somewhere definite. Somewhere not too far away perhaps. Who were his friends?'

'Come off it, he didn't have any.' Brady chuckled. 'Except for the female variety. The original sexual athlete, the Gunner. Never happy unless he had three or four birds on the go at once.'

'What about Mona Freeman?' Miller said. 'He was going to marry her.'

'She was a mug if she believed him.' Brady shook his

45

head. 'She's still in Holloway. Conspiracy to defraud last year.'

'All right then,' Miller said. 'Get out the street directory and let's take a look at the map. Something might click while you're looking at it.'

Brady had grown old on the streets of the city and had developed an extraordinary memory for places and faces, the minutiae of city life. Now he unfolded the map at the back of his pocket directory and examined the area around the infirmary. He gave a sudden grunt. 'Doreen Monaghan.'

'I remember her,' Miller said. 'Little Irish girl of seventeen just over from the bogs. She thought the sun shone out of the Gunner's backside.'

'Well, she isn't seventeen any longer,' Brady said. 'Has a flat in a house in Jubilee Terrace less than a quarter of a mile from here. Been on the game just over a year now.'

'Let's go then.' Miller grinned. 'And don't forget that right of his whatever happens. He's only got to connect once and you won't wake up till next Friday.'

Five

When the Gunner hurried across the courtyard and turned into the side street at the rear of the infirmary, he hadn't the slightest idea what he was going to do next. Certainly he had no particular destination in mind although the icy coldness of the wet flags beneath his bare feet told him that he'd better find one quickly.

The rain was hammering down now which at least kept

the streets clear and he paused on a corner to consider his next move. The sign above his head read Jubilee Street and triggered off a memory process that finally brought him to Doreen Monaghan who at one time had worshipped the ground he walked on. She'd written regularly during the first six months of his sentence when he was at Pentonville, but then the letters had tailed off and gradually faded away. The important thing was that she lived at 15, Jubilee Terrace and might still be there.

He kept to the back streets to avoid company and arrived at his destination ten minutes later, a tall, decaying Victorian town house in a twilight area where a flat was high living and most families managed on one room.

The fence had long since disappeared and the garden was a wilderness of weeds and brambles, the privet hedge so tall that the weight of the heavy rain bowed it over. He paused for a moment and looked up. Doreen had had the top floor flat stretching from the front of the house to the rear and light showed dimly through a gap in the curtains which was encouraging.

When he went into the porch there was an innovation, a row of independent letter boxes for mail, each one neatly labelled. Doreen's name was there all right underneath the one at the end and he grinned as he went in through the hall and mounted the stairs. She was certainly in for one hell of a surprise.

The lady in question was at that moment in bed with an able seaman of Her Majesty's Royal Navy home on leave from the Far East and already regretting the dark-skinned girls of Penang and Singapore who knew what it was for and didn't charge too much.

47

A member of the oldest profession in the world, she had long since discovered that its rewards far exceeded anything that shop or factory could offer and salved her conscience with a visit to the neighbouring church of Christ the King every Monday for confession followed by Mass.

Her sailor having drifted into the sleep of exhaustion, she gently eased herself from beneath the sheets, pulled on an old kimono and lit a cigarette. Having undressed in something of a hurry, his uniform lay on the floor beside a chair and as she picked it up, a leather wallet fell to the floor. There must have been eighty or ninety pounds in there—probably his leave money. She extracted a couple of fivers, slipped them under the edge of the mat, then replaced the wallet.

He stirred and she moved across to the dressing-table and started to put on her stockings. He pushed himself up on one elbow and said sleepily. 'Going out, then?'

'Three quid doesn't get you squatter's rights you know,' she said. 'Come on now, let's have you out of there and dressed. The night isn't half over and I've things to do.'

At that moment there was a knock at the door. She straightened, surprise on her face. The knocking continued, low but insistent.

She moved to the door and said softly, 'Yes?'

The voice that replied was muffled beyond all recognition. 'Come on, Doreen, open up,' it called. 'See what Santa's brought you.'

'Who is it?' the sailor called, an edge of alarm in his voice.

Doreen ignored him, opened the door on its chain and peered out. Sean Doyle stood there in a pool of water, soaked to the skin, hair plastered to his skull, the scarlet hospital dressing-gown clinging to his lean body like a second skin.

He grinned, the old wicked grin that used to put her on her back in five seconds flat. 'Come on then, darling, I'm freezing to death out here.'

So complete was the surprise, so great the shock of seeing him that she unhooked the chain in a kind of dazed wonder and backed slowly into the room. As the Gunner moved in after her and closed the door the sailor skipped out of bed and pulled on his underpants.

'Here, what's the bloody game?' he demanded.

The Gunner ignored him, concentrating completely on Doreen whose ample charms were prominently displayed for the girdle of her kimono, loosely fastened, had come undone.

'By God, but you're a sight for sore eyes,' he said, sincere admiration in his voice.

Having had time to take in the Gunner's bedraggled appearance, the sailor's alarm had subsided and there was an edge of belligerency in his voice when he spoke again, 'I don't know who the hell you are, mate, but you'll bloody well get out of it fast if you know what's good for you.'

The Gunner looked him over and grinned amiably. 'Why don't you shut up, sonny?'

The sailor was young, active and muscular and fancied himself as a fighting man. He came round the end of the bed with a rush, intending to throw this rash intruder out on his ear and made the biggest mistake of his life. The Gunner's left foot slipped forward, knee turned slightly in. The sailor flung the sort of punch that he had seen used frequently and with great success on the films. The Gunner swayed a couple of inches and the punch slid across his shoulder. His left fist screwed into the sailor's solar plexus, his right connected with the edge of the jaw, slamming him back against the far wall from which he re-

49

bounded to fall on his face unconscious.

The Gunner turned, untying the cord of his dressing-gown. 'How've you been keeping them, darlin'?' he demanded cheerfully.

'But Gunner—what happened?' she said.

'They had me in the infirmary for a check-up. One of the screws got a bit dozy so I took my chance and hopped it. Got any clothes?'

She opened a drawer, took out a clean towel and gave it to him, an expression of wonder still on her face. 'No—nothing that would do for you.'

'Never mind—I'll take this bloke's uniform.' He turned her round and slapped her backside. 'Find me something to drink, there's a girl. It was no joke out there in this rig-out on a night like this.'

She went into the kitchen and he could hear her opening cupboards as he stripped and scrubbed himself dry. He had the sailor's trousers and shirt on and was trying to squeeze his feet into the shoes when she returned.

He tossed them into the corner in disgust. 'No bloody good. Two sizes too small. What have you got there?'

'Sherry,' she said. 'It's all I could find. I was never much of a drinker—remember?'

The bottle was about half-full and he uncorked it and took a long swallow. He wiped a hand across his mouth with a sigh of pleasure as the wine burned its way into his stomach.

'Yes, I remember all right.' He emptied the bottle and dropped it on the floor. 'I remember lots of things.'

He opened her kimono gently, and his sigh seemed to echo into forever. Still sitting on the edge of the bed, he pulled her close to him, burying his face in her breasts.

She ran her fingers through his hair and said urgently, 'Look, Gunner, you've got to get moving.'

'There's always time for this,' he said and looked up at her, his eyes full of grey smoke. 'All the time in the world.'

He fell back across the bed, pulling her down on top of him and there was a knock on the door.

Doreen jumped up, pulling her kimono about her and demanded loudly. 'Who is it?'

The voice that replied was high and clear. 'Mrs. Goldberg, dear. I'd like a word with you.'

'My landlady,' Doreen whispered and raised her voice. 'Can't it wait?'

'I'm afraid not, dear. It really is most urgent.'

'What am I going to do?' Doreen demanded desperately. 'She's a funny old bird. She could make a lot of trouble for me.'

'Does she know you're on the game?' the Gunner demanded.

'At fifteen quid a week for this rat-trap? What do you think?'

'Fair enough.' The Gunner rolled the unconscious sailor under the bed, lay on it quickly, head propped up against a pillow and helped himself to a cigarette from a packet on the bedside locker. 'Go on, let her in now. I'm just another client.'

Mrs. Goldberg called out again impatiently and started to knock as Doreen crossed to the door and opened it on the chain. The Gunner heard the old woman say, 'I must see you, my dear. It's very, very urgent.'

Doreen shrugged and unfastened the chain. She gave a cry of dismay as the door was pushed back sending her staggering across the room to sprawl across the Gunner on the bed.

Nick Miller moved in, Brady at his side, the local patrolman behind them, resplendent in black crash helmet and foul-weather gear.

51

'All right then, Gunner,' Miller said cheerfully. 'Let's be having you.'

The Gunner laughed out loud. 'Another five minutes and I'd have come quietly, Mr. Miller, but to hell with this for a game of soldiers.'

He gave the unfortunate Doreen a sudden, violent push that sent her staggering into Miller's arms, sprang from the bed and was into the kitchen before anyone could make a move. The door slammed in Brady's face as he reached it and the bolt clicked home. He turned and nodded to the young patrolman, a professional rugby player with the local team, who tucked his head into his shoulder and charged as if he was carving his way through a pack of Welsh forwards.

In the kitchen, the Gunner tugged ineffectually at the window, then grabbed a chair and smashed an exit. A second later, the door caved in behind him as the patrolman blasted through and sprawled on his face.

There was a fallpipe about five feet to one side. Without hesitation, the Gunner reached for the rotting gutter above his head, swung out into the rain and grabbed at the pipe as the gutter sagged and gave way.

He hung there for a moment, turned and grinned at Miller who leaned out of the window, arm outstretched and three feet too short.

'No hard feelings, Mr. Miller. See you in church.'

He went down the pipe like a monkey and disappeared into the darkness and rain below. Miller turned and grinned at Brady. 'Still in his bare feet, did you notice? He always was good for a laugh.'

They returned to the bedroom to find Doreen weeping passionately. She flung herself into Brady's arms the moment he appeared. 'Oh, help me, Mr. Brady. As God's my judge I didn't know that divil was coming here this night.'

52

Her accent had thickened appreciably and Brady patted her bottom and shoved her away. 'You needn't put that professional Irish act on with me, Doreen Monaghan. It won't work. I'm a Cork man meself.'

There was a muffled groan from under the bed. Brady leaned down and grabbed a foot, hauling the sailor into plain view, naked except for his underpants.

'Now I'd say that just about rounds the night off,' Miller said to the big Irishman and they both started to laugh.

Mrs. Goldberg, seventy and looking every year of it with her long jet ear-rings and a patina of make-up that gave her a distinct resemblance to a death mask, peered round the door and viewed the splintered door with horror.

'Oh, my God,' she said. 'The damage. Who's going to pay for the damage?'

The young patrolman appeared behind her, looking white and shaken. Miller moved forward, ignoring Mrs. Goldberg for the moment. 'What happened to you?'

'Thought I'd better get a general call out for Doyle as soon as possible, Sergeant, so I went straight down to my bike.'

'Good lad,' Brady said. 'That's using your nut.'

'They've been trying to get in touch with Sergeant Miller for the last ten minutes or so.'

'Oh, yes,' Miller said. 'Anything important?'

'Chief Superintendent Mallory wants you to meet him at Dob Court, Sergeant. That's off Gascoigne Street on the north side of Jubilee Park. The beat man found a woman there about twenty minutes ago.' Suddenly he looked sick. 'Looks like another Rainlover killing.'

.   .   .   .

There were at least a dozen patrol cars in Gascoigne Street when Miller and Brady arrived in the Mini-Cooper and the Studio, the Forensic Department's travelling laboratory, was just drawing up as they got out and moved along the wet pavement to Dob Court.

As they approached, two men emerged and stood talking. One was Detective Inspector Henry Wade, Head of Forensic, a fat balding man who wore horn-rimmed spectacles and a heavy overcoat. He usually smiled a lot, but now he looked grim and serious as he wiped rain from his glasses with a handkerchief and listened to what Detective Chief Superintendent George Mallory of Scotland Yard's Murder Squad was saying to him.

He nodded and moved away and Mallory turned to Miller. 'Where were you?'

He was forty-five years of age, crisp, intelligent, the complete professional. The provincials he had to work with usually didn't like him, which suited him down to the ground because he detested inefficiency in any form and had come across too much of it for comfort on his forays outside London.

He thoroughly approved of Miller with his sharp intelligence and his law degree, because it was in such men that the salvation of the country's out-dated police system lay. Under no circumstances would he have dreamt of making his approval apparent.

'Brady and I had a lead on Doyle.'

'The prisoner who escaped from the infirmary? What happened?'

Miller told him briefly and Mallory nodded. 'Never mind that now. Come and have a look at this.'

The body lay a little way inside the Alley covered with a coat against the heavy rain until the Studio boys could get a tarpaulin rigged. The constable who stood beside it held his torch close as Mallory lifted the raincoat.

'From the looks of it her neck is broken just like the others,' Mallory said, 'but the first thing we've got to do is find out who she is. Typical of a lot of these girls these days there isn't any kind of identification whatsoever in her handbag.'

Miller looked down at the waxen face turned sideways awkwardly, the eyes staring into eternity. When he spoke, it was with difficulty.

'I think I can help you there, sir.'

'You know her?'

'Her name is Packard, sir,' Miller said hoarsely. 'Grace Packard.'

Six

The Gunner went through the back gate of the yard at the rear of Doreen's house and ran like a hare, turning from one street into another without hesitation, completely forgetting his bare feet in the excitement of the moment.

When he paused in a doorway for a breather, his heart was pounding like a trip-hammer, but not because he was afraid. On the contrary, he found himself in the grip of a strange exhilaration. A psychologist might have found a reason in the sudden release from confinement after two and a half years in a prison cell. The Gunner only knew that he was free and he lifted his face up to the rain and laughed out loud. The chase was on. He would lose it in the end, he knew that, but he'd give them a run for their money.

He moved towards the end of the street and paused. A woman's voice said clearly, 'Able-fox-victor come in please. I have a 952 for you.'

He peered round the corner and saw a police car parked, window open as a beat constable in helmet and cape leaned down to speak to the driver. The Gunner retreated hastily and trotted towards the far end of the street. He was no more than half-way along when a police motor cyclist turned the corner and came towards him. The man saw him at once and came on with a sudden burst of speed, engine roaring. The Gunner ran across the street and ducked into a narrow entry between two houses.

He found himself in a small courtyard faced by a stone wall a good fifteen feet high and in one corner was an old wash-house of the type common to late Victorian houses. He pulled himself up on to the sloping roof as the patrolman pounded into the entry blowing his whistle, and reached for the top of the wall, sliding over silently as the policeman arrived.

The sound of the whistle faded as he worked his way through a network of backyards and alleys that stretched towards the south side of Jubilee Park. He stopped once as a police car's siren sounded close by and then another lifted on the night air in the middle distance. He started to run again. The bastards were certainly doing him proud.

Ten minutes later he had almost reached the park when another siren not too far in front of him made him pause. It was standard police procedure on this sort of chase, he knew that, intended to confuse and bewilder the quarry until he did something stupid.

But the Gunner was too old a fox for that one. The park was out. What he needed now was somewhere to lie up for a few hours until the original excitement had died down.

He retraced his steps and turned into the first side street. It was flanked by high walls and on the left, a massive wooden gate carried the sign *Henry Crowther and Sons—Transport*. It seemed just the sort of place he was looking for and for once his luck was in. There was the usual small judas with a yale lock set in the main gate. Someone had left it on the latch for it opened to his touch.

He found four trucks parked close together in a cobbled yard. There was a house at the other end and light streamed between the curtains of a ground floor window.

When he peered inside he saw a white-haired old woman sitting in front of a bright coal fire watching television. She had a cigarette in one hand and what looked like a glass of whisky in the other. He envied her both and was conscious of his feet for the first time since leaving Doreen's flat. They were cold and raw and hurt like hell. He hobbled across the yard towards a building on the right of the house and went in through doors which stood open. It had been a stable in years gone by, but from the looks of things was now used as a workshop or garage.

Wooden stairs went up through a board floor to what had obviously been the hayloft. It was in almost total darkness and seemed to be full of drums of oil and assorted junk. A half-open wooden door creaked uneasily and rain drifted in on the wind. A small wooden platform jutted out ten feet above the cobbles and a block and tackle hung from a loading hook.

He had a good view of the house and the yard, which was important, and sank down on an old tarpaulin and started to massage his feet vigorously. They hadn't felt like this since Korea and he shuddered as old memories of frostbite and comrades who had lost toes and even feet in that terrible retreat south during the first winter campaign, came back to him.

The gate clicked in the darkness below and he straightened and peered out. Someone hurried across the yard and opened the front door. As light streamed out, he saw that it was a young woman in a raincoat with a scarf bound around her head, peasant-fashion. She looked pretty wet and the Gunner smiled as she went inside and closed the door.

He leaned against the wall and stared into the rain, hunger gnawing at his stomach. Not that there was anything he could do about that. Later, perhaps, when all the lights had gone out in the house he might see if he had lost any of his old skill. Shoes and something to eat and maybe an old raincoat—that's all he needed. If he could make it as far as the Ring Road there were any one of half a dozen transport cafés where long-distance lorry drivers pulled up for rest and a meal. All he had to do was get himself into the back of a truck and he could be two hundred miles away by breakfast.

He flinched, dazzled by light that poured from one of the second floor windows. When he looked across he could see the girl standing in the doorway of what was obviously her bedroom. The wind lifted, driving rain before it and the judas gate creaked. The Gunner peered cautiously into the darkness, imagining for a moment that someone else had arrived, then turned his attention to the bedroom again.

The girl didn't bother to draw the curtains, secure in the knowledge that she was cut off from the street by the high wall and started to undress, obviously soaked to the skin.

The Gunner watched with frank and open admiration. Two and a half years in the nick and the only female company a monthly visit from his Aunty Mary, a seventy-year-old Irish woman with a heart of corn whose visits with their acid asides on authority, the peelers as she still insisted on calling them, and life in general, always kept him laughing for at least a week afterwards. But this? Now this was different.

The young woman dried off with a large white towel, then examined herself critically in the mirror. Strange how few women looked their best in the altogether, but she was more than passable. The black hair almost reached the pointed breasts and a narrow waist swelled into hips that were perhaps a trifle too large for some tastes, but suited the Gunner down to the ground.

When she dressed again, she didn't bother with a suspender belt. Simply pulled on a pair of hold-up stockings, black pants and bra, then took a dress from the wardrobe. He'd heard they were wearing them short since he'd gone down, but this was ridiculous. Not only was it half-way up her thighs, but crocheted into the bargain so you could see through it like the tablecloth Aunty Mary had kept in the parlour when he was a kid.

She stood at the dressing table and started to brush her hair, perhaps the most womanly of all actions, and the Gunner felt strangely sad. He'd started off by fancying a bit of the usual and why not? He'd almost forgotten what it tasted like and the business with Doreen had certainly put him in the mood. But now, lying there in the loft with the rain falling, he felt like some snotty-nosed kid with his arse out of his pants, looking in at what he could never have and no one to blame but himself.

She tied her hair back with a velvet ribbon, crossed to the door and went out, switching off the light. The Gunner sighed and eased back slightly and below in the yard there was the scrape of a foot on stone.

. . . .

Jenny Crowther was twenty-two years of age, a practical, hard-headed Yorkshire girl who had never visited London in her life, but in her crocheted mini-dress and dark stockings she would have passed in the West End without comment.

'Feeling better, love?' her grandmother enquired as she entered the room.

Jenny nodded, rubbing her hands as she approached the fire. 'It's nice to be dry.'

'Eh, Jenny love,' the old woman said. 'I don't know how you can wear yon dress. I can see your knickers.'

'You're supposed to, Gran.' The old woman stared in blank amazement across a gulf that was exactly fifty years wide and the girl picked up the empty coal scuttle. 'I'll get some coal, then we'll have a nice cup of tea.'

The coal was in a concrete bunker to the left of the front door and when she opened it, light flooded across the yard, outlining her thighs clearly through the crocheted dress as she paused, looking at the rain. She took an old raincoat from a peg, hitched it over her shoulders, went down the steps and lifted the iron trap at the base of the coal bunker. There was no sound and yet she turned, aware from some strange sixth sense of the danger that threatened her. She caught a brief glimpse of a dark shape, the vague blur of a face beneath a rain hat, and then great hands had her by the throat.

. . . .

The Gunner went over the edge of the platform, hung for a moment at the end of the block and tackle, then dropped to the cobbles. He moved in fast, smashing a fist into the general area of the other man's kidneys when he got close enough. It was like hitting a rock wall. The man flung the girl away from him and turned. For a moment, the Gunner saw the face clearly, lips drawn back in a snarl. An arm swept sideways with amazing speed, bunched knuckles catching him on the side of the head, sending him back against one of the trucks. The Gunner went down on one knee and the girl's attacker went past him in a rush. The judas banged and the man's running steps faded along the back street.

As the Gunner got to his feet, Ma Crowther called from the doorway, 'Make another move and I'll blow your head off.'

She was holding a double-barrelled shotgun, the barrels of which had been sawn down to nine inches in length, transforming it into one of the most dangerous and vicious weapons in the book.

Jenny Crowther moved away from the wall, a hand to her throat and shook her head. 'Not him, Gran. I don't know where he came from, but it was a good job he was around.'

The Gunner was impressed. Any other bird he'd ever known, even the really hard knocks, would have been on their backs after an experience like that, but not this one.

'Which mob were you in then, the Guards?' he demanded.

The girl turned to look at him, grinning instantly and something was between them at once, unseen perhaps, but almost physical in its strength. Like meeting like, with instantaneous recognition.

She looked him over, taking in the sailor's uniform, the

bare feet and laughed, a hand to her mouth. 'Where on earth did you spring from?'

'The loft,' the Gunner told her.

'Shall I get the police, love?' Ma Crowther asked.

The Gunner cut in quickly. 'Why bother the peelers about a little thing like this? You know what it's like on a Saturday night. A bloke has a few pints, then follows the first bit of skirt he sees. Sometimes he tries to go a bit too far like the geezer who just skipped, but it's all come out in the wash. Once it's reported in the papers, all the old dears will think he screwed you, darlin', even if he didn't,' he assured the girl gaily.

'Here, just a minute,' the old woman said. 'Bare feet and dressed like a sailor. I know who you are.' She turned to the girl and said excitedly, 'They've just had a flash on Northern Newscast. This is Gunner Doyle.'

'Gunner Doyle?' the girl said.

'The boxer. Your Dad used to take me to see him. Topped the bill at the Town Hall a couple of times. Doing five years at Manningham Gaol. They took him into the infirmary because they thought he was ill and he gave them the slip earlier this evening.'

The girl stood looking at him, legs slightly apart, a hand on her hip and the Gunner managed a tired, tired grin. 'That's me, the original naughty boy.'

'I don't know about that,' she said. 'But you're bleeding like a stuck pig. Better come inside.' She turned and took the shotgun from the old woman's grasp. 'It's all right, Gran. He won't bite.'

'You forgot something,' the Gunner said.

She turned in the doorway. 'What's that, then?'

'What you came out for in the first place.' He picked up the coal scuttle. 'Lad's work, that's what my Aunty Mary always used to say.'

He got down on his knees to fill it. When he straightened and turned wearily, the girl said, 'I don't know why, but I think I like your Aunty Mary.'

The Gunner grinned. 'She'd go for you, darlin'. I'll tell you that for nothing.'

He swayed suddenly and she reached out and caught his arm in a grip of surprising strength. 'Come on then, soldier, you've had enough for one night,' and she drew him into the warmth.

Seven

Faulkner frowned, enormous concentration on his face as he leaned over the drawing board and carefully sketched in another line. When the door bell rang he ignored it and continued working. There was another more insistent ring. He cursed softly, covered the sketch with a clean sheet of cartridge paper and went to the door.

He opened it to find Chief Superintendent Mallory standing there, Miller at his shoulder. Mallory smiled politely. 'Mr. Faulkner? Chief Superintendent Mallory. I believe you've already met Detective Sergeant Miller.'

Faulkner showed no particular surprise, but his eyes widened slightly when he looked at Miller. 'What is all this? Tickets for the policeman's ball?'

Mallory's manner was dangerously gentle. 'I wonder if we could have a few words with you, sir?'

Faulkner stood to one side, ushering them into the studio with a mock bow. 'Be my guest, Superintendent.'

He closed the door and as he turned to face them, Mallory said in a calm, matter-of-fact voice, 'We're making enquiries concerning a Miss Packard, Mr. Faulkner. I understand you might be able to help us?'

Faulkner lit a cigarette and shrugged. 'To the best of my knowledge I've never even heard of her.'

'But she was with you earlier this evening at Joanna Hartmann's party,' Miller put in.

'Oh, you mean Grace?' Faulkner nodded. 'I'm with you now. So the viper's discovered it can sting, has it? Has he made a formal complaint?'

'I'm afraid I don't understand you, sir,' Mallory said. 'Grace Packard is dead. Her body was found in an alley called Dob Court not far from here less than an hour ago. Her neck was broken.'

There was a short silence during which both policemen watched Faulkner closely, waiting for some reaction. He seemed genuinely bewildered and put a hand to his forehead. 'Either of you feel like a drink?'

Mallory shook his head. 'No thank you, sir.'

'Well, I do.' He moved to the fire and tossed his cigarette into the flames. 'You say she was found about an hour ago?'

'That's right.' Faulkner glanced up at the clock. It was just coming on to eleven thirty-five and Mallory said, 'What time did she leave here?'

Faulkner turned slowly. 'Who said she was here at all?' He looked at Miller with a frown. 'Have you been bothering Joanna?'

Miller shook his head. 'When I telephoned, the party was still going strong from the sound of things. I spoke to the maid. She told me that you and the girl had left together.'

'All right—she was here, but for no more than ten minutes. I left at half-ten.'

'Which would indicate that she was murdered almost immediately,' Mallory said.

'Is this another of those Rainlover things?'

'We can't be sure yet. Let's say it falls into a familiar pattern.'

'Two in two days.' Faulkner was by now quite obviously over the initial shock. 'He's getting out of hand.'

Miller watched his every move, slightly puzzled. The man actually seemed to be enjoying the whole sorry business. He wondered what Faulkner had in his veins instead of blood and the big man said, 'I hope you won't mind me asking, but am I first on the list?'

'This is an informal interview, sir, solely to help us in our enquiries,' Mallory told him. 'Of course you're perfectly entitled to have your solicitor present.'

'Wouldn't dream of dragging him away from the party,' Faulkner said. 'He deserves it. You just fire away. I'll do anything I can to help.'

'You made a rather puzzling remark when we first came in,' Miller said. 'Something about a viper discovering that it could sting. What did you mean by that?'

'I might as well tell you, I suppose. I've been working rather hard lately and completely forgot about Joanna's birthday party. A friend, Mr. Jack Morgan, called for me and we stopped in at The King's Arms in Lazer Street for a quick one. While we were there, the girl came in.'

'And you got into conversation?' Mallory said.

'On the contrary, I picked her up quite deliberately. She was waiting for her boy friend and he was late. I invited her to the party.'

'Why did you do that, sir?'

'Because I knew it would be infested by a miserable bunch of stuffed shirts and I thought she might liven things up a bit. She was that sort of girl. Ask Miller, he

65

was paying enough attention to her himself from what I could see. An honest tart. Hair out of a bottle and a skirt that barely covered her backside.'

'You were at the party for about twenty minutes before I left,' Miller said. 'You couldn't have stayed for long.'

'About half an hour in all.'

'And the girl left with you?'

'You already know that, for Christ's sake.' He swung on Mallory. 'Are you sure you won't have that drink?'

'No, sir.'

'Then I will.' He went behind the bar and reached for a bottle. 'All of a sudden, things seem to be taking a rather nasty turn.'

Mallory ignored the remark. 'You say she was here for no more than ten minutes.'

'That's right.'

'I would have thought she'd have stayed longer.'

'If I'd brought her back to sleep with me, the poor little bitch would be alive now, but I didn't.'

'Why *did* you bring her back?'

'To pose for me.' He swallowed a large whisky and poured himself another. 'I offered her five quid to come back and pose for me.'

For a brief moment Mallory's composure slipped. He glanced at Miller in bewilderment and Faulkner said, 'As it happens I'm a sculptor. That little lot on the dais behind you is a commission I'm working on at the moment for the new Sampson building. The Spirit of Night. This is just a rough draft, so to speak—plaster on wire. I thought a fifth figure might give more balance. I brought Grace back with me to stand up there with the others so I could see.'

'And for that you paid her five pounds?'

'Ten, as a matter of fact. I wanted to know and I wanted

to know right then. She happened to be available.'

'And what did you decide, sir?' Mallory asked.

'I'm still thinking about it. Well, what happens now?'

'Oh, we'll have to make further enquiries, sir,' Mallory said. 'We'll probably have to see you again, of course, you realise that.'

They walked to the door and Faulkner opened it for them. 'What about her boy friend, Superintendent? Harold, I think she called him.'

'I don't follow you, sir.'

Faulkner laughed boyishly. 'I suppose I'd better come clean. He arrived just as we were leaving The King's Arms. There was something of a scene. Nothing I couldn't handle, but he was pretty angry—at the girl more than me.'

'That's very interesting, sir,' Mallory said. 'I'll bear it in mind.'

He went out. As Miller moved to follow him, Faulkner tapped him on the shoulder. 'A private word, Sergeant,' he said softly and the smile had left his face. 'Stay away from my fiancée in future. One likes to know when a friend is a friend. The trouble with all you bloody coppers is that you're on duty twenty-four hours a day.'

There was a sudden viciousness in his voice, but Miller refused to be drawn. 'Good night, Mr. Faulkner,' he said formally and went out.

Faulkner slammed the door and turned with a frown. For a while he stood there looking thoughtful, then moved back to the drawing board. He removed the clean sheet of cartridge paper, disclosing a sketch of the four statues. After a while he picked up his pencil and started to add an additional figure with bold, sure strokes.

．　　　．　　　．　　　．　　　．

Outside in the street, it was still raining heavily as Miller and Mallory got into the Chief Superintendent's car where Jack Brady waited with the driver.

'What did you think?' Mallory demanded.

Miller shrugged. 'It's hard to say. He's not the sort you meet every day of the week. Did you buy his story about taking the girl back to the studio to pose for him?'

'It's crazy enough to be true, we just can't tell at this stage. He's certainly right about one thing—the girl's boy friend wants checking out.' He turned to Brady. 'You can handle that one. The fiancé's name is Harold, that's all we know. The girl's father should be able to give you the rest. When you get the address, go straight round and bring him down to Central for questioning.'

'What about me, sir?' Miller asked.

'You can go back to that damned party. See Joanna Hartmann and check Faulkner's story. I still don't understand why he left so early. I'll see you at Central as well when you've finished. Get cracking then—I'll drop Brady off.'

His car moved away into the rain. Miller watched it go and sighed heavily as he got into the Mini-Cooper. His second visit to Joanna Hartmann's that night was something he didn't fancy one little bit.

Eight

The party had just about folded and all the guests had departed except for Jack Morgan and Frank Marlowe who sat at the bar with Joanna and her aunt, having a final drink before leaving.

The door bell chimed and Joanna looked up in surprise. 'Now, who on earth can that be?'

'Probably Bruno,' her aunt remarked acidly. 'Returning to tell you that all is forgiven.'

'Well, it won't work—not this time.' Joanna was annoyed. 'He can stew for a while.'

There was another ring and Frank Marlowe started to rise. 'I'd better go . . .'

'No, I'll handle it. I'll see him myself.'

She opened the door, braced for her encounter and found Nick Miller standing there. 'Why, Nick,' she said in bewilderment.

'Could I come in for a moment?'

'Certainly.' She hesitated. 'I'm afraid nearly everyone's gone home. We're just having a final drink. Why don't you join us?'

'I'd better not,' he said. 'To tell you the truth, I'm here on business.'

As she closed the door, she stiffened, then turned very slowly. 'Bruno? Something has happened to Bruno?'

Miller shook his head quickly. 'He's perfectly all right —I've just been speaking to him. There was a girl here earlier—a girl called Grace Packard. He brought her with him, didn't he?'

Jack Morgan got up from his stool and came forward. 'That's right, but she left some time ago. Look here, Miller, what is this?'

'As I said, I've already spoken to Faulkner. She went back to his studio with him and left at approximately ten-thirty. She was found by a police officer less than fifteen minutes later in an alley a couple of streets away.'

There was a shocked gasp from Mary Beresford and Marlowe said in a whisper, 'You mean she's dead?'

'That's right. Murdered. Her neck was broken, probably by a sharp blow from the rear.'

'The Rainlover,' Mary Beresford said so quietly that it might have been a sigh.

'It could be,' Miller said. 'On the other hand that kind of killer tends to work to a pattern and it's a little close to his last one.' He turned to Morgan. 'You've been here all the time?'

'Since I arrived at eighty-thirty or so.'

'I can confirm that,' Joanna said quickly. 'We all can.'

'Look here,' Marlowe said. 'Can we know where we stand? Is this an official call?'

'Just an enquiry.' Miller turned to Joanna again. 'I understand from your fiancé that he didn't stay very long. Isn't that rather unusual considering that it was your birthday party?'

'Bruno's very much a law unto himself,' she said calmly.

Mary Beresford came in under full sail. 'Oh, for heaven's sake tell the truth about him for once, Joanna. He didn't stay long because he was asked to leave.'

'And why was that?'

'I should have thought it sufficiently obvious. You were here—you saw what happened. He picked that little tart up in a saloon bar and brought her here with the deliberate intention of ruining the party for everyone.'

'Aunt Mary—please,' Joanna said.

'It's true, isn't it?' The old woman's eyes glittered fiercely. 'He arrived dressed like a tramp as usual and with twenty minutes was trying to break the place up.'

Miller turned enquiringly. Jack Morgan picked up the two halves of the wooden chopping block that lay on the bar. 'Bruno's latest parlour trick.'

'Karate?'

'That's right. Imagine what a blow like that would do to somebody's jaw.'

A brown belt who was soon to face re-grading to first Dan, Miller could have told him in detail. Instead he looked at Marlowe speculatively. 'That bruise on your face—did he do that?'

'Look here,' Marlowe said angrily. 'I don't know what all this is leading up to, but if you think I'm laying a complaint against him you're mistaken. There was a rather undignified squabble—there usually is when Bruno's around. Nothing more.'

'And he left with Grace Packard. You must have found that rather upsetting, Joanna.'

'God knows, but she's had enough practice by now,' Mary Beresford said. 'You say he took her home with him?'

'That's right, but apparently she only stayed ten minutes or so.'

'A likely story.'

'Confirmed by the time the body was found. He says that he gave her ten pounds to pose for him. Would you say that was likely?'

Frank Marlowe laughed harshly. 'More than that—typical.'

Joanna had gone very white, but hung on to her dignity with everything she had left. 'As I've already said, he's very much a law unto himself.'

'He's been working on a special commission,' Jack Morgan said. 'One of the most important he's had. It started as a single figure four or five weeks ago and now comprises a group of four. He was discussing with me earlier the question of adding a fifth to give the thing balance.'

Miller nodded. 'Yes, he did mention that.'

71

'Then why did you have to ask?' Joanna Hartmann said sharply.

Miller frowned. 'I'm afraid I don't follow you.'

'Are we to take it that my fiancé is under some kind of suspicion in this business?'

'Routine, Joanna, pure routine at the moment. But it has to be done, you must see that surely.'

'I don't at all,' she said hotly. 'What I do see is that you were a guest in my house earlier this evening because I had imagined you a friend.'

'Rubbish,' Miller said crisply. 'You asked me to your party for one reason only. Because my brother is probably the most influential man in Northern Television and you're worried because you've heard there's talk of taking off your series at the end of this season.'

'How dare you?' Mary Beresford said. 'I'll complain to your superiors.'

'You can do what you damned well like,' Miller helped himself to a cigarette from a box on the table and smiled calmly. 'With my present service and including certain special payments my annual salary at the moment as a Detective Sergeant is one thousand three hundred and eighty-two pounds, Mrs. Beresford. It might interest you to know that every penny of it goes for income tax. Gives me a wonderful feeling of freedom when I'm dealing with people like you.'

He turned back to Joanna Hartmann. 'Whether you like it or not you've got a few unpleasant facts to face. Number one as far as I'm concerned is that Grace Packard was murdered within an hour of leaving this flat in company with your fiancé, so don't start trying to get on your high horse because we have the impudence to suggest that he might be able to help us with our enquiries.'

'I'm Mr. Faulkner's solicitor,' Jack Morgan said. 'Why

wasn't I present when he was questioned?'

'Why not ask him? He was certainly offered the privilege.' Miller turned very quickly, moved to the door and opened it. 'I'll probably have to see you again, Miss Hartmann,' he said formally. 'We'd appreciate it if you'd make yourself available during the next couple of days.'

'But Miss Hartmann's due in London tomorrow for an important business conference,' Frank Marlowe said.

'I can't prevent her going,' Miller said, 'but it would certainly be a great pity if Faulkner happened to need her and she wasn't here.'

He closed the door and chuckled grimly as he went along the corridor to the lift. He'd certainly stirred things up there. It would be more than interesting to see what the outcome, if any, would be.

.   .   .   .   .

The heavy silence after Miller had gone out was first broken by Frank Marlowe. 'I don't like the smell of this—don't like it at all.'

'Neither do I,' Jack Morgan said.

Joanna went up the steps to the door, opened a cupboard and took out a sheepskin coat. She pulled it on quickly.

'Did you come in your car, Jack?'

'Yes.'

'Good . . . I'd like you to run me round to Bruno's.'

Her aunt put a hand on her arm as if she would restrain her. 'For goodness' sake, Joanna, don't be a fool. Stay out of this.'

Joanna turned on her fiercely. 'You don't like him, do you, Aunt Mary. You never did. Because of that you want

73

to believe that he's somehow mixed up in this business. Well, I never will.'

The old woman turned away, suddenly looking her age and Frank Marlowe said, 'Want me to come?'

Joanna shook her head. 'Better not. Would you mind hanging on till we get back?'

'I'll be here.'

Jack Morgan opened the door for her and as Joanna turned, her aunt made a final try, 'Joanna,' she said sharply. 'You must listen to me. It's for your own good. Think of your career. You can't afford to get mixed up in the kind of scandal this could cause.'

Joanna ignored her completely. 'Ready, Jack?' she said and led the way out.

.   .   .   .   .

They didn't talk during the drive to Bruno's place, but when Morgan pulled in at the kerb and switched off the engine, she put a hand on his arm.

'You've known Bruno a long time, Jack, longer than any of us. You don't believe he could . . .'

'Not a chance,' he told her emphatically. 'He's a wild man, I'll give you that, but I couldn't accept the kind of suspicions Nick Miller obviously holds for a moment.'

'That's all I wanted to hear.' She smiled her relief. 'Now let's go up and have a word with him.'

But they were wasting their time. There was no reply to their insistent knocking at Bruno's door. After five minutes of fruitless effort, Morgan turned to her and said gently, 'Better leave it for now, Joanna. He's probably had enough for one night.'

She nodded wearily. 'All right, Jack, take me home.

74

We'll try again in the morning. I'll cancel my trip to London.'

On the other side of the door, Faulkner listened to the footsteps fade as they descended the stairs. His head was hurting again. My God, but it was hurting. He took a couple of the pills the doctor had given him, poured himself a large whisky and stood at the window and looked out into the night.

Rain spattered against the glass and he rested his aching forehead against it. But it didn't help. Quite suddenly it was as if he was suffocating. Air, that's what he needed—the cold air of night to drive away this terrible pain. He grabbed his trenchcoat and hat and let himself out quickly.

Nine

'Last time I saw you in the ring was when you fought Terry Jones for the area title,' Ma Crowther said. 'I thought you had it in your pocket till he gave you that cut over the eye and the ref stopped the fight in the third.'

'I always did cut too easily,' the Gunner said. 'If it hadn't been for that I could have gone right to the top. The Boxing Board took my licence away after the Terry Jones fight on medical advice. Just a vale of tears, isn't it?'

He looked anything but depressed sitting there at the table wearing an old sweater the girl had found him and a pair of boots that had belonged to her father. He had already worked his way through three fried eggs, several rashers of bacon and half a loaf of bread and was now on his third cup of tea.

75

'You're a funny one and no mistake.' Jenny Crowther shook her head. 'Doesn't anything ever worry you?'

'Life's too short, darlin'.' He helped himself to a cigarette from the old woman's packet. 'I shared a cell once with a bloke who was big on this Yoga lark. You've got to learn to relaxez vous. Live for today and use the talents the good Lord's given you.'

Jenny laughed helplessly. 'I think that's marvellous. Considering the way you make a living.'

He wasn't in the least embarrassed. 'So I scrounge a few bob where I can. The kind of people I hit can afford it. Insured up to the hilt they are. I don't go around duffing up old women in back street shops.'

'The original Robin Hood,' she said acidly. 'And what happens when someone gets in your way on a job? Do you go quietly or try to smash your way through?'

She piled the dirty dishes on to a tray and went into the kitchen. The Gunner moved across to the fire and sat in the opposite chair to the old woman. 'Is she always as sharp as that?'

'She has to be, lad, running an outfit like this.'

'You mean she's in charge?'

'Her Dad passed on a couple of months back—cerebral haemorrhage. Jenny was a hairdresser, a good one too, but she dropped that and took over here. Been trying to keep things going ever since.'

'Having trouble, then?'

'Only what you'd expect. We've eight drivers and two mechanics and there isn't one who wouldn't take advantage if he could. And then there's the foreman, Joe Ogden. He's the worst of the lot. He's shop steward for the union. Always quoting the book at her, making things as difficult as he can.'

'And why would he do that?'

76

'You've seen her, haven't you?' She poured herself another whisky. 'What about you? Where do you go from here?'

He shrugged. 'I don't know, Ma. If I can get to the Ring Road I could snatch a lift to any one of a dozen places.'

'And then what?' He made no answer and she leaned across and put a hand on his knee. 'Don't be a fool, lad. Give yourself up before it's too late.'

Which was exactly what the Gunner had been thinking, but he didn't say so. Instead, he got to his feet and grinned. 'I'll think about it. In any case there's nothing for you or Jenny to worry about. I'll clear out of here in an hour or so when it's a bit quieter, if that's all right with you.'

He went into the kitchen and found the girl at the sink, an apron around her waist, washing the dishes. 'Need any help?'

'You can dry if you like.'

'Long time since I did this.' He picked up a tea towel.

'Even longer before you do it again.'

'Heh, what have I done?' he demanded.

'It's just that I can't stand waste,' she said. 'I mean look at you. Where on earth do you think you're going to go from here? You won't last long out there with every copper for miles around on the watch for you.'

'Whose side are you on then?'

'That's another thing. You can't be serious for a moment—not about anything.'

She returned to the dishes and the Gunner chuckled. 'I'm glad you're angry anyhow.'

'What's that supposed to mean?'

'Better than no reaction at all. At least you're interested.'

'You'll be lucky. The day I can't do better I'll jump off Queen's Bridge.'

But she was smiling and some of the tension had gone out of her when she returned to the washing-up. 'I was having an interesting chat with your gran,' the Gunner said. 'Seems you've got your hands full at the moment.'

'Oh, we get by.'

'Sounds to me as if you need a good man round the place.'

'Why, are you available?'

He grinned. 'I wish I was, darlin'.'

The judas gate banged outside and steps echoed across the yard. Jenny Crowther frowned. 'That's funny, I dropped the latch when I went out earlier.'

'Anyone else got a key?'

'Not as far as I know. I'll see who it is. You'd better stay here.'

He waited, the kitchen door held open slightly so that he could see what took place. Ma Crowther appeared from the other room and watched as Jenny opened the front door.

The man who pushed his way inside wore a donkey jacket with leather patches on the shoulders and had obviously had a drink. He was hefty enough with arms that were a little too long, but his face was puffed up from too much beer and the weak mouth the biggest giveaway of all.

'And what might you want at this time of night, Joe Ogden?' Ma Crowther demanded.

'Leave this to me, Gran,' Jenny said calmly. 'Go on now. I'll be in in a minute.'

The old woman went back into the sitting-room reluctantly and Jenny closed the door and turned to face Ogden. She held out her hand. 'You used a key to open the outside gate. I don't know where you got it from, but I want it.'

He smiled slyly. 'Nay, lass, I couldn't do that. I like to be able to come and go.' He took a step forward and put his hand on the wall so that she was caged in the corner by the sitting-room door. 'We could get along just fine, you and me. Why not be sensible? A lass like you's got better things to be doing than trying to run a firm like this. Keeping truckies in their place is man's work.'

He tried to kiss her and she twisted her head to one side. 'I'm going to give you just five seconds to get out of here. If you don't, I'll send for the police and lay a complaint for assault.'

He jumped back as if he had been stung. 'You rotten little bitch,' he said, his face red and angry. 'You won't listen to reason, will you? Well, just remember this—I'm shop steward here. All I have to do is say the word and every man in the place walks out through that gate with me—they'll have no option. I could make things very awkward for you.'

She opened the door w.thout a word. He stood there glowering at her, then moved out. 'All right, miss,' he said viciously. 'Don't say I didn't warn you.'

She closed the door and turned, shaking with rage. 'Ill kill him. I'll kill the bastard,' she said and then broke down and sobbed, all the worry and frustration of the weeks since her father's death welling up to the surface.

Strong arms pulled her close and a hand stroked her hair. 'Now then, darlin', never say die.' She looked up and the Gunner grinned down at her. 'Only one way to handle a situation like this. Put the kettle on, there's a good girl. I'll be back in five minutes.'

He kissed her full on the mouth and before she could

say anything, opened the door and went out into the night.

.   .   .   .

Joe Ogden paused on the corner, swaying slightly for he was still about three-parts drunk. So she wanted it the hard way did she? Right—then that was the way she could have it. He'd show the bitch—by God he would. By the time he was finished she'd come crawling, begging him to sort things out for her and then he'd call the tune all right.

He crossed the street and turned into a narrow lane, head down against the driving rain, completely absorbed by a series of sexual phantasies in which Jenny Crowther was doing exactly as she was told. The lane was badly lit by a number of old-fashioned gas lamps, long stretches of darkness in between and the pavement was in a bad state of repair, the flags lifting dangerously.

The Gunner descended on him like a thunderbolt in the middle of one of the darker stretches and proceeded to take him apart savagely and brutally in a manner that was as exact as any science.

Ogden cried out in pain as he was propelled into the nearest brick wall with a force that took the breath out of his body. He swung round, aware of the pale blur of a face and swung a fist instinctively, catching the Gunner high on the right cheekbone.

It was the only hit he was to make that night. A boot caught him under the right kneecap, a left and a right screwed into his stomach and a knee lifted into his face as he keeled over, for the Gunner was never one to allow the Queensberry rules to get in his way in this sort of affair.

Ogden rolled over in the rain and the Gunner kicked

him hard about the body half a dozen times, each blow judged to a nicety. Ogden lay there, face against the pavement, more frightened than he had ever been in his life, expecting to meet his end at any moment.

Instead, his assailant squatted beside him in the darkness and said in a strangely gentle voice, 'You don't know who I am, but I know you and that's all that matters. Now listen carefully because I'm only going to say this once. You'll get your cards and a week's pay in the post Monday. In the future, you stay away from Crowther's yard. Make any kind of trouble at all, union or otherwise, and I'll get you.' He grabbed a handful of Ogden's hair. 'Understand?'

'Yes.' Ogden could hardly get the word out as fear seized him by the throat.

'See that you do. Now where's the key to the outside gate?'

Ogden fumbled in his left hand pocket, the Gunner took the yale key from him, slammed him back hard against the pavement and walked away.

Ogden got to his knees, dizzy with pain and pulled himself up against the wall. He caught a brief glimpse of the Gunner running through the lighted area under one of the lamps and then he was alone again. Quite suddenly, and for the first time since childhood, he started to cry, dry sobs tearing at his throat as he turned and stumbled away through the darkness.

.   .   .   .   .

Crouched by the open doorway in the loft above the old barn in the exact positon the Gunner had occupied earlier, the Rainlover waited patiently, wondering whether the man would return.

81

The door opened for the second time in ten minutes and the girl appeared, framed against the light, so close that he could see the worry on her face. He started to get up and beyond through the darkness, there was the creaking of the judas gate as it opened. A moment later, the Gunner appeared.

He paused at the bottom of the steps and tossed the key up to Jenny. 'This is yours.'

She glanced at it briefly. 'What happened?'

'Oh, you might say we came to an understanding. He's agreed not to come back. In return he gets his cards and a week's pay, first post Monday morning.'

She tilted his head to one side and examined the bruise that was spreading fast under his right eye. 'Some understanding. You'd better come in and let me do something about that.'

She turned and the Gunner followed her. After he had closed the door, the yard was dark again, but something moved there in the shadows making no more noise than the whisper of dead leaves brushing across the ground in the autumn. The judas gate creaked slightly and closed with a soft click. In the alley, footfalls faded into the rain.

.   .   .   .   .

The Gunner emptied the glass of whisky she had given him with a sigh of satisfaction and turned his head to the light as she gently applied a warm cloth to the bruise under his eye.

'What happened to the old lass, then?'

'I told her to go to bed. It's late.'

He glanced at the clock. 'You're right. I'll have to be off soon.'

'No hurry. You'll stand a better chance later on.'

'Maybe you're right.'

He was suddenly tired and with the whisky warm in his stomach, contented in a way that he hadn't been for years. It was pleasant there by the cheerful fire with just the one lamp in the corner and the solid, comfortable furniture. She gave him a cigarette and lit a paper spill at the fire for a light.

He took one of the easy chairs and she sat on the rug, her legs tucked underneath her. The Gunner smoked his cigarette slowly from long habit, making it last, and watched her. Strange, but he hadn't felt like this about a woman before. She had everything a man could ever want —a body to thank God for, a pleasant face, strength, character. He pulled himself up short. This was beginning to get out of hand. Trouble was it had been so damned long since he'd been within smelling distance of a bird that probably one of those forty-five-year-old Toms from the back of the market would have looked remarkably like the Queen of the May.

She turned and smiled. 'And what's going on inside that ugly skull of yours now?'

'Just thinking how you're about the best-looking lass I've seen in years.'

'Not much of a compliment,' she scoffed. 'Not when you consider where you've been lately.'

'Been reading up on me, have you?'

She shrugged. 'I caught the final newscast on television. You'd plenty of competition, by the way. There's been a woman murdered earlier tonight on the other side of Jubilee Park.'

'Another of these Rainlover things?'

'Who else could it be?' She shivered and added slowly, 'When I was alone in the kitchen earlier I got to thinking that maybe that man out there in the yard ...'

83

'Was the Rainlover?' The Gunner shook his head emphatically. 'Not a chance. The fact that he's seen off this poor bitch earlier is proof enough of that. They always work to a pattern these blokes. Can't help themselves. The chap who jumped you had something a damned sight more old-fashioned on his mind.'

She frowned. 'I don't know, I was thinking that maybe I should report it to the police.'

She hesitated as well she might. Her father had left mother and daughter a business which was worth in cash and property some fifteen thousand pounds yet he had never considered himself as anything other than working class. His daughter was of the same stubborn breed and had been raised to obey the usual working class code which insisted that contact with the police, no matter what the reason, was something to be avoided at all costs.

'And what were you going to tell them?' demanded the Gunner. 'That Sean Doyle, with every copper for miles around on his tail, stopped to save you from a fate worse then death, so you fed him and clothed him and sent him on his way rejoicing because you figured you owed him something?' He chuckled harshly. 'They'll have you in a cell in Holloway before you know what's hit you.'

She sighed. 'I suppose you're right.'

'Of course I am.' With some adroitness he changed the subject. 'So I was on the telly, was I?'

'Oh, they did quite a feature on the great Gunner Doyle.'

'Free publicity is something I can always use. I hope they mentioned I was the best second-storey man in the North of England.'

'Amongst other things, including the fact that you were the most promising middle-weight since the war, a contender for the crown until women and booze and fast

84

cars got in the way. They said you were the biggest high-liver the ring had seen since somebody called Jack Johnson.'

'Now there's a compliment if you like.'

'Depends on your point of view. The commentator said that Johnson had ended up in the gutter without a penny. They seemed to be drawing some kind of comparison.'

There was a cutting edge to her voice that needled the Gunner and he said hotly, 'Well just for the record, darlin', there's a few things they've missed out like the way I cut so badly that refs used to stop fights I was winning because they'd get worried about the blood pouring all over my face. In that last fight with Terry Jones I got cut so much I was two weeks in hospital. I even needed plastic surgery. They took my licence away so I couldn't box any more. Any idea how I felt?'

'Maybe it was rough, Gunner, life often is, but it didn't give you a licence to steal.'

'Nay, lass, I don't need any excuses.' He grinned. 'I had a few sessions with a psychiatrist at the Scrubs first time I got nicked. He tried to make out that I'd gone bent to get my own back on society.'

'What's your version?'

'Chance, darlin', time and chance, that's what happened to me. When the fight game gave me up I'd about two hundred quid in the bank and I was qualified to be just one thing. A bloody labourer. Anything seemed better than that.'

'So you decided to try crime?'

'Not really. It just sort of happened. I was staying in the Hallmark Hotel in Manchester, trying to keep up appearances while I tried to con my way into a partnership with a bloke I knew who was running a gambling club. When the deal folded, I was so broke I couldn't even pay the bill. One night I noticed a bloke in the bar with a wallet full of fivers. Big bookie in from the races.'

He stared into the fire, silent for a moment and as he started to speak again, she realised that in some strange way he was re-living that night in every detail.

'He was staying on the same floor as me five rooms along. There was a ledge outside my window, only about a foot wide mind you, but it was enough. I've always had a head for heights ever since I was a kid, always loved climbing. I don't know, maybe if things had been different I might have been a real climber. North face of the Eiger and all that sort of stuff. Those are the blokes with the real guts.'

'What happened?' she said.

'I worked my way along the ledge at about two in the morning, got in through his window and lifted the wallet and him snoring the whole time.'

'And you got away with it?'

'No trouble at all. Just over six hundred nicker. I ask you, who'd have gone labouring after a touch like that? My fortune was made. As I said, I've always had a head for heights and that kind of thing is a good number. You don't need to work with anyone else which lowers the chance of getting nicked.'

'They got you though, didn't they?'

'Twice, that's all, darlin'. Once when I fell forty feet at the back of the Queen's Hotel in Leeds and broke a leg. The second time was when I got nicked at that new hotel in the Vandale Centre. Seems they had one of these electronic eyes switched on. The scuffers were in before I knew what hit me. Oh, I gave them quite a chase over the roofs, but it was all for laughs. I'd been recognised for one thing.'

He yawned and shook his head slightly, suddenly very,

very tired. 'Better get moving I suppose. You don't want me hanging round here in the morning.'

The cigarette dropped from his hand to the carpet. She picked it up and tossed it into the fire and the Gunner sighed, leaning back in the comfortable old chair. Very softly Jenny Crowther got up and reached for the rug that was draped over the back of the settee.

As she covered the Gunner, his hand slid across her thigh and he said softly, 'Best looking lass I've seen in years.'

She didn't move, aware that he was already asleep, but gently disengaged his hand and tucked it under the rug. She stood there for quite a while looking down at that reckless face, almost childlike in repose. In spite of the scar tissue around the eyes and the permanently swollen cheekbones, it was handsome enough, a man's face whatever else he was and her thigh was still warm where he had touched her.

Perhaps it was as well that sleep had overtaken him so suddenly before things had taken their inevitable course— although she would have had no particular objections to that in principle. By no means promiscuous, she was like most young people of her generation, a product of her day and the sexual morality of earlier times meant nothing to her.

But loving, even in that sense, meant some kind of involvement and she couldn't afford that. Better that he should go after an hour or two's sleep. She turned off the light and went and stood at the window, her face against the cold glass, rain hammering hard against it, wondering what would happen to him, wondering where he would run to.

Ten

Narcia Place lay in an area that provided the local police force with one of its biggest headaches. The streets followed each other upon a pattern that was so exact as to be almost macabre. Sooty plane trees and solid terrace houses, once the homes of the lower middle classes on their way up, but now in multiple occupation due to an influx of immigrants since the war. Most of the whites had left. Those who found it impossible stayed and hated.

It was almost 12.15 when Jack Brady arrived in a Panda car provided by the local station. The whole street was dark and still in the heavy rain and when he rapped the old-fashioned cast-iron knocker on the door of number ten there was no immediate response. The driver of the Panda car vanished into the entry that led to the back yard without a word and Brady tried again.

It was at least five minutes before a window was pushed up above his head and a voice called, 'What the hell you think you're playing at this time in the morning?'

'Police,' Brady replied. 'Open up and be sharp about it. I haven't got all night.'

The window went down and the driver of the Panda car emerged from the entry. 'Any joy?'

'Just stuck his head out of the window,' Brady said. 'Get round to the back yard, just in case he tries to scarper.'

But there was no need for at that moment, the bolt was drawn and the front door opened. Brady pushed it back quickly and went in. 'Harold Phillips?'

'That's me—what is this?'

His feet were bare and he wore an old raincoat. Brady

looked him over in silence and Harold swallowed, his black eyes flickering restlessly. He looked hunted and was very obviously scared.

Brady smiled in an avuncular manner and put a hand on his shoulder. 'I'm afraid I've got some bad news for you, son. I understand you're engaged to be married to a Miss Grace Packard?'

'That's right.' Harold went very still. 'What's happened? She been in an accident or something?'

'Worse than that, son. She was found dead earlier tonight in an alley called Dob Court on the other side of Jubilee Park.'

Harold stared at him for a long moment, then started to puke. He got a hand to his mouth, turned and fled into the kitchen. Brady found him leaning over the sink, a hand on the cold water tap.

After a while Harold turned, wiping his mouth with the back of one hand. 'How did it happen?'

'We're not certain. At the moment it looks as if her neck was broken.'

'The Rainlover?' The words were almost a whisper.

'Could be.'

'Oh, my God.' Harold clenched a fist convulsively. 'I had a date with her tonight. We were supposed to be going dancing.'

'What went wrong?'

'I was late. When I turned up she'd got involved with another bloke.'

'And she went off with him.' Harold nodded. 'Do you know who he was?'

Harold shook his head. 'Never seen him before, but the landlord seemed to know him. That's the landlord of The King's Arms near Regent Square.'

'What time was this?'

89

'About half eight.'

'Did you come straight home afterwards?'

'I was too upset so I walked around in the rain for a while. Then I had a coffee in the buffet at the railway station. Got home about half nine. Me mum was in bed so I took her a cup of tea and went myself.'

'Just you and your mother live here?'

'That's right.'

'She goes to bed early then?'

'Spends most of her time there these days. She isn't too well.'

Brady nodded sympathetically. 'I hope we haven't disturbed her.'

Harold shook his head. 'She's sleeping like a baby. I looked in on my way down.' He seemed much more sure of himself now and a strange half-smile played around his mouth like a nervous tic that couldn't be controlled. 'What happens now?'

'I'd like you to come down to Central if you wouldn't mind, just to have a few words with Chief Superintendent Mallory—he's in charge of the case. The girl's father is already there, but we need all the assistance we can get. You could help a lot. Give us details of her friends and interests, places she would be likely to visit.'

'Glad to,' Harold said. 'I'll go and get dressed. Only be five minutes.'

He went out and the Panda driver offered Brady a cigarette. 'Quite a technique you have. The silly bastard thinks he's got you eating out of his hand.'

'Glad you noticed,' Brady said, accepting the cigarette and a light. 'We'll make a copper out of you yet.'

There was a white pill box on the mantelpiece and he picked it up and examined the label. It carried the name of a chemist whose shop was no more than a couple of

90

streets away. *The Capsules—one or two according to instructions—it is dangerous to exceed the stated dose.*

Brady opened the box and spilled some of the white and green capsules into his palm. 'What you got there?' the Panda man demanded.

'From the look of them I'd say it's what the doctor gave my wife last year when she burnt her hand and couldn't sleep for the pain. Canbutal. Half a dozen of these and you'd be facing your Maker.'

He replaced the box on the mantelpiece, a slight frown on his face. 'Tell you what,' he said to the Panda driver. 'You go and wait for us in the car and bang the door as hard as you like on the way out.'

The young constable, old before his years and hardened to the vagaries of C.I.D. men, left without a word, slamming the door so hard that the house shook. Brady went and stood at the bottom of the stairs, but heard no sound until a door opened and Harold appeared buttoning his jacket on the way down.

'What was all that then?' he demanded. 'Thought the house was falling down.'

'Just my driver on his way out to the car. I think the wind caught the door. Ready to go?'

'Whenever you are.' Harold took down his raincoat and struggled into it as he made for the door. 'Fame and fortune here I come. Who knows, I might be selling my story to the *Sunday News* before I'm finished.'

With an effort of will, Brady managed to stop himself from assisting him down the steps with a boot in the backside. Instead he took a deep breath and closed the door behind him with infinite gentleness. He was beginning to feel sorry for Harold's mother.

.   .   .   .   .   .

It was chance more than anything else that led Miller to The King's Arms after leaving Joanna Hartmann's flat. His quickest route back to Central C.I.D. took him along Lazer Street and the pub stood on the corner. It was the light in the rear window which caused him to brake suddenly. The landlord would have to be interviewed sooner or later to confirm the circumstances of Grace Packard's meeting with Faulkner and Morgan, but there was no reason why that couldn't wait till morning.

The real truth was that Miller was more interested in the disturbance that had taken place, the trouble with the girl's boy friend which Faulkner had hinted at. 'Nothing I couldn't handle,' he had said. The sort of phrase Miller would have expected from some back street tearaway, indicating a pattern of violence unusual and disturbing in a man of Faulkner's education and background.

He knocked on the back door and after a while it was opened on a chain and Harry Meadows peered out. He grinned his recognition for they were old friends.

'What's this then, a raid?'

Miller went in as Meadows unchained the door. 'A few words of wisdom, Harry, that's all.'

'Nothing stronger?'

'Only if you've got a cup of tea to put it in.'

'Coming up.'

Miller unbuttoned his coat and went across to the fire. The kitchen was large, but cluttered with crates of bottled beer and cases of whisky. It was warm and homely with the remains of the supper still on the table and the old sofa on the other side of the fireplace looked very inviting.

'See you've got another killing on your hands,' Meadows said as he came back into the room with a mug of tea.

'Where did you hear that?'

'Late night news on the radio. Not that they were giving much away. Just said the body of a woman had been found near Jubilee Park.'

'Dob Court to be precise.' Miller swallowed some of his tea, coughing as the whisky in it caught at the back of his throat.

'Dob Court? That's just round the corner from here.' Meadows looked grim. 'Was it anyone I knew?'

'A girl called Grace Packard.'

Meadows stared at him, the skin tightening visibly across his face. Quite suddenly he went to the sideboard, opened a bottle of brandy and poured a large dose into the nearest glass. He swallowed it down and turned, shuddering.

'She was in here earlier tonight.'

'I know, Harry, that's why I'm here. I understand there was some trouble.'

Meadows helped himself to another brandy. 'This is official then?'

'Every word counts so take your time.'

Meadows was looking a lot better as the brandy took effect. He sat down at the table. 'There's a bloke called Faulkner comes in here a lot. Only lives a couple of streets away. He was in here earlier tonight with a friend of his, a solicitor called Morgan. Nice bloke. He handled the lease of this place for me when I decided to buy last year.'

'What time did they come in?'

'Somewhere around half-eight.'

'Who else was here?'

'Nobody. Trade's been so bad in the evenings since this Rainlover business started that I've had to lay off the bar staff.'

'I see. When did the girl arrive?'

'About five minutes after the other two.'

'You knew her name, so presumably she'd been in before?'

'Two or three times a week, usually with a different bloke and she wasn't too particular about their ages either.'

'Was she a Tom?'

'That's the way it looked to me.'

'And what about this boy friend of hers?'

'You mean Harold?' Meadows shrugged. 'He's met her in here maybe half a dozen times. I don't even know his second name.'

'Was he picking up her earnings?'

'Could be, I suppose. He didn't look so tough to me, but you can never tell these days.'

Miller nodded. 'All right, what happened between Faulkner and the girl?'

'She sat on a stool at one end of the bar and he told me to give her a drink. It seems he and Morgan were going on to some posh do and Faulkner got the idea it might be fun to take the girl. She must have liked the idea because they all left together.'

'And then Harold arrived.'

'That's right and he didn't like what he found. Ended up taking a punch at Faulkner who got very nasty with him. I had to intervene. In fact I told Morgan to tell him he needn't come back. I've had about as much as I can take.'

'He's been mixed up in this sort of trouble before then?'

'Too damned much for my liking. When he loses his temper he's a raving madman, that one. Doesn't know what he's doing. He was in here one Saturday night a couple of months back and a couple of market porters came in. You know what they're like—rough lads—they started taking the mickey out of his posh voice and so on.

94

He took them both out in the alley, gave them a hell of a beating.'

'Did you report it?'

'Come off it, Mr. Miller. I've got the reputation of the house to think of. I only put up with him because most of the time he's a real gent and why should I cry over a couple of tearaways like that? They asked for it, they got it.'

'A point of view,' Miller started to button his coat. 'Strange in a man of his background, all this violence.'

Meadows hesitated perceptibly. 'Look, I don't know if this is any use to you, but he was in here on his own one night, not exactly drunk, but well on the way. We were talking about some court case in the evening paper. Three blokes who'd smashed up an old-age pensioner for the three or four quid that was in her purse. I said blokes like that were the lowest form of animal life. He leaned across the bar and took me by the tie. "No, they're not, Harry," he said. "The lowest form of animal life is a screw".'

In other days the man who turned the key in the lock had been called a warder. In more enlightened times he was known as a prison officer, but to anyone who had ever served time he was a screw, hated and despised.

'You think he's been inside?' Miller said.

Meadows shrugged. 'Sounds crazy, I know, but I've reached the stage where I could believe anything about that one.' He opened the door. 'You don't think he killed Grace Packard, do you?'

'I haven't the slightest idea. What happened to Harold after the others left, by the way? You didn't tell me that.'

'I offered him a drink and he told me where to go and went out after them. Funny thing was he turned up again about five minutes afterwards full of apologies. Said he

95

was sorry he'd lost his temper and so on. Then he tried
to get Faulkner's address out of me.'

'He knew his name then?'

'Apparently he'd heard me use it during the fuss when
I called out to Faulkner to lay off.'

'Did you give him the address?'

'Do I look as if I came over on a banana boat?'
Meadows shrugged. 'Mind you, there's always the telephone book.'

'As you say.' Miller punched him lightly in the shoulder.
'See you soon, Harry.'

He went. Crossed the yard through the heavy rain.
Meadows watched him climb into the Cooper, then closed
the door.

.   .   .   .   .

Miller went up the steps of the Central Railway Station and paused to light a cigarette in the porch. The
match flared in his cupped hands briefly illuminating the
white face and dark eyes. Here and there in the vast con-
course a lounger stiffened, turned and faded briskly into
the night which was no more than Miller had intended for
the railway station of any great city is the same the world
over, a happy hunting ground for wrongdoers of every
description.

He moved across to the buffet by the ticket barrier and
looked in through the window. The young woman he was
searching for was sitting on a stool at one end of the tea
bar. She saw him at once, for there were few things in life
that she missed, and came out.

She was about twenty-five years of age with a pleasant,
open face and her neat tweed suit was in excellent taste.
She might have been a schoolteacher or someone's pri-

vate secretary. In fact she had appeared before the local bench on no fewer than five occasions for offences involving prostitution and had recently served three months in a detention centre.

She nodded familiarly. ' 'Evening, Mr. Miller, or should I say good morning?'

'Hello, Gilda. You must be hard up to turn out on a night like this with a bloody maniac hanging around out there in the rain.'

'I can look after myself.' When she lifted her umbrella he saw that the ferrule had been sharpened into a wicked looking steel point. 'Anyone makes a grab at me gets this through the eyes.'

Miller shook his head. 'You think you can take on the whole world, don't you? I wonder what you'll look like ten years from now.'

'Just older,' she said brightly.

'If you're lucky, only by then you'll be down to a different class of customer. Saturday night drunks at a quid a time for a quickie round the back of the station.'

She wasn't in the least offended. 'We'll see. What was it you wanted?'

'I suppose you heard there was a girl killed earlier tonight?'

'That's right. Other side of the park, wasn't it?'

'Her name was Grace Packard. I've been told she was on the game. Is that true?'

Gilda showed no particular surprise. 'Kinky looking little tart, all plastic mac and knee boots.'

'That's it.'

'She tried working the station about six months ago. Got herself into a lot of trouble.'

'What kind?'

97

'Pinching other people's regulars, that sort of thing. We moved her on in the end.'

'And how did you manage that?' She hesitated and he said harshly, 'Come on, Gilda, this is murder.'

'All right,' she said reluctantly. 'I asked Lonny Brogan to have a word with her. She took the point.'

'I can imagine she would after hearing what that big ape had to say,' Miller said. 'One other thing, did anyone pimp for her?'

Gilda chuckled contemptuously. 'Little half-baked kid with a face like the underbelly of a fish and black side-boards. Harold something or other. Christ knows what she saw in him.'

'You saw her give him money?'

'Plenty of times—mostly to get rid of him from what I could see.'

He nodded. 'All right, Gilda, I'll be seeing you.'

'Oh, Mr. Miller,' she said reprovingly. 'I hope you don't mean that the way it sounds.'

Her laughter echoed mockingly from the vaulted ceiling as he turned and walked away.

Eleven

When Brady and Harold entered the general office at Central C.I.D. it was bustling with activity for no man might reasonably expect to see his bed on a night like this. Brady left Harold on an uncomfortable wooden bench with the Saturday sport's paper and went in to Chief Superintendent Mallory who was using Grant's office.

Mallory was shaving with a battery-operated electric razor and reading a report at the same time. His white shirt was obviously fresh on and he looked crisp and alert in spite of the hour.

'I've got the girl's boy friend outside,' Brady said. 'Phillips his name is—Harold Phillips.'

'What's your first impression?'

'Oh, there's something there all right. For a start, he's an unpleasant little bastard.'

'You can't hang a man for that.'

'There's a lot more to it than that.'

Brady gave him the gist of his conversation with Harold and when he was finished, Mallory nodded. 'All right, let's have him in.'

When Brady called him, Harold entered with a certain bravado and yet his nervousness was betrayed in the muscle that twitched in his right cheek.

Mallory greeted him with extreme politeness. 'Good of you to come at this hour, Mr. Phillips. We appreciate it.'

Harold's confidence received a king-size boost and he sat down in the chair Brady brought forward and gave Mallory a big man-of-the-world smile. 'Anything I can do, Superintendent. You've only got to say.'

Brady offered him a cigarette. As he was lighting it, there was a knock on the door and Miller glanced in. He was about to withdraw, but Mallory shook his head and beckoned him inside. Miller closed the door behind him and took up a position by the window without a word.

'Now then, sir, just to get the record straight, you are Mr. Harold Phillips of 10, Narcia Place?' Mallory began.

'That's me.'

'I'm given to understand that you and Miss Grace Packard were engaged to be married. Is that correct?'

'I suppose you could say that in a way.' Harold

99

shrugged. 'I bought her a ring a couple of months back, but nothing was really official. I mean we hadn't set a date or anything.'

'I understand, sir. Now I wonder if you'd mind going over the events of last night again. I know you've already discussed this with Constable Brady, but it would help me to hear for myself.'

'Well, as I told Mr. Brady, I had a date with Grace at half-eight.'

'Just one moment, sir. What happened before that? What time did you get home from work?'

Harold smiled bravely. 'To tell you the truth I'm not actually working at the moment, Superintendent. It's my back you see. I had this accident about a year ago so I have to be very careful.'

Mallory looked sympathetic. 'That must be difficult for you. You were saying that you had an appointment with Miss Packard at eight-thirty?'

'That's right. In The King's Arms, the one near Regent Square on the corner of Lazer Street.'

'And you kept that appointment?'

'I was a couple of minutes late. When I got there she was leaving with two blokes.'

'Who were they?'

'I don't know—never seen 'em before.'

'Did she often do this sort of thing?'

Harold sighed heavily. 'I'm afraid she did. She was sort of restless, if you know what I mean. Always looking for something new.'

It sounded like a line from a bad television play, but Mallory simply nodded and went on, 'What happened when you arrived and found her leaving with these two men?'

'I tried to stop her, tried to reason with her, but she

wouldn't listen.' Harold flushed. 'Then one of them got hold of me—great big bloke he was. He twisted my hand in one of these judo locks or something. Put me down on my face. That's when the landlord moved in and told 'em to clear off.'

'And what did you do then, sir?'

Harold frowned as if trying to remember. 'Oh, had a drink with the landlord—on the house.'

'Did you go straight home afterwards?'

'No, like I told Mr. Brady, I was too upset. I walked around in the rain for a while, then I had a coffee in the station buffet. Got home about half-nine. Me mum was in bed so I took her a cup of tea and went myself.'

Mallory had been making notes. He added a sentence and as he glanced up, Miller said, 'Excuse me, sir, I've been expecting a message.'

He went out into the main office, picked up the telephone on his desk and rang through to Mallory. 'Miller here, sir. He's lying.'

'That's certainly nice to know,' Mallory said calmly. 'I'll be straight out.'

He put down his phone and smiled brightly at Harold. 'I'll only be a moment.' He got to his feet and said to Brady, 'See that Mr. Phillips gets a cup of tea, will you Constable? There should be some left in the pot.'

He found Miller sitting on the edge of his desk drinking someone else's coffee. Mallory sat down in the chair and started to fill his pipe. 'Nasty little bastard, isn't he?'

'He may have his moments, but they must be few and far between,' Miller said. 'To start with I've seen Harry Meadows, the landlord of The King's Arms. After the fuss, he offered Harold a drink on the house. Harold told him to get stuffed and went off after the others. Five minutes later he returned full of apologies to claim his free glass.'

'Now why would he do that?' Mallory said thoughtfully.

'Apparently he spent the time trying to pump Meadows. Wanted to know where Faulkner lived.'

'You mean he actually knew Faulkner by name?'

'Oh, yes, he made that clear enough. He'd heard Meadows use it during the argument.'

Mallory grinned like the Cheshire cat, the first time Miller had ever seen him smile. 'Well that's a nice fat juicy lie he's told us for a start.'

'There's more,' Miller said. 'Grace Packard was on the game. Worked the station until the rest of the girls moved her on a month or two back. According to my informant she had a boy friend who picked up her earnings pretty regularly. The description fits our Harold exactly.'

Mallory got to his feet. 'Let's go back in.'

Harold was half-way through his third cigarette and glanced round nervously when the door opened. 'Sorry about that, Mr. Phillips,' Mallory said. He smiled heartily and held out his hand. 'Well, I don't think we need to detain you any longer. You can go back to bed now.'

Harold's mouth gaped. 'You mean you don't need me any more?'

'That's right. The information you've given us will be most helpful. I can't thank you enough for turning out at this hour in the morning. It's that kind of co-operation that helps us beat these things you know.' He turned to Brady who came to attention briskly. 'See that Mr. Phillips gets home will you, Constable?'

'See to it myself, sir.' Brady put a hand under Harold's

102

elbow, looking more avuncular than ever. 'Have you home in fifteen minutes, sir.'

Harold grinned. 'Be seeing you, Superintendent,' he said and went out of the room like a turkey-cock.

Mallory sat down and put a match to his pipe. 'No harm in letting him think he's out of the wood for a few hours. When we pull him in again in the morning the shock will just about cripple him.'

'You really think he's got something to hide, sir?' Miller demanded.

'He's lying when he says he doesn't know Faulkner by name—that's for a start. Then there's this business about the girl—the fact that he was pimping for her.'

'It still doesn't add up to murder.'

'It never does to start with, Sergeant. Suppositions, inaccuracies, statements that don't really hold water—that's all we ever have to work with in most cases. For example, Phillips says that he walked the streets for a while after leaving the pub, then had a coffee at the station buffet. How many people would you say use that buffet on a Saturday night?'

'Thousands, sir.'

'Exactly. In other words it would be unreasonable to expect some sort of personal identification by any of the buffet staff. Another thing—as far as we can judge at the moment, the girl was killed at around half-ten.'

'And Phillips was home at nine-thirty and in bed ten minutes or so later. What was it he said? That he took his mother a cup of tea?'

'Interesting thing about Mrs. Phillips,' Mallory said. 'Brady had to kick on the door for a good five minutes before he could rouse Phillips. There wasn't a bleat from the old girl. In fact Phillips told him she was sleeping like a baby.'

Miller frowned. 'That doesn't make very good sense.'

'Even more interesting was the bottle of Canbutal capsules Brady found on the mantelpiece. A couple of those things and you wouldn't hear a bomb go off in the next street.'

'Might be an idea to check with her doctor in the morning, just to get a complete picture.'

Mallory nodded. 'Brady can handle that.' He got to his feet. 'I'm going over to the Medical School now. We've hauled Professor Murray out of bed. He's going to get cracking on the post-mortem just as soon as the Forensic boys have finished with her. You'd better get a couple of hours' sleep in the rest room. If I want you, I'll phone.'

Miller helped him on with his coat. 'What about Faulkner?'

Mallory shook his head. 'I never had much of a hunch about him, not in the way I do about Phillips.'

'I'm afraid I can't agree with you there, sir.'

For a moment, Mallory poised on the brink of one of those sudden and terrible wraths for which he was famous. With a great effort he managed to control himself and said acidly, 'Don't tell me you're going to solve this thing in a burst of intuitive genius, Miller?'

'Meadows had some very interesting things to say about him, sir,' Miller said patiently. 'There's a pattern of violence there that just doesn't fit in a man of his background. He uses force too easily, if you follow me.'

'So do I when the occasion calls for it,' Mallory said. 'Is that all you have to go on?'

'Not exactly, sir. He had a pretty strange conversation with Meadows one night when he was drunk. Meadows got the impression that he'd been inside.'

Mallory frowned. 'Did he indeed? Right, get on to C.R.O. in London. Tell them it's for me. Say I want everything they have on Faulkner by breakfast. I'll discuss it with you then.'

The door banged behind him and Miller grinned softly. For a moment there, just for a moment, it had looked as if they were going to clash. That moment would come again because George Mallory was a stubborn man and Nick Miller was a sleeping partner in a business so large that he didn't need to put himself out to anyone for the sake of keeping his job. Not God or even Chief Superintendents from New Scotland Yard. An interesting situation. He lit a cigarette, picked up Mallory's telephone and asked for Information Room.

Twelve

The small rest room was badly overcrowded and there was hardly room to move between the camp beds which had been specially imported. Miller slept badly which was hardly surprising. There was an almost constant disturbance at what seemed like five minute intervals throughout the night as colleagues were sent for and the rain continued to hammer relentlessly against the window pane above his head.

At about seven a.m. he gave up the struggle, got a towel and went along the corridor to the washroom. He stood under a hot shower for a quarter of an hour, soaking the tiredness away and then sampled the other end of the scale, an ice-cold needle spray for precisely thirty seconds just to give himself an appetite.

He was half-way through a plate of bacon and eggs and

on his third cup of tea in the canteen when Brady found him. The big Irishman eased himself into the opposite chair and pushed a flimsy across the table.

'Hanley in Information asked me to give you that. Just come in from C.R.O. in London.'

Miller read it quickly and took a deep breath. 'Quite a lad when he gets going, our Bruno. Where's Mallory?'

'Still at the post-mortem.'

Miller pushed back his chair. 'I'd better get over to the Medical School then. You coming?'

Brady shook his head. 'I still haven't contacted Mrs. Phillips' doctor. Mallory told me to wait till after breakfast. Said there was no rush. I'll be across as soon as I've had a word with him.'

'I'll see you then,' Miller said and left quickly.

.   .   .   .   .

The mortuary was at the back of the Medical School, a large, ugly building in Victorian Gothic with stained glass windows and the vaguely religious air common to the architecture of the period.

Jack Palmer, the Senior Technician, was sitting in his small glass office at the end of the main corridor and he came to the door as Miller approached.

'Try and arrange your murders at a more convenient hour next time will you,' he said plaintively. 'My first Saturday night out in two months ruined. My wife was hopping mad, I can tell you.'

'My heart bleeds for you, Jack,' Miller said amiably. 'Where's the top brass?'

'Having tea inside. I shouldn't think you rate a cup.'

Miller opened the door on the other side of the office and went into the white-tiled hall outside the theatre. Mallory was there, seated at a small wooden table talking to Henry Wade, the Head of Forensic, and Professor Stephen Murray, the University Professor of Pathology, a tall, spare Scot.

Murray knew Miller socially through his brother and greeted him with the familiarity of an old friend. 'You still look as if you've stepped straight out of a whisky advert, Nick, even at eight-fifteen in the morning. How are you?'

'Fine—nothing that a couple of weeks' leave wouldn't cure.' Miller turned to Mallory. 'I've just been handed the report on Faulkner from C.R.O.'

'Anything interesting?'

'I think you could say that, sir. Harry Meadows wasn't wrong—he does have a record. Fined twice for assault and then about two years ago he ran amok at some arty Chelsea party.'

'Anybody hurt?'

'His agent. Three broken ribs and a fractured jaw. Faulkner's a karate expert so when he loses his temper it can have rather nasty results.'

'Did they send him down?'

'Six months and he did the lot. Clocked one of the screws and lost all his remission.'

'Anything known against him since?'

'Not a thing. Apparently some sort of psychiatric investigation was carried out when he was inside so there's quite an interesting medical report. Should be along soon.'

Mallory seemed curiously impatient. 'All right, all right, we'll talk about it later.' He turned to Professor Murray. 'What do you think then, is this another Rainlover thing or isn't it?'

'That's for you to decide,' Murray said. 'I'm the last man to make that kind of prediction—I've been at this game too long. If you mean are there any obvious differences between this murder and the others, all I can say is yes and leave you to form your own conclusions.'

'All right, Professor, fire away.'

Murray lit a cigarette and paced up and down restlessly. 'To start with the features which are similar. As in all the other cases, the neck was broken cleanly with a single powerful blow, probably a blunt instrument with a narrow edge.'

'Or the edge of the hand used by an expert,' Miller suggested.

'You're thinking of karate, I suppose,' Murray smiled faintly. 'Always possible, but beware of trying to make the facts fit your own suppositions, Nick. A great mistake in this game, or so I've found.'

'What other similarities were present, Professor?' Mallory asked, obviously annoyed at Miller's interruption.

'No physical ones. Time, place, weather—that's what I was meaning. Darkness and rain—the lonely street.'

'And the features in this one that don't fit?' Henry Wade said. 'What about those?'

'Recent bruising on the throat, another bruise on the right cheek as if someone had first grabbed her angrily around the neck and then struck her a violent blow, probably with his fist. The death blow came afterwards. Now this is a very real departure. In the other cases, there was no sign of violence except in the death blow itself. Quick, sharp, clean, obviously totally unexpected.'

'And in this case the girl obviously knew what was coming,' Mallory said.

Henry Wade shook his head. 'No, I'm afraid that won't work, sir. If she was attacked by an unknown assailant, she'd have put up some sort of a struggle, even if it was only to get her nails to his face. We didn't find any signs that would indicate that such a struggle took place.'

'Which means that she stood there and let someone knock her about,' Mallory said. 'Someone she knew.'

'I don't see how we can be certain of that, sir.' Miller couldn't help pointing out what seemed an obvious flaw. 'She was on the game after all. Why couldn't she have been up that alley with a potential customer?'

Again the irritation was noticeable in Mallory's voice. 'Would she have stood still while he grabbed her throat, fisted her in the face? Use your intelligence, Sergeant. It's quite obvious that she took a beating from someone she was perfectly familiar with and she took it because she was used to it.'

'I think the Superintendent's got a point, Nick,' Henry Wade said. 'We're all familiar with the sort of relationship a prostitute has with her minder. Beatings are the order of the day, especially when the pimp thinks his girl isn't coughing up all her earnings and the women take their hidings quietly, too. God knows why. I suppose a psychiatrist would have an answer.'

'True enough,' Miller admitted.

'And there's one important point you're forgetting,' Wade added. 'In every Rainlover case yet he's always taken some memento. Either an article of clothing or a personal belonging. That doesn't seem to have happened here.'

'Anything else, Miller?' Mallory enquired.'

'Was there any cash in her handbag, sir?'

'Two or three pounds in notes and silver.'

'Faulkner said he gave her a ten-pound note.'

Exactly, Sergeant.' Mallory gave him a slight, ironic smile. 'Any suggestions as to what happened to it?'

'No, sir.' Miller sighed. 'So we're back to Harold Phillips?'

'That's right and I want him pulled in now. You can take Brady with you.'

'And Faulkner, sir?'

'Oh, for God's sake, Sergeant, don't you ever take no for an answer?'

There was an electric moment and then Murray cut in smoothly. 'All very interesting, gentlemen, but you didn't allow me to finish my story. If it's of any use to you, the girl had intercourse just before her death.'

Mallory frowned. 'No suggestion of rape, is there?'

'None whatsoever. In view of the conditions I would say the act took place against the wall and definitely with her consent. Of course one can't judge whether under threat or not.'

Mallory got to his feet. 'Only another nail in his coffin.' He turned to Miller. 'Go and get Phillips now and bring the clothes he was wearing last night. I'll expect you back within half an hour.'

There was a time to argue and a time to go quietly. Miller went without a word.

.   .   .   .   .

Miller met Brady coming down the steps of the main entrance of the Town Hall. 'You look as if you've lost a quid and found a tanner,' he told Miller. 'What's up?'

'We've got to pull Harold Phillips in right away. Mallory thinks he's the mark.'

'Harold—the Rainlover?' Brady said incredulously.

Miller shook his head. 'Could be this wasn't a Rainlover killing, Jack. There were differences—I'll explain on the way.'

'Did you and Mallory have a row or something?' Brady asked as they went down the steps to the Mini-Cooper.

110

'Not quite. He's got the bit between his teeth about Harold and I just don't see it, that's all.'

'And what about Faulkner?'

'The other side of the coin. Mallory thinks exactly as I do about Harold.'

'He could change his mind,' Brady said as they got in the car. 'I've just seen a report from Dwyer, the beat man who found the body and got slugged.'

'How is he?' Miller said as he switched on the ignition and drove away.

'A bit of concussion, that's all. They're holding him in the infirmary for observation. There's an interesting tit-bit for you in his report though. Says that about ten minutes before finding the body, he bumped into a bloke leaving the coffee stall in Regent Square.'

'Did he recognise him?'

'Knows him well—local resident. A Mr. Bruno Faulkner.'

The Mini-Cooper swerved slightly as Miller glanced at him involuntarily. 'Now that is interesting.'

He slowed suddenly, turning the car into the next street and Brady said, 'Now where are we going? This isn't the way to Narcia Street.'

'I know that coffee stall,' Miller said. 'Run by an old Rugby pro called Sam Harkness. He usually closes about nine on a Sunday morning after catching the breakfast trade.'

Brady shook his head sadly. 'Mallory is just going to love you for this. Ah well, a short life and a merry one.' He eased back in the seat and started to fill his pipe.

.   .   .   .   .   .

Rain drifted across Regent Square in a grey curtain and

111

when Miller braked to a halt, there were only two customers at the coffee stall, all-night taxi drivers eating fried egg sandwiches in the shelter of the canopy. Miller and Brady ran through the rain and Harkness turned from the stove, a frying pan in his hand.

'Oh, it's you, Mr. Miller. Looking for breakfast?'

'Not this time, Sam,' Miller said. 'Just a little information. You know about last night's murder in Dob Court?'

'Don't I just? Cars around here most of the night. Did all right out of it in tea and wads, I can tell you.'

'I've just been looking at Constable Dwyer's report on what happened. He says he called here about ten past ten.'

'That's right.'

'I understand you had a customer who was just leaving —a Mr. Bruno Faulkner according to Dwyer.'

Harkness nodded and poured out a couple of teas. 'Artist. Lives round the corner from here. Regular customer of mine. Turns out at any old time in the a.m. when he's run out of fags. You know what they're like, these blokes.'

'And it was cigarettes he wanted last night was it?' Brady asked.

'He bought twenty Crown King-size. As a matter of fact I'm waiting for him to look in again. He left a pair of gloves—lady's gloves.'

He searched under the counter and produced them. They were in imitation black leather, heavily decorated with pieces of white plastic and diamanté, cheap and ostentatious—the sort of thing that was to be found in any one of a dozen boutiques which had sprung up in the town of late to cater for the needs of young people.

'Rather funny really,' Harkness said. 'He pulled them out of his pocket when he was looking for change. I said they were hardly his style. He seemed a bit put out to me.

112

Tried to make out they were his fiancée's, but that was just a load of cobblers if you ask me. She's been here with him—his fiancée I mean—Joanna Hartmann. You see her on the telly all the time. Woman like that wouldn't wear this sort of rubbish.'

Amazing how much people told you without being asked. Miller picked up the gloves. 'I'll be seeing Mr. Faulkner later this morning, Sam. I'll drop these in at the same time.'

'Probably still in bed with the bird they belong to,' Harkness called. 'Bloody artists. I should be so lucky.'

'So Faulkner had Grace Packard's gloves in his pocket,' Brady said when they got back to the Mini-Cooper. 'So what? He didn't deny having her at his flat. He'll simply say she left the gloves by mistake or something.'

Miller handed him the gloves, took out his wallet and produced a pound note. 'This is on me, Jack. Take a taxi to the Packard house. I don't suppose the mother's in too good a state, but see if the father can give you a positive identification on those gloves. Come straight on to Narcia Street from there. I'll be waiting for you.'

'Mallory isn't going to like this.'

'That's just too bloody bad. How far did you get with Mrs. Phillips' doctor?'

'He wouldn't discuss it on the phone. It's that Indian bloke—Lal Das. You know what these wogs are like. Give 'em an inch and they'll take a mile every time.'

'All right, Jack, all right, I'll see him myself,' Miller said, an edge to his voice for the kind of racial prejudice that seemed to be part of the make-up of so many otherwise decent men like Brady was guaranteed to bring out the worst in him.

'Half an hour then,' Brady said, checking his watch. 'That's all it should take.'

113

'I'll wait for you outside.' Miller watched him run across to one of the taxis, got into the Mini-Cooper and drove away quickly.

Thirteen

Lal Das, to whom Brady had referred so contemptuously, was a tall, cadaverous Indian. A Doctor of Medicine and a Fellow of the Royal College of Physicians, he could have secured a senior post in a major hospital any time he wanted and yet he preferred to run a large general practice in one of the less salubrious parts of the city. He had a national reputation in the field of drug addiction and, in this connection, Miller had frequently sought his advice.

The Indian had just finished breakfast and was working his way through the Sunday supplements when Miller was shown in. Das smiled and waved him to a seat. 'Just in time for coffee.'

'Thanks very much.'

'Business or did you just happen to be in the neighbourhood?'

Miller took the cup of coffee the Indian handed to him and shook his head. 'You had a call earlier—a query concerning a Mrs. Phillips of 10, Narcia Street.'

The Indian nodded. 'That's right. The officer who spoke to me wasn't terribly co-operative. Wouldn't tell me what the whole thing was about, so I simply refused to give him the information he required until I knew more about it. A doctor/patient relationship can only function satisfactorily when there is an atmosphere of complete

114

trust. I would only be prepared to discuss a patient's case history and private affairs in exceptional circumstances.'

'Would murder be extreme enough?' Miller asked.

Lal Das sighed and put down his cup carefully. 'I think you'd better tell me about it. I'll judge for myself.'

'Fair enough. The man at the centre of things is the woman's son—Harold Phillips. Presumably he's a patient of yours also?'

An expression of real distaste crossed the Indian's face. 'For my sins. A particularly repellant specimen of present-day youth.'

'He had a girl friend called Grace Packard. Ever meet her?'

Das shook his head. 'I notice you use the past tense.'

'She was murdered last night. Naturally Harold was called upon to explain his movements, especially as he'd had some sort of row with her earlier in the evening. His story is that he was home by nine-thirty. He says that his mother was in bed and that he took her a cup of tea and went himself.

'So his mother is his alibi?'

'That's about the size of it. The murder was committed around ten-fifteen you see.'

Das nodded. 'But what is it you want from me? Surely it's straightforward enough.'

'It might have been if something rather strange hadn't occurred. Two police officers went to Narcia Street just after midnight to bring Harold in for questioning. They had to kick on the door for a good five minutes before he showed any signs of life. His mother failed to put in an appearance at all. He said she was sleeping like a baby and hadn't been very well, but according to the officer in charge, no one could have slept through such a disturbance.'

115

'Unless drugged of course,' Das said.

'He did find a box of Canbutal capsules on the mantelpiece, which seemed to offer a solution.'

'So what you're really wondering is whether or not Mrs. Phillips could have been in bed and asleep when Harold returned home—whenever that was.'

'Naturally—I understand Canbutal is pretty powerful stuff. I also understand that it's not usually prescribed in simple cases of insomnia.'

Das got to his feet, went to the fireplace and selected a black cheroot from a sandalwood box. 'What I tell you now must be treated in the strictest confidence. You're right about Canbutal. It works best in cases where the patient cannot sleep because of extreme pain. It's as close to the old-fashioned knock-out drops as you can get.'

'Mrs. Phillips must be pretty ill to need a thing like that.'

'Cancer.'

There was a moment of silence as if darkness had drifted into the room. Miller took a deep breath and went on, 'Does Harold know?'

'She doesn't know herself. She's had bronchial trouble for years. She thinks this is the same thing she gets every winter only a little worse than usual. She'll go very quickly. Any time, any day.'

'What kind of an effect would the Canbutal have—can she be awakened, for example?'

'That would depend on the amount taken. Mrs. Phillips is on a dosage of two each night. She visits me once a week and I give her a prescription for a week's supply. As a matter of fact I saw her yesterday morning.'

'But she definitely could be awakened even an hour or two after having taken a couple of these things?'

'Certainly. Mind you, it depends on what you mean by

awakened. What took place might seem like a dream to her afterwards—there might not even be a memory of it.'

Miller got to his feet. 'Very helpful—very helpful indeed.'

They went out into the hall and Das opened the door for him. 'Do you intend to arrest young Phillips? Is there really a case against him?'

'I've been ordered to take him in again for further questioning,' Miller said. 'I can't be more definite than that. I suppose you've heard that Grant's in hospital after a car accident? That means the Scotland Yard man, Chief Superintendent Mallory, is in charge. If you want to go any further with this, he's the man to see.'

'I'm concerned with one thing only,' Das said. 'The welfare of Mrs. Phillips. I would hope that you could keep the seriousness of this business from her until the last possible moment. If you intend to question her then I think I should be there.'

'As I said, I'm going round to pick up her son now,' Miller told him. 'And there are obviously certain questions I must put to his mother. You're perfectly at liberty to come with me. In fact I'd welcome it.'

'Very well,' Das said. 'I'll follow in my own car. You'll wait for me before entering?'

'Certainly,' Miller said and he went down the steps to the Mini-Cooper and drove away.

.   .   .   .   .

Brady was standing in the doorway of a newsagent's shop just round the corner from Narcia Street and he ran across the road through the heavy rain and scrambled into the Mini-Cooper as Miller slowed.

117

'Not bad timing,' he said. 'I've only just got here.' He produced the gloves. 'The girl's father recognised these straightaway. He bought them for her as a birthday present. She was with him at the time. He even remembers the shop. That boutique place in Grove Square.'

'Good enough,' Miller said. 'I've seen Das. He tells me you only prescribe Canbutal when a patient can't sleep because of pain.'

'So the old girl's in a bad way?'

'You could say that. Das is following on behind, by the way. He's coming in with us, just in case she gets a funny turn or anything.'

'Good enough,' Brady said.

A horn sounded behind them as Das arrived. Miller moved into gear, drove round the corner into Narcia Street and pulled up outside number ten.

When Harold opened the door there was a momentary expression of dismay on his face that was replaced in an instant by a brave smile.

'Back again then?' he said to Brady.

'This is Detective Sergeant Miller,' Brady said formally. 'He'd like a few words with you.'

'Oh, yes.' Harold glanced at Das curiously. 'What are you doing here?'

'I'm interested in one thing only,' Das said. 'Your mother's welfare. In her present state of health she can't stand shocks so I thought it better to be on hand.'

They all went into the living-room and Miller said, 'I wonder whether you'd mind getting dressed, sir? We'd like you to come down to Central C.I.D. with us.'

'I've already been there once,' Harold said. 'What is this?'

'Nothing to get excited about, son,' Brady said kindly. 'One or two new facts have come up about the girl and

118

Chief Superintendent Mallory thinks you might be able to help him, that's all.'

'All right then,' Harold said. 'Give me five minutes.'

He went out and Brady picked up the box of Canbutal capsules from the mantelpiece. 'These are what she's been taking,' he said, holding them out to Miller.

Das took the box, opened it and spilled the capsules out on his palm. He frowned. 'I gave her the prescription for these at two-thirty yesterday afternoon. She's taken three since then.' He put the capsules back into the box. 'I think I'd better go up and see her.'

'All right,' Miller said. 'I'll come with you.'

'Is that absolutely necessary?'

Miller nodded. 'I must ask her to confirm Harold's story—can't avoid it. Better with you here surely.'

'I suppose so. It might help for the present if you could handle it other than as a police enquiry though. Is there really any need to upset her at this stage?'

'I'll do what I can.'

Das obviously knew his way. They went up the stairs and he opened the door that stood directly opposite. The curtains were still half-drawn and the room was grey and sombre. The furniture was many years old, mainly heavy Victorian mahogany and the brass bed had now become a collector's item if only its occupant had realised that fact.

She was propped against the pillows, eyes closed, head turned slightly to one side, the flesh drawn and tight across the bones of her face. Someone on the way out. Miller had seen it before and he knew the signs. Death was a tangible presence, waiting over there in the shadows to take her out of her misery like a good friend.

Das sat on the bed and gently touched her shoulder. 'Mrs. Phillips?'

The eyes fluttered open, gazed at him blindly, closed.

119

She took several deep breaths, opened her eyes again and smiled weakly. 'Doctor Das.'

'How are you today, Mrs. Phillips. Little bit better?'

The Indian's slightly sing-song voice was incredibly soothing carrying with it all the compassion and kindness in the world.

'What day is it, Doctor?' She was obviously muddled and bewildered, the effects of the drug Miller surmised.

'Sunday, my dear. Sunday morning.'

She blinked and focussed her eyes on Miller. 'Who—who are you?'

Miller came forward and smiled. 'I'm a friend of Harold's, Mrs. Phillips. He was supposed to meet me last night, but he didn't turn up. I thought I'd better call and see if everything was all right.'

'He's about somewhere,' she said in a dead voice. 'A good boy, Harold. He brought me some tea when he came in.'

'When would that be, Mrs. Phillips?' Miller said softly.

'When?' She frowned, trying to concentrate. 'Last night, I think. That's right—it was last night when he came in.' She shook her head. 'It gets harder to remember.'

'Did Harold tell you that he brought you tea last night, Mrs. Phillips?'

'I don't know—I don't remember. He's a good boy.' Her eyes closed. 'A good boy.'

Behind them the door opened and Harold appeared. 'What's going on here?' he demanded angrily.

'Your mother is very ill,' Das said. 'I must make arrangements to have her admitted to hospital at once.' He held up the box of Canbutal capsules. 'Did you know she has been increasing her dosage? Didn't I warn you that the effects could be disastrous?'

Harold had turned very pale. Brady appeared behind him and took his arm. 'Come on, son,' he said. 'Let's go.'

They moved to the head of the stairs and Miller went after them. 'Are those the clothes you were wearing last night?' he asked Harold.

Harold turned, answering in a kind of reflex action, 'Sure.' Then it dawned on him and fear showed in his eyes. 'Here, what is this?'

'Take him down,' Miller said and turned away.

Das closed the bedroom door quietly. 'Things don't look too good for him, do they?'

'He's in for a bad time, that's as much as I can say at the moment. What about her? Anything I can do?'

'Don't worry. They have a telephone next door. I'll ring for an ambulance and stay with her till it comes. You'll keep me posted?'

Miller nodded and they went downstairs. When he opened the door, rain drifted to meet him, pushed across the slimy cobbles by the wind. He looked down towards the Mini-Cooper where Harold sat in the rear with Brady.

'Sunday morning,' he said. 'What a hell of a way to make a living.'

'We all have a choice, Sergeant,' Das told him.

Miller glanced at him sharply, but nothing showed in that brown, enigmatic face. He nodded formally. 'I'll be in touch,' and moved out into the rain.

Fourteen

When they reached Central C.I.D. they took Harold to the Interrogation Room where, in spite of his angry protests, he was relieved of his trousers.

'What the hell do you think you're playing at?' he demanded. 'I've got my rights, just like anyone else.'

'Our lab boys just want to run a few tests, son, that's all,' Brady informed him. 'If they come out right, you'll be completely eliminated from the whole enquiry. You'd like that, wouldn't you?'

'You go to hell,' Harold shouted furiously. 'And you can knock off the Father Christmas act.'

There was a knock on the door and a constable entered carrying a pair of police uniform trousers. 'Better get into those and do as you're told,' Miller said, tossing them across. 'You'll make it a lot easier on yourself in the long run.' He turned to Brady. 'I've got things to do. I'll see you later.'

The medical report on Faulkner which C.R.O. had promised was waiting on his desk. He read it through quickly, then again, taking his time. When he was finished, he sat there for a while, staring into space, a frown on his face. He finally got up and crossed to Mallory's office taking the report with him.

The Chief Superintendent was seated at his desk examining a file and glanced up impatiently. 'Took you long enough. What's going on then?'

'Brady's got him in the Interrogation Room now, sir. His trousers have gone over to Forensic for examination. I understand Inspector Wade's got one of the Medical

School serologists to come in. You should get a quick result.'

'You saw the mother?'

Miller told him what had taken place at Narcia Street. 'From the looks of her, I wouldn't give her long.'

Mallory nodded. 'So Master Harold could have awakened her at any time with that cup of tea, that seems to be what it comes down to. From what the doctor says she wouldn't know whether it was yesterday or today in her condition.'

'That's about the size of it.'

'Good show.' Mallory rubbed his hands together. 'I'll let him stew for a while then get to work. I don't think he'll last long.'

'You sound pretty certain.'

'You're a smart lad, Miller, so I'm going to tell you something for your own good. You don't know what it's all about up here in the sticks. I've been on more murder investigations than you've had hot dinners. You get an instinct for these things, believe me. Harold Phillips killed that girl—I'd stake my reputation on it.'

'And what about Faulkner? He's still a strong possibility in my book. Have you read Constable Dwyer's report yet on what happened last night?'

'I know what you're going to say,' Mallory said. 'He saw Faulkner at a coffee stall in Regent Square just before the murder took place.'

'Something he conveniently forgot to mention to us when we questioned him.'

'Perfectly understandable in the circumstances.'

Miller produced the gloves and tossed them down on the desk. 'Those belonged to Grace Packard. Faulkner left them at the coffee stall by mistake.'

123

Mallory picked them up, frowning. 'You mean you've been there this morning?'

'That's right. Brady told me about Dwyer's report. I thought I might as well call at the coffee stall on my way to pick young Phillips up, just to see what the proprietor had to say.'

'I thought I told you I wanted Phillips picked up right away?' Mallory demanded harshly.

'So I wasted ten minutes. Would it interest you to know that when those gloves dropped out of Faulkner's pocket he told the owner of the coffee stall they belonged to his fiancée? Now why would he do that?'

Mallory laughed in his face. 'Because he didn't want him to know he'd been out with another woman or is that too simple for you?'

'But a great many people already knew he'd been in Grace Packard's company that night. Everyone at the party saw him leave with her. Why tell the bloke at the coffee stall such a silly lie at this stage?'

'I think you're placing far too much importance on a very minor incident.'

'But is it minor, sir? Inspector Wade reminded us earlier that in every other incident the Rainlover had taken some item or another from the victim. He said that didn't seem to have happened in this case. Can we be certain of that knowing about these gloves?'

'So we're back to the Rainlover again?' Mallory shook his head. 'It won't fit, Miller. There are too many other differences.'

'All right,' Miller said. 'But I still think Faulkner has a lot of explaining to do. To start with he was in the girl's company and his reasons for taking her back to the flat were eccentric enough to be highly suspect.'

'Not at all,' Mallory countered. 'Typical behaviour according to his friends and past record.'

'He was in the immediate area of the murder only minutes before it took place, we've two witnesses to that. And he lied about the girl's gloves to Harkness.'

'Why did he visit the coffee stall? Did Harkness tell you that?'

'To buy cigarettes.'

'Was this the first time?'

'No, he frequently appeared at odd hours for the same reason.'

'Can you imagine what a good defence counsel would do with that?'

'All right,' Miller said. 'It's circumstantial—all of it, but there are too many contributing factors to ignore. Take this pattern of violence for example. Unusual in a man of his background. I've got the medical report on him here.'

He handed it across and Mallory shook his head. 'I haven't got time. Tell me the facts.'

'It's simple enough. He was involved in a serious car accident about six years ago—racing at Brand's Hatch. His skull was badly fractured, bone fragments in the brain and so on. He was damned lucky to pull through. His extreme aggressiveness has been a development since then. The psychiatrists who examined him at Wandsworth were definitely of the opinion that the behaviour pattern was a direct result of the brain damage, probably made worse by the fragments of bone which the surgeons had been unable to remove. The pattern of violence grew worse during his sentence. He was involved in several fights with prisoners and attacked a prison officer. He was advised to enter an institution for treatment on his discharge, but refused.'

'All right, Miller, all right.' Mallory held up both hands defensively. 'You go and see him—do anything you like. I'll handle Harold.'

'Thank you, sir,' Miller said formally.

He got the door half-open and Mallory added, 'One more thing, Miller. A quid says Harold Phillips murdered Grace Packard.'

'Fair enough, sir.'

'And I'll give you odds of five-to-one against Bruno Faulkner.'

'Well, I don't really like to take the money, but if you insist, sir.' Miller grinned and gently closed the door.

. . . .

It was at that precise moment in another part of the city that the man known as the Rainlover opened his Sunday newspaper and found Sean Doyle staring out at him from the middle of page two. He recognised him instantly and sat there staring at the picture for a long moment, remembering the girl standing in the lighted doorway and the darkness and the rain falling.

He had unfinished business there, but first it would be necessary to get rid of the man. Of course he could always telephone the police anonymously, give them the address, tell them that Doyle was in hiding there. On the other hand, they would probably arrest the girl also for harbouring him.

The solution, when it came, was so simple that he laughed out loud. He was still laughing when he put on his hat and coat and went out into the rain.

. . . . .

Miller got no reply to his persistent knocking at Faulkner's door and finally went down the stairs to the flat below where someone was playing a tenor, cool and clear, so pure that it hurt a little.

The instrumentalist turned out to be an amiable West Indian in dark glasses and a neat fringe beard. He took off the glasses and grinned hugely.

'Aint's I seen you play piano at Chuck Lazer's club?'

'Could be,' Miller told him.

'Man, you were the most. Someone told me you was a John.' He shook his head. 'I tell you, man, you get some real crazy cats around these nights. Sick in the head. They'll say anything. You coming in?'

'I'm looking for Bruno Faulkner. Any idea where he might be? I can't get a reply.'

The West Indian chuckled. 'Sunday's his brick smashing day.'

'Come again?'

'Karate, man. He goes to the Kardon Judo Centre every Sunday morning for a workout. Of course if he can't find any bricks to smash he'd just as soon smash people.' He tapped his head. 'Nutty as a fruit cake. He don't need the stuff, man. He's already there.'

'Thanks for the information,' Miller said. 'See you sometime.'

'The original wild man from Borneo,' the West Indian called as he went down the stairs. 'That the best you Western European civilisation cats can do? The day is coming, man! The day is coming!'

From the sound of it, he was on the stuff himself, but Miller had other fish to fry and he got into the Mini-Cooper and drove away quickly.

Miller himself had been an ardent student of both judo and karate for several years. A brown belt in both, only the pressure of work had prevented him from progressing further. Although he did most of his own training at the police club, he was familiar with the Kardon Judo Centre and knew Bert King, the senior instructor, well.

There were two dojos and King was in the first supervising free practice with half a dozen young schoolboys. He was a small, shrunken man with a yellowing, parchment-like skin and a head that seemed too large for the rest of him. He was a fourth Dan in both judo and aikido and incredible in action on the mat as Miller knew to his cost.

King came across, all smiles. 'Hello, Sergeant Miller. Not seen you around much lately.'

'Never have the time, Bert,' Miller said. 'I'm looking for a man called Faulkner. Is he here?'

King's smile slipped a little, but he nodded. 'Next door.'

'You don't think much of him?' Miller demanded, quick to seize any opportunity.

'Too rough for my liking. To tell you the truth he's been on the borderline for getting chucked out of the club for some time now. Forgets himself, that's the trouble. Loses his temper.'

'Is he any good?'

'Karate—second Dan and powerful with it. He's good at the showy stuff—smashing bricks, beams of wood and so on. His judo is nowhere. I'll take you in. He's on his own.'

Faulkner wore an old judogi which had obviously been washed many times and looked powerful enough as he worked out in front of the full-length mirrors at one end of the dojo, going through the interminable and ritualistic exercises without which no student can hope to attain any

128

standard at all at karate. His kicks were one of his strongest features, very high and fast.

He paused to wipe the sweat from his face with a towel and noticed his audience. He recognised Miller at once and came forward, a sneer on his face.

'Didn't know you allowed coppers in here, Bert, I'll have to reconsider my membership.'

'Sergeant Miller's welcome here any time,' King said, his face flushed with anger. 'And I'd be careful about going on the mat with him if I were you. You could get a nasty surprise.'

Which was a slight exaggeration judging from what Miller had just seen, but Faulkner chuckled softly. 'And now you're tempting me—you really are.'

King went out and Faulkner rubbed his head briskly. 'I'm beginning to get you for breakfast, dinner and tea. Rather boring.'

'I can't help that,' Miller said and produced Grace Packard's gloves from his pocket. 'Recognise these?'

Faulkner examined then and sighed. 'Don't tell me. I left them at Sam Harkness's coffee stall in Regent Square last night. As I remember, I pulled them out of my pocket when looking for some loose change. He said something about them not being my style.'

'And you told him they belonged to your fiancée.'

'I know, Miller, very naughty of me. They were the Packard girl's. She left them at the flat.'

'Why did you lie about it to Harkness?'

'Be your age—why should I discuss my private affairs with him?'

'You've never seemed to show that kind of reluctance before.'

Faulkner's face went dark. 'Anything else, because if not I'd like to get on with my work-out?'

'You've had that. You've got a lot of explaining to do, Faulkner. A hell of a lot.'

'I see. Am I going to be arrested?'

'That remains to be seen.'

'So I'm still a free agent?' He glanced at his watch. 'I'll be here for another twenty minutes, Miller. After that I'll shower for five minutes, dress and take a taxi to my flat. If I have to see you, I'll see you there and nowhere else. Now good morning to you.'

He turned and stalked across the mat to the mirrors, positioned himself and started to practice front kicks. Strangely enough Miller didn't feel angry at all. In any case the flat would be preferable to the judo centre for the kind of conversation he envisaged. The important thing was that there was something there, something to be brought into the light. He was certain of that now. He turned and went out quickly, his stomach hollow with excitement.

Fifteen

The Gunner came awake slowly, yawned and stretched his arms. For a moment he stared blankly around him, wondering where he was and then he remembered.

It was quiet there in the comfortable old living-room— so quiet that he could hear the clock ticking and the soft patter of the rain as it drifted against the window.

The blanket with which Jenny Crowther had covered him had slipped down to his knees. He touched it gently for a moment, a smile on his mouth, then got to his feet and stretched again. The fire was almost out. He dropped to one knee, raked the ashes away and added a little of the kindling he found in the coal scuttle. He waited until the flames were dancing and then went into the kitchen.

He filled the kettle, lit the gas stove and helped himself to a cigarette from a packet he found on the table. He went to the window and peered out into the rain-swept yard and behind him, Jenny Crowther said, 'Never stops, does it?'

She wore an old bathrobe and the black hair hung straight on either side of a face that was clear and shining and without a line.

'No need to ask you if you slept well,' he said. 'You look as if they've just turned you out at the mint.'

She smiled right down to her toes and crossed to the window, yawning slightly. 'As a matter of fact I slept better than I have done for weeks. I can't understand it.'

'That's because I was here, darlin',' he quipped. 'Guarding the door like some faithful old hound.'

'There could be something in that,' she said soberly.

There was an awkward pause. It was as if neither of them could think of the right thing to say next, as if out of some inner knowledge they both knew that they had walked a little further towards the edge of some quiet place where anything might happen.

She swilled out the teapot and reached for the caddy and the Gunner chuckled. 'Sunday morning—used to be my favourite day of the week. You could smell the bacon frying all the way up to the bedroom.'

'Who was doing the cooking?'

'My Aunt Mary of course.' He tried to look hurt. 'What kind of a bloke do you think I am? The sort that keeps stray birds around the place?'

'I'm glad you put that in the plural. Very honest of you.'

131

On impulse, he moved in behind her and slid his arms about her waist, pulling her softness against him, aware from the feel of her that beneath the bathrobe she very probably had nothing on.

'Two and a half bleeding years in the nick. I've forgotten what it's like.'

'Well, you needn't think you're going to take it out on me.'

She turned to glance over her shoulder, smiling and then the smile faded and she turned completely, putting a hand up to his face.

'Oh, Gunner, you're a daft devil, aren't you?'

His hands cupped her rear lightly and he dropped his head until his forehead rested against hers. For some reason he felt like crying, all choked up so that he couldn't speak, just like being a kid again, uncertain in a cold world.

'Don't rub it in, lass.'

She tilted his chin and kissed him very gently on the mouth. He pushed her away firmly and held her off, a hand on each shoulder. What he said next surprised even himself.

'None of that now. You don't want to be mixed up with a bloke like me. Nothing but a load of trouble. I'll have a cup of tea and something to eat and then I'll be off. You and the old girl had better forget you ever saw me.'

'Why don't you shut up?' she said. 'Go and sit down by the fire and I'll bring the tea in.'

He sat in the easy chair and watched her arrange the tray with a woman's instinctive neatness and pour tea into two cups. 'What about the old girl?'

'She'll be hard on till noon,' Jenny said. 'Needs plenty of rest at her age.'

He sat there drinking his tea, staring into the fire and

132

she said softly, 'What would you do then if this was an ordinary Sunday?'

'In the nick?' He chuckled grimly. 'Oh, you get quite a choice. You can go to the services in the prison chapel morning and evening—plenty of the lads do that, just to get out of their cells. Otherwise you're locked in all day.'

'What do you do?'

'Read, think. If you're in a cell with someone else you can always play chess, things like that. If you're at the right stage in your sentence they let you out on to the landing for an hour or so in the evening to play table tennis or watch television.'

She shook her head. 'What a waste.'

He grinned and said with a return to his old flippancy, 'Oh, I don't know. What would I be doing Sundays on the outside? Spend the morning in the kip. Get up for three or four pints at the local and back in time for roast beef, Yorkshire pud and two veg. I'd have a snooze after that, work me way through the papers in the afternoon and watch the telly in the evening. What a bloody bore.'

'Depends who you're doing it with,' she suggested.

'You've got a point there. Could put an entirely different complexion on the morning in the kip for a start.'

She put down her cup and leaned forward. 'Why not go back, Gunner? There's nowhere to run to. The longer you leave it, the worse it will be.'

'I could lose all my remission,' he said. 'That would mean another two and a half years.'

'Are you certain you'd lose all of it?'

'I don't know. You have to take your chance on that sort of thing.' He grinned. 'Could have been back now if things had turned out differently last night.'

'What do you mean?' He told her about Doreen and what had happened at her flat. When he finished, Jenny

133

shook her head. 'What am I going to do with you?'

'I could make a suggestion. Two and a half years is a hell of a long time.'

She examined him critically and frowned. 'You know I hadn't realised it before, but you could do with a damned good scrub. You'll find a bathroom at the head of the stairs and there's plenty of hot water. Go on. I'll make you some breakfast while you're in the tub.'

'All right then, all right,' he said good-humouredly as she pulled him to his feet and pushed him through the door.

But he wasn't smiling when he went upstairs and locked himself in the bathroom. *Two and a half years*. The thought of it sent a wave of coldness through him, of sudden, abject despair. If only that stupid screw hadn't decided to sneak off to the canteen. If only he hadn't tried to touch up the staff nurse. But that was the trouble with life, wasn't it? Just one big series of ifs.

    .   .   .   .   .

He was just finishing dressing when she knocked on the door and said softly, 'Come into my room when you've finished Gunner—it's the next door. I've got some clean clothes for you.'

When he went into her room she was standing at the end of the bed bending over a suit which she had laid out. 'My father's,' she said. 'Just about the right fit I should say.'

'I can't take that, darlin',' the Gunner told her. 'If the coppers catch me in gear like that they'll want to know where it came from.'

She stared at him, wide-eyed. 'I hadn't thought of that.'

'If I go back it's got to be just the way I looked when I

turned up here last night otherwise they'll want to know where I've been and who's been helping me.'

The room was strangely familiar and he looked around him and grinned. 'You want to get a curtain for that window, darlin'. When I was in the loft last night I could see right in. Quite a view. One I'm not likely to forget in a hurry.' He sighed and said in a whisper, 'I wonder how many times I'll think of that during the next two and a half years.'

'Look at me, Gunner,' she said softly.

When he turned she was standing at the end of the bed. She was quite naked, her bathrobe on the floor at her feet. The Gunner was turned to stone. She was so lovely it hurt. She just stood there looking at him calmly, waiting for him to make a move, the hair like a dark curtain sweeping down until it gently brushed against the tips of the firm breasts.

He went towards her slowly, reaching out to touch like a blind man. Her perfume filled his nostrils and a kind of hoarse sob welled up in his throat.

He held her tightly in his arms, his head buried against her shoulder and she smoothed his hair and kissed him gently as a mother might a child. 'It's all right, Gunner. Everything's going to be all right.'

Gunner Doyle, the great lover. He was like some kid presented with the real thing for the first time. His hands were shaking so much that she had to unbutton his shirt and trousers for him. But afterwards it was fine, better than he had ever known it before. He melted into her flesh as she pulled him close and carried him away into warm, aching darkness.

.   .   .   .   .

135

Afterwards—a long time afterwards, or so it seemed—the telephone started to ring. 'I'd better see who it is.' She slipped from beneath the sheets, and reached for her bathrobe.

The door closed softly behind her and the Gunner got up and started to dress. He was fastening his belt when the door opened again and she stood there staring at him looking white and for the first time since he had known her, frightened.

He took her by the shoulders. 'What's up?'

'It was a man,' she said in a strained voice. 'A man on the phone. He said to tell you to get out fast. That the police would be here any time.'

'Jesus,' he said. 'Who was it?'

'I don't know,' she said and cracked suddenly. 'Oh, Gunner, what are we going to do?'

'You stay put, darlin', and carry on as normal,' he said, going to the bed and pulling on the boots she had given him. 'I'm the only one who has to do anything.'

He yanked the sweater over his head and she grabbed his arm. 'Give yourself up, Gunner.'

'First things first, darlin'. I've got to get out of here and so far away that the coppers don't have a hope of connecting me with you and the old girl.'

She looked up into his face for a moment then turned to the dressing-table and opened her handbag. She took out a handful of loose coins and three pound notes.

When she held the money out to him he tried to protest, but she shook her head. 'Better take it, just in case you decide to keep on running. I'm not holding you to anything.' She went to the wardrobe and produced an old single-breasted raincoat. 'And this. It was my father's. No use to him now.'

Suddenly she was the tough Yorkshire lass again,

136

rough, competent, completely unsentimental. 'Now you'd better get out of here.'

He pulled on the coat and she led the way into the passageway. The Gunner started towards the stairs and she jerked his sleeve. 'I've got a better way.'

He followed her up another flight of stairs, passing several doors which obviously led to upper rooms. At the top, they were confronted by a heavier door bolted on the inside and protected by a sheet of iron against burglars.

She eased back the bolts and the door swung open in the wind giving him a view of a flat roof between two high gables. There was a rail at one end and on the other side of it the roof sloped to the yard below.

'If you scramble over the gable end,' she said, pointing to the left, 'you can slide down the other side to the flat roof of a metalworks next door. Nothing to it for you —I've done it myself when I was a kid. You'll find a fire escape that'll take you all the way down into the next alley.'

He stared at her dumbly, rain blowing in through the open doorway, unable to think of anything to say. She gave him a sudden fierce push that sent him out into the open.

'Go on—get moving, you bloody fool,' she said and slammed the door.

He had never felt so utterly desolate, so completely cut-off from everything in his life. It was as if he had left everything worth having back there behind that iron door and there was nothing he could do about it. Not a damned thing.

He followed her instructions to the letter and a minute or so later hurried along the alley on the far side and turned into the street at the end.

137

He kept on walking in a kind of daze, his mind else-where, turning from one street into the other in the heavy rain. About ten minutes later he found himself on the edge of Jubilee Park. He went in through a corner entrance, past the enigmatic statue of good Queen Victoria, orb in one hand and sceptre in the other, and walked aimlessly into the heart of the park.

He didn't see a living soul which was hardly surprising considering the weather. Finally he came to an old folks' pavilion, the kind of place where pensioners congregated on calmer days to gossip and play dominos. The door was locked, but a bench beside it was partially sheltered from the rain by an overhanging roof. He slumped down, hands thrust deep into the pockets of the old raincoat and stared into the grey curtain. He was alone in a dead world. Completely and finally alone.

Sixteen

When Faulkner got out of the taxi there was no sign of Nick Miller. Faulkner was surprised, but hardly in a mood to shed tears over the matter. He hurried up to his flat, unlocked the door and went in. The fire had almost gone out and he took off his wet raincoat, got down on one knee and started to replenish it carefully. As the flames started to flicker into life the door bell sounded.

He opened it, expecting Miller, and found Joanna and Jack Morgan standing there.

'Surprise, surprise,' Faulkner said.

'Cut it out, Bruno,' Morgan told him. 'We had a visit

from Nick Miller early this morning and what he told us wasn't funny.'

Faulkner took Joanna's coat. 'This whole thing is beginning to annoy me and there's a nasty hint of worse to come. Visions of a lonely cell with two hard-faced screws, the parson snivelling at my side as I take that last walk along the corridor to the execution room.'

'You should read the papers more often. They aren't hanging murderers this season.'

'What a shame. No romance in anything these days, is there?'

Joanna pulled him round to face her. 'Can't you be serious for once? You're in real trouble. What on earth possessed you to bring that girl back here?'

'So you know about that, do you?'

'Miller told us, but I'd still like to hear about it from you,' Morgan said. 'After all, I am your lawyer.'

'And that's a damned sinister way of putting it for a start.'

The door bell rang sharply. In the silence that followed, Faulkner grinned. 'Someone I've been expecting. Excuse me a moment.'

.　　　.　　　.　　　.　　　.

When Miller left the judo centre he was feeling strangely elated. At the best of times police work is eighty per cent instinct—a special faculty that comes from years of handling every kind of trouble. In this present case his intuition told him that Faulkner had something to hide, whatever Mallory's opinion might be. The real difficulty was going to be in digging it out.

He sat in the car for a while, smoking a cigarette and thinking about it. Faulkner was a highly intelligent man

139

and something of a natural actor. He enjoyed putting on a show and being at the centre of things. His weakness obviously lay in his disposition to sudden, irrational violence, to a complete emotional turnabout during which he lost all control or at least that's what his past history seemed to indicate. If only he could be pushed over the edge . . .

Miller was filled with a kind of restless excitement at the prospect of the encounter to come and that was no good at all. He parked the car beside the corner gate of Jubilee Park, buttoned his trenchcoat up to the chin and went for a walk.

He didn't mind the heavy rain—rather liked it, in fact. It somehow seemed to hold him safe in a small private world in which he was free to think without distraction. He walked aimlessly for twenty minutes or so, turning from one path to another, not really seeing very much, his mind concentrated on one thing.

If he had been a little more alert he would have noticed the figure of a man disappearing fast round the side of the old folks' shelter as he approached, but he didn't and the Gunner watched him go, heart in mouth, from behind a rhododendron bush.

.　　　.　　　.　　　.　　　.

When Miller walked into the flat and found Joanna Hartmann and Morgan standing by the fire he wasn't in the least put out for their presence suited him very well indeed.

He smiled and nodded to the woman as he unbuttoned his damp raincoat. 'We seem to have seen rather a lot of each other during the past twenty-four hours.'

'Is there any reason why I shouldn't be here?' she demanded coldly.

'Good heavens no. I've just got one or two loose ends to tie up with Mr. Faulkner. Shouldn't take more than five minutes.'

'I understand you've already asked him a great many questions,' Morgan said, 'and now you intend to ask some more. I think we have a right to know where we stand in this matter.'

'Are you asking me as his legal representative?'

'Naturally.'

'Quite unnecessary, I assure you.' Miller lied smoothly. 'I'm simply asking him to help me with my enquiries, that's all. He isn't the only one involved.'

'I'm happy to hear it.'

'Shut up, Jack, there's a good chap,' Faulkner cut in. 'If you've anything to say to me, then get on with it, Miller. The sooner this damned thing is cleared up, the sooner I can get back to work.'

'Fair enough.' Miller moved towards the statues. 'In a way we have a parallel problem. I understand you started five weeks ago with one figure. In a manner of speaking, so did I.'

'A major difference if I might point it out,' Faulkner said. 'You now have five while I only have four.'

'But you were thinking of adding a fifth, weren't you?'

'Which is why I paid Grace Packard to pose for me, but it didn't work.' Faulkner shook his head. 'No, the damned thing is going to be cast as you see it now for good or ill.'

'I see.' Miller turned from the statues briskly. 'One or two more questions if you don't mind. Perhaps you'd rather I put them to you in private.'

'I've nothing to hide.'

'As you like. I'd just like to go over things again briefly. Mr. Morgan called for you about eight?'

'That's right.'

141

'What were you doing?'

'Sleeping. I'd worked non-stop on the fourth figure in the group for something like thirty hours. When it was finished I took the telephone off the hook and lay on the bed.'

'And you were awakened by Mr. Morgan?'

'That's it.'

'And then went to The King's Arms where you met Grace Packard? You're quite positive you hadn't met her previously?'

'What are you trying to suggest?' Joanna interrupted angrily.

'You don't need to answer that, Bruno,' Morgan said.

'What in the hell are you both trying to do . . . hang me? Why shouldn't I answer it? I've got nothing to hide. I should think Harry Meadows, the landlord, would be the best proof of that. As I recall, I had to ask him who she was. If you must know I thought she was on the game. I wasn't looking forward to the party and I thought she might liven things up.'

'And you met her boy friend on the way out?'

'That's it. He took a swing at me so I had to put him on his back.'

'Rather neatly according to the landlord. What did you use . . . judo?'

'Aikido.'

'I understand there was also some trouble at the party with Mr. Marlowe?'

Faulkner shrugged. 'I wouldn't have called it trouble exactly. Frank isn't the physical type.'

'But you are—or so it would seem?'

'What are you trying to prove?' Joanna demanded, moving to Faulkner's side.

'Just trying to get at the facts,' Miller said.

Morgan moved forward a step. 'I'd say you were aiming at rather more than that. You don't have to put up with this, Bruno.'

'Oh, but I do.' Faulkner grinned. 'It's beginning to get rather interesting. All right, Miller, I've an uncontrollable temper, I'm egotistical, aggressive and when people annoy me I tend to hit them. They even sent me to prison for it once. Common assault—the respectable kind, by the way, not the nasty sexual variety.'

'I'm aware of that.'

'Somehow I thought you might be.'

'You brought the girl back here to pose for you and nothing else?'

'You know when she got here, you know when she left. There wasn't time for anything else.'

'Can you remember what you talked about?'

'There wasn't much time for conversation either. I told her to strip and get up on the platform. Then I saw to the fire and poured myself a drink. As soon as she got up there I knew it was no good. I told her to get dressed and gave her a ten-pound note.'

'There was no sign of it in her handbag.'

'She slipped it into her stocking top. Made a crack about it being the safest place.'

'It was nowhere on her person and she's been examined thoroughly.'

'All right, so the murderer took it.'

Miller decided to keep the information that the girl had had intercourse just before her death to himself for a moment. 'There was no question of any sexual assault so how would the murderer have known where it was?'

There was a heavy silence. He allowed it to hang there for a moment and continued, 'You're quite sure that you and the girl didn't have an argument before she left?'

Faulkner laughed harshly. 'If you mean did I blow my top, break her neck with one devastating karate chop and carry her down the back stairs into the night because she refused my wicked way with her, no. If I'd wanted her to stay the night she'd have stayed and not for any ten quid either. She came cheaper than that or I miss my guess.'

'I understand she was found in Dob Court, Sergeant?' Morgan said.

'That's right.'

'And are you seriously suggesting that Mr. Faulkner killed the girl here, carted her downstairs and carried her all the way because that's what he would have to have done. I think I should point out that he doesn't own a car.'

'They took my licence away last year,' Faulkner admitted amiably. 'Driving under the influence.'

'But you did go out after the girl left?'

'To the coffee stall in Regent Square.' Faulkner made no attempt to deny it. 'I even said hello to the local bobby. I often do. No class barriers for me.'

'He's already told us that. It was only five or ten minutes later that he found Grace Packard's body. You left Joanna's gloves on the counter. The proprietor asked me to pass them on.'

Miller produced the black and white gloves and handed them to Joanna Hartmann who frowned in puzzlement. 'But these aren't mine.'

'They're Grace Packard's,' Faulkner said. 'I pulled them out of my pocket when I was looking for some change, as you very well know, Miller. I must have left them on the counter.'

'The man at the coffee stall confirms that. Only one difference. Apparently when he commented on them, you said they belonged to Joanna.'

144

Joanna Hartmann looked shocked, but Faulkner seemed quite unperturbed. 'He knows Joanna well. We've been there together often. I'd hardly be likely to tell him they belonged to another woman, would I? As I told you earlier, it was none of his business, anyway.'

'That seems reasonable enough surely,' Joanna said.

Miller looked at her gravely. 'Does it?'

She seemed genuinely puzzled. 'I don't understand. What are you trying to say?'

Morgan had been listening to everything, a frown of concentration on his face and now he said quickly, 'Just a minute. There's something more here, isn't there?'

'There could be.'

For the first time Faulkner seemed to have had enough. The urbane mask slipped heavily and he said sharply, 'I'm beginning to get rather bored with all this. Is this or is it not another Rainlover murder?'

Miller didn't even hesitate. 'It certainly has all the hall-marks.'

'Then that settles it,' Morgan said. 'You surely can't be suggesting that Mr. Faulkner killed the other four as well?'

'I couldn't have done the previous one for a start,' Faulkner said. 'I just wasn't available.'

'Can you prove that?'

'Easily. There were three statues up there two days ago. Now there are four. Believe me, I was occupied. When Jack called for me last night I hadn't been out of the flat since Thursday.'

'You still haven't answered my question, Sergeant,' Morgan said. 'The gloves . . . you were getting at some-thing else, weren't you?'

'In killings of this kind there are always certain details not released to the Press,' Miller said. 'Sometimes because they are too unpleasant, but more often because public knowledge of them might prejudice police enquiries.'

He was on a course now which might well lead to disaster, he knew that, and if anything went wrong there would be no one to help him, no one to back him up. Mallory would be the first to reach for the axe, but he had gone too far to draw back now.

'This type of compulsive killer is a prisoner of his own sickness. He not only has the compulsion to kill again. He can no more alter his method than stop breathing and that's what always proves his undoing.'

'Fascinating,' Faulkner said. 'Let's see now, Jack the Ripper always chose a prostitute and performed a surgical operation. The Boston Strangler raped them first then choked them with a nylon stocking. What about the Rainlover?'

'No pattern where the women themselves are concerned. The eldest was fifty and Grace Packard was the youngest. No sexual assault, no perversions. Everything neat and tidy. Always the neck broken cleanly from the rear. A man who knows what he's doing.'

'Sorry to disappoint you, but you don't need to be a karate expert to break a woman's neck from the rear. One good rabbit punch is all it takes.'

'Possibly, but the Rainlover has one other trademark. He always takes something personal from his victims.'

'A kind of *memento mori*? Now that is interesting.'

'Anything special?' Morgan asked.

'In the first case it was a handbag, then a headscarf, a nylon stocking and a shoe.'

'And in Grace Packard's case a pair of gloves?' Faulkner suggested. 'Then tell me this, Miller? If I was content with one shoe and one stocking previously why

146

should it suddenly be necessary for me to take two gloves? A break in the pattern, surely?'

'A good point,' Miller admitted.

'Here's another,' Joanna said. 'What about the ten-pound note? Doesn't that make two items missing?'

'I'm afraid we only have Mr. Faulkner's word that it existed at all.'

There was a heavy silence. For the first time Faulkner looked serious—really serious. Morgan couldn't think of anything to say and Joanna Hartmann was just plain frightened.

Miller saw it as the psychological moment to withdraw for a little while and smiled pleasantly. 'I'd better get in touch with Headquarters, just to see how things are getting on at that end.'

Faulkner tried to look nonchalant and waved towards the telephone. 'Help yourself.'

'That's all right. I can use the car radio. I'll be back in five minutes. I'm sure you could all use the break.'

He went out quickly, closing the door softly behind him.

Faulkner was the first to break the silence with a short laugh that echoed back to him, hollow and strained. 'Well, now, it doesn't look too good, does it?'

Seventeen

Harold Phillips was hot and uncomfortable. The Interrogation Room was full of cigarette smoke and it was beginning to make his eyes hurt. He'd already had one

147

lengthy session with Chief Superintendent Mallory and he hadn't liked it. He glanced furtively across the room at the stony-faced constable standing beside the door.

He moistened his lips. 'How much longer then?'

'That's up to Mr. Mallory, sir,' the constable replied.

The door opened and Mallory returned, Brady following him. 'Did they get you a cup of tea?' the Superintendent asked.

'No, they didn't,' Harold answered in an aggrieved tone.

'That's not good enough—not good enough at all.' He turned to the constable. 'Fetch a cup of tea from the canteen on the double for Mr. Phillips.'

He turned, smiling amiably and sat at the table. He opened a file and glanced at it quickly as he started to fill his pipe. 'Let's just look at this again.'

In the silence which followed the only sound was the clock ticking on the wall and the dull rumble of thunder somewhere far off in the distance.

'Sounds like more rain then,' Harold commented.

Mallory looked up. His face was like stone, the eyes dark and full of menace. He said sharply and angrily, 'I'm afraid you haven't been telling the truth, young man. You've been wasting my time.'

The contrast between this and his earlier politeness was quite shattering and Harold started to shake involuntarily. 'I don't know what you mean,' he stammered. 'I've told you everything I can remember.'

'Tell him the truth, son,' Brady put in, worried and anxious. 'It'll go better with you in the long run.'

'But I am telling him the bleeding truth,' Harold cried. 'What else does he want—blood? Here, I'm not having any more of this. I want to see a lawyer.'

'Lie number one,' Mallory said remorselessly. 'You told

148

us that you didn't know the name of the man you'd had the argument with at The King's Arms. The man who went off with Grace Packard.'

'That's right.'

'The landlord remembers differently. He says that when you came back to the pub to take him up on his offer of a drink on the house, you already knew the name of the person concerned. What you'd really come back for was his address only the landlord wouldn't play.'

'It's a lie,' Harold said. 'There isn't a word of truth in it.'

'He's ready to repeat his statement under oath in the box,' Brady said.

Mallory carried on as if he hadn't heard. 'You told us that you were home by half-nine, that you took your mother a cup of tea and then went to bed. Do you still stick to that story?'

'You ask her—she'll tell you. Go on, just ask her.'

'We happen to know that your mother is a very sick woman and in severe pain most of the time. The pills the doctor gave to make her sleep needed to be much stronger than usual. Her dosage was two. We can prove she took three yesterday. Medical evidence would indicate that it would be most unlikely that you would have been able to waken her at the time you state.'

'You can't prove that,' Harold sounded genuinely indignant.

'Possibly not,' Mallory admitted candidly, 'but it won't look good, will it?'

'So what. You need evidence in a court of law—real evidence. Everybody knows that.'

'Oh, we can supply some of that as well if you insist. You told us that after leaving The King's Arms you didn't see Grace Packard again, that you walked round the

149

streets for a while, had a coffee at the station buffet and went home, arriving at half-nine.'

'That's right.'

'But you found time for something else, didn't you?'

'What are you talking about?'

'You had intercourse with someone.'

Harold was momentarily stunned. When he spoke again he was obviously badly shaken. 'I don't know what you mean.'

'I wouldn't try lying again if I were you. You asked for evidence, real evidence. I've got some for you. For the past couple of hours your trousers, the trousers you were wearing yesterday have been the subject of chemical tests in our laboratory. They haven't finished yet by any means, but I've just had a preliminary report that indicates beyond any shadow of a doubt that you were with a woman last night.'

'Maybe someone forgot to tell you, son,' Brady put in, 'but Grace Packard had intercourse just before she died.'

'Here, you needn't try that one.' Harold put out a hand defensively. 'All right, I'll tell you the truth. I did go with a woman last night.'

'Who was she?' Mallory asked calmly.

'I don't know. I bumped into her in one of those streets behind the station.'

'Was she on the game?' Brady suggested.

'That's it. Thirty bob for a short time. You know how it goes. We stood against the wall in a back alley.'

'And her name?' Mallory said.

'Do me a favour, Superintendent. I didn't even get a clear look at her face.'

'Let's hope she hasn't left you something to remember her by,' Brady said grimly. 'Why didn't you tell us about this before?'

Harold had obviously recovered some of his lost confidence. He contrived to look pious. 'It isn't the sort of thing you like to talk about, now is it?'

The constable came in with a cup of tea, placed it on the table and whispered in Mallory's ear. The Chief Superintendent nodded, got to his feet and beckoned to Brady.

'Miller's on the phone,' he said when they got into the corridor.

'What about Harold, sir?'

'Let him stew for a few minutes.'

He spoke to Miller from a booth half-way along the corridor. 'Where are you speaking from?'

'Phone box outside Faulkner's place,' Miller told him. 'He's up there now with his lawyer and Joanna Hartmann.'

'You've spoken to him then?'

'Oh, yes, thought I'd give him a breather, that's all. We've reached an interesting stage. You were right about the gloves, sir. He didn't even attempt to deny having had them. Gave exactly the reason for lying about them at the coffee stall that you said he would.'

Mallory couldn't help feeling slightly complacent. 'There you are then. I don't like to say I told you so, but I honestly think you're wasting your time, Miller.'

'Don't tell me Harold's cracked?'

'Not quite, but he's tying himself up in about fifty-seven different knots. I think he's our man. More certain of it than ever.'

'But not the Rainlover?'

'A different problem, I'm afraid.'

'One interesting point, sir,' Miller said. 'Remember Faulkner told us he gave the girl ten pounds?'

'What about it?'

'What he actually gave her was a ten-pound note. He

says she tucked it into her stocking top. Apparently made some crack about it being the safest place.'

'Now that is interesting.' Mallory was aware of a sudden tightness in his chest that interfered with his breathing—an old and infallible sign. 'That might just about clinch things if I use it in the right way. I think you'd better get back here right away, Miller.'

'But what about Faulkner, sir?'

'Oh, to hell with Faulkner, man. Get back here now and that's an order.'

He slammed down the phone and turned to Brady who waited, leaning against the wall. 'Miller's just come up with an interesting tit-bit. Remember Faulkner said he gave the girl ten pounds for posing for him. He's just told Miller it was actually a ten-pound note. Now I wonder what our friend in there would do with it.'

'Always assuming that he's the man we want, sir,' Brady reminded him.

'Now don't you start, Brady,' Mallory said. 'I've got enough on my hands with Miller.'

'All right, sir,' Brady said. 'Put a match to it if he had any sense.'

'Which I doubt,' Mallory chuckled grimly. 'Can you imagine Harold Phillips putting a match to a ten-pound note?' He shook his head. 'Not on your life. He'll have stashed it away somewhere.'

At that moment Henry Wade appeared from the lift at the end of the corridor and came towards them, Harold's trousers over his arm.

'Anything else for me?' Mallory demanded.

Wade shook his head. 'I'm afraid not. He was with a woman, that's all I can tell you.'

'Nothing more?'

Wade shrugged. 'No stains we can link with the girl if

152

that's what you mean. Sometimes if you're lucky you can test the semen for its blood group factor. About forty per cent of males secrete their blood group in their body fluids. Of course it won't work if the subject isn't a member of that group. In any case you need a large specimen and it's got to be fresh. Sorry, sir.'

Mallory took a deep breath. 'All right, this is what we do. We're all going back in there. I want you to simply stand with the trousers over your arm and say nothing, Wade. Brady—just look serious. That's all I ask.'

'But what are you going to try, sir?' Brady demanded.

'A king-size bluff,' Mallory said simply. 'I'm simply betting on the fact that I'm a better poker player than Harold Phillips.'

Eighteen

Nick Miller replaced the receiver and stepped out of the telephone box into the heavy rain. Mallory's instructions had been quite explicit. He was to drop the Faulkner enquiry and return to Headquarters at once and yet the Scotland Yard man was wrong—Miller still felt certain about that. It was nothing he could really put his finger on, something that couldn't be defined and yet when he thought of Faulkner his stomach went hollow and his flesh crawled.

But orders were orders and to disobey this one was to invite the kind of reaction that might mean the end of his career as a policeman. When it finally came down to it he wasn't prepared to throw away a life that had come to

153

mean everything to him simply because of a private hunch that could well be wrong.

He crossed to the Mini-Cooper, took out his keys and, above his head, the studio window of Faulkner's flat dissolved in a snowstorm of flying glass as a chair soared through in a graceful curve that ended in the middle of the street.

. . . . .

There was a heavy silence after Miller left and Faulkner was the first to break it. He crossed to the bar and poured himself a large gin. 'I can feel the noose tightening already. Distinctly unpleasant.'

'Stop it, Bruno!' Joanna said sharply. 'It just isn't funny any more.'

He paused, the glass half-way to his lips and looked at her in a kind of mild surprise. 'You surely aren't taking this thing seriously?'

'How else can I take it?'

Faulkner turned his attention to Morgan. 'And what about you?'

'It doesn't look too good, Bruno.'

'That's wonderful. That's bloody marvellous.' Faulkner drained his glass and came round from behind the bar. 'How long have you known me, Jack? Fifteen years or is it more? I'd be fascinated to know when you first suspected my homicidal tendencies.'

'Why did you have to bring that wretched girl back with you, Bruno? Why?' Joanna said.

He looked at them both in turn, his cynical smile fading. 'My God, you're both beginning to believe it, aren't you? You're actually beginning to believe it.'

'Don't be ridiculous.' Joanna turned away.

154

He swung her round to face him. 'No, you're afraid to give it voice, but it's there in your eyes.'

'Please, Bruno . . . you're hurting me.'

He pushed her away and turned on Jack. 'And you?'

'You've a hell of a temper, Bruno, no one knows that better than I do. When you broke Pearson's jaw it took four of us to drag you off him.'

'Thanks for the vote of confidence.'

'Face facts, Bruno. Miller's got a lot to go on. All circumstantial, I'll grant you that, but it wouldn't look good in court.'

'That's your opinion.'

'All right, let's look at the facts as the prosecution would present them to a jury. First of all there's your uncontrollable temper, your convictions for violence. The medical report when you were in Wandsworth said you needed psychiatric treatment, but you refused. That won't look good for a start.'

'Go on—this is fascinating.'

'You bring Grace Packard back here late at night and give her ten pounds to pose for you for two or three minutes.'

'The simple truth.'

'I know that—I believe it because it's typical of you, but if you think there's a jury in England that would swallow such an explanation you're crazy.'

'You're not leaving me with much hope, are you?'

'I'm not finished yet.' Morgan carried on relentlessly. 'No more than a couple of minutes after she left you went out after her. You bought cigarettes at that coffee stall in Regent Square and she was killed not more than two hundred yards away a few minutes later. And you had her gloves—can you imagine what the prosecution would try to make out of that one?'

Faulkner seemed surprisingly calm considering the circumstances. 'And what about the ten-pound note? If it didn't exist why should I bother to mention it in the first place?'

'A further complication . . . all part of the smokescreen.'

'And you believe that?'

'I think a jury might.'

Faulkner went to the bar, reached for the gin bottle and poured himself another drink. He stood with his back to them for a moment. When he finally turned, he looked calm and serious.

'A good case, Jack, but one or two rather obvious flaws. You've laid some stress on the fact that I had Grace Packard's gloves. I think it's worth pointing out that I had them before she was killed. In any case, the gloves are only important if you maintain that Grace Packard was killed by the Rainlover. Have you considered that?'

'Yes, I've considered it,' Morgan said gravely.

'But if I am the Rainlover then I killed the others and you'd have to prove that was possible. What about the woman killed the night before last for example? As I told you when you called for me last night, I'd been working two days non-stop. Hadn't even left the studio.'

'The body was found in Jubilee Park no more than a quarter of a mile from here. You could have left by the back stairs and returned inside an hour and no one the wiser. That's what the prosecution would say.'

'But I didn't know about the murder, did I? You had to tell me. Don't you remember? It was just after you arrived. I was dressing in the bedroom and you spoke to me from in here.'

Morgan nodded. 'That's true. I remember now. I asked if you'd heard about the killing, picked up the paper and discovered it was Friday night's.' He seemed to go rigid and added in a whisper, 'Friday night's.'

He went to the chair by the fire, picked up the newspaper that was still lying there as it had been on his arrival the previous evening. 'Final edition, Friday 23rd.' He turned to Faulkner. 'But you don't have a paper delivered.'

'So what?'

'Then how did you get hold of this if you didn't leave the house for two days?'

Joanna gave a horrified gasp and for the first time Faulkner really looked put out. He put a hand to his head, frowning. 'I remember now. I ran out of cigarettes. I was tired . . . so tired that I couldn't think straight and it was raining hard, beating against the window.' It was almost as if he was speaking to himself. 'I thought the air might clear my head and I needed some cigarettes so I slipped out.'

'And the newspaper?'

'I got it from the old man on the corner of Albany Street.'

'Next to Jubilee Park.'

They stood there in tableau, the three of them, caught in a web of silence and somewhere in the distance thunder echoed menacingly. Morgan was white and strained and a kind of horror showed in Joanna's face.

Faulkner shook his head slowly as if unable to comprehend what was happening. 'You must believe me, Joanna, you must.'

She turned to Morgan. 'Take me home, Jack. Please take me home.'

Faulkner said angrily, 'I'll be damned if I'll let you go like this.'

As he grabbed at her arm she moved away sharply, colliding with the drawing board on its stand, the one at

157

which Faulkner had been working earlier. The board went over, papers scattering and his latest sketch fell at her feet, a rough drawing of the group of four statues with a fifth added.

There was real horror on her face at this final, terrible proof. As she backed away, Morgan picked up the sketch and held it out to Faulkner. 'Have you got an explanation for this, too?'

Faulkner brushed him aside and grabbed Joanna by both arms. 'Listen to me—just listen. That's all I ask.'

She slapped at him in a kind of blind panic and Morgan tried to pull Faulkner away from her. Something snapped inside Faulkner. He turned and hit Morgan back-handed, sending him staggering against the bar.

Joanna ran for the door. Faulkner caught her before she could open it and wrenched her around, clutching at the collar of her sheepskin coat.

'You're not leaving me, do you hear? I'll kill you first!'

Almost of their own volition his hands slid up and around her throat and she sank to her knees choking. Morgan got to his feet, dazed. He staggered forward, grabbed Faulkner by the hair and pulled hard. Faulkner gave a cry of pain, releasing his grip on the woman's throat. As he turned, Morgan picked up the jug of ice water that stood on the bar top and tossed the contents into his face.

The shock seemed to restore Faulkner to his senses. He stood there swaying, an almost vacant look on his face and Morgan went to Joanna and helped her to her feet.

'Are you all right?'

She nodded, without speaking. Morgan turned on Faulkner. 'Was that the way it happened, Bruno? Was that how you killed her?'

Faulkner faced them, dangerously calm. His laughter,

when it came, was harsh, completely unexpected.

'All right—that's what you've been waiting to hear, isn't it? Well, let's tell the whole bloody world about it.'

He picked up a chair, lifted it high above his head and hurled it through the studio window.

.   .   .   .   .

Miller hammered on the door and it was opened almost immediately by Jack Morgan. Joanna Hartmann was slumped into one of the easy chairs by the fire, sobbing bitterly and Faulkner was standing at the bar pouring himself another drink, his back to the door.

'What happened?' Miller demanded.

Morgan moistened dry lips, but seemed to find difficulty in speaking. 'Why don't you tell him, Jack?' Faulkner called.

He emptied his glass and turned, the old sneer lifting the corner of his mouth. 'Jack and I were at school together, Miller—a very old school. The sort of place that has a code. He's finding it awkward to turn informer.'

'For God's sake, Bruno, let's get it over with,' Morgan said savagely.

'Anything to oblige.' Faulkner turned to Miller. 'I killed Grace Packard.' He held out his wrists. 'Who knows, Miller, you might get promoted over this.'

Miller nodded slowly. 'You're aware of the seriousness of what you're saying?'

'He admitted it to Miss Hartmann and myself before you arrived,' Morgan said wearily. He turned to Bruno. 'Don't say anything else at this stage, Bruno. You don't need to.'

'I'll have to ask you to accompany me to Central C.I.D. Headquarters,' Miller said.

He delivered a formal caution, produced his handcuffs and snapped them over Faulkner's wrists. Faulkner smiled. 'You enjoyed doing that, didn't you?'

'Now and then it doesn't exactly make me cry myself to sleep,' Miller took him by the elbow.

'I'll come with you if I may,' Morgan said.

Faulkner smiled briefly, looking just for that single instant like an entirely different person, perhaps that other self he might have been had things been different.

'It's nice to know one's friends. I'd be obliged, Jack.'

'Will Miss Hartmann be all right?' Miller asked.

She looked up, her eyes swollen from weeping and nodded briefly. 'Don't worry about me. Will you come back for me, Jack?'

'I'll leave you my car.' He dropped the keys on top of the bar.

'Nothing to say, Joanna?' Faulkner demanded.

She turned away, her shoulders shaking and he started to laugh. Miller turned him round, gave him a solid push out on to the landing and Morgan closed the door on the sound of that terrible weeping.

Nineteen

It was quiet in the Interrogation Room. The constable at the door picked his nose impassively and thunder sounded again in the distance, a little nearer this time. Harold held the mug of tea in both hands and lifted it to his lips. It was almost cold, the surface covered by a kind of unpleasant scum that filled him with disgust. He shuddered and put the mug down on the table.

'How much longer?' he demanded and the door opened.

Mallory moved to the window and stood there staring out into the rain. Wade positioned himself at the other end of the table and waited, the trousers neatly folded over one arm.

Harold was aware of a strange, choking sensation in his throat. He wrenched at his collar and glanced appealingly at Brady who had closed the door after the constable who had discreetly withdrawn. The big Irishman looked troubled. He held Harold's glance for only a moment, then dropped his gaze.

'What did you do with the tenner?' Mallory asked without turning round.

'Tenner? What tenner?' Harold said.

Mallory turned to face him. 'The ten-pound note the girl had in her stocking top—what did you do with it?'

'I've never handled a ten-pound note in my life.'

'If you'd had any sense you'd have destroyed it, but not you.' Mallory carried on as if there had been no interruption. 'Where would you change it at that time of night —a pub? Or what about the station buffet—you said you were there.'

The flesh seemed to shrink visibly on Harold's bones. 'What the hell are you trying to prove?'

Mallory picked up the phone and rang through to the C.I.D. general office. 'Mallory here,' he told the Duty Inspector. 'I want you to get in touch with the manager of the buffet at the Central Station right away. Find out if anyone changed a ten-pound note last night. Yes, that's right—a ten-pound note.'

Harold's eyes burned in a face that was as white as paper. 'You're wasting your time.' He was suddenly belligerent again. 'They could have had half a dozen ten-pound notes through their hands on a Saturday night for all you know, so what does it prove?'

'We'll wait and see shall we?'

Harold seemed to pull himself together. He sat straighter in his chair and took a deep breath. 'All right, I've had enough. If you're charging me, I want a lawyer. If you're not, then I'm not staying here another minute.'

'If you'll extend that to five I'll be more than satisfied,' Mallory said.

Harold stared at him blankly. 'What do you mean?'

'I'm expecting a chap from the lab to arrive any second. We just want to give you a simple blood test.'

'Blood test? What for?'

Mallory nodded to Wade who laid the trousers on the table. 'The tests the lab ran on these trousers proved you were with a woman last night.'

'All right—I admitted that.'

'And the post-mortem on Grace Packard indicated she'd had intercourse with someone just before she died.'

'It wasn't with me, that's all I know.'

'We can prove that one way or the other with the simplest of tests.' It was from that point on that Mallory started to bend the facts. 'I don't know if you're aware of it, but it's possible to test a man's semen for his blood group factor.'

'So what?'

'During the post-mortem on Grace Packard a semen smear was obtained. It's since been tested in the lab and indicates a certain blood group. When the technician gets here from the lab he'll be able to take a small sample of your blood and tell us what your group is within a couple of minutes—or perhaps you know already?'

Harold stared wildly at him and the silence which enveloped them all was so heavy that suddenly it seemed

162

almost impossible to breathe. His head moved slightly from side to side faster and faster. He tried to get up and then collapsed completely, falling across the table.

He hammered his fist up and down like a hysterical child. 'The bitch, the rotten stinking bitch. She shouldn't have laughed at me! She shouldn't have laughed at me!'

He started to cry and Mallory stood there, hands braced against the table, staring down at him. There was a time when this particular moment would have meant something, but not now. In fact, not for some considerable time now.

Quite suddenly the whole thing seemed desperately unreal—a stupid charade that had no substance. It didn't seem to be important any longer and that didn't make sense. Too much in too short a time. Perhaps what he needed was a spot of leave.

He straightened and there was a knock at the door. Brady opened it and a constable handed him a slip of paper. He passed it to Mallory who read it, face impassive. He crumpled it up in one hand and tossed it into the waste bin.

'A message from Dr. Das. Mrs. Phillips died peacefully in her sleep fifteen minutes ago. Thank God for that anyway.'

.   .   .   .   .

'It would be easy to say I told you so, Miller, but there it is,' Mallory said.

Miller took a deep breath. 'No possibility of error, sir?'

'None at all. He's given us a full statement. It seems he waited outside Faulkner's flat, saw Faulkner and the girl go in and followed her when she came out. He pulled her

163

into Dob Court where they had some kind of reconciliation because she allowed him to have intercourse with her and she gave him the ten-pound note.'

'What went wrong?'

'God alone knows—I doubt if we'll ever get a clear picture. Apparently there was some sort of argument to do with Faulkner and the money. I get the impression that after the way he had treated him, Phillips objected to the idea that Faulkner might have had his way with the girl. The money seemed to indicate that he had.'

'So he killed her?'

'Apparently she taunted him, there was an argument and he started to hit her. Lost his temper completely. Didn't mean to kill her of course. They never do.'

'Do you think a jury might believe that?'

'With his background? Not in a month of Sundays.' The telephone rang. Mallory picked up the receiver, listened for a moment, then put it down. 'Another nail in the coffin. It seems the manager of the station buffet has turned up the assistant who changed that ten-pound note last night. Seems she can identify Phillips. He was a regular customer. She says he was in there about a quarter to eleven.'

'The bloody fool,' Miller said.

'They usually are, Miller, and a good thing for us, I might add.'

'But what on earth is Faulkner playing at? I don't understand.'

'Let's have him in and find out shall we?'

Mallory sat back and started to fill his pipe. Miller opened the door and called and Faulkner came in followed by Jack Morgan.

Faulkner looked as if he didn't have a care in the world. He stood in front of the desk, trenchcoat draped from his

164

shoulders like a cloak, hands pushed negligently into his pockets.

Mallory busied himself with his pipe. When it was going to his satisfaction, he blew out the match and looked up. 'Mr. Faulkner, I have here a full and complete confession to the murder of Grace Packard signed by Harold Phillips. What have you got to say to that?'

'Only that it would appear that I must now add a gift for prophecy to the list of my virtues,' Faulkner said calmly.

Morgan came forward quickly. 'Is this true, Superintendent?'

'It certainly is. We've even managed to turn up the ten-pound note your client gave the girl. Young Phillips changed it at the station buffet before going home.'

Morgan turned on Faulkner, his face white and strained. 'What in the hell have you been playing at, for God's sake? You told us that you killed Grace Packard.'

'Did I?' Faulkner shrugged. 'The other way about as I remember it. You told me.' He turned to Mallory. 'Mr. Morgan, like all lawyers, Superintendent, has a tendency to believe his own arguments. Once he'd made up his mind I was the nigger in the woodpile, he couldn't help but find proof everywhere he looked.'

'Are you trying to say you've just been playing the bloody fool as usual?' Morgan pulled him round angrily. 'Don't you realise what you've done to Joanna?'

'She had a choice. She could have believed in me. She took your road.' Faulkner seemed completely unconcerned. 'I'm sure you'll be very happy together. Can I go now, Superintendent?'

'I think that might be advisable,' Mallory said.

Faulkner turned in the doorway, the old sneer lifting the corner of his mouth as he glanced at Miller. 'Sorry about that promotion—better luck next time.'

After he had gone there was something of a silence. Morgan just stood there, staring wildly into space. Quite suddenly he turned and rushed out without a word.

Miller stood at the window for a long moment, staring down into the rain. He saw Faulkner come out of the main entrance and go down the steps. He paused at the bottom to button his trenchcoat, face lifted to the rain, then walked rapidly away. Morgan appeared a moment later. He watched Faulkner go then hailed a taxi from the rank across the street.

Miller took out his wallet, produced a pound note and laid it on Mallory's desk. 'I was wrong,' he said simply.

Mallory nodded. 'You were, but I won't hold that against you. In my opinion Faulkner's probably just about as unbalanced as it's possible to be and still walk free. He'd impair anyone's judgement.'

'Nice of you to put it that way, but I was still wrong.'

'Never mind.' Mallory stood up and reached for his coat. 'If you can think of anywhere decent that will still be open on a Sunday afternoon I'll buy you a late lunch out of my ill-gotten gains.'

'Okay, sir. Just give me ten minutes to clear my desk and I'm your man.'

.   .   .   .   .

The rain was falling heavier than ever as they went down the steps of the Town Hall to the Mini-Cooper. Miller knew a restaurant that might fit the bill, an Italian place that had recently opened in one of the northern suburbs of the city and he drove past the infirmary and took the car through the maze of slum streets behind it

166

towards the new Inner Ring Road.

The streets were deserted, washed clean by the heavy rain and the wipers had difficulty in keeping the screen clear. They didn't speak and Miller drove on mechanically so stunned by what had happened that he was unable to think straight.

They turned a corner and Mallory gripped his arm. 'For God's sake, what's that?'

Miller braked instinctively. About half-way along the street, two men struggled beside a parked motorcycle. One of them was a police patrolman in heavy belted stormcoat and black crash helmet. The other wore only shirt and pants and seemed to be barefooted.

The policeman went down, the other man jumped for the motorcycle and kicked it into life. It roared away from the kerb as the patrolman scrambled to his feet, and came straight down the middle of the street. Miller swung the wheel, taking the Mini-Cooper across in an attempt to cut him off. The machine skidded wildly as the rider wrenched the wheel, and shaved the bonnet of the Mini-Cooper with a foot to spare, giving Miller a clear view of his wild, determined face. *Gunner Doyle*. Well this was something he *could* handle. He took the Mini-Cooper round in a full circle across the footpath, narrowly missing an old gas lamp, and went after him.

.   .   .   .   .

It was at that precise moment that Jack Morgan arrived back at Faulkner's flat. He knocked on the door and it was opened almost at once by Joanna Hartmann. She was very pale, her eyes swollen from weeping, but seemed well in control of herself. She had a couple of dresses over one arm.

167

'Hello, Jack, I'm just getting a few of my things together.'

That she had lived with Faulkner on occasions was no surprise to him. She moved away and he said quickly, 'He didn't kill Grace Packard, Joanna.'

She turned slowly. 'What did you say?'

'The police had already charged the girl's boy friend when we got there. They have a full confession and corroborating evidence.'

'But Bruno said . . .'

Her voice trailed away and Morgan put a hand on her arm gently. 'I know what he said, Joanna, but it wasn't true. He was trying to teach us some sort of lesson. He seemed to find the whole thing rather funny.'

'He doesn't change, does he?'

'I'm afraid not.'

'Where is he now?'

'He went out ahead of me. Last I saw he was going for a walk in the rain.'

She nodded briefly. 'Let's get out of here then—just give me a moment to get the rest of my things.'

'You don't want to see him?'

'Never again.'

There was a hard finality in her voice and she turned and went into the bedroom. Morgan followed and stood in the entrance watching. She laid her clothes across the bed and added one or two items which she took from a drawer in one of the dressing tables.

There was a fitted wardrobe against the wall, several suitcases piled on top. She went across and reached up in vain.

'Let me,' Morgan said.

He grabbed the handle of the case which was bottom of

the pile and eased it out. He frowned suddenly. 'Feels as if there's something in it.'

He put the case on the bed, flicked the catches and opened the lid. Inside there was a black plastic handbag, a silk headscarf, a nylon stocking and a high-heeled shoe.

Joanna Hartmann started to scream.

Twenty

Strange, but it was so narrowly avoiding Miller in the park which finally made the Gunner's mind up for him, though not straight away. He waited until the detective had disappeared before emerging from the rhododendron bushes, damp and uncomfortable, his stomach hollow and empty.

He moved away in the opposite direction and finally came to another entrance to the park. Beyond the wrought iron gate he noticed some cigarette machines. He found the necessary coins from the money Jenny had given him, extracted a packet of ten cigarettes and a book of matches and went back into the park.

He started to walk again, smoking continuously, one cigarette after the other, thinking about everything that had happened since his dash from the infirmary, but particularly about Jenny. He remembered the first time he had seen her from the loft, looking just about as good as a woman could. And the other things. Her ironic humour, her courage in a difficult situation, even the rough edge of her tongue. And when they had made love she had given every part of herself, holding nothing back—something

169

he had never experienced in his life before. *And never likely to again* . . .

The thought pulled him up short and he stood there in the rain contemplating an eternity of being on his own for the first time in his life. Always to be running, always to be afraid because that was the cold fact of it. Scratching for a living, bedding with tarts, sinking fast all the time until someone turned him in for whatever it was worth.

The coppers never let go, never closed a case, that was the trouble. He thought of Miller. It was more than an hour since the detective had walked past the shelter and yet at the memory, the Gunner felt the same panic clutching at his guts, the same instinct to run and keep on running. *Well, to hell with that for a game of soldiers.* Better to face what there was to face and get it over than live like this. There was one cigarette left in the packet. He lit it, tossed the packet away and started to walk briskly towards the other side of the park.

.   .   .   .   .

A psychologist would have told him that making a definite decision, choosing a course of action, had resolved his conflict situation. The Gunner would have wondered what in the hell he was talking about. All he knew was that for some unaccountable reason he was cheerful again. One thing was certain—he'd give the bastards something to think about.

On the other side of the park he plunged into the maze of back streets in which he had been hunted during the previous night and worked his way towards the infirmary. It occurred to him that it might be fun to turn up in the very room from which he had disappeared. But there were certain precautions to take first, just to make certain that

the police could never link him with Jenny and her grandmother.

A few streets away from the infirmary he stopped in a
back alley at a spot where houses were being demolished
as fast as the bulldozers could knock them down. On the
other side of a low wall, a beck that was little more than a
fast-flowing stream of filth rushed past and plunged into
a dark tunnel that took it down into the darkness of the
city's sewage system.

He took off the raincoat, sweater, boots and socks and
dropped them in. They disappeared into the tunnel and
he emptied his pockets. Three pound notes and a handful
of change. The notes went fluttering down followed by the
coins—all but a sixpenny piece. There was a telephone
box at the end of the street...

He stood in the box and waited as the bell rang at the
other end, shivering slightly as the cold struck into his
bare feet and rain dripped down across his face. When she
answered he could hardly get the coin into the slot for
excitement.

'Jenny? It's the Gunner. Is anyone there?'

'Thank God,' she said, relief in her voice. 'Where are
you?'

'A few hundred yards from the infirmary. I'm turning
myself in, Jenny. I thought you might like to know that.'

'Oh, Gunner.' He could have sworn she was crying, but
that was impossible. She wasn't the type.

'What about the police?' he asked.

'No one turned up.'

'No one turned up?' he said blankly.

A sudden coldness touched his heart, something
elemental, but before he could add anything Jenny said,
'Just a minute, Gunner, there's someone outside in the
yard now.'

A moment later the line went dead.

'You fool,' the Gunner said aloud. 'You stupid bloody fool.'

Why on earth hadn't he seen it before? Only one person could possibly have known he was at the house and it certainly wasn't Ogden who hadn't even seen his face. But the other man had, the one who had attacked Jenny outside the door in the yard.

The Gunner left the phone box like a greyhound erupting from the trap and went down the street on the run. He turned the corner and was already some yards along the pavement when he saw the motorcycle parked at the kerb half-way along. The policeman who was standing beside it was making an entry in his book.

The policeman glanced up just before the Gunner arrived and they met breast-to-breast. There was the briefest of struggles before the policeman went down and the Gunner swung a leg over the motorcycle and kicked the starter.

He let out the throttle too fast so that the machine skidded away from the kerb, front wheel lifting. It was only then that he became aware of the Mini-Cooper at the other end of the street. As he roared towards it, the little car swung broadside on to block his exit. The Gunner threw the bike over so far that the footrest brought sparks from the cobbles, and shaved the bonnet of the Mini-Cooper. For a brief, timeless moment he looked into Miller's face, then he was away.

.   .   .   .

In the grey afternoon and the heavy rain it was impossible to distinguish the features of the man in the yard at any distance and at first Jenny thought it must be Ogden.

172

Even when the telephone went dead she felt no panic. It was only when she pressed her face to the window and saw Faulkner turn from the wall no more than a yard away, a piece of the telephone line still in his right hand that fear seized her by the throat. She recognised him instantly as her attacker of the previous night and in that moment everything fell neatly into place. The mysterious telephone call, the threat of the police who had never come —all to get rid of the only man who could have protected her.

'Oh, Gunner, God help me now.' The words rose in her throat, almost choking her as she turned and stumbled into the hall.

The outside door was still locked and bolted. The handle turned slowly and there was a soft, discreet knocking. For a moment her own fear left her as she remembered the old woman who still lay in bed, her Sunday habit. Whatever happened she must be protected.

Ma Crowther lay propped against the pillows, a shawl around her shoulders as she read one of her regular half-dozen Sunday newspapers. She glanced up in surprise as the door opened and Jenny appeared.

'You all right, Gran?'

'Yes, love, what is it?'

'Nothing to worry about. I just want you to stay in here for a while, that's all.'

There was a thunderous knocking from below. Jenny quickly extracted the key on the inside of her grandmother's door, slammed it shut and locked it as the old woman called out to her in alarm.

The knocking on the front door had ceased, but as she went down the stairs, there was the sound of breaking glass from the living-room. When she looked in he was smashing the window methodically with an old wooden clothes prop from the yard. She closed the door of the room, locked it on the outside and went up to the landing.

Her intention was quite clear. When he broke through the flimsy interior door, which wouldn't take long, she would give him a sight of her and then run for the roof. If she could climb across to the metalworks and get down the fire escape there might still be a chance. In any case, she would have led him away from her grandmother.

The door suddenly burst outwards with a great splintering crash and Bruno Faulkner came through with it, fetching up against the opposite wall. He looked up at her for a long moment, his face grave, and started to unbutton his raincoat. He tossed it to one side and put his foot on the bottom step. There was an old wooden chair on the landing. Jenny picked it up and hurled it down at him. He ducked and it missed him, bouncing from the wall.

He looked up at her still calm and then howled like an animal, smashing the edge of his left hand hard against the wooden banister rail. The rail snapped in half, a sight so incredible that she screamed for the first time in her life.

She turned and ran along the landing to the second staircase and Faulkner went after her. At the top of the stairs she was delayed for a moment as she wrestled with the bolt on the door that led to the roof. As she got it open, he appeared at the bottom.

She ran out into the heavy rain, kicked off her shoes and started up the sloping roof, her stocking feet slipping on the wet tiles. She was almost at the top when she slipped back to the bottom. Again she tried, clawing desperately towards the ridge riles as Faulkner appeared from the stairway.

She stuck half-way and stayed here, spread-eagled, caught like a fly on paper. And he knew it, that terrible

174

man below. He came forward slowly and stood there looking up at her. And then he laughed and it was the coldest laugh she had ever heard in her life.

He started forward and the Gunner came through the door like a thunderbolt. Faulkner turned, swerved like a ballet dancer and sent him on his way with a back-handed blow that caught him across the shoulders. The Gunner lost his balance, went sprawling, rolled beneath the rail at the far end and went down the roof that sloped to the yard below.

.   .   .   .   .

The Gunner skidded to a halt outside Crowther's yard and dropped the motorcycle on its side no more than four or five minutes after leaving the phone box. He went for the main gate on the run and disappeared through the judas as the Mini-Cooper turned the corner.

It was Mallory who went after him first, mainly because he already had his door open when Miller was still braking, but there was more to it than that. For some reason he felt alive again in a way he hadn't done for years. It was just like it used to be in the old days as a young probationer in Tower Bridge Division working the docks and the Pool of London. A punch-up most nights and on a Saturday anything could happen and usually did.

The years slipped away from him as he went through the judas on the run in time to see the Gunner scrambling through the front window. Mallory went after him, stumbling over the wreckage of the door on his way into the hall.

He paused for a brief moment, aware of the Gunner's progress above him and went up the stairs quickly. By the time he reached the first landing, his chest was heaving

175

and his mouth had gone bone dry as he struggled for air, but nothing on earth was going to stop him now.

As he reached the bottom of the second flight of stairs, the Gunner went through the open door at the top. A moment later there was a sudden sharp cry. Mallory was perhaps half-way up the stairs when the girl started to scream.

Faulkner had her by the left ankle and was dragging her down the sloping roof when Mallory appeared. In that single moment the whole thing took on every aspect of some privileged nightmare. His recognition of Faulkner was instantaneous, and at the same moment, a great many facts he had refused to face previously, surfaced. As the girl screamed again, he charged.

In his day George Mallory had been a better than average rugby forward and for one year Metropolitan Police light - heavyweight boxing champion. He grabbed Faulkner by the shoulder, pulled him around and swung the same right cross that had earned him his title twenty-seven years earlier. It never even landed. Faulkner blocked the punch, delivered a forward elbow strike that almost paralysed Mallory's breathing system and snapped his left arm like a rotten branch with one devastating blow with the edge of his right hand. Mallory groaned and went down. Faulkner grabbed him by the scruff of the neck and started to drag him along the roof towards the railing.

.   .   .   .   .

For Miller it was as if somehow all this had happened before. As he came through the door and paused, thunder split the sky apart overhead and the rain increased into a solid grey curtain that filled the air with a strange, sibilant rushing sound and reduced visibility to a few yards.

176

He took in everything in a single moment. The girl with her dress half-ripped from her body, crouched at the foot of the sloping roof crying hysterically, and Faulkner who had now turned to look towards the door, still clutching Mallory's coat collar in his right hand.

Faulkner. A strange fierce exhilaration swept through Miller, a kind of release of every tension that had knotted up inside him during the past twenty-four hours. A release that came from knowing that he had been right all along.

He moved in on the run, jumped high in the air and delivered a flying front kick, the devastating mae-tobi-geri, full into Faulkner's face, one of the most crushing of all karate blows. Faulkner staggered back, releasing his hold on Mallory, blood spurting from his mouth and Miller landed awkwardly, slipping in the rain and falling across Mallory.

Before he could scramble to his feet, Faulkner had him by the throat. Miller summoned every effort of will-power and spat full in the other man's face. Faulkner recoiled in a kind of reflex action and Miller stabbed at his exposed throat with stiffened fingers.

Faulkner went back and Miller took his time over getting up, struggling for air. It was a fatal mistake for a blow which would have demolished any ordinary man had only succeeded in shaking Faulkner's massive strength. As Miller straightened, Faulkner moved in like the wind and delivered a fore-fist punch, knuckles extended, that fractured two ribs like matchwood and sent Miller down on one knee with a cry of agony.

Faulkner drew back his foot and kicked him in the stomach. Miller went down flat on his face. Faulkner lifted his foot to crush the skull and Jenny Crowther staggered forward and clutched at his arm. He brushed her away as one might a fly on a summer's day and turned back to Miller. It was at that precise moment that the Gunner reappeared.

.   .   .   .   .

The Gunner's progress down the sloping roof had been checked by the presence of an ancient Victorian cast iron gutter twice the width of the modern variety. He had hung there for some time contemplating the cobbles of the yard thirty feet below. Like Jenny in a similar situation, he had found progress up a steeply sloping bank of Welsh slate in heavy rain a hazardous undertaking. He finally reached for the rusting railings above his head and pulled himself over in time to see Faulkner hurl the girl from him and turn to Miller.

The Gunner, silent on bare feet, delivered a left and a right to Faulkner's kidneys that sent the big man staggering forward with a scream of pain. As he turned, the Gunner stepped over Miller and let Faulkner have his famous left arm screw punch under the ribs followed by a right to the jaw, a combination that had finished no fewer than twelve of his professional fights inside the distance.

Faulkner didn't go down, but he was badly rattled. 'Come on then, you bastard,' the Gunner yelled. 'Let's be having you.'

Miller pushed himself up on one knee and tried to lift Mallory into a sitting position. Jenny Crowther crawled across to help and pillowed Mallory's head against her shoulder. He nodded, face twisted in pain, unable to speak and Miller folded his arms tightly about his chest and coughed as blood rose into his mouth.

There had been a time when people had been glad to pay as much as fifty guineas to see Gunner Doyle in

178

action, but up there on the roof in the rain, Miller, the girl and Mallory had a ringside seat for free at his last and greatest battle.

He went after Faulkner two-handed, crouched like a tiger. Faulkner was hurt—hurt badly, and the Gunner had seen enough to know that his only chance lay in keeping him in that state. He swayed to one side as Faulkner threw a punch and smashed his left into the exposed mouth that was already crushed and bleeding from Miller's efforts. Faulkner cried out in pain and the Gunner gave him a right that connected just below the eye and moved close.

'Keep away from him,' Miller yelled. 'Don't get too close.'

The Gunner heard only the roar of the crowd as he breathed in the stench of the ring—that strange never-to-be-forgotten compound of human sweat, heat, and embrocation. He let Faulkner have another right to the jaw to straighten him up and stepped in close for a blow to the heart that might finish the job. It was his biggest mistake. Faulkner pivoted, delivering an elbow strike backwards that doubled the Gunner over. In the same moment Faulkner turned again, lifting the Gunner backwards with a knee in the face delivered with such force that he went staggering across the roof and fell heavily against the railing. It sagged, half-breaking and he hung there trying to struggle to his feet, blood pouring from his nose and mouth. Faulkner charged in like a runaway express train, shoulder down and sent him back across the railing. The Gunner rolled over twice on the way down, bounced across the broad iron gutter and fell to the cobbles below.

Faulkner turned slowly, a terrifying sight, eyes glaring, blood from his mouth soaking down into his collar. He snarled at the three of them helpless before him, grabbed at the sagging iron railing and wrenched a four-foot

179

length of it free. He gave a kind of animal-like growl and started forward.

Ma Crowther stepped through the door at the head of the stairs, still in her nightdress, clutching her sawn-off shotgun against her breast. Faulkner didn't see her, so intent was he on the task before him. He poised over his three victims, swinging the iron bar high above his head like an executioner, and she gave him both barrels full in the face.

Twenty-one

It was almost nine o'clock in the evening when Miller and Jenny Crowther walked along the second floor corridor of the Marsden Wing of the General Infirmary towards the room in which they had put Gunner Doyle.

They walked slowly because Miller wasn't in any fit state to do anything else. His body seemed to be bruised all over and he was strapped up so tightly because of his broken ribs, that he found breathing difficult. He was tired. A hell of a lot had happened since that final terrible scene on the roof and with Mallory on his back, he had been the only person capable of handling what needed to be done. A series of pain-killing injections weren't helping any and he was beginning to find difficulty in thinking straight any more.

The constable on the chair outside the door stood up and Miller nodded familiarly. 'Look after Miss Crowther for a few minutes will you, Harry? I want a word with the Gunner.'

The policeman nodded, Miller opened the door and

went in. There was a screen on the other side of the door and beyond it the Gunner lay propped against the pillows, his nose broken for the fourth time in his life, his right leg in traction, fractured in three places.

Jack Brady sat in a chair on the far side of the bed reading his notebook. He got up quickly. 'I've got a statement from him. He insists that he forced his way into the house last night; that Miss Crowther and her grandmother only allowed him to stay under duress.'

'Is that a fact?' Miller looked down at the Gunner and shook his head. 'You're a poor liar, Gunner. The girl's already given us a statement that clarifies the entire situation. She says that when you saved her from Faulkner in the yard, she and her grandmother felt that they owed you something. She seems to think that's a good enough defence even in open court.'

'What do you think?' the Gunner said weakly.

'I don't think it will come to court so my views don't count. You put up the fight of your life back there on the roof. Probably saved our lives.'

'Oh, get stuffed,' the Gunner said. 'I want to go to sleep.'

'Not just yet. I've got a visitor for you.'

'Jenny?' The Gunner shook his head. 'I don't want to see her.'

'She's been waiting for hours.'

'What in the hell does she want to see me for? There's nothing to bleeding well say, is there? I'll lose all my remission over this little lot. I'm going back to the nick for another two and a half years plus anything else the beak likes to throw at me for the things I've done while I've been out. On top of that I'll be dragging this leg around behind me like a log of wood for the rest of my life when I get out.'

181

'And a bloody good thing as well,' Brady said brutally. 'No more climbing for you, my lad.'

'I'll get her now,' Miller said. 'You can see her alone. We'll wait outside.'

The Gunner shrugged. 'Suit yourself.'

Miller and Brady went out and a second later, the girl came round the screen and stood at the end of the bed. Her face was very pale and there was a nasty bruise on her forehead, but she was still about fifty times better in every possible way than any other woman he'd ever met. There was that strange choking feeling in his throat again. He was tired and in great pain. He was going back to goal for what seemed like forever and for the first time he was afraid of the prospect. He felt just like a kid who had been hurt. He wanted to have her come round the bed and kiss him, smooth back his hair, pillow his head on her shoulder.

But that was no good—no good at all. What he did now was the most courageous thing he had ever done in his entire life, braver by far than his conduct on the roof when facing Faulkner.

He smiled brightly. 'Surprise, surprise. What's all this?'

'I've been waiting for hours. They wouldn't let me in before. Gran sends her regards.'

'How is she?' The Gunner couldn't resist the question. 'They tell me she finished him off good and proper up there. How's she taken it? Flat on her back?'

'Not her—says she'd do it again any day. They've told you who he was?' The Gunner nodded and she went on, 'I was in such a panic when he started smashing his way in that I locked her in the bedroom and forgot all about the shotgun. She keeps it in the wardrobe. She had to shoot the lock off to get out.'

'Good job she arrived when she did from what they tell me.'

There was a slight silence and she frowned. 'Is anything wrong, Gunner?'

'No—should there be?'

'You seem funny, that's all.'

'That's me all over, darlin'. To tell you the truth I was just going to get some shut-eye when you turned up.'

Her face had gone very pale now. 'What is it, Gunner? What are you trying to say?'

'What in the hell am I supposed to say?' He snapped back at her, genuinely angry. 'Here I am flat on my back like a good little lad. In about another month they'll stick me in a big black van and take me back where I came from. That's what you wanted, isn't it?'

She had gone very still. 'I thought it was what *you* wanted—really wanted.'

'And how in the hell would you know what I want?'

'I've been about as close to you as any woman could get and . . .'

He cut in sharply with a laugh that carried just the right cutting edge to it. 'Do me a favour, darlin'. No bird gets close to me. Just because I've had you between the sheets doesn't mean I've sold you the rights to the story of my life for the Sunday papers. It was very nice—don't get me wrong. You certainly know what to do with it, but I've got other fish to fry now.'

She swayed. For a moment it seemed as if she might fall and then she turned and went out. The Gunner closed his eyes. He should have felt noble. He didn't. He felt sick and afraid and more alone than he had ever done in his life before.

.   .   .   .   .

183

The girl was crying when she came out of the room. She kept on going, head-down and Miller went after her. He caught her, swung her round and shoved her against the wall.

'What happened in there?'

'He made it pretty clear what he really thinks about me, that's all,' she said. 'Can I go now?'

'Funny how stupid intelligent people can be sometimes,' Miller shook his head wearily. 'Use your head, Jenny. When he left your house he was wearing shoes and a raincoat, had money in his pocket—money you'd given him. Why did he telephone you?'

'To say he was giving himself up.'

'Why was he barefooted again? Why had he got rid of the clothes you gave him? Why did he come running like a bat out of hell when you were in danger?'

She stared at him, eyes wide and shook her head. 'But he was rotten in there—he couldn't have done more if he'd spat on me.'

'Exactly the result he was hoping for, can't you see that?' Miller said gently. 'The biggest proof of how much he thinks of you is the way he's just treated you.' He took her arm. 'Let's go back inside. You stay behind the screen and keep your mouth shut and I'll prove it to you.'

The Gunner was aware of the click of the door opening, there was a soft footfall and he opened his eyes and looked up at Miller. 'What do you want now, copper?'

'Congratulations,' Miller said. 'You did a good job—on the girl, I mean. Stupid little tart like that deserves all she gets.'

It was all it took. The Gunner tried to sit up, actually tried to get at him. 'You dirty bastard. She's worth ten of you—any day of the week. In my book you aren't fit to clean her shoes.'

184

'Neither are you.'

'The only difference between us is I know it. Now get to hell out of here and leave me alone.'

He closed his eyes as Miller turned on heel and limped out. The door clicked and there was only the silence. He heard no sound and yet something seemed to move and then there was the perfume very close.

He opened his eyes and found her bending over him. 'Oh, Gunner,' she said. 'Whatever am I going to do with you?'

.   .   .   .   .

Miller sat on the end of Mallory's bed to make his report. The Chief Superintendent had a room to himself in the private wing as befitted his station. There were already flowers in the corner and his wife was due to arrive within the hour.

'So you've left them together?' Mallory said.

Miller nodded. 'He isn't going to run anywhere.'

'What about the leg? How bad is it?'

'Not too good, according to the consultant in charge. He'll be lame for the rest of his life. It could have been worse, mind you.'

'No more second-storey work at any rate,' Mallory commented.

'Which could make this injury a blessing in disguise,' Miller pointed out.

Mallory shook his head. 'I hardly think so. Once a thief always a thief and Doyle's a good one—up there with the best. Clever, resourceful, hightly intelligent. When you think of it, he hasn't done anything like the time he should have considering what he's got away with in the past. He'll find something else that's just as crooked, mark my words.'

Which was probably true, but Miller wasn't going down without a fight. 'On the other hand if he hadn't been around last night Jenny Crowther would have been number five on Faulkner's list and we'd have been no further forward. I'd also like to point out that we'd have been in a damn bad way without him up there on the roof.'

'Which is exactly how the newspapers and the great British public will see it, Miller,' Mallory said. 'You needn't flog it to death. As a matter of interest I've already dictated a report for the Home Secretary in which I state that in my opinion Doyle had earned any break we can give him.'

Miller's tiredness dropped away like an old cloak. 'What do you think that could mean—a pardon?'

Mallory laughed out loud. 'Good God, no. If he's lucky, they'll release him in ten months on probation as they would have done anyway if he hadn't run for it.'

'Fair enough, sir.'

'No, it isn't, Miller. He'll be back. You'll see.'

'I'm putting my money on Jenny Crowther.' Miller got to his feet. 'I'd better go now, sir. You look as if you could do with some sleep.'

'And you look as if you might fall down at any moment.' Miller turned, a hand on the door and Mallory called, 'Miller?'

'Yes, sir?'

'Regarding that little wager of ours. I was right about Phillips—he killed Grace Packard just as I said, but taking everything else into consideration I've decided to give you your pound back, and no arguments.'

He switched off the light with his good hand and Miller went out, closing the door softly behind him.

He took the lift down to the entrance hall and found Jack Brady standing outside the night sister's small glass office talking to her. They turned as Miller came forward and the sister frowned.

'You look awful. You should be in your bed, really you should.'

'Is that an invitation, Sister?' Miller demanded and kissed her on the cheek.

Brady tapped out his pipe and slipped a hand under Miller's arm. 'Come on, Nick, let's go.'

'Go where?'

'The nearest pub. I'd like to see what a large whisky does for you, then I'll take you home.'

'You're an Irish gentleman, Jack. God bless you for the kind thought.'

They went out through the glass doors. The rain had stopped and Miller took a deep breath of fresh, damp air. 'Hell is always today, Jack, never tomorrow. Have you ever noticed that?'

'It's all that keeps a good copper going,' Brady said and they went down the steps together.

Toll for the Brave

Contents

Prologue: Nightmare

They were beating the Korean to death in the next room, all attempts to break him down having failed completely. He was a stubborn man and, like most of his countrymen, held the Chinese in a kind of contempt and they reacted accordingly. The fact that Republic of Korea troops had the highest kill ratio in Vietnam at that time didn't exactly help matters.

There were footsteps outside, the door opened and a young Chinese officer appeared. He snapped his fingers and I got up like a good dog and went to heel. A couple of guards were dragging the Korean away by the feet, a blanket wrapped about his head to keep the blood off the floor. The officer paused to light a cigarette, ignoring me completely, then walked along the corridor and I shuffled after him.

We passed the interrogation room, which was something to be thankful for, and stopped outside the camp commandant's office at the far end. The young officer knocked, pushed me inside and closed the door.

Colonel Chen-Kuen was writing away busily at his desk. He ignored me for quite some time, then put down his pen and got to his feet. He walked to the window and glanced outside.

'The rains are late this year.'

I couldn't think of anything to say in answer to that pearl of wisdom, didn't even know if it was expected. In any

193

event, he didn't give me a chance to make small talk and carried straight on, still keeping his back to me.

'I am afraid I have some bad news for you, Ellis. I have finally received instructions from Central Committee in Hanoi. Both you and General St. Claire are to be executed this morning.'

He turned, his face grave, concerned and said a whole lot more, though whether or not he was expressing his personal regret, I could not be sure for it was as if I had cut the wires, his mouth opening and closing soundlessly and I didn't hear a word.

He left me. In fact, it was the last time I ever saw him. When the door opened next I thought it might be the guards come to take me, but it wasn't. It was Madame Ny.

She was wearing a uniform that looked anything but People's Republic and had obviously been tailored by someone who knew his business. Leather boots, khaki shirt and a tunic which had been cut to show off those good breasts of hers to the best advantage. The dark eyes were wet with tears, tragic in the white face.

She said, 'I'm sorry, Ellis.'

Funny, but I almost believed her. Almost, but not quite. I moved in close so that I wouldn't miss, spat right in her face, opened the door and went out.

The young officer had disappeared, but a couple of guards were waiting for me. They were hardly more than boys, stocky little peasants out of the rice fields who gripped their AK assault rifles too tightly like men who weren't as used to them as they should be. One of them went ahead, opened the end door and motioned me through.

The compound was deserted, not a prisoner in sight. The gate stood wide, the watch towers floated in the morning mist. Everything waited. And then I heard the sound of marching feet and St. Claire came round the corner with the young Chinese officer and two guards.

In spite of the broken jump boots, the tattered green fatigues, he still looked everything a soldier ever could be. He marched with that crisp, purposeful movement that only the regular seems to acquire. Every step meant something. It was as if the Chinese were with him; as if he were leading.

He had the Indian sign on them, there was no doubt of that which is saying something for the Chinese do not care for the Negro overmuch. But then, he was something special and like no man I have known before or since.

He paused and looked at me searchingly, then smiled that famous St. Claire smile that made you feel you were the only damned person that mattered in the wide world. I moved to his side and we set off together. He increased his pace and I had to jump to it to stay level with him. We might have been back at Benning, drill on the square, and the guards had to run to keep up with us.

Colonel Chen-Kuen's rains came as we went through the gate, in that incredible instant downpour that you only get with the monsoon. It didn't make the slightest difference to St. Claire and he carried on at the same brisk pace so that one of the guards had to run past to get in front of us to lead the way.

In other circumstances it could have been funny, but not now. We plunged through the heavy, drenching downpour into the forest and took a path that led down towards the river a mile or more away.

A couple of hundred yards further on we entered a broad clearing that sloped steeply into the trees. There were mounds of earth all over the place, as nice a little cemetery as you could wish for, but minus the headstones naturally.

The young officer called us to a halt, his voice hard and

195

flat through the rain. We stood and waited while he had a look round. There didn't seem much room to spare, but he obviously wasn't going to let a little thing like that worry him. He selected a spot on the far side of the clearing, found us a couple of rusting trenching shovels that looked as if they had seen plenty of service and went and stood in the shelter of the trees with two of the guards and smoked cigarettes, leaving one to watch over us as we set to work.

The soil was pure loam, light and easy to handle because of the rain. It lifted in great spadefuls that had me knee-deep in my own grave before I knew where I was. And St. Claire wasn't exactly helping. He worked at it as if there was a bonus at the end of the job, those great arms of his swinging three spadefuls of dirt into the air for every one of mine.

The rain seemed to increase in a sudden rush that drowned all hope. I was going to die. The thought rose in my throat like bile to choke on and then it happened. The side of the trench next to me collapsed suddenly, probably because of the heavy rain, leaving a hand and part of a forearm protruding from the earth, flesh rotting from the bones.

I turned away blindly, fighting for air, and lost my balance, falling flat on my face. At the same moment the other wall of the trench collapsed across me.

As I struggled for life, I was aware that St. Claire had started to laugh, that deep, rich, special sound that seemed to come right up from the roots of his being. It didn't make any kind of sense at all but I had other things to think of now. The stink of the grave was in my nostrils, my eyes. I opened my mouth to scream and soil poured in choking the life out of me in a great wave of darkness that blotted out all light . . .

1 World's end

The dream always ended in exactly the same way—with me sitting bolt upright in bed, screaming like any child frightened in the dark, St. Claire's laughter ringing in my ears which was the most disturbing thing of all.

And as always during the silence that followed, I waited with a kind of terrible anxiety for something to happen, something I dreaded above all things and yet could not put a name to.

But as usual, there was nothing. Only the rain brushing against the windows of the old house, driven by a wind that blew stiffly across the marshes from the North Sea. I listened, head turned, waiting for a sign that never came, shaking slightly and sweating rather a lot which was exactly how Sheila found me when she arrived a moment later.

She had been painting—still clutched a palette and three brushes in her left hand and the old terry towelling robe she habitually wore was streaked with paint. She put the palette and brushes down on a chair, came and sat on the edge of the bed, taking my hands in hers.

'What is it, love? The dream again?'

When I spoke my voice was hoarse and broken. 'Always the same—always. Accurate in every detail, exactly as it was until St. Claire starts to laugh.'

I started to shake uncontrollably, teeth grinding together in intense stress. She had the robe off in a moment, was

197

under the sheets, her arms pulling me into the warmth of that magnificent body.

And as always, she knew exactly what she was doing for fear turns upon itself endlessly like a mad dog unless the cycle can be broken. She kissed me repeatedly, hands gentle. For a little while, comfort, then by some mysterious alchemy, she was on her back, thighs spreading to receive me. An old story between us, but one which never palled and at such moments, the finest therapy in the world—or so I told myself.

* * *

Englishmen who have served with the American forces in Vietnam aren't exactly thick on the ground, but there are more of us around than most people realise. Having said that, to disclose what I'd been doing for the past three years, in mixed company, was usually calculated to raise most eyebrows, and in some instances could be guaranteed to provoke open hostility.

The party where I had first met Sheila Ward was a case in point. It had turned out to be a stuffy, pseudo-intellectual affair. I was thoroughly bored and didn't seem to know a soul except my hostess. When she finally had time for me I had done what seemed the sensible thing and got good and drunk, something at which I was fairly expert in those days.

Unfortunately, she didn't seem to notice and insisted on introducing me to a sociologist from the London School of Economics who by some minor miracle known only to academics, had managed to obtain a doctorate for a thesis on structural values in Revolutionary China without ever having actually visited the country.

The information that I had spent three of the best years

of my young life serving with the American Airborne in Vietnam including a sizeable stretch in a North Vietnamese prison camp, had the same effect as if he had been hit by a rather heavy truck.

He told me that I was about as acceptable in his eyes as a lump of dung on his shoe which seemed to go down well with the group who'd been hanging on his every word, but didn't impress me one little bit.

I told him what he could do about it in pretty fluent Cantonese which—surprisingly in an expert on Chinese affairs—he didn't seem to understand.

But someone else did which was when I met Sheila Ward. Just about the most spectacular woman I'd ever seen in my life. Every man's fantasy dream. Soft black leather boots that reached to her thighs, a yard or two of orange wool posing as a dress, shoulder-length auburn hair framing a strong peasant face and a mouth which was at least half a mile wide. She could have been ugly, but her mouth was her saving grace. With that mouth she was herself alone.

'You can't do that to him,' she said in fair Chinese. 'They'd give you at least five years.'

'Not bad,' I told her gravely, 'But your accent is terrible.'

'Yorkshire,' she said. 'Just a working class girl from Doncaster on the make. My husband was a lecturer at Hong Kong University for five years.'

The conversation was interrupted by my sociologist friend who tried to pull her out of the way and started again so I punched him none too gently under the breastbone, knuckles extended, and he went down with a shrill cry.

I don't really remember what happened after that except that Sheila led me out and no one tried to get in the way.

I do know that it was raining hard, that I was leaning up against my car in the alley at the side of the house beneath a street lamp.

She buttoned me into my trenchcoat and said soberly, 'You were pretty nasty in there.'

'A bad habit of mine these days.'

'You get in fights often?'

'Now and then.' I struggled to light a cigarette. 'I irritate people or they annoy me.'

'And afterwards you feel better?' She shook her head 'There are other ways of relieving that kind of tension or didn't it ever occur to you?'

She had a bright red oilskin mac slung around her shoulders against the rain so I reached inside and cupped a beautifully firm breast.

She said calmly, 'See what I mean?'

I leaned back against the car, my face up to the rain. 'I can do several things quite well besides belt people. Latin declensions which comes of having gone to the right kind of school and I can find true north by pointing the hour hand of my watch at the sun or by shoving a stick into the ground. And I can cook. My monkey is delicious and tree rats are my speciality.'

'Exactly my type,' she said. 'I can see we're going to get along fine.'

'Just one snag,' I told her. 'Bed.'

She frowned. 'You didn't lose anything when you were out there did you?'

'Everything intact and in full working order, ma'am.' I saluted gravely. 'It's just that I've never been any good at it. A Chinese psychiatrist once told me it was because my grandfather found me in bed with the Finnish au pair when I was fourteen and beat all hell out of me with a blackthorne he prized rather highly. Carried it all the way

200

through the desert campaign. He was a general, you see, so he naturally found it difficult to forgive me when it broke.'

'On you?' she said.

'Exactly, so I don't think you'd find me very satisfactory.'

'We'll have to see, won't we?' She was suddenly the lass from Doncaster again, the Yorkshire voice flat in the rain. 'What do you do with yourself—for a living, I mean?'

'Is that what you call it?' I shrugged. 'The last of the dinosaurs. Hunted to extinction. I enjoy what used to be known in society as private means—lots of them. In what little time I have to spare, I also try to write.'

She smiled at that, looking so astonishingly beautiful that things actually stopped moving for a moment. 'You're just what I've been seeking for my old age.'

'You're marvellous,' I said. 'Also big, busty, sensuous . . .'

'Oh, definitely that,' she said. 'I never know when to stop. I'm also a lay-out artist in an advertising agency, divorced and thirty-seven years of age. You've only seen me in an artificial light, love.'

I started to slide down the side of the car and she got a shoulder under my arm and went through my clothes.

'You'll find the wallet in my left breast pocket,' I murmured.

She chuckled. 'You daft ha'p'orth. I'm looking for the car keys. Where do you live?'

'The Essex coast,' I told her. 'Foulness.'

'Good God,' she said. 'That must be all of fifty miles away.'

'Fifty-eight.'

She took me back to her flat in the King's Road, just for the night. I stayed a month, which was definitely all I could

201

take of the hub of the universe, the bright lights, the crowds. I needed solitude again, the birds, the marshes, my own little hole to rot in. So she left her job at the agency, moved down to Foulness and set up house with me.

* * *

Oscar Wilde once said that life is a bad quarter of an hour made up of exquisite moments. She certainly gave me plenty of those in the months that followed and that morning was no exception. I started off in my usual frenzy and within minutes she had gentled me into making slow, meaningful love and with considerably more expertise than when we had first met. She'd definitely taken care of that department.

Afterwards I felt fine, the fears of the hour before dawn a vague fantasy already forgotten. I kissed her softly under her rigid left nipple, tossed the sheets to one side and went into the bathroom.

A medical friend once assured me that the shock of an ice-cold shower was detrimental to the vascular system and liable to reduce life expectancy by a month. Admittedly he was in his cups at the time but I had always found it an excellent excuse for spending five minutes each morning under a shower that was as hot as I could bear.

When I returned to the bedroom Sheila had gone, but I could smell coffee and realised that I was hungry. I dressed quickly and went into the sitting-room. There was a log fire burning on the stone hearth and she had her easel set up in front of it.

She was standing there now in her old terry towelling robe, the palette back in her left hand, dabbing vigorously at the canvas with a long brush.

202

'I'm having coffee,' she said without turning round. 'I've made tea for you. It's on the table.'

I poured myself a cup and went and stood behind her. It was good—damn good. A view from the house, the saltings splashed with sea-lavender, the peculiarly luminous light reflected by the slimy mud flats, blurring everything at the edges. Above all, the loneliness.

'It's good.'

'Not yet.' She worked away busily in one corner without turning her head. 'But it will be. What do you want for breakfast?'

'I wouldn't dream of disturbing the muse.' I kissed her on the nape of the neck. 'I'll take Fritz for a walk.'

'All right, love.'

The brush was moving very quickly now, a frown of concentration on her face. I had ceased to exist so I got my hunting jacket from behind the door and left her to it.

* * *

I have been told that in some parts of America, Airedales are kept specifically to hunt bears and they are excellent swimmers, a useful skill in an area like Foulness. But not Fritz who was Sheila's one true love, a great, shaggy bundle in ginger and black, amiable to a degree in spite of a bark that could be heard half a mile away. He had ceased to frighten even the birds and was terrified of water, objecting to even the mildest wetting of his paws. He romped ahead of me along the rutted grassy track and I followed.

Foulness—Cape of Birds, the Saxons called it and they were here in plenty. I have always had a liking for solitude and no more than fifty-odd miles from London, I rotted gently and in the right place for it. Islands and mist and sea walls to keep out the tide, built by the Dutch centuries ago. Creeks, long grass, stirring to change colour as if brushed by an invisible presence, the gurgle of water everywhere and the sea creeping in like a ghost in the night to take the unwary.

The Romans had known this place, Saxon outlaws hidden here from the Normans, and now Ellis Jackson pretended for the moment that this was all there was.

In the marshes autumn is the saltings purple and mauve with the sea lavender, the damp smell of rotting vegetation. Birds calling constantly, lifting from beyond the sea wall uneasily, summer dead and winter yet to come. Gales blowing in off the North Sea, the wind moaning endlessly.

Was this all there was—truly? A bottle a day and Sheila Ward to warm the bed? What was I waiting for, here at the world's end?

Somewhere in the far distance I heard shooting. Heavy stuff from the sound of it. It stirred something deep inside, set the adrenalin surging only I didn't have an MI6 carbine to hang on to and this wasn't the Mekong Delta. This was a grazing marsh on the tip of Foulness in quiet Essex and the shooting came from the Ministry of Defence Proof and Experimental Artillery ranges at Shoeburyness.

Fritz was somewhere up ahead exploring and out of sight. He suddenly appeared over a dyke about fifty yards ahead, plunged into a wide stretch of water and swam strongly to the other side, disappearing into the reeds.

A moment later, he started to bark frantically, a strange new sound for him that seemed to have fear in it. There was a single rifle shot and the barking ceased.

Birds lifted out of the marsh in great clouds. The beating of their wings filled the air and when they had passed, they left an uncanny stillness.

I ran into the mist calling his name. I found his body

a minute later sprawled across the rutted track. From the look of things he had been shot through the head with a high velocity bullet for most of the skull had disintegrated. I couldn't really take it in because it didn't make any kind of sense. This wasn't a place where one found strangers. The Ministry were tough about that because of the experimental ranges. Even the locals had to produce a pass at certain checkpoints when leaving or returning to the general area. I had one myself.

A small wind touched my cheek coldly, there was a splashing and as I turned something moved in the tall reeds to my right.

* * *

North Vietnamese regular troops wear khaki, but the Viet Cong have their own distinctive garb of conical straw hat and black pyjamas. Many of them still use the old Browning Automatic rifle or the MI carbine that got most American troops through the Second World War.

But not the one who stepped out of the reeds some ten or fifteen yards to my right. He held what looked like a brand new AK47 assault rifle across his chest, the best that China could provide. Very probably the finest assault rifle in the world.

He was as small as they usually were, a stocky little peasant out of some rice field or other. He was soaked to the knees, rain dripped from the brim of his straw hat, the black jacket was quilted against the cold.

I took a couple of cautious steps back. He said nothing, made no move at all, just stood there, holding the AK at the high port. I half-turned and found his twin standing ten yards to my rear.

If this was madness, it had been a long time coming. I

cracked completely, gave a cry of fear, jumped from the track into the reeds and plunged into the mist, knee-deep in water.

A wild swan lifted in alarm, great wings beating so close to me that I cried out again and got my arms to my face. But I kept on moving, coming up out of the reeds on the far side close to the old grass-covered dyke that kept the sea back in its own place.

I crouched against it, listening for the sounds of pursuit. Somewhere back there in the marsh there was a disturbance, birds rising in alarm. It was enough. I scrambled over the dyke, dropped to the beach below and ran for my life.

* * *

Sheila was still at the easel in front of the fire when I burst into the cottage. I made it to a wing-backed chair near the door and fell into it. She was on her knees beside me in an instant.

'Ellis? Ellis, what is it?'

I tried to speak, but the words wouldn't come and there was real fear in her eyes now. She hurried to the sideboard and returned with a glass of whisky.

I spilled more than I got down, my hand shaking as if I was in high fever. I had left the door open behind me and it swung to and fro in the wind. As she got up to close it, there was the patter of feet.

She said, 'There's a lovely old boy and mud up to the eyebrows.'

Fritz padded round to the front of the chair and shoved his nose at my hand.

* * *

There had always been a chance that this would happen ever since Tay Son. The psychiatrists had hinted as much, for the damage was too deep. I started to cry helplessly like a child as Fritz nuzzled my hand.

Sheila was very pale now. She pushed my hair back from my brow as if I were a small untidy boy and kissed me gently.

'It's going to be all right, Ellis. Just trust me.'

The telephone was in the kitchen. I sat there, clutching my empty whisky glass, staring into space, tears running down my face.

I heard her say, 'American Embassy? I'd like to speak to General St. Claire, please. My name is Mrs. Sheila Ward. There was a pause and then she said, 'Max, is that you?' and closed the door.

She came out in two or three minutes and knelt in front of me. 'Max is coming, Ellis. He's leaving at once. He'll be here in an hour and a half at the most.'

She left me then to go and get dressed and I hung on to that thought. That Max was coming. Black Max. Brigadier-General James Maxwell St. Claire, Congressional Medal of Honour, D.S.C., Silver Star, Medaille Militaire, from Anzio to Vietnam, every boy's fantasy figure. Black Max was coming to save me as he had saved me, body and soul, once before in the place they called Tay Son.

2 Forcing House Number One

On a wet February evening in 1966 during my second year at Sandhurst, I jumped from a railway bridge to a freight train passing through darkness below. I landed on a pile of coke, but the cadet who followed me wasn't so lucky. He dropped between two trucks and was killed instantly.

We were drunk, of course, which didn't help matters. It was the final link in a chain of similar stupidities and the end of something as far as I was concerned. Harsh words were said at the inquest, even harsher by the commandant when dismissing me from the Academy.

Words didn't exactly fail my grandfather either, who being a major-general, took it particularly hard. He had always considered me some kind of moral degenerate after the famous episode with the Finnish au pair at the tender age of fourteen and this final exploit gave him the pleasure of knowing that he had been right all along.

My father had died what is known as a hero's death at Arnhem during the Second World War. My mother, two years later. So, the old man had had his hands on me for some considerable time. Why he had always disliked me so was past knowing and yet hatred is as strong a bond as loving so that when he forbade me his house, there was a kind of release.

The army had been his idea, not mine. The family tradition, or the family curse depending which way you looked at it, so now I was free after twenty-odd years of some kind of servitude or other and thanks to my mother's money, wealthy by any standards.

Perhaps because of that—because it was my choice and mine alone—I flew to New York within a week of leaving the Academy and enlisted for a period of three years in the United States Army as a paratrooper.

●　　　●　　　●

It could be argued that the jump from that railway bridge was a jump into hell for in a sense it landed me in Tay

208

Son, although eighteen months of a different kind of hell intervened.

I flew into the old French airport at Ton Son Nhut in July, 1966, one of two hundred replacements for the 801st Airborne Division. The pride of the army and every man a volunteer as paratroopers are the world over.

A year later, only forty-eight of that original two hundred were still on active duty. The rest were either dead, wounded or missing, thirty-three in one bad ambush alone in the Central Highlands which I only survived myself along with two others by playing dead.

So, I discovered what war was all about—or at least war in Vietnam. Not set-piece battles, not trumpets on the wind, no distant drum to stir the heart. It was savage street fighting in Saigon during the *Tet* offensive. It was the swamps of the Mekong Delta, the jungles of the Central Highlands, leg ulcers that ate their way through to the bone like acid and leeches that fastened on to your privates and could only be removed with the lighted end of a cigarette.

In a word, it was survival and I became rather an expert in that particular field, came through it all without a scratch until the day I was taking part in a routine search and destroy patrol out of Din To and was careless enough to step on a *punji* stake, a lethal little booby trap much favoured by the Viet Cong. Fashioned from bamboo, needle-sharp, stuck upright in the ground amongst the elephant grass and smeared with human excrement, it was guaranteed to produce a nasty, festering wound.

It put me in hospital for a fortnight and a week's leave to follow, which brought me directly to that fateful day in Pleikic when I shambled around in the rain, trying to arrange some transportation to Din To where I had to rejoin my unit. I managed to thumb a lift in a Medevac helicopter that was flying in medical supplies—the worst day's work in my life.

*   *   *

We were about fifty miles out of Din To when it happened, flying at a thousand feet over paddy fields and jungle, an area stiff with Viet Cong and North Vietnamese regular troops.

A flare went up suddenly about a quarter of a mile to the east of us. There was the burnt-out wreck of a small Huey helicopter in the corner of a paddy field and the man who waved frantically from the dyke beside it was in American uniform.

When we were about thirty feet up, a couple of heavy machine guns opened up from the jungle no more than fifty yards away and at that range they couldn't miss. The two pilots were wearing chest protectors, but it didn't do them any good. I think they must have both died instantly. Certainly the crew chief did, for standing in the open doorway in his safety belt, he didn't have a chance.

The only surviving crew member, the medic, was huddled in the corner, clutching a bloody arm. There was an MI6 in a clip beside him. I grabbed for it, but at the same moment the aircraft lifted violently and I was thrown out through the open door to fall into the mud and water of the paddy field below.

The helicopter bucked twenty or thirty feet up into the air, veered sharply to the left and exploded in a great ball of fire, burning fuel and debris scattering like shrapnel.

I managed to stand, plastered with mud and found myself looking up at the gentleman on the dyke who was pointing an AK47 straight at me. It was no time for heroics, especially as forty or fifty North Vietnamese regular troops swarmed out of the jungle a moment later.

The Viet Cong would have killed me out of hand, but not these boys. Prisoners were a valuable commodity to them, for propaganda as well as intelligence purposes. They marched me into the jungle surrounded by the whole group, everyone trying to get in on the act.

There was a small camp and a young officer who spoke excellent English with a French accent and gave me a cigarette. Then he went through my pockets and examined my documents.

Which was where things took a more sinister turn. In action, it was the practice to leave all personal papers at base, but because I had only been in transit after medical treatment, I was carrying everything, including my British passport.

He said slowly, 'You are English?'

There didn't seem to be much point in denying it. 'That's right. Where's the nearest consul?'

Which got me a fist in the mouth for my pains. I thought they might kill me then, but I suppose he knew immediately how valuable a piece of propaganda I would make.

They kept me alive—just—for another fortnight until they found it possible to pass me on to a group moving north for rest and recuperation.

And so, at last, I came to Tay Son. The final landing place of my jump from that railway bridge into darkness, a year and a half before.

* * *

My first sight of it was through rain at late evening as we came out of a valley—a great, ochre-painted wall on the crest above us.

I'd seen enough Buddhist monasteries to recognise it for

211

what it was, only this one was different. A watch tower on stilts at either side of the main gate, a guard in each with a heavy machine gun. Beyond, in the compound, there were several prefabricated huts.

Having spent three days stumbling along on the end of a rope at the tail of a column of pack mules, I had only one aim in life which was to find a corner to die in. I tried to sit and someone kicked me back on my feet. They took the mules away, leaving only one guard for me. I stood there, already half-asleep, the rain drifting down through the weird, half-light that you get in the highlands just before dark.

And then an extraordinary thing happened. A man reported dead by the world's press came round the corner of one of the huts with three armed guards trailing behind him, a black giant in green fatigues and jump boots, Chaka, King of the Zulu nation, alive and shaking the earth again.

Brigadier-General James Maxwell St. Claire, the pride of the Airborne, one of the most spectacular figures thrown up by the army since the Second World War. A legend in his own time—Black Max.

His disappearance three months earlier had provoked a scandal that had touched the White House itself for, as a Medal of Honour man, he had been kept strictly out of the line of fire since Korea, had only found himself in Vietnam at all as a member of a fact-finding commission reporting directly to the president himself.

The story was that St. Claire was visiting a forward area helicopter outfit when a red alert went up. One of the gun ships was short of a man to operate one of its door-mounted M6o's. St. Claire, seizing his chance of a little action, had insisted on going along. The chopper had gone down in flames during the ensuing action.

He changed direction and crossed the compound so briskly that his guards were left trailing. Mine presented his AK and St. Claire shoved it to one side with the back of his hand.

I came to attention. He said, 'At ease, soldier. You know me?'

'You inspected my outfit at Din To just over three months ago, sir.'

He nodded slowly. 'I remember and I remember you, too. Colonel Dooley pointed you out to me specially. You're English. Didn't I speak to you on parade?'

'That's right, General.'

He smiled suddenly, my first sight of that famous St. Claire charm and put a hand on my shoulder. 'You look bushed, son. I'll see what I can do, but it won't be much. This is no ordinary prison camp. The Chinese run this one personally. Forcing house number one. The commander is a Colonel Chen-Kuen, one of the nicest guys you ever met in your life. Amongst other things, he's got a Ph.D. in psychology from London University. He's here for one reason only. To take you apart.'

There was an angry shout and a young officer appeared from the entrance of one of the huts. He pulled out an automatic and pointed it at St. Claire's head.

St. Claire ignored him. 'Hang on to your pride, boy, you'll find it's all you have.'

He went off like a strong wind and they had to run to keep up with him, the young officer cursing wildly. Strange the sense of personal loss as I found myself alone again but I was no longer tired—St. Claire had taken care of that at least.

They left me there for another hour, long enough for the evening chill to eat right into my bones and then a door opened and an n.c.o. appeared and called to my guard who kicked my leg viciously and sent me on my way.

Inside the hut, I found a long corridor, several doors opening off. We stopped at the end one and after a while it opened and St. Claire was marched out. There was no time to speak for a young officer beckoned me inside.

The man behind the desk wore the uniform of a colonel in the Army of the People's Republic of China, presumably the Chen-Kuen St. Claire had mentioned.

The eyes lifted slightly at the corners, shrewd and kindly in a bronzed healthy face and the lips were well-formed and full of humour. He unfolded a newspaper and held it up so that I could see it. The *Daily Express* printed in London five days earlier according to the date. *English war hero dies in Vietnam.* The headline sprawled across the front page.

I said 'They must have been short of news that day.'

His English was excellent. 'Oh, I don't think so. They all took the story, even *The Times*.' He held-up a copy. 'They managed to get an interview with your grandfather. It says here that the general was overwhelmed by his loss, but proud.'

I laughed out loud at that one and the colonel said gravely, 'Yes, I found that a trifle ironic myself when one considers his intense dislike of you. Almost pathological. I wonder why?'

A remark so penetrating could not help but chill the blood, but I fought back. 'And what in hell are you supposed to be—a mind reader?'

He picked up a manilla file. 'Ellis Jackson from birth to death. It's all there. We must talk about Eton some time. I've always been fascinated by the concept of the place. The Sandhurst affair was certainly a great tragedy. You got the dirty end of the stick there.' He sighed heavily, as if feeling

214

the whole thing personally and keenly. 'In my early years as a student at London University, I read a novel by Ouida in which the hero, a Guards officer in disgrace, joins the French Foreign Legion. Nothing changes, it appears.'

'That's it exactly,' I said. 'I'm here to redeem the family honour.'

'And yet you hated the idea of going into the army,' he said. 'Hated anything military. Or is it just your grandfather you hate?'

'Neat enough in theory,' I said. 'On the other hand, I never met anyone yet who had a good word for him.'

I could have kicked myself at the sight of his smile, the satisfaction in his eyes. Already I was telling him things about myself. I think he must have sensed what was in my mind for he pressed a button on the desk and stood up.

'General St. Claire spoke to you earlier, I believe?'

'That's right.'

'A remarkable man—gifted in many directions, but arrogant. You may share his cell for a while.'

'An enlisted man with the top brass. He might not like that.'

'My dear Ellis, our social philosophy does not recognise such distinctions between human beings. He must learn this. So must you.'

'*Ellis.*' It gave me a strange, uncomfortable feeling to be called by my Christian name. Too intimate under the circumstances, but there was nothing I could do about it. The door opened and the young officer entered.

Chen-Kuen smiled amicably and put a hand on my shoulder. 'Sleep, Ellis—a good, long sleep and then we speak again.'

What was it St. Claire had said of him? *One of the nicest guys you've ever met?* The father I'd never known perhaps and my throat went dry at the thought of it. Deep

215

waters certainly—too damned deep and I turned and got out of there fast.

*　　*　　*

During the journey to Tay Son, we had made overnight stops twice at mountain villages. I had been put on display, a rope around my neck, as an example of the kind of mad-dog mercenary the Americans were using in Vietnam, a murderer of women and children.

It almost got me just that, the assembled villagers baying for my blood like hounds in full cry and each time, the earnest young officer, a dedicated disciple of Mao and Uncle Ho, intervened on my behalf. I must survive to learn the error of my ways. I was a typical product of the capitalist imperialist tradition. I must be helped. Simple behaviourist psychology, of course. The blow followed by kindness so that you never knew where you were.

Something similar happened on leaving Colonel Chen-Kuen's office. I was marched across the compound to one of the huts which turned out to be the medical centre.

The young officer left me in charge of a guard. After a while, the doctor appeared, a small, thin woman in an immaculate white coat with steel spectacles, a face like tight leather and the smallest mouth I've ever seen in my life. She bore an uncanny resemblance to my grandfather's housekeeper during my early childhood, a little, vinegary lowland Scot who had never been able to forgive John Knox and therefore hated all things male. I could taste the castor oil for the first time in years and shuddered.

She sat down at her desk and the door opened again and another woman entered. A different proposition entirely. She was one of those women whose sensuality was so much a part of her that even the rather unflattering tunic and

216

skirt of her uniform, the knee-length leather boots, could not hide it.

Her hair was jet black, parted in the centre, worn in two plaits wound into a bun at the back in a very Eastern European style, which wasn't surprising in view of the fact that her mother, as I discovered later, was Russian.

The face was the face of one of those idols to be seen in temples all over the East. The Earth Mother who destroys all men, great, hooded, calm eyes, wide, sensual mouth. One could strive on her forever, seeking the sum total of all pleasures and finding, in the end, that the pit was bottomless.

She had only the slightest of accents and her voice was indescribably beautiful. I am Madame Ny. I am to be your instructor.

'Well, I don't know what that's supposed to mean,' I said, 'But it sounds nice.'

The old doctor spoke to her in Chinese. Madame Ny nodded. 'You will undress now, Mr. Jackson. The doctor wishes to examine you.'

I was so tired that undressing was an effort, but I finally made it down to my underpants. The doctor glanced up from a file she was examining, frowned in exasperation.

Madame Ny said, 'Everything, please, Mr. Jackson.'

I tried to keep it light. 'Even the Marine Corps let you keep this much on.'

'You are ashamed to be seen so and by a doctor?' She seemed genuinely surprised. 'There is nothing obscene in the human form. A most unhealthy attitude.'

'That's me,' I said. 'Cold showers just never seemed to work.'

She leaned down to speak to the doctor and again they examined a file between them, presumably mine.

I peeled off like a good boy and waited. I must have

217

stood there for twenty minutes or more and during that time various individuals, both men and women, came and went with files and papers. A study in conscious humiliation.

When it had presumably been judged I'd been punished enough, the doctor stood up abruptly and went to work. She gave me a thorough and competent examination, I'll say that for her, even to the extent of taking blood and urine samples.

Finally, she pulled forward a chair, sat down and proceeded to examine my genitals with scrupulous efficiency. It was the kind of free-from-infection check that soldiers the world over get every few months. That didn't make it any easier to take, especially with Madame Ny standing at her shoulder and following every move.

I squirmed, mainly at the old girl's rough handling and Madame Ny said softly, 'You find this disturbing, is it not so, Mr. Jackson? A basic, clinical examination carried out by a woman old enough to be your mother and yet you find it shameful.'

'Why don't you jump off?' I told her.

Her eyes widened as if gaining sudden insight. 'Ah, but I see now. Not shameful, but frightening. You are afraid in such situations.'

She turned, spoke to the old doctor who nodded and they walked out on me before I could say a word. I wasn't tired any more but I found it difficult to think straight. I felt as angry and frustrated as any schoolboy, humiliated before the class for no good reason.

I had just struggled back into my clothes when Madame Ny returned with the young officer. She had a paper in her hand which she placed on the desk.

She picked up a pen and offered it to me. 'You will sign this now, please.'

There were five foolscap pages, closely typed and all in Chinese. 'You'll have to read the small print for me,' I told her. 'I haven't got my spectacles with me.'

'Your confession,' the young officer cut in. 'A factual account of your time in Vietnam as an English mercenary lured by the Americans.'

I told him what to do with the paper in an English phrase so vulgar that he obviously didn't understand. But Madame Ny did.

She smiled faintly. 'A physical impossibility, I fear, Mr. Jackson. You will sign in the end, I assure you, but we have plenty of time. All the time in the world.'

She left again and the young officer told me to follow him. We crossed the compound through the rain and entered the monastery itself, a place of endless passages and worn stone steps although, surprisingly, lit by electricity.

The passage we finally turned into was obviously at the highest level, so long it faded into darkness; and, quite plainly, I heard a guitar.

As we advanced, the sound became even plainer and then someone started to sing a slow blues in a deep, mellow voice that reached out to touch everything around.

'Now gather round me people,
Let me tell you the true facts.
That tough luck has struck me
And the rats is sleeping in my hat.'

The door had two guards outside and was of heavy black oak. The young officer produced a key about twelve inches long to unlock it and it took both hands to turn.

The room was surprisingly large and lit by a single electric bulb. There was a rush mat on the stone floor and

219

two wooden cots. St. Claire sat on one of them a guitar across his knees.

He stopped playing. 'Welcome to Liberty Hall, Eton. It isn't much, but it's the London Hilton compared to most of the accommodation around here.'

I don't think I've ever been happier to see anyone in my life.

* * *

He produced a pack of American cigarettes. 'You use these things?'

'Officer's stock?' I said.

He shook his head. 'They're being nice to me at the moment. They might give me a pack a day for a whole month, or simply cut off the supply from tomorrow morning.'

'Pavlovian conditioning?'

'That's it exactly. They have one set idea and you better get used to it. To drive you to the edge of insanity, to tear you apart, then they'll put you together again in their image. Even their psychology is Marxian. They believe each of us has his thesis, his positive side and his antithesis, the dark side of his being. If they can find out what that is, they encourage its growth until it becomes the strongest part of your nature. Once that happens, you begin to doubt every moral or decent worthwhile thing you've been taught.'

'They don't seem to be getting very far with you.'

'You could say I'm inclined to be set in my ways.' He smiled. 'But they're still trying and my instructor is the best. Chen-Kuen himself. That's just another name for interrogator, by the way.'

'I've already met mine,' I said and told him about Madame Ny and what had happened at the medical centre.

220

He listened intently and shook his head when I was finished. 'I've never come across her myself, but then you won't have contacts with many people at all. I haven't met another prisoner face-to-face since I've been here. Even the sessions in the Indoctrination Centre, where they feed you Chinese and Marxism by the hour, are all strictly private. You sit in an enclosed booth with headphones and a tape recorder.'

I made the obvious point. 'If what you're saying is true, why have they put me in with you?'

'Search me.' He shrugged. 'First I knew was when Chen-Kuen called me in, told me every last damn thing about you there was to know and said you'd be joining me.'

'But there must be a purpose?'

'You can bet your sweet life there is. Could be he just wants to observe our reactions. Two rats in a cage. That's all we are to him.'

I kicked a chair out of the way, walked to one of the tiny windows and stared out into the rain.

St. Claire said softly, 'You're too up-tight, son. You'll need to cool it if you're going to survive round here. The state you're in now, you'd crack at the first turn of the screw.'

'But not you,' I said. 'Not Black Max.'

He was off the bed and I was nailed to the wall. The face was devoid of all expression, carved from stone, the face of a man who would kill without the slightest qualm, had done so more times than he could probably remember.

He said very slowly in a voice like a cut-throat razor, 'They have a room down below here they call the Box. I could tell you what it's like, but you wouldn't begin to understand. They locked the door on me for three weeks and I walked out. Three weeks of being back in the womb and I walked out.'

He released me and spun around like a kid, arms out-stretched, smiling like the sun breaking through after rain.

'Jesus, boy, but you should have seen their faces.'

'How?' I said. 'How did you do it?'

He tossed me another cigarette. 'You've got to be like the Rock of Gibraltar. So sure of yourself that nothing can touch you.'

'And how do you get like that?'

He lay back, head pillowed on one arm. 'I did a little Judo at Harvard when I was a student. After the war, when I was posted to Japan with the occupation army, I took it further, mainly for something to do. First I discovered *Karate*, then a lethal little item called *aikido*. I'm black belt in both.'

It was said casually, a statement of fact, no particular pride in the voice at all.

'And then a funny thing happened,' he continued. 'I was taken to meet an old Zen priest, eighty or ninety years old and all of seven stone. The guy who took me was a *judo* black belt. In the demonstration that followed, the old man remained seated and he attacked him from the rear.'

'What happened?'

'The old man threw him time and time again. He told me afterwards that his power came from the seat of reflex control, what they call the tanden or second brain. Usually developed by long periods of meditation and special breath-ing exercises. It's all just a Japanese development of the ancient Chinese art of Shaolin Temple Boxing and even that was imported from India with Zen Buddhism.'

He was beginning to lose me. 'Just how far did you go with all this stuff yourself?'

'Zen Buddhism, Confuscianism, Taoism. I've boned up on them all. Studied Chinese Boxing in every minute of my spare time for nearly four years at a Zen monastery about forty miles out of Tokio in the mountains. I thought I knew it all when I started and found I knew nothing.'

'And what's it all come down to?'

'Ever read the *Daw-Der-Jung* by Lao Tzu, the Old Master?' He shrugged. 'No, I guess you wouldn't. He says, amongst other things, that when one wishes to expand one must first contract. When one wishes to rise, one must first fall. When one wishes to take, one must first give. Meekness can overcome hardness and weakness can overcome strength.'

'And what in the hell is all that supposed to add up to?'

'You've got to be able to relax completely, just like a cat. That way you develop *ch'i*. It's a kind of intrinsic energy. When it's accumulated in the *tan t'ien*, a point just below the navel, it has an elemental force greater than any physical strength can hope to be. There are various breathing exercises which can help you along the way. A kind of self-hypnotism.'

He proceeded to explain one in detail and the whole thing seemed so ridiculous that for the first time it occurred to me that his imprisonment might have affected him for the worst.

I suppose it must have shown on my face for he laughed out loud. 'You think I'm crazy, don't you? Well, not yet, boy. Not by a mile and a half. You listen to me and maybe you stand a ten percent chance of getting through this place in one piece. And now I'd get some sleep if I were you while you've got the chance.'

He dismissed me by picking up a book, a paperback edition of *The Thoughts of Mao Tse Tung*. By then, I was past caring about anything. Even the short walk to my bed was an effort.

But the straw mattress seemed softer than anything I had ever known, the sensation of easing aching limbs

223

almost masochistic in the pleasure it gave. I closed my eyes, poised on the brink of sleep and started to slither into darkness, all tension draining out of me. A bell started to jangle somewhere inside my head, a hideous frightening clamour that touched the raw nerve endings like a series of electric shocks.

I was aware of St. Claire's warning cry and the door burst open and the young officer who had delivered me re-appeared, a dozen soldiers at his back and three of them with bayonets fixed to their AKs. They penned St. Claire to the wall, roaring like a caged tiger. The others were armed only with truncheons.

'Remember what I told you, boy,' St. Claire called and then I was taken out through the door on the run and helped on the way by the young officer's boot.

I was kicked and beaten all the way along the passage and down four flights of stone stairs, ending up in a corner against a wall, cowering like an animal, arms wrapped around my head as some protection against those flailing truncheons.

I was dragged to my feet, half-unconscious, the clothes stripped from my body. There was a confusion of voices then an iron door clanged shut and I was alone.

* * *

It was like those odd occasions when you awaken to utter darkness at half-past three in the morning and turn back fearfully to the warmth of the blankets, filled with a sense of dreadful unease, of some horror beyond the understanding crouched there on the other side of the room.

Only this was for always, or so it seemed. There were no blankets to turn into. Three weeks St. Claire had survived in here. *Three weeks*. Eternity could not seem longer.

224

I took a hesitant step forward and blundered into a stone wall. I took two paces back, hand outstretched and touched the other side. Three cautious paces brought me to the rear wall. From there to the iron-plated door was four more.

A stone womb. And cold. Unbelievably cold. A trap at the bottom of the door opened, yellow light flooding in. Some sort of metal pan was pushed through and the trap closed again.

It was water, fresh and cold. I drank a little, then crouched there beside the door and waited.

* * *

I managed to sleep, probably for some considerable period, which wasn't surprising in view of what I had been through and awakened slowly to the same utter darkness as before.

I wanted to relieve myself badly, tried hammering on the door with no effect whatsoever and was finally compelled to use one of the corners which was hardly calculated to make things any more pleasant.

How long had it been? Five hours or ten? I sat there listening intently, straining my ears for a sound that would not come and suddenly it was three-thirty in the morning again and it was waiting for me over there in the darkness, some nameless horror that would end all things.

I felt like screaming. Instead, I started to fight back. First of all I tried poetry, reciting it out loud, but that didn't work too well because my voice seemed to belong to someone else which made me feel more alarmed than ever. Next, I tried working my way through books I'd read. Good, solid items that took plenty of time. I did a fair job on *Oliver Twist* and could recite *The Great Gatsby* almost word-for-word anyway, but I lost out on *David Copperfield* half-way through.

It was about then that I found myself thinking about St. Claire for he was already a kind of mythical hero figure as far as the American Airborne forces were concerned. St. Claire and his history were as much a part of recruit training as practising P. L. F.s or learning how to take an MI6 to pieces and putting it together again blindfold.

Brigadier-General James Maxwell St. Claire, himself alone from the word go. Son of a Negro millionaire who'd made his first million out of insurance and had never looked back. No silver spoon, just eighteen carat gold. Harvard—only the best—and then he'd simply walked out and joined the paratroops as a recruit back in nineteen forty-one.

Captured in Italy in forty-three, as a sergeant, he'd escaped to fight with Italian partisans in the Po marshes, ending up in command of a force of four hundred that fought a German infantry division to a standstill in three days. That earned him a field commission and within a year he was captain and dropping into Brittany a week before D-day with units of the British Special Air Service.

He'd earned his Medal of Honour in Korea in nineteen fifty-two. When a unit of Assault Engineers had failed to blow a bridge the enemy were about to cross in strength, St. Claire had gone down and blown it up by hand, himself along with it. By then no one in the entire American Army was particularly surprised when he was fished out of the water alive.

And his appetite for life was so extraordinary. Women, liquor and food in that order, but looking back on it all now, I see that above all, it was action that his soul craved for and a big stage to act on.

God, but I was cold and shaking all over, my limbs trembling uncontrollably. I wrapped my arms around my-

226

self and hung on tight, not that that was going to do me much good. I think it was then that I remembered what St. Claire had said, recalled even a line or two of some Taoist poem he had quoted. *In motion, be like water, at rest like the mirror.*

I had nothing to lose, that was for certain, so I sat cross-legged and concentrated on recalling every step of the breathing exercises he had described to me. His method of developing this mysterious *ch'i* he had talked about.

I tried to relax as much as possible, breathing in through the nose and out through the mouth. I closed my eyes, not that it made much difference, and covered my right ear with my left hand. I varied this after five minutes by covering my left ear with my right hand. After a further five minutes, I covered both ears, arms crossed.

It was foolishness of the worst kind, even if it was a technique a couple of thousand years old according to St. Claire, but at least my limbs had stopped shaking and the sound of the breathing was strangely peaceful. I was no longer conscious of the stone floor or of the cold, simply floated there in the cool darkness, listening to my breathing.

It was like the sea upon the shore, a whisper through leaves in a forest at evening, a dying fall. Nothing.

* * *

They had me in there for eight days during which time I grew progressively weaker. Using St. Claire's technique, I slid into a self-induced trance almost at will, coming out of it, as far as I could judge afterwards, at fifteen or twenty hour intervals.

During the whole period no one appeared, no one spoke. I never again saw the small trap in the door open although

227

I did discover several more containers of water, presumably pushed through while I was in a trance. There was never any food.

Towards the end, conditions were appalling. The place stank like a sewer for obvious reasons and I was very weak indeed—very light-headed. And I was never conscious of dreaming, of thinking of anything at all, except at the very end of things when I experienced one of the most vivid and disturbing dreams of my life.

*　　*　　*

I was lying naked on a small bed and it was not dark. I was no longer in the Box for I could see again, a pale, diffused golden glow to things that was extraordinarily pleasant. It was warm. I was cocooned in warmth which was hardly surprising for the room was full of steam.

A voice called, slightly distorted, like an echo from far away. 'Ellis? Are you there, Ellis?'

I raised my head and saw Madame Ny standing no more than a yard away from me. She was wearing her uniform skirt and the leather boots, but had taken off her tunic. Underneath, she was wearing a simple white cotton blouse.

The blouse was soaking up the steam like blotting paper and as I watched, a nipple blossomed on the tip of each breast and then the breasts themselves materialised as if by magic as the thin material became saturated.

It was one of the most erotic things I have ever seen in my life, electrifying in its effect and my body could not help but respond. She came over beside the bed, leaned down and put a hand on me.

I tried to push her away and she smiled gently and said, still in that distorted, remote voice, 'But there's nothing to be ashamed of, Ellis. Nothing to fear.'

She unfastened the zip at the side of her uniform skirt and slipped out of it. Underneath she was wearing a pair of cotton pants as damp with steam as the blouse. She took them off with a complete lack of concern, then sat on the edge of the bed and unbuttoned the blouse.

Her breasts were round and full, wet with moisture from the steam, incredibly beautiful. I was shaking like a leaf in a storm as she reached out and pulled my face against them.

'Poor Ellis.' The voice echoed into the mist. 'Poor little Ellis Jackson. Nobody loves him. Nobody.' And then she pushed me away so that she could look into my face and said, 'But I do. I love you, Ellis.'

And then she rolled on to her back, the thighs spreading to receive me and her mouth was all the sweetness in life, the fire of my climax such a burning ecstasy that it had me screaming out loud.

I came awake to that scream in the darkness of the Box again, the stench of the place in my nostrils and for some reason found myself standing up straight and screaming out loud again, a blank defiance at the forces ranged against me.

There was a rattle of bolts and a moment later, the door opened and a great shaft of yellow light flooded in.

*   *   *

They were all there, the young officer and his men and Colonel Chen-Kuen, Madame Ny at his shoulder, very correct in full uniform including a regulation peaked cap with a red star in the front. She looked white and shocked. No, more than that—distressed, but not Chen-Kuen. He was simply interested in how well I'd stood up to things, the complete scientist.

229

I stood swaying from side-to-side while they busied themselves with a door next to mine. When it swung open, there was only darkness inside and then St. Claire stepped out.

He had a body on him like the Colossus of Rhodes, hewn out of ebony, pride in his face as he stood there, his nakedness not concerning him in the slightest. He caught sight of me and his eyes widened. He was across the passage in two quick strides, an arm about me as I reeled.

'Not now, Ellis—not now you've got this far,' he said. 'We walk to the medical centre on our own two feet and shag this lot.'

Which gave me the boost I needed, that and the strength of his good right arm. We made it under our own steam, out through the main entrance, crossed the compound to the medical hut through a thin, cold rain falling through the light of late evening.

Once there, they parted us and I found myself alone in a small cubicle wrapped in a large towel after a warm shower. The old doctor appeared, gave me a quick check, then an injection in my right arm and left.

I lay there staring up at the ceiling and the door clicked open. It was a day for surprises. Madame Ny appeared at the side of the bed. There were tears in her eyes and she dropped to her knees beside the bed and reached for my hand.

'I didn't know they would do that, Ellis. I did not know.'

For some obscure reason I believed her, or perhaps it didn't really matter to me any more, but in any event, I have never felt comfortable in the presence of a woman's tears.

I said, 'That's all right. I made it in one piece, didn't I?'

She began to cry helplessly, burying her face against my chest. Very gently, I started to stroke her hair.

*　*　*

The weeks that followed had a strange, fantasy air to them and things dropped into a routine. I still shared the room with St. Claire and each morning at six o'clock we were taken together to the Indoctrination Centre. Once there, we were separated to sit in small, enclosed booths in headphones, listening to interminable tapes.

The indoctrination stuff was mainly routine. Marx and Lenin to start with, then Mao Tse-tung until the old boy was pouring out of our ears. None of it ever really got through to me although I have noticed in later years that I have a pronounced tendency to argue in most situations using Marxian terminology. St. Claire was a great help to me in this respect. It was he who pointed out the real and tangible flaws in Mao's works. For example, that everything he had written on warfare was lifted without acknowledgement from Sun Tzu's *The Art of War* written in 500 B.C. As the Jesuits have it, one corruption is all corruption and I could never again accept any of the great man's writings at face value.

Five hours a day were devoted to learning Chinese. In one of many interviews with me, Chen-Kuen told me that this was to help promote a closer understanding between us, an explanation which never made much sense to me. On the other hand, languages were something I'd always been good at and it gave me something to do.

Each afternoon I had a long session of 'instruction' with Madame Ny which St. Claire made me report in detail to him each night, although that was only one of our activities. He taught me *karate* and *aikido,* subjected me to

231

lengthy and complicated breathing exercises, all designed to make me fit enough to face up to the day when we were going to crash out of there, his favourite phrase.

But he was the original polymath. Philosophy, psychology, military strategy from Sun Tzu and Wu Ch'i to Clausewitz and Liddell Hart, literature, and poetry in particular, for which he had a great love. He insisted that we talked in Chinese and even gave me lessons on his guitar.

Every minute had to be filled to use up as much as possible of that burning energy. He was like a caged tiger waiting his chance to spring.

I once tried to sum him up and could only come up with words like witty, attractive, brave, totally unscrupulous, amoral. All I know, and still believed at the end of things, was that he was the most complete man I have ever known. If anyone ever lived with total spontaneity, bringing it right up from the core of his being, it was he.

*   *   *

My relationship with Madame Ny was perhaps the strangest part of the whole affair.

I was taken to her office in a room on the second floor of the monastery each afternoon. There were always two guards in the corridor, but inside, we were quite alone.

It was a comfortable room, surprisingly so, although I suspect now that was mainly by design. Chinese carpets on the floor, a modern desk and swivel chairs, a filing cabinet, water colours on the wall and a very utilitarian looking psychiatrist's couch in black leather.

It became very plain from the beginning that these were psycho-analytical sessions. That she was out to strip me to the bone.

Not that I objected, for it quickly became a game of

question and answer—my kind of answer—that I rather enjoyed playing and the truth is that I wanted to be with her. Looked forward to being in her company.

From the beginning, she was calm and a little remote, insisted on calling me Ellis, yet never by any remark or action, referred to that emotional breakdown at my bedside on the evening they had released me from the Box.

What I could not erase from my mind was the memory of that strange dream, an erotic fantasy so real that to see her simply get up and stretch or stand at the window, a hand on her hip, was enough to send my pulse up by a rate of knots.

A great deal of her questioning, I didn't mind. Childhood and my relationship with my grandfather, schooling, particularly the years at Eton which seemed to fascinate her. She seemed surprised that the experience hadn't turned me into a raving homosexual and asked searching and vaguely absurd questions about masturbation which only succeeded in bringing out the comic in me.

We spent a month in this way and it became obvious to me that she was becoming more and more impatient. One day she stood up abruptly after one particularly feeble joke, took off her tunic and walked to the window where she stood in the pale sunshine, angrier than I had ever seen her.

From that angle, half-turned away from me, it became obvious that her breasts managed very well without the benefit of such a western appurtenance as a brassière and I could see the line of them sloping to the nipples as the sunlight filtered through the thin cotton.

'All men are at least three people, Ellis,' she said. 'What they appear to be to others, what they think they are and what they really are. Your great fault is to accept people at face value.'

233

'Is that a fact?' I said mockingly.

She turned on me in anger, made a visible effort to control it, went to the door. 'Come with me.'

We didn't go very far. Through a door at the end of the corridor which led to a gallery above what was obviously the central half of the old temple. There was a statue of Buddha at the far end, flickering candles, the murmur of voices at prayer from a group of Zen monks in yellow robes.

Madame Ny said, 'If I asked you who was the commander of Tay Son you would say Colonel Chen-Kuen of the Army of the People's Republic.'

'So what?'

'The commander is down there at this moment.'

The monks had risen to their feet, their Abbot magnificent in saffron robes at their head. He glanced up at that moment and looked straight at me before moving on. *Colonel Chen-Kuen.*

We returned to her office in silence. I sat down and she said, 'So, nothing is as it seems, not even Ellis Jackson.'

I made no reply and an orderly came in with the usual afternoon pot of China tea and tiny porcelain cups. It was unfailingly and deliciously refreshing. She passed me a cup without comment and I took the first long sip with a sigh of pleasure and knew, almost instantly, that I was in trouble.

I slipped into another slot in time, my arms seemed frozen in space. The orderly had re-appeared, I seemed to see him in a distorted mirror, Madame Ny opening a drawer in the desk and taking out a case containing a row of hypodermic syringes.

Her voice came from some other place, but with surprising clarity. 'We are not making the kind of progress I would wish, Ellis, and time is limited. We must try other

234

means. Nothing painful. Just two simple injections. First, Pentathol, what you call, mistakenly, the truth drug.' I felt no pain, no pain at all as the needle went in. 'Next, a small dose of Methedrine.'

I knew what that was. Speed, the hippies called it in New York. *Speed kills, wasn't that the phrase?*

I was floating and for a moment saw myself in the chair, Madame Ny bringing her chair round to be near me, the orderly going out, closing the door behind him. Sometimes I was conscious of what I said, sometimes the conversation seemed the murmur of the sea on a distant shore, but always I talked, and one thing above all came to me with frightening vividness, just like the dream in the Box.

* * *

Helga Jorgenson wasn't really Finnish except through her husband. Swedish by origin, she had arrived at my grandfather's house in the Chilterns during the early summer of my fourteenth year. Widowed the previous year, she was thirty-five years of age with long ash blonde hair and what seemed to my hot young mind the most voluptuous figure I had ever seen. And she was the kindest person I have ever known—always smiling, always with time for me.

We were thrown together a great deal. I'd had a bad bout of glandular fever and the doctor had thought it better that I take it easy at home for the rest of that half instead of returning to school.

It was the happiest summer of my life for by chance, my grandfather was asked by the War Department to sit on an Anglo-American mutual defence committee which took him to London frequently and finally to Washington for a month.

235

I taught her to ride, we played tennis and went for long, rambling walks, lay in the grass to eat our sandwiches and talked and talked in a way I hadn't been able to talk to anyone in my life before. I was at the age when the sap is rising and she was a beautiful, sensual woman in her prime, used to a man and denied one.

She was in the habit of kissing me good night with a pat on the cheek that always sent a shudder of delight through me. That and the smell of her filled my mind and bed with erotic fantasies that were perfectly normal for my age.

The Tuesday in July when disaster struck was a day of intense heat, a day of utter stillness when even the birds found difficulty in singing. Helga swung in a hammock under the beech trees in the garden in a bikini and old straw hat. I lay on the ground underneath and read, for the fourth time in a month, a book I had just discovered that summer. *The Great Gatsby* by Scott Fitzgerald.

Strange, the small things that live in memory. The ladybird on my arm, sweat on my face and when I rolled over, the sight of her body through the mesh of the hammock above me.

One arm dangled limply over the side, fingers slack. On impulse, I reached up to touch them. She was half asleep which explained her instinctive response. The fingers tightened in mine and the stomach turned hollow inside of me, more fear than ecstasy. I got to my feet slowly, half-unwilling, pulled by the hand.

She had taken off the top half of her bikini—the heat, I suppose—and lay there, the straw hat tipped across closed eyes. A shaft of pale afternoon sun touching the breasts with fire.

I started to tremble and the ache where the ache is bound to be in such instances, was unbearable. She smiled lazily, the eyes half-opened then widened as if she only at that moment realised what was happening.

She pulled free without embarrassment and eased up the bra, leaning forward to fasten it at the back.

'I was half-asleep.'

I was trembling visibly and noticing, she frowned in genuine concern and took my hands.

'I'm sorry,' I said for it was all I could think to say.

'But that's stupid,' she replied. 'There was nothing wrong, Ellis, nothing to be ashamed of. To be so attracted at the sight of a pretty woman is normal and healthy.'

Not that I really believed her for I had been branded clean to the bone too early and rugby and cold showers had never provided much of an answer. I searched for something to say and was saved from an unexpected source. Thunder had rumbled on the horizon of things on several occasions during the past hour and now, the heavens split wide open directly above us with a sound like the last trump and the rains came.

Helga laughed and cried above the roaring, 'Let's make a run for it, Ellis. Beat you to the house.'

She was off in a second and I slipped on starting so that she was several yards in front of me, a pale yellow flash in the grey curtain. I slipped again at the side of the drive and finally made it into the conservatory liberally splashed with mud.

'Slow coach,' she called from the landing at the top of the stairs then disappeared.

The house was quiet for it was market day and the cook had gone into town in the estate car for the afternoon. I climbed the stairs slowly, trying to catch my breath and went into her bedroom.

Helga was standing in front of the dressing table, drying her hair with a white bath towel. She turned, laughing. 'Oh, what a sight you are. Here, let me.'

She wiped the mud splashes from my body quickly then started to dry my hair, shaking her head in a kind of mock gravity. 'Poor Ellis. Poor little Ellis Jackson.'

The pale yellow bikini had tightened with the rain so that she might have had nothing on, but it wasn't that. A kind of desperate yearning not to be poor little Ellis any more, I suppose.

I kissed her clumsily and with no finesse whatsoever. Her smile faded. She didn't look angry, only solemn.

What happened then was a product of many things and she was no more to blame than I was. The situation was against us and I think she loved me in a way. There was her own need admittedly, but also, she saw mine. That this was only a symbol. That no one had ever given me real, honest-to-God-all-the-way affection and love in my life.

She kissed me very deliberately her mouth opening like a flower so that I could feel her tongue and the ache in my groin was unbelievable.

I tried to pull away from her, but she held me close and put a hand on me very deliberately. 'There's nothing to be ashamed of. Nothing at all.'

The rest was as dreamlike and unreal as everything that had gone before. She was so gentle, so calm. She took off her bikini, dried herself, then did the same for me. I was trembling violently when she pulled me across to the bed and fell back, pillowing my face against her breasts.

'Poor Ellis. Poor little Ellis Jackson. Nobody loves him. Nobody loves him but me.'

And then her mouth fastened on mine and she opened her thighs and drew me into her and the pleasure, the terrible, aching fire that burned its way through caused me to cry out in agony.

I pushed myself up on my hands, riding her like a young bull and saw, in the triple mirror above the dressing table, three images of my grandfather standing in the open doorway, the wrath of God on his face, his favourite black-thorne in his hand.

The stick descended once, twice across my back, snapping in half as I broke free.

'You dirty little animal,' he bellowed. 'Get out! Get out!'

I cowered from his wrath, filled with such fear and shame as I had never known. Helga tried to stand. He struck her back-handed across the face.

'This is how you repay me, is it?' he shouted. 'Cuckolding me with my own grandson.'

I heard no more for he kicked me out of the door and slammed it shut. I heard the bolt click into place and crept to my room.

What happened in there, I do not know, but she left that night on the London train and I returned to Eton the following day, doctor or no doctor.

I never saw Helga again.

* * *

I was still half under the influence of the drug as I came to the end.

'Cuckolding me with my own grandson,' a voice was saying. 'Cuckolding me with my own grandson.'

Madame Ny seemed excited. She leaned close and shook me by the chin. 'This is the first time you've remembered that bit, am I right?'

I nodded and said dully, 'What does it mean?'

'That she was your grandfather's mistress. It explains everything. Her age, for example. As you said, she was no ordinary au pair girl, but a mature woman in her prime. He must have picked her very carefully. His anger was the anger of the old bull seeing a younger take what he considers to be rightfully his. He has never been able to forgive you.'

'My mouth's as dry as a bone,' I said.

'That's usual.' She poured water into a glass. 'You are not angry with me?'

I swallowed about a pint and wiped my mouth. 'Why should I be? You've taught me something in helping me to remember. Why should I be ashamed because of that old bastard?'

She said calmly, 'Your sex life has not been satisfactory, am I right?'

'Bloody awful,' I said. 'I'm attracted by anything in skirts and feel as guilty as hell about it. And my performance, I've been given to understand, is only second league variety.'

'You think this will change now?'

'You tell me. You're the expert.'

She shook her head slowly. 'No, not yet.'

I was still not quite with it as she stood up, went over to the door and locked it. She turned, the sun from the window putting gold flecks in the dark eyes and started to unbutton the cotton blouse as she walked towards me.

'Poor Ellis,' she said softly. 'Poor little Ellis Jackson. Nobody loves him. Nobody loves him, but me.'

And when I took her, on the couch so thoughtfully provided, I was back there in the bedroom at the old house again, the rain thundering into the dry ground outside, drifting in through the open window in a fine spray. And the fear was there again, mingling with the fierce, abrasive joy, sending my heart pounding, waiting for the wrath of God to burst in through the door. But this time, there was no nemesis, no nameless terror. This time there was the most complete release I have ever known.

Madame Ny stifled a cry, presumably because of the

240

guards and gasped my name, but the name on my lips was Helga's name and in that final moment of complete release it was Helga I had taken at last.

* * *

I did not tell St. Claire. Not then, for nagging away at the back of my mind was his warning about the technique they employed. To find a man's antithesis, his weakness, that of which he was ashamed and to bring it out into the open until it became the dominant factor in his personality.

But she had not done that. She had taken an open, running sore in my personality and changed it for the good. Why, I did not know, could not even comprehend, although the events of the next few weeks led me to only one conclusion.

On the following day when I was delivered to her for my session, she was cool and correct, giving no sign of what had happened the previous day. As for me, I burned for her, it was as simple as that.

She paced the room, delivering a lecture on the Marxian dialectic with every evidence of conviction. 'You must see, Ellis,' she said. 'That it is we who will win and you who will lose. History is against you.'

I wasn't particularly interested in the march of world communism for she paused only a couple of feet away from me, a hand on the desk.

I pulled her on to my knee and kissed her hard, cupping a hand over her left breast. She pushed against me, one arm sliding behind my neck and then, abruptly, stood up and went and locked the door.

* * *

241

From then on, I was hooked and so was she. Each afternoon the talk grew less, the activity on the couch increased. She filled my thoughts to the extent that it interfered seriously with my ability to concentrate on anything else.

St. Claire couldn't help but know that something had changed. He brought it up on several occasions, usually in a half-bantering way, but I always insisted stoutly that there was nothing wrong.

'You can't trust them,' he said fiercely. 'You realise that, don't you? Not even her.'

But I didn't believe him, went blundering on to the final bitter end and only myself to blame.

* * *

It was a hot, sultry afternoon towards the end of May, with everything waiting for the monsoon to come. She seemed curiously distant, remote and far away, even troubled, though she denied it when I asked her.

God, but it was hot, the lull before the storm and our bodies were sticky with sweat and yet she held on to me passionately asking me over and over again, eyes closed in ecstasy, if I loved her, a thing she had never done before.

She had locked the door as usual, of that I was certain, and yet I was suddenly aware of the slightest of breezes and started to turn, but too late.

A long bamboo pole, the type used as a mock sword in *kendo* fighting, tapped me gently on the shoulder. Madame Ny's eyes filled with horror and she pushed me away, hands against my chest.

Chen-Kuen stood in the centre of the room, the door open behind him, dressed in his Abbot's robe, the *kendo* pole extended. As Madame Ny stood up, I tried to get between them in some gesture of protection.

'My dear Ellis, there's no need for that,' Chen-Kuen said. 'No need at all.'

I turned to look at her. She was already into her skirt and buttoning her blouse. Her face was very calm, no passion there, no fear—*nothing*.

How foolish a man can be without his trousers. I pulled mine on, hands shaking as I fastened the belt and the truth of it all, the unavoidable fact rose in my mouth like bile.

'It was all planned,' I said. 'Every last step.'

'But of course,' she said.

And then an even more staggering thought hit me. 'The dream when I was in the Box—the steam room.'

She smiled in a kind of satisfaction and that I could not forgive. I punched her solidly in the mouth and only a fraction later, Chen-Kuen delivered a basic *do* cut to the side of my head with his wooden sword that nearly unseated my brains.

In spite of that, it took three of them to get me downstairs and out into the compound. St. Claire came out of the medical centre at the same time, a single guard with him and one of my guards chose that particular moment to sink the butt of his rifle into my ribs.

I went truly crazy for a short while, a rage against everything living, turned and delivered a reverse elbow strike that splintered half his chest cage.

At least a dozen guards rushed out from the monastery entrance at Chen-Kuen's call and swarmed all over me. There was another voice, too, raised in a trumpet call as Black Max arrived, like Jove descending, to help me out.

Everything he had taught me, I used. Short, devastating screw punches that focussed the *ch'i* power so that internal organs were damaged beyond repair, edge of the hand

243

blows that splintered bone, but it could only end in one way.

I think it was the butt of an AK47 that connected with my skull and I went down into the dust amongst the whirling feet. St. Claire was still at it, I heard his voice, but then that too slipped away from me.

I came back to life in half-darkness, a little light streaming in through a barred window. I groaned, there was a sudden movement and St. Claire was beside me.

'Take it easy, boy. Nice and easy.'

There was the rattle of a pan, he raised my head and I sipped a little water. My skull was twice its normal size or so was the impression.

I felt the area in question gingerly and St. Claire said, 'No fracture as far as I can see.'

'Where are we?'

'A punishment cell on the ground floor. What happened up there today?'

I didn't even attempt to evade that one and told him in finest detail.

He shook his head when I was finished. 'Why in hell didn't you tell me, boy? I warned you. She wasn't liberating you. She was chaining you up tighter than ever.'

'To what end?' I demanded.

'Search me.' He shrugged. 'Not that it matters.'

I managed to sit up, aware of something in his voice. 'What's that supposed to mean?'

'One of those guards died an hour ago. Ruptured spleen.'

I took a deep breath. 'You made me too good, Max.'

'Hell, no,' he said. 'It could have been me. No way of knowing.'

I said slowly, 'Are you trying to say they might put us away for good for this one?'

'They've failed with me anyway,' he said. 'No percentage in continuing and we're both dead already in case you've forgotten.'

We didn't get the chance to discuss the matter further for a moment or so later, the door opened and they took him away.

* * *

The young officer called us to a halt, his voice hard and flat through the rain. We stood and waited while he had a look round. There didn't seem to be much room to spare, but he obviously wasn't going to let a little thing like that worry him. He selected a spot on the far side of the clearing, found us a couple of rusting trenching shovels that looked as if they had seen plenty of service and went and stood in the shelter of the trees with two of the guards and smoked cigarettes, leaving one to watch over us as we set to work.

It wasn't going to take very long, either. The soil was pure loam, light and easy to handle because of the rain. It lifted in great spadefuls that had me knee-deep in my own grave before I knew where I was. St. Claire wasn't exactly helping. He worked as if there was a bonus at the end of the job, those great arms of his swinging three spadefuls of dirt into the air for every one of mine.

The rain seemed to increase in a sudden rush that drowned all hope. I was going to die. The thought rose in my throat like bile to choke on and then it happened. The side of the trench next to me collapsed suddenly, probably because of the heavy rain, leaving a hand and part of a forearm protruding from the earth, flesh rotting from the bones.

The stench was unbelievable and I turned away blindly,

fighting for air, and lost my balance, falling flat on my face. At the same moment the other wall of the trench collapsed across me.

The stink of the grave was in my nostrils, my eyes. I opened my mouth to scream and then a hand like iron fastened around my collar and dragged me free.

As I surfaced, St. Claire pulled me upright one-handed, holding his trenching shovel in the other. There was something in his eyes when he asked me if I was all right, a kind of madness, and behind him, the guard ran to the edge of the trench and leaned over, shouting angrily.

St. Claire swung the spade back-handed like a war-axe, the rusting edge catching the guard across the side of the neck, killing him instantly. He had the man's AK47 in his great hands before the body hit the ground, pushed it on to full automatic and fired a long burst that sent the young officer and the other two guards diving for cover.

I didn't need the shove in the back St. Claire gave me, but it certainly helped me on my way. I was into the trees, head-down before the first shots whispered through the branches above my head. A moment later, I emerged into another clearing of elephant grass perhaps fifty yards wide, a dozen or more water buffalo grazing peacefully.

I hesitated and St. Claire arrived in time to give me another violent push. 'Keep moving,' he cried. 'If they catch us in the open we've had it.'

He fired a couple of rounds towards the water buffalo who stampeded madly in two or three different directions and I started to run again, ploughing through the elephant grass in a straight line.

The ground on the other side sloped steeply through heavy undergrowth between the trees, a length of vines and brush that made for hard going, needle thorns tearing at my fatigues and then, the bank tilted and we went

246

down into the river, riding a wave of loose soil.

Crossing wasn't particularly difficult. The bottom was firm and the water in no place more than chest deep. It was perhaps thirty yards wide and St. Claire was across before me, simply because he could move faster. When I finally made it he was already on one knee behind a curtain of vines, covering me with the AK.

I lay there face down, choking for a minute or so and finally managed to catch my breath.

'You did fine, boy, just fine,' he said.

'They'll cut us into little pieces after this one.'

'Only if they catch us.'

'Then what are we waiting for?'

'It's a hundred and seventy miles to the demarcation line,' he said calmly. 'We aren't going to make it on one rifle and whatever's left in the magazine.'

The young officer and the other two guards arrived at the same moment a few yards down stream on the other side. They entered the water without hesitation and started to wade across.

'Now,' I whispered when they were half-way, rifles raised above their heads.

He shook his head and pushed the AK on semi-automatic. 'I want their gear. There's no telling how many rounds are left in this thing so get ready to use your hands.'

Not that there was any need. They came out of the water to a spit of sand, the officer in the lead and St. Claire took all three with single shots fired so rapidly they sounded like one continuous roll.

We stripped the bodies of everything worth having. Water bottles, bayonets and rubber ponchos from the two soldiers, an AK for me, several hundred rounds of ammunition, the young officer's pistol and three grenades. They had not been carrying any rations which was hardly sur-

247

prising under the circumstances, but that was the least of our worries.

When we'd got all that we needed, we threw the bodies into the river. The whole business had taken no longer than five minutes and we moved back into the shelter of the jungle.

I still couldn't take it all in, so brief had been the time lapse from the grave to life again. I leaned against a tree, shaking all over. St. Claire pulled his poncho over his head and picked up his AK.

'Now hear me, boy, and hear me good,' he said. 'Because I'll only say this once. Walk, don't run, that's the first rule of the jungle. We stand a chance because of the monsoon. We keep to the high country and live off the land. Monkey and parrot make fine eating when there's nothing else to be had. Under no circumstances do we ever approach a village. Even the *montagnards* aren't to be trusted. Do as I say and you'll live. Take it any other way and you're on your own.'

'That's fine by me,' I said. 'You're the boss.'

'A hundred and seventy miles to the demarcation line.' His face cracked open into that famous St. Claire smile. 'But we'll make it, boy. Thirty days at the outside.'

But he was wrong. We were in the jungle all of June and the best part of July. Fifty-two days of living like animals, of hit-and-run, of kill-or-be-killed. Fifty-two days until the Sunday afternoon near Khe Sanh when we were spotted in a clearing by a Huey helicopter flying in supplies to an A.R.V.N. strongpoint.

And so I came out of the jungle, but by no means the same man who went in.

3 The sound of thunder

Instantaneous recall, the psychologists call it—every last detail of past experience floating to the surface so that one not only remembers, one lives it again with as much reality as the day it happened.

I sat there in the chair in the cottage, the whisky glass still clutched firmly in my right hand. Sheila was standing by the window smoking a cigarette, looking out, the dog crouching at her feet.

It turned its head to look at me as I moved in the chair, got up lazily and padded towards me. Something caught at my throat, half growl, half moan of agony and the glass cracked in my hand.

The dog stopped dead in its tracks and Sheila started forward, a terrible anxiety on her face.

'Ellis, what is it?' she asked.

I got to my feet and backed away. 'Get him out of here. For God's sake, get him out of here.'

She stood there, puzzlement on her face, then moved to the kitchen door and called softly to Fritz. He went to her instantly, passed into the kitchen and she closed the door.

She crossed the room quickly, put her hands on my shoulders and pushed me down in the chair. 'It's only Fritz, Ellis,' she said calmly. 'There's nothing to worry about.'

I said, 'Fritz is dead. I saw him out there in the marsh with a bullet through his head.'

'I see,' she said. 'And when was this?'

Her calmness had the wrong kind of effect in the circumstances. I grabbed her arms above the elbows and held on tight. 'They were out there, Sheila. The Viet Cong. I saw them.'

The fear in her eyes broke through to the surface like scum on a pond, terrible to see and she struggled to free herself. 'You need another drink, Ellis. Let me get you one.'

She went into the kitchen, closing the door behind her and I sat there, suspended in that terrible dream. The slight tinkle of the extension bell on the telephone on the table by the window brought me back to reality.

To have lifted the receiver would have warned her that I was listening in. Instead, I got up and moved to the serving hatch in the wall between the sitting-room and the kitchen.

It was open perhaps half-an-inch; enough for me to see part of her face, her hand clutching the receiver. The voice was subdued and full of anxiety.

'No, I must speak to Doctor O'Hara personally. It's absolutely vital.'

Sean O'Hara. The best that Harley Street could provide. I might have known.

She said, 'Sean? This is Sheila Ward. Yes, it's Ellis. I think you should get down here right away. He's worse than I've ever known him. He came in in a terrible state just now and said he'd seen Viet Cong in the marsh. It's as if he's regressed to Vietnam.' There was a pause that seemed interminable. 'No, I'll be fine. I phoned Max St. Claire earlier. He should be here soon.'

As she replaced the receiver, I kicked open the door. The Airedale was on me in a second as she cried out, his teeth bared, muzzle an inch from my leg.

She got him by the collar and hauled him away. I said, 'So I've cracked wide open, have I? Regressed to Vietnam?

250

Well, I'll show you! I know what I saw out there. Now I'll prove it.'

I kept a couple of shot-guns in the umbrella stand by the door. I took the 16-bore, pulled a cartridge belt over my head and was out of the front door while she was still struggling to control the dog.

* * *

Rain kicked into my face, cold and sharp. This was real, this could surely be no dream and I breathed in the damp salt air and moved along the rutted track.

They were shooting again at Shoeburyness, the quiet thunder of heavy guns just as before and I paused, a coldness passing through me that sapped that new confidence which had sent me out of the cottage with blood in my eye. Had anything happened—truly? Was it then or now?

I fought against it and succeeded for the moment. Once I had survived in country like this when other men had died. I hadn't come through the worst that Vietnam had to offer to finally go to pieces in a salt marsh on the edge of the North Sea. The dog I could not explain, did not even attempt to, but the two men. Now they *had* been real for the only other explanation was so terrible that my mind refused to contemplate it for a moment.

The 16-bore was a single barrel slide repeater and took six .662 cartridges. As lethal a weapon as you could hope for at close quarters. I loaded it quickly and left the cart track a little further on, moving along a narrow, treacherous path through the marsh. A step to one side in some places could put you into the kind of bog that would swallow you up for all time.

I had to tread softly, but not just because the going

was dangerous. The wild life of the marsh lurked on every side, widgeon, mallard, wild duck and teal. Any real disturbance from me and they would rise into the rain, trumpeting their alarm to the wide world.

But then I was a part of all this; had survived too long to be anything but cunning in the ways of the Delta country. Had survived by beating the V.C. at their own game. They were good, but not good enough. Waiting for me out there in the swamp—waiting for me to declare myself. To make a mistake, as they always did. Well, two could play at that game. I crouched down in a thicket of reeds, the 16-bore ready and waited as I had waited so many times before for a sound, the briefest of murmurs, anything to indicate an alien presence.

* * *

There was no hero's welcome when I returned from Vietnam, the climate of opinion was against it and I was weighed in the balance and found wanting along with every other mercenary who had fought in other men's wars since nineteen forty-five.

My grandfather made an attempt, for medals, I suppose, were something he could understand and I had enough of those, God knows. But it didn't work. I found an older man with moist eyes and a tendency to stare into space for lengthy periods without speaking. I left him, after ten uncomfortable days, to those better qualified to care for him than I and returned to London.

What happened then had a kind of inevitability to it. A reasonably rapid slide to nowhere with the statutory bottle of Scotch a day and by a kind of personal choice. An urge to self-destruction. Old friends, who had greeted me with something like warmth, soon learned to avoid me.

Nothing, it seemed, could stop me from running head-down into nowhere.

And then Black Max re-entered my life to save me for the second time as I was sliding down the wall beside the entrance to the saloon bar of a pub at the western end of Milner Street off the Kings Road, the landlord having ejected me for his good and my own.

It was raining hard and I was just beginning to go when the car swung into the kerb, an Alfa Romeo G.T. Veloce, the colour of spring daffodils. The voice calling my name was from the other end of a dark tunnel, something from dream-time.

'Ellis? Ellis, is that you?'

I opened my eyes and managed to focus with some difficulty. He was in dress uniform, returning to his hotel—as I found later—from a reception at the American Embassy.

'It's raining, Max,' I said. 'Your medals will get rusty.'

His laughter shook the street from one end to the other. 'By God, Ellis, but it's good to see you.'

Which was exactly how I felt. Tay Son again in the rain and our first meeting. Remembering that, I started to cry helplessly like a child. I suppose it was then that he realised just how sick I was.

*   *   *

It was raining again now, blowing in across the marsh in a slanting curtain. Somewhere in the distance, birds lifted in alarm and I heard a car engine.

I cut through a patch of reeds and scrambled up on top of the nearest dyke. There was only one person it could be. I caught a brief glimpse of the Alfa Romeo, a smudge of yellow vivid in the grey morning as it turned off the side road into the cart track leading across the marsh.

I ran along the top of the dyke throwing caution to the winds, mainly because it took me three-quarters of the way across that section of the marsh, jumped down at the far end and ran, knee-deep through water, the 16-bore held across my chest.

I was conscious of the Alfa's engine, birds calling in alarm and then it stopped abruptly. I suppose I knew at once what had happened—knew as if the whole thing had happened before.

I came out through the reeds and found the Alfa forty yards to the right of me. One of the Viet Cong stood in the centre of the track, covering St. Claire who was getting out of the car. He was in uniform and wore his own private version of a general officer's overcoat, a kind of British warm with fur collar.

He towered over his assailant and stood, hands on hips. The V.C. raised the AK threateningly. What happened then was purely reflex, the soldier's instinct for action for it seemed to me that he intended to shoot St. Claire dead.

Where a man is concerned, a shot-gun is deadly up to twenty yards and I had forty to go which meant I very probably was running to my death, but at least it would give St. Claire a chance to save himself, or so it seemed to me then.

I went in on the run, mouth open in a *banzai* cry savage enough to split the world in two, firing from the hip as I went.

The V.C. swung round, loosing off a quick burst, an involuntary action, his bullets raising fountains to the right of me.

It was the only chance he got for St. Claire had him in an instant stranglehold from the rear, falling backwards, one knee raised to break his spine as they fell.

The other V.C. stepped out of the reeds on the far side of the Alfa. I cried a warning and loosed off another of my useless shots. St. Claire rolled, grabbing for the first man's AK, firing it smoothly in the same moment, a long burst slashing through the reeds, sending the other man jumping for cover.

St. Claire rolled into the ditch and stayed low. After a while, he waved and fired a quick burst into the reeds to cover me while I ran to join him. There were a couple of shots in reply, but I made it in one piece, sliding over the edge of the ditch.

He grinned, 'For a guy who's supposed to be be coming apart at the seams, you looked pretty good out there. Just like old times.'

'Doesn't anything ever throw you?' I demanded.

'Life's too short, boy. I've told you that before.' He nodded towards the first V.C. who was lying in the middle of the track. 'Okay, sweetheart, so what are the Viet Cong doing in the Essex marshes?'

'Christ knows,' I said. 'I thought I was going out of my mind when they jumped me earlier and Sheila certainly did. That's why she phoned you. She's even got Sean O'Hara coming down at the double complete with hypo and tranquillisers.'

'So she's on her own back there?' He frowned. 'That isn't so good in the circumstances and we certainly aren't going to find the answer to this thing by hanging around here. What I need right now is a telephone.'

'So what do you suggest?'

'You get into the Alfa. Keep your head down, but get her started. I'll give you some covering fire and we'll make a run for it.'

He moved a little way further along the ditch and fired

three or four shots into the reeds on the other side of the road. I didn't wait for an answer, wasn't even sure if one came. I crawled across to the Alfa and wormed my way behind the wheel, dumping the shot-gun on the rear seat.

I shouted to St. Claire, starting the engine and moving into gear at the same moment. He loosed off a long burst into the reeds and was into the passenger seat, head-down as I moved off, accelerating so sharply that the rear wheels kicked up a great curtain of mud and filth.

I went down the track at fifty miles an hour, a hair-raising speed considering the conditions, crossed the un-fenced dyke over the main stream without slowing at all and skidded to a halt on the cobbled yard of the cottage within a couple of minutes of leaving the scene of the ambush.

There was no time for conversation and within a second of stopping I was out of the Alfa and running for the door calling her name, St. Claire close behind.

I don't know what happened as I went through the door for this part of the affair is not too clear to me, but I certainly went down the steps into the sitting-room head first with the appropriate result.

* * *

I came to my senses to find myself lying on the couch, though perhaps floating would be a better word for it. Once again, it was as if I was disembodied, as if nothing phy-sical existed for me at all.

I was filled with the most dreadful nausea so that my stomach seemed to turn inside out. I rolled over, fell to the floor and was violently sick.

I lay there for a while. There was something hard underneath me, something painful and when I sat up,

I found it was the 16-bore. I picked it up and used it as a prop to get upright for I found it almost impossible to keep my feet.

The door to the bedroom was open and the light was on. I called Sheila's name or thought I did for no sound came from my mouth, then floated towards the open doorway.

Something waited for me in there, something terrible and yet it was not to be avoided and I was drawn towards the door inexorably.

The first thing I saw was the blood in a scarlet crescent splashed across the white painted wall. Sheila lay in the centre of the room, quite naked except for a sheet entwined round one leg, as if she had tripped over it while trying to run. The back of her skull had been smashed like an eggshell.

St. Claire lay back across the bed, one knee raised, as naked as she except for the dog tags around his neck that he never took off, an old affectation.

Only it wasn't St. Claire when I got close. It wasn't anybody, for there was no face—only the bloody pulp left by a couple of shot-gun cartridges fired at close range.

I turned to run, found myself still clutching the 16-bore and threw it away from me with a cry. There was someone standing in the doorway watching me, I knew that, but who it was impossible to say for it was as if I fainted and everything around me melted into darkness.

*   *   *

Once, skin-diving in Cornwall using aqualung equipment, I had valve trouble with my reserve bottle of air and only just made it to the surface in time. It was like that now, kicking hard, struggling with everything I had to rise through cold water towards a small patch of light.

I made it at last, breaking through to the surface, gasping for air, and found myself naked under an ice-cold shower, held there by a burly individual with close-cropped hair and a broken nose.

I tried to push his hands away and found there was no strength in me at all. My hands seemed to rise in slow motion, to float as if suspended in water, then to drift down again.

The man who was holding me called over his shoulder, 'Doctor, he's coming out of it.'

The voice echoed inside my head, I seemed to float over the side of the bath, which was surely impossible, and Sean O'Hara appeared in the doorway.

He was handsome enough in his own decadent Irish way with a face on him like Oscar Wilde or Nero himself and a mane of silver hair that made him look more like an actor than what he was, which was, quite simply, one of the finest psychiatrists in Western Europe.

I said, 'Now then, you old bastard. Still getting your own back on the bloody English at fifty guineas a session?'

He didn't smile, not even an attempt which was unusual for he could laugh at the drop of a hat, but then, so did everything else seem strange. Even my voice sounded as if it belonged to a stranger.

He took down my bathrobe from behind the door and held it open for me. 'Get this on, Ellis, there's a good lad and come along with me.'

I was perfectly calm, no anxiety at all, conscious of no particular feeling about anything. Simply floated, trapped in that strange, dreamlike state.

Sean waited patiently while I fiddled with the belt, then put a hand on my shoulder. 'All right, then, let's get it over.'

The sitting-room seemed crowded with people, all men I had never seen before, two in shirt sleeves on the floor making various measurements. There was a uniformed policeman at the door, the sudden flash of a camera bulb. Everyone stopped talking.

I waited patiently while Sean and a small, brisk, dark-haired man in gold-rimmed spectacles talked in low tones then Sean turned and took my arm.

'We'll go into the bedroom now, shall we, Ellis?'

And it was waiting for me, there behind the half-open door. That nameless horror which had haunted my dreams for so many months. My throat went dry, I was conscious of my heart pounding and found it difficult to breathe. I tried to pause and Sean drew me relentlessly on.

When he pushed the door open with his foot, the first thing I saw was the blood in a great scarlet crescent splashed across the white-painted wall.

I turned, clutching at him as the earth moved. 'A dream,' I said brokenly. 'I thought it was a dream.'

'No dream, Ellis,' he said gravely. 'This happened. This has to be faced.'

He pushed me forward into the room.

* * *

They put me on a chair in the kitchen and someone produced a cup of tea. It tasted like something out of a sewer and I lurched to the sink and vomited. I turned wearily and a young constable helped me across to my chair again as Sean O'Hara and the man in the gold-rimmed spectacles appeared.

'How do you feel now, Ellis?' Sean asked.

'I'll live, I suppose.' Again, the voice seemed to come from somewhere outside me.

He produced a small white pill box from his pocket, opened it and shook three or four of the familiar purple capsules into his palm.

I told you how lethal these things can be. I gave Sheila your prescription for another twenty-one last Wednesday. From what's left in here, I calculate you must have taken ten or twelve of the bloody things earlier. If I hadn't arrived when I did, you'd be dead by now.'

'Which was presumably what Mr. Jackson intended,' the man in the gold-rimmed spectacles put in. 'Isn't that so, sir?'

'As you know, this whole area is owned by the Defence Ministry.' Sean put in. 'Superintendent Dix here, of the Special Branch, is in charge of security.'

I seemed to experience some difficulty in focussing my eyes when I turned to Dix. 'What are you trying to say? That I tried to commit suicide after knocking them both off? I didn't even take those bloody pills.'

I brought out this last bit with such violence that the young constable on the door stirred uneasily.

'So you can't remember, sir?' Dix produced a tiny bottle. 'Not surprising if you were on this.'

I seemed to have moved into one of those stages when I wasn't worried again. I said, 'And what might that be?'

'L.S.D. We found it in your bedside locker.'

'Well, I've news for you,' I told him. 'I've never touched that stuff in my life.'

'We've already taken blood samples while you were unconscious, sir. There's really no way out, you know.'

'Tell me about the Viet Cong, Ellis,' Sean said quietly.

I looked at them both, faces grave, waiting for what I had to say. Even the young constable had taken an involuntary step closer. It was then that I noticed the open door, the men outside, all waiting.

There was a new arrival, a paratroop major in the kind of uniform which had been tailored in Savile Row, red beret tilted at the exact regulation angle, a lazy, fleshy, amiable face except for the eyes which were like lumps of jagged glass. I knew him, that was the intriguing thing, but couldn't remember where from. He nodded slightly as if to encourage me.

'You think I'm mad, don't you?' I said. 'Well, they were out there and Max and I took them on. That's cold, hard fact and there's the body of the man he killed lying up there on the track to prove it.'

Dix shook his head. 'Nothing there, Mr. Jackson. Not a damned thing.'

In the silence which followed I seemed to wait for another blow from the axe. It came soon enough.

Dix said, 'As you know, this whole area is Defence Ministry property so we check on people's movements, regular movements, rather carefully. Mrs. Ward, for instance, was in the habit of going up to London every Thursday.'

'To see her eight-year-old son.' I nodded. 'She was divorced. Her husband had custody.'

He shook his head. 'Her husband has been lecturing at the University of Southern California for the past two years, sir. There never was a son.'

I gazed at him stupidly and Sean said, 'She spent the whole day at Max's flat, Ellis, whenever she was in town.'

I came apart at the seams, put my head down on my folded arms and fought for survival, great waves flowing over me.

Through the roaring, I heard Sean O'Hara say, 'Any further attempts at this stage would be quite useless. The hallucinatory state which follows L.S.D. can last for days. Typical clinical symptoms. I think we should commit him

261

to Marsworth Hall as soon as may be and I'll arrange for some intensive treatment. He's quite obviously a danger to himself and everyone else in his present state.'

Marsworth Hall, a staging house for Broadmoor, last stop for the criminally insane. Sean gave them a day a week as consultant free. Such interesting cases, as he had once told me. The prospect of those gates closing on me for ever was so terrible that I staggered to my feet, reaching out to him frantically.

'They were there. They did exist.'

'And Fritz?' he said gently. 'You told Sheila they shot him yet he's outside now, tied up in his kennel. Would you like to see him?'

And then I remembered—remembered the one thing that had happened which shouldn't have. A complete impossibility.

'The dog that was shot,' I cried. 'It wasn't Fritz—it couldn't have been. It jumped off the dyke and swam fifty yards through deep water.' They stared at me, puzzled. I said, 'Fritz can't swim.'

The silence which followed was like that iron gate swinging shut. Someone coughed and Dix nodded briefly.

The young constable took my arm. 'All right, sir, if you'll come with me.'

I twisted in a half-circle, broke his arm with one blow and threw him out through the door to clear a path for me. Fear—complete panic, call it what you like, but I went berserk.

They moved in on me like a rugby scrum and my bathrobe was torn off within seconds which left me naked as the day I was born. *Tom-a-Bedlam running amok.* Next came the chains.

I gave a fair account of myself, sent one man back screaming as his ribs went, broke another's jaw and then the paratroop major moved in and kicked me in the stomach, perfect *karate*, the foot flicking upwards only when the knee was waist-high.

Not that it was enough, that's what having *ch'i* does for you. I moved in on him, hands raised, remembering who he was at the same time. My first half at Eton, his last. The wall game. Hilary Vaughan, the pride of the school. Brains and brawn, poetry and boxing. No one could ever make him out, especially when he entered the army.

He knew that I had recognised him, saw it in my eyes and frowned involuntarily, as if it didn't make sense— as if it was something he hadn't expected. In any event, it was round about then that the rugby scrum won and I went down under the sheer weight.

But it took six of the bastards to get me out to the car, handcuffs or no handcuffs.

4 Time out of mind

Marsworth Hall was the kind of eighteenth century country house you seem to find in England and nowhere else. Not quite as large as Blenheim Palace, but not much smaller. There was a twenty-foot perimeter wall topped by what was very obviously a recent innovation—an electrified wire fence and we were admitted through electronically operated gates.

It was rather like Tay Son, at least in atmosphere. Dusk was falling and there was a strange lack of people. In fact, during the time I was there, I saw no other patients at all.

Sean dealt with the formalities, handing me over at once to two male nurses. They were of a type to be expected. Large, intimidating men, one with the flattened nose and scar tissue around the eyes peculiar to those who have boxed a great deal and both had the efficient, no nonsense air about them that one associates with ex-Guards' n.c.o.s.

The more reasonable of the two was called Thompson and the ex-boxer, Flattery. They took me to a shower room where I was thoroughly washed down with the aid of the usual Ministry of Works carbolic soap, then provided with pyjamas, the trousers of which had an elasticated top and there was no cord to the dressing gown.

We went up to the top floor in a small lift and Thompson unlocked a door directly opposite while Flattery clutched my arm which gave me my first real insight into the man's character. He held me in an unnecessarily vice-like grip that left the arm half-paralysed. I had thought he would be Irish but when he spoke, it was obvious that he came from Liverpool.

'In you go,' he said and gave me a shove.

It was a fine and private place, bed, wardrobe, locker, private lavatory, except when someone looked in through the spy hole in the door and there was a view of the grounds between bars.

'Now what?' I demanded.

'Now nothing.' He chuckled harshly. 'We lead a very quiet life here and we like it that way, but if you want trouble, you can have it.'

Thompson, who had looked vaguely uneasy during this speech, said in a much more conciliatory tone, 'I wouldn't get into bed yet if I were you. Dr. O'Hara wants to see you before he goes.'

The door closed and I was alone, yet not alone, my

mind racing in an effort to keep up with the dozens of different thoughts and images that bubbled to the surface.

I lay down on the bed and tried to relax and found it impossible for I was still subject to sudden changes in consciousness. One moment I was myself and thinking clearly and objectively again, the next, someone else entirely, outside of things, floating in a kind of hiatus, unable to make even two and two add up to four any more.

I forced myself back to that morning, starting with the dream and progressing through each incredible incident, looking for some pattern. And yet what pattern could I hope to find? If what Sean O'Hara had indicated was true, then I had never really wakened from that dream at dawn and the whole day was simply a continuation of it.

Time passed—an hour, perhaps two. I heard steps on one occasion and an eye appeared at the peephole in the door. Constant surveillance, which made sense. I had, after all, attempted suicide once that day. Even thinking about that made the hackles rise, made me feel viciously angry as if my whole being rebelled against the idea.

It was round about then that footsteps sounded outside again, the key rattled in the lock and Flattery ushered Sean O'Hara in. Sean dismissed him and stood against the closed door for a while, his face grave.

'How do you feel now, Ellis?'

'I'd say that was a reasonably stupid question.'

'Perhaps. Would you care for a cigarette?'

It tasted foul which surprised me for he only smoked a very exclusive brand of Sullivan. I made a face and stubbed the cigarette out.

He had been watching me searchingly and nodded his head slightly. 'Only to be expected. Your whole body chemistry's up the creek.'

'And what's that supposed to mean?'

He sat on the end of the bed. 'I've just had the necessary tests run through in the lab here. Blood, urine, saliva—the usual things.'

I knew what he was going to say, of course, just by looking at him, yet had to hear the cold facts spoken out loud.

'All right, surprise me.'

'That you'd taken those capsules was something I was reasonably certain of—the tests only confirm it. I didn't want to believe in the L.S.D. bit, but that's a hard fact of life now also. How long have you been taking it?'

'You tell me.'

He got angry, the Irish in him exploding to the surface. 'God damn it, man, I've been trying to help you find yourself again for nearly a year now and not just for those bloody fees you're always cracking on about. I liked you—still do, if it comes to that. You went through an experience out there in Vietnam that would have finished most men and stayed on your own two feet. Problems, yes, but nothing we couldn't put right. But L.S.D.' He got up and moved to the window. 'Of all things for a man with your background to take, that was the worst you could have chosen. The effect on anyone suffering from even the slightest instability can be incalculable.'

I said slowly, 'Anything I could say would be a complete waste of time and energy so just tell me one thing, then go. What happens now?'

He shrugged. 'It seems there's a security element involved. Something to do with the work St. Claire was doing. We'll know more tomorrow. They'll be coming to see you.'

'Superintendent Dix?'

He shook his head. 'No, it seems a Major Vaughan will be handling it. A paratroop officer but he's tied up with intelligence in some way. He was up at the cottage.'

'A good man with his boot,' I said. 'Now I think I'll go to bed, Sean. I don't think there's much more either of us can say at the moment and I'm tired.'

I turned my back on him, took off my dressing gown and climbed between the sheets. He knocked on the door and said, 'I'm afraid the light will have to be left on all night. I'm sorry about that.'

'That's all right.' I said. 'You seem to forget I'm the original expert on this kind of thing. In a manner of speaking, I've been here before.'

The door closed. I lay there staring up at the ceiling. After a while I heard the key again and Thompson entered with a half-pint mug which he put down against the wall by the door.

He smiled awkwardly. 'I thought you might like a cup of tea.'

'What's wrong?' I demanded. 'Did O'Hara warn you not to get too close? Where's your pal?'

'Flattery?' He shrugged. 'Half-way to the village by now. He likes his beer. It's his night off and you made him late which he'll hold against you. I'd watch that if I were you.'

He went out, the door closed again and for the last time that night and I was finally alone. I looked across at the mug of tea on the floor by the door. For some reason it reminded me of the Box. Tay Son all over again and I fell asleep and dreamt of Madame Ny.

* * *

Surprisingly, I slept quite well and was finally awakened at seven-thirty by Thompson and Flattery who appeared together bringing my breakfast on a tray. Porridge without cream, lukewarm scrambled egg, and cold, brittle toast.

267

They left me to eat it and returned in a quarter of an hour and took me along to the shower room.

Lying there in bed I had somehow felt myself again, slightly light-headed, but no more than that. It was only when I got on my feet and started to walk that I realised I was still in trouble. The walls undulated slightly, the corridor stretched into infinity. There was that peculiar feeling of being somehow outside of myself again.

Yet I was still capable of rational thought or so it seemed. Still able to make some kind of judgement about things. Flattery, for example, was different—different in his attitude to me. It was as if he had been spoken to—warned off, perhaps.

Yet it was more subtle than that. There was a new interest in the way he looked at me, a kind of calculation in the eyes, I noticed that particularly, especially when I was shaving in front of a small mirror with an electric razor they provided. He watched me only when he thought I wasn't looking at him and glanced away when I did. And his hand on my arm was considerably more gentle than it had been the previous night when they took me back along the corridor.

My feet seemed to spurn the ground and I moved in slow motion, seemingly in perfect control and yet it must have showed for Thompson cried out something unintelligible, the voice distorted in an echo chamber again, and grabbed my other arm.

The lift door opened at the same moment and Sean O'Hara appeared. He took in the situation at a glance, I suppose, for I was conscious of him running forward, mouth opening and closing as if he were talking.

The next thing I knew, I was on the bed in my room, staring up at the light bulb which for some reason was the size of a balloon and then, just like that, there was a kind of click inside my head and the bulb jumped back to normal size.

Flattery waited at the door and Thompson was holding a tray for Sean who was in the act of filling a hypodermic. I struggled up and he turned instantly and moved to my side.

'Are you going to stick that thing in me or not?' I demanded.

He glanced at the hypo, smiled and dropped it into the tray Thompson held out to him. 'How do you feel?'

'A little weak, but I can think straight. For a while there, I was in that dream world again.'

He nodded gravely. 'I'm afraid this kind of thing will continue for some days. At least if you know what's happening, it won't frighten you. You're lucky. On the dosage you took, most people would either be dead now or hopelessly insane.'

'You always were a comfort.'

He smiled with something like warmth which in the circumstances surprised me. 'You'd better rest now. I don't really think you're up to interviews yet. Major Vaughan's here. He was hoping you might be in a fit state to talk to him, but I can always put him off.'

'No thanks.' I stood up. 'I'd like to get it over with as soon as possible. I've always preferred to know the worst or had you forgotten?'

'Fair enough. By far the best way of looking at things. I'll go down now and check that he's ready for you and you can follow at your own pace with Flattery.'

* * *

Flattery's hand on my arm was still gentle and he called me sir a couple of times. Quite a turnabout. He went along

269

the corridor past the lift and he unlocked a door at the far end and ushered me through. I found myself standing at the end of a narrow steel bridge, not much more than a catwalk that spanned the courtyard at the rear of the main block, obviously constructed to give quick access to the east wing. It was roofed with some kind of transparent plastic, but the sides were open to the four winds and protected only by a three-foot rail.

The early morning sunshine was momentarily dazzling. I averted my eyes quickly as I started to cross and got the shock of my life as St. Claire's yellow Alfa Romeo turned into the courtyard sixty feet below.

I grabbed for the rail and waited, heart pounding. The door swung open, long, lovely legs, a flash of several hundred poundsworth of leopard-skin coat and then she was out clutching a formal-looking leather briefcase. Tall, proud, beautiful—skin not quite as dark as St. Claire's, hair wholly Negroid and proud of it.

She glanced up casually and saw me and called my name instantly. I closed my eyes, finally convinced the whole world really had gone mad and almost went over the rail.

* * *

Helen St. Claire was her brother's especial pride. Brains and beauty, he used to say, and I knew her history backwards long before I ever met her. As a medical student, prizes all along the way. After taking her M.D. she'd branched out into general psychiatry, finally specialising in behaviourist therapy with children.

But we'd never met, not until that famous occasion when St. Claire had discovered me sliding down the wall of that pub in Milner Street, had re-entered my life to save it for a second time.

He was due back in Paris the following day where he was something big with NATO Intelligence Headquarters at Versailles and had insisted on taking me back with him to the apartment at Auteuil with the cantilevered terrace that hung in space over the Seine giving the kind of view of Paris that seized you by the throat.

Helen was living with him at that time—working in a children's hospital and researching for a Ph.D. at the Sorbonne in her spare time which for some reason he completely failed to mention to me. She wasn't exactly expecting me either, for when we arrived on that first night, she had just finished dressing to go out to dinner and was waiting for her escort who, when he arrived, turned out to be a seventy-year-old Austrian Professor of Chemical Psychiatry at the Sorbonne.

A fine time they had between them over me. For a month, she dropped everything, watched over me like a broody hen. Never a hope of a drink did I have until the first week was over and my system was clear of the damn stuff and I was ten years younger and eating again.

After that, another kind of therapy. Paris in depth. She arranged a careful schedule day-by-day. You name it, we saw it. Churches, galleries, every historical building worth a footnote. And in between, gay meals at pavement cafés where she drank champagne which I insisted on because I was strictly regulated to coffee, tea or mineral water. Versailles, the woods at St. Germaine sheltering under a beech tree from a sudden shower.

She was a couple of years older than me, a vital, beautiful girl, utterly dedicated to her work and I was in love with her up to and including that final week of torture when St. Claire had to fly to Washington unexpectedly and we were left alone. I wanted her more than I'd ever wanted any woman, a constant itch that wouldn't go away.

Just to be near her was hell in a hundred subtle ways. To watch her sit down, get up, move around the place, reach for things, the skirt of a sky blue dress she was fond of at the time sliding six inches up her thigh . . . but she was St. Claire's sister. There was a kind of honour involved.

In the end, of course, my depression showed. She came in one night and found me on drink number one, a small scotch admittedly for by then she had established the pleasing fact that I wasn't really an alcoholic.

She asked me what was wrong and I told her, my natural tendency to over-dramatise anything bursting forth in a wonderful little scene that was as good as anything Noël Coward ever wrote. At the end, she had smiled gravely, taken my by the hand and had led me to her bedroom.

What had happened then was the greatest humiliation possible. Nothing I did, no amount of careful lovemaking, had the slightest effect on her. She caressed me in a calm, impersonal way, and certainly kissed me with considerable affection, but there was nothing else. I finally pleasured myself, if that is the word for it, and rolled off that magnificent body feeling utterly miserable.

Three nights like that was all I could take. She was beautiful, superbly intelligent and one of the most genuinely compassionate people I have ever met. Perhaps it was all sublimated so that there was nothing left over. Certainly there wasn't what I wanted, needed, if you like, as some kind of reassurance, although of what, I am not quite sure.

And so I fled from her, to London and the slippery slope. To grab at a lifeline called Sheila Ward, to decay a little bit more each day in the Foulness Marshes.

*   *   *

I was shown into a room on the ground floor which had

obviously once been a small drawing-room and still had great style with a gilt mirror over an Adam fireplace and white and blue Wedgwood plaques on the walls.

Sean was sitting behind a modern desk. There were a couple of easy chairs, bookshelves and a row of filing cabinets, but the main incongruity was the bars at the long windows, their shadows slanting across the Chinese carpet in the pale morning sunshine.

'Yours?' I asked.

He nodded. 'Very nice, but we can't even put in an electrical plug without getting permission from the Ministry. The whole place is under some kind of preservation order.' He faltered into temporary silence and then added with some force, 'Look, I'm on your side, Ellis. All right?'

'I never doubted it.' I said. 'Now wheel him in and let's get it over with.'

I moved to the window and looked out across green lawn to a fringe of beech trees. Rooks lifted lazily in the clear air, came down again. It was all very autumnal, very English out there beyond the bars.

Hilary Vaughan said, 'Hello, Ellis, it's been a long time.'

He was still in uniform, his red beret vivid in the sunlight. He had come through a door in the panelling to one side which I had failed to notice earlier and which now stood ajar.

'A long time since what?' I asked.

'You fagged for me during my last half at Eton or had you forgotten?'

'There was an oaf called Chambers,' I said. 'Played for the first eleven. Used to take a cricket stump to us if he thought we weren't being nippy enough. You caught him giving me a thrashing one day and broke his nose.'

'He took over the family business against all advice and

went broke in three years,' he said. 'Merchant banking. He never was up to much.'

He pulled off his beret, took a file out of his briefcase and sat down at the desk. 'They shouldn't have chucked you out of the Academy.'

'It didn't exactly break my heart.'

'You never wanted to go in the first place, did you?'

'You seem to know.'

'They why did you go to Vietnam?'

I helped myself to a cigarette from a box on the table. 'It seemed like a good idea at the time.'

He tapped one of the papers on the desk. 'This is a copy of your confidential report on file at the Pentagon, *A born soldier with outstanding qualities of leadership.* That's a direct quote. Bronze star, Vietnamese Cross of Valour plus the D.S.C. they gave you and St. Claire for escaping. That adds up to quite a record.'

'It should also read somewhere *Unfit for further service,*' I pointed out. 'Or did you miss that choice bit of information? Nutty as a fruitcake, although they put it more politely.'

'The general must have been proud of you.'

'You can stick the general where grandma had the pain.' I stubbed my cigarette out impatiently. 'What in the hell has all this got to do with what happened yesterday, anyway?'

I can see now that he was only feeling his way, had wanted to get me talking. He said, 'Okay, what *did* happen yesterday?'

'All right,' I said. 'I woke up yesterday morning, took a dose of L.S.D. large enough to kill most people so that I could have hallucinations about the Viet Cong chasing me through the marshes. This naturally led to my mistress sending a cry for help to my best friend who came galloping to the rescue, then decided to get into bed and screw her instead which left me no alternative but to blast them both and then do the only decent thing.'

He laughed, head back, his whole body shaking. 'You have a gift for the apt phrase, old lad, I'll give you that.'

He had a good face, I noticed that in an abstracted sort of way as he leaned back. Fleshy, perhaps, and there was certainly arrogance there, but it had been a mistake to think him amiable. A soldier's face—a scholar's also and one thing was certain. Here was an utterly ruthless man. A Regency buck born out of his time. The kind who would play cards all night, find half-an-hour for his mistress then face his man at ten paces under the trees at dawn and put a bullet between his eyes.

He said casually, 'Did you know that your friend, Mrs. Ward, was an active Marxist when she was an art student?' I stared at him blankly and he carried straight on. 'Those visits of hers to St. Claire's place on Thursdays when he was in town—they were a fact as Dix told you last night. Do you think they were having it off?'

I stood up and walked to the window. 'I wasn't her keeper. We certainly weren't in love or anything like that. It was a kind of mutual aid society. She looked after me in her way and I looked after her in mine. If she and Max were up to anything, then it was their own business.'

'On the other hand, she could have been simply giving him progress reports on you?'

'That's possible. He worried about me.'

Vaughan looked at the paper in front of him again. 'One thing does strike me as very odd. You come in from the marsh raving away and she immediately phones for General St. Claire.'

'I've had breakdowns of one kind and another before and he's always come running,' I said. 'We had a special

275

relationship, just like Britain and America.'

'But why did she wait so long before phoning your psychiatrist? They both had to pass through the Special Branch point at Landwich on their way to Foulness. I have the records here and Dr. O'Hara was booked through an hour and a half later than the general.'

I wasn't thinking too straight and there was an ache at the back of my head which had to be felt to be believed. I said, 'Look, what in the hell are you driving at?'

He ignored my question and said instead, 'Now tell me again what happened yesterday in that damned marsh, only the truth this time or at least what you remember as the truth.'

It didn't take long and when I was finished he sat for quite some time, chin in hands. I said, 'Yes, I know, typical hallucinatory symptoms after taking L.S.D., isn't that what Sean O'Hara said?'

'But you said you didn't take L.S.D.'

'The tests he's run on me indicate otherwise. A massive dose. I'm slipping from this world into the next so often at the moment that I don't know where I am.'

'Then who gave it to you?' he cut in sharply. I stared at him blankly. 'If you didn't take it yourself, then someone administered it to you. It's quite simple. A few drops soaked into a lump of sugar. Dropped into your tea perhaps or a cup of coffee.'

I stared at him in genuine horror and he said gently, 'It had to be her, Ellis, there *is* no one else.'

He was right, of course, had to be if what I remembered was the truth of things. I said hoarsely, 'But why? Why should she do that to me?'

'You'd be surprised just how much sense this whole affair does make,' he said. 'Your story, for instance.'

I was thunderstruck. 'You mean you believe it?'

'It makes a damn sight more sense than the other one.'

'Then you also believe I didn't murder them?'

He produced from the file a photo of that body sprawled across the bed, one knee raised, face obliterated.

'Well, you certainly didn't kill St. Claire, old lad.' He smiled beautifully. 'You see, that isn't him.'

5 *Action by night*

I grabbed at a chair to steady myself and turned it over, going down on one knee. There was a cry of alarm and Helen St. Claire came in through that door in the panelling like a strong wind, Sean O'Hara a step behind her.

I managed a smile. 'I wondered who in the hell this cunning bastard had out there.'

They got me into the chair which Sean had set upright again, but she couldn't manage even the trace of a smile in return for mine. She was all worry and concern.

'Ellis, you look like hell. What did they do to you?'

'Never mind that.' I turned to Vaughan. 'What proof have you?'

'Me!' Helen cut in. 'Major Vaughan spoke to me on the phone in Paris yesterday afternoon and asked me to come as soon as possible. I flew in at nine last night to find him waiting for me.'

'I took her straight to the Pathology Department at St. Bede's where they were holding the bodies.' Vaughan put in.

'It wasn't Max,' she said. 'It was as simple as that. I just knew, in spite of all those terrible injuries. Oh, he

277

was the right colour and size, but it just wasn't him. Christ, I've never felt so relieved in my life.'

There were actually tears in her eyes. I patted that lovely face and said to Vaughan, 'You'll have to come up with something a little more concrete than that, surely?'

'We have,' he said. 'Or rather, Dr. St. Claire did. A question of the middle finger on the right hand.'

'Max put it into the cog wheels of an old-fashioned mangle when he was ten,' she said. 'The end was nipped off. It's the sort of thing that wouldn't be noticed. The end of the finger looks quite normal, there's even a nail, but when he puts his hands together you see that the middle finger of the right hand is a quarter of an inch less than the other. When I was a little girl he used to put his hands together to show me. It was a kind of joke between us.'

I nodded, trying hard to take it all in for I was already beginning to feel tired. The shock had been too great.

I said to Vaughan. 'All right, what's it all about?'

'Let's look at all possibilities,' he said. 'St. Claire is an important man. Has direct responsibility for all Intelligence activities within the NATO alliance and a unique background in Far Eastern affairs, particularly Chinese. He's been heavily involved behind the scenes in the Paris peace talks over Vietnam.'

'And you think someone's snatched him?'

'I think it's the most likely explanation of what's happened. The only feasible one.' He took another photo from his briefcase and passed it across. 'Recognise him?'

It was Colonel Chen-Kuen, not a hair out of place and smiling faintly.

I said, 'I'll never forget him as long as I live. St. Claire and I picked him out of several hundred photos the CIA showed us after our escape.'

'I was aware of that.' He put the photo back in its place.

'He's been head of Chinese Intelligence Section C, which is their Western European Sector, for about a year now operating out of Tirana in Albania.'

'And you think he's behind this business? You think he's got Max?'

'Perhaps.' He shrugged. 'At the moment we're struggling in the dark.

It was Sean O'Hara who made the obvious point. 'If they wanted to lay their hands on General St. Claire, why not get on with it? Why all this tomfoolery concerning Ellis?'

'Look at it this way,' Vaughan said. 'If they'd simply kidnapped St. Claire, everyone would have known it within hours. There would have been a world-wide stink. Questions in the U.N. The lot. But if they could make it seem that he was dead . . .'

'So the Ward woman was working for them?'

'She had to be.'

'And yet they killed her,' Helen said softly.

'The kind of people they are. Anything for the cause. I don't know who the substitute for your brother was. Probably some poor devil off the docks somewhere carefully selected beforehand.'

'And how would they get into the Foulness area?' Sean said. 'I've always had to produce a pass myself.'

Vaughan shrugged. 'Determined men could get ashore at the River Crouch end with very little trouble.'

I shook my head which was hurting even more by then. 'But they must have known they wouldn't stand much of a chance of getting away with a thing like that. Of the body passing muster.'

'Why not?' he said. 'General St. Claire was seen to enter the area. Was checked through the Special Branch point and stated his destination as your cottage. With Sheila

279

Ward's phone call to Dr. O'Hara to damn you utterly, I'd say they had a fair chance that the body in question would be automatically accepted as that of the general.'

'And Sheila?'

'Probably thought she was to be a witness against you and the idea was that you were to be dead yourself, remember.'

The pain was terrible now. I turned blindly, pushing my head into Helen's shoulder and Sean said anxiously, 'What is it, Ellis?'

I told him and he went out quickly. Helen said, 'I'm going to stay in the village for a few days to be near you, Ellis. They didn't have a room vacant at the inn but the landlord has very kindly let me have the old Mill cottage by the bridge that he usually rents out during the summer.'

I think she was talking to keep me going. In any event Sean re-entered within a couple of minutes with a hypodermic and gave me an injection.

'That should help you sleep. As I said earlier, I'm afraid you'll be subject to various rather unpleasant symptoms for the next few days.'

I said to Vaughan, 'What about Max?'

'We'll be doing everything we can, but it's one hell of a difficult situation. We haven't a thing to go on. You'll still have to be held in official custody, but I'm hoping it won't be for long.'

I was going to argue, but I was too damn tired. Sean rang the bell on the desk and Flattery came in. 'Take Mr. Jackson to his room and keep a close eye on him. I'll see him later this afternoon.'

Flattery took me by the arm and helped me outside. When we went up in the lift he put an arm about my shoulders.

'You lean on me, sir,' he said. 'You don't look too good.'

A change for the better indeed and I took full advantage of his offer, particularly when we got out of the lift and started across the narrow catwalk.

And then, half-way across, one of his feet became inextricably mixed in mine and his strong right arm was no longer in evidence as I went headlong, rolling towards the railing. I distinctly felt his foot planted squarely in the small of my back, helping me on my way to roll under the bottom rail and drop sixty feet to the flagstones below.

I grabbed at the rail, one leg already in space and then another voice echoed with mine and Thompson came running along the catwalk from the far end.

They got me on my feet between them, Flattery repeating several times that he simply couldn't understand how it had happened. A nasty accident narrowly averted, that seemed to be the general feeling.

But not to me. God knows what Sean had pumped into me for I was already half-asleep as they put me to bed, but still awake enough to remember the feel of that foot in the back, to notice the look in Flattery's eyes as he went out backwards, closing the door and locking it.

Flattery, for reasons best known to himself, had just tried to murder me. A hell of a thought to go to sleep on.

* * *

Caught between the shadow lines of sleep and wakening when strange things fill the mind, his face seemed to float up out of darkness, full of malevolence. I blinked a couple of times, murmuring disjointed words and when I opened my eyes again, he was still there, crouched over me. The expression had changed to one of apparent concern.

'Are you all right, Mr. Jackson?'

I pushed myself up on one elbow. 'What time is it?'

'About seven o'clock, sir. You've slept like a log all day. Dr. O'Hara would like to see you.'

I nodded slowly, my mind still dulled from whatever it was Sean had given me. 'All right, where is he?'

'Downstairs, sir. Shall I give you a hand?'

I shook my head wearily. 'No, I'll be all right, but I'd like a shower. I feel half-doped.'

'Dr. O'Hara did say he was in something of a hurry, sir. I understand he wants to start back for London as soon as possible.'

I was still half-asleep and doped up to the eyeballs so that the memory of the incident on the catwalk earlier in the day had faded considerably, just another part of the mad pattern of my dreams like that look on his face as I awakened.

I had my back to him as I pulled on my dressing gown and turning rather quickly, caught him off guard, that expression of utter malevolence on his face again. I suppose it was that which saved me for in spite of his sudden, genial smile I was as wary as a cat as I moved out in the corridor.

'Where's Thompson?'

'Night off,' he said, pausing to close my door. 'Lucky devil. His second Saturday this month.'

'So you're in charge tonight?'

'That's it, sir.'

All this delivered in bluff, genial tones that put my teeth on edge because I didn't believe a word of it. I moved along the corridor towards the door to the catwalk, fighting to clear the greyness from my head.

Flattery said, 'Not that way tonight, sir, raining like hell it is.'

I paused at the lift doors. He reached over my shoulder and pressed one of the buttons. The doors slid open instantly only there was no lift, just a couple of steel cables rising out of a dark cavity.

It had all happened so quickly that it almost succeeded for I was completely off-balance. He gave me a shove in the back that sent me staggering forward. I grabbed for the steel cables, twisted round in a circle and gave him both feet in the chest as he leaned in through the entrance.

It was hardly a crippling blow, for most of the energy in the thrust of my body was expended in getting me back to safety, but it certainly sent him staggering back into the opposite wall. I made it to firm ground and ran a yard or two along the corridor, turning to face him.

'Who put you up to it, Flattery?'

He stood up slowly, wiping blood from his mouth, madness in his eyes. 'Bloody little squirt,' he said. 'I'll show you. No one to help you up here. Dr. O'Hara just left after phoning through to see how you were. I told him you were all tucked up for the night.'

He moved fast for such a big man, the boxer in him coming out. He swung a tremendous right that would have broken my jaw if it had landed. I swerved slightly allowing him to plunge past me and slashed him across the kidneys with the edge of my hand. He went flat on his face with a cry, got up almost at once and lurched forwards, hands reaching to destroy, all his science forgotten.

I grabbed for his right wrist with both hands, twisting it round and up. I gave it an extra twist to dislocate the shoulder then ran him head-first into the wall.

He was moaning with pain, blood on his face and I dropped to one knee. 'I've asked you a question.'

He had plenty of animal courage, I'll give him that and told me where to go in pretty fair Anglo-Saxon.

'All right,' I said. 'So you're a hard man.'

I got him by the scruff of the neck, dragged him across

283

to the lift and positioned him with his head over the edge. Then I stood up, a foot in his back to hold him steady and put my finger on the button.

'You'll be able to see it coming.' I said. 'A lovely way to go.'

I pressed the button and the cables moved. It was all it took. He broke wide open with a cry of fear, struggling furiously under my foot. I took my finger off the button and dropped to one knee beside him. He tried to move back, but I held him fast, his head still on the block.

'Now start talking.'

'I met this bloke in the village pub last night. Fruity as hell. Bow tie, shaven head, that sort of thing. Said his name was Dallywater.'

'So what happened?'

'He was doing all the buying. One double after another. At first I thought he was just some old queer on the make, then he started talking about you.'

'And turned out to have friends who would find it convenient if I met with an accident?'

He nodded. 'That's it, but it took him four hours to get around to it. We ended up in his room.'

'How much?'

He coughed and spat blood into the darkness of the shaft. 'A thousand quid. A hundred down—the rest to come afterwards. He gave me the first instalment there and then. I couldn't believe it.'

'You bloody fool,' I said. 'You'd have got paid off all right, but not with any nine hundred pounds. Who was behind this?'

Not that I expected an answer to that one and he shook his head. 'All I know is, his name isn't Dallywater. It's Pendlebury.'

'How do you know that?'

'I had a look inside his car afterwards. He'd left one of the quarter lights open. There were some visiting cards in the glove compartment. I've got one with me. Right-hand ticket pocket. And there was a book written under the same name with his picture on the back.'

'What kind of book?'

'Something to do with the east. Buddhism and that sort of stuff. *The Great Mystery*, that was it.'

I found the visiting card. *Rafe Pendlebury, Sargon House, Sidbury*. Sidbury, as I remembered, was somewhere near the Mendip Hills.

I gave the button another brief jab and Flattery cried out. 'I've told you the truth, I swear it, only he isn't there now. Told me he was leaving this morning. That he'd be in touch.'

I hoisted him to his feet and propped him against the wall. He stayed there, blood oozing from the smashed mouth and nose, his right arm held at an awkward angle. I suppose what happened then was the catalyst for everything that followed for until that moment I intended to take him to whoever was in charge of the place, insist that they contacted O'Hara and Hilary Vaughan as quickly as possible.

As I turned to press the button to bring the lift up, he came to life and lunged forward, his one good arm aimed for my back again, a repeat of his earlier performance. I pivoted sideways, he brushed against me and went headlong into the shaft without a cry.

When I brought the lift up, he was sprawled on top, his head twisted to one side in a way which could only mean his neck was broken. He was dead all right—no escaping that or the fact that it was going to look as if I'd killed him.

Getting out of there seemed in that single moment in

time the most sensible thing I could do. I brought the lift up level with the opening and locked it back on to the automatic system which meant that he would ride up and down on top, hidden from view, until some maintenance man or other decided to check the shaft. From now on, I had to play it wholly by ear and needed more than a little luck, but then it was time for some of that. Things had certainly been running the other way for long enough. I got into the lift and took it down to the first floor.

When the doors opened, I peered out into a deserted corridor. Somewhere a radio played faintly and rain drummed against the window to the left. I stepped out and the lift doors closed behind me quietly.

I turned and saw the indicator light move down to the ground floor. It paused fractionally, then started to rise again. I turned, noticed a door opposite marked *Bathroom* and was inside in a moment.

I stood in darkness, the door open a crack and watched as the lift indicator came to rest and the doors opened. A couple of male nurses emerged, one of them a West Indian.

They moved along the corridor together and I heard the West Indian say, 'Not me, man. On a night like this I stay close to home. How about a game of cards later?'

The other man seemed to agree and moved off down the corridor and the West Indian opened the door of what was obviously his room and went in.

It occurred to me then that the bathroom was perhaps not the safest of places in which to avoid detection. I noticed a door marked *Linen* on the other side of the lift and moved across. Inside, it was not much more than a closet with white wooden shelves loaded with blankets and sheets.

The move had certainly been a judicious one for as I

286

peered out through the crack of the door, the West Indian emerged from his room in a bathrobe, a towel over one arm, a plastic toilet bag swinging from his other hand. He was whistling cheerfully, went into the bathroom and closed the door. The inside bolt moved into place with a definite click and the taps were turned on.

I didn't hesitate. I was out of the linen closet in a second, half-a-dozen quick strides took me to his door and I stepped inside.

It was larger than I had expected and extremely well furnished with a fitted carpet and Scandinavian bedroom suite. There was even a portable television on a table at the foot of the bed.

The wardrobe was well stocked with clothes. I helped myself to some corduroy slacks and a pair of suede chukka boots with elastic sides which looked as if they'd stay on in spite of being a size too large. There were three or four sweaters on the shelves and I simply grabbed the first one that came to hand, a heavy Norwegian job, and a pair of socks.

There was an overcoat behind the door, I was going to take it, then discovered an old faded Burberry trench-coat underneath. A much better proposition altogether. A cautious check on the corridor and I was back inside the linen closet.

I kept my pyjamas on—simply pulled the pants and sweater over them. The chukka boots were too large as I had surmised, but not uncomfortably so, and the Burberry I buttoned to the neck and turned up the collar.

There was an inevitability to it all now. It was as if the whole thing was already marked out and I was trapped by events, borne along inexorably towards a destination as yet unknown to me. I knew that, quite suddenly, with complete certainty and it gave me a strange feeling of confidence when I stepped into the corridor and opened the lift doors.

The basement seemed the safest place to go. The last place for anyone to be at half-past eight on a Saturday night whereas there was certain to be staff around at the ground floor level.

When the doors opened, I pressed the second floor button and quickly stepped out into the passage. The doors closed behind me and as the lift ascended, I moved forward between white painted walls.

At the far end, I found two or three steps leading to a stout wooden door, rain seeping through. It was bolted top and bottom. I eased them free, opened the door and found myself in a small dark area, steps leading up to the courtyard above.

I went up the steps without hesitation, hands in pockets, for it seemed to me that to look in any way out of the ordinary would be the worst possible thing.

But I was as yet only half free as I walked briskly across the courtyard and went along the side of the main block. I didn't fancy my chances with that electrified fence which only left the main gate and that meant transport.

I took my one chance, running across the lawn at the front of the house towards the beech trees, those same trees I had seen earlier that day from behind bars and made it in what seemed like record time considering my condition.

Now here is a strange thing. At that time and for some time afterwards, I felt better than I had at any stage since the game began, gripped by a fierce exhilaration that reminded me strongly of that moment on the other side of the river from Tay Son with St. Claire at the start of our incredible journey. It certainly provided me with the fuel for what was to follow.

I moved through the trees and positioned myself in the bushes at a point where I noticed that the road down from the main block turned at right angles for the final run to the gate. It seemed reasonable to suppose that any vehicle coming that way would have to slow right down.

Within five minutes, a private car appeared, to be followed by another very quickly. Neither of them was suitable for my purposes. I waited hopefully for another quarter of an hour, getting wetter and wetter, wondering whether I might stand there all night when suddenly there was the roaring of a much larger engine and an old three ton Bedford truck rolled out of the night. It stopped altogether, then moved forward slowly as the driver negotiated the bend.

When I clambered over the tailgate, I saw in the light of the lamps at the edge of the drive that the thing was empty except for a couple of small packing cases. Which left me only one place to go and as the truck increased speed, I stood on the tailgate, hauled myself up on top of the canvas tilt and lay face down and prayed.

I suppose it was the rain which helped more than anything for by now it was hammering down with real force. When we reached the gates, the truck braked to a halt, but left the engine ticking over.

I closed my eyes tight and tried to make myself even smaller as feet clattered down the steps of the single-storeyed guard house. They moved to the rear of the truck, paused as someone peered over the tailgate and then a voice called something unintelligible. The gates creaked open and we moved out into the road.

I gave it a couple of minutes, then raised my head and saw to my horror that we were already approaching the outskirts of the village. I crawled backwards, scrambled down on to the tailgate and got ready to jump as the truck slowed to negotiate a narrow bridge. A moment later, I was rolling over twice on wet grass at the side of the road.

I sat up, for some reason choking back laughter and the truck faded into the night. But there was another sound, a steady, rather monotonous creaking, a regular heavy splashing. I moved to the parapet of the bridge, looked across and saw an old mill water wheel turning in the fast-flowing stream.

The old mill cottage by the bridge, wasn't that what Helen said? I found it on the other side, a white painted fence with *Mill House* on a board on the gate and the cottage itself beyond, Elizabethan from the look of it, with a thatched roof.

I moved round to the side and found that Alfa parked there, glistening in the rain in the light of a lamp above the door. I peered through the window into a surprisingly modern kitchen and saw Helen standing at the stove, stirring a pan.

That flair for drama of mine coming to the surface again, I simply opened the door and stepped inside. She whirled round, a frown on her face, then stood there, staring at me in utter amazement.

'Ellis!'

'In the flesh,' I said.

She crossed to me with a kind of rush, flung her arms around my neck and kissed me—and with real passion. One hell of an improvement on Paris.

I said, 'You'll get wet. I'm soaking.'

'That's obvious.' She started to unbutton my Burberry. 'Dr. O'Hara left here for London not ten minutes ago. According to him, you were nicely tucked up for the night. Now what's going on?'

She stood there clutching the wet Burberry looking more beautiful than any woman had a right to do and clever with it—two doctorates and another on the way. So I decided on the direct approach.

'I've killed a man,' I said simply. 'Or at least that's the way it's going to look when they find him.'

* * *

When I finally finished, we were sitting facing each other on the opposite sides of the table. She believed me, there was no doubt about that, but her distress was plain.

'But why, Ellis? What could be the motive?'

'All right,' I said. 'Accepting Vaughan's version of things, an important part of the original plan was quite simply that I should appear to be a raving lunatic under the influence of dangerous drugs who then committed suicide. Fortunately for me, I vomited most of the poison and Sean arrived in time to do exactly the right thing.'

'I know that,' she said. 'Go on.'

'Now the fact that I'm alive, no matter how guilty I look, is more than inconvenient because it means there's always a chance that if I keep on yelling loudly enough, someone might take a little notice.'

'Not take things quite so much for granted, you mean?'

'Exactly. Much better if poor, raving Ellis Jackson throws himself off the catwalk or jumps down the lift shaft. If either of those things had happened it would have been accepted as a second, only this time successful, attempt at suicide.'

'But not by Vaughan, surely?'

'Dead right, only they don't know how far their little scheme's come unstuck already, do they?'

She shook her head slowly. 'Even so, this Flattery business is terrible. You should have stayed, Ellis. Now things look blacker than ever.'

'Oh, no they don't.' I produced the visiting card. 'Not as long as I've got this. The mysterious Mr. Pendlebury's

291

got some explaining to do. There'll be an R.A.C. handbook in the Alfa. Give me the keys.'

'What do you want that for?'

'To find out exactly where Sidbury is.'

'You don't mean to say you intend to go chasing off after this wretched man yourself.'

'Have you any objections?'

She appeared to hesitate, then sighed heavily, reached for her handbag and took out the keys which she threw across the table.

'For such a clever man you can sometimes be incredibly stupid, Ellis, but have it your own way.'

I went out into the rain, unlocked the Alfa and got into the driving seat. I found the R.A.C. handbook and looked up Sidbury in the gazetteer. It was there all right. Population one hundred and twenty. One pub, one garage and not much else, on the edge of the Mendip Hills not far from Wells. I had a look at the map then returned to the cottage.

Helen was not in the kitchen. I opened the far door and found myself in a pleasant, oak-beamed lounge. There was a stone hearth large enough to roast an ox and a log fire burned brightly. She was sitting beside it, her hand on the telephone.

'Who are you thinking of calling—Vaughan?'

'I can't,' she said. 'He phoned earlier to say he'd been called to Paris for a NATO Intelligence conference to discuss this whole affair.'

'When does he get back?'

'Sometime tomorrow morning. He's flying in on the RAF Support Command mail plane first thing.'

'All right, that rules him out for the moment which only leaves Sean and he'll still be en route for London.'

'I could always phone the police.'

'You could at that, but the way things look at the moment, I suspect they'd be more inclined to clap me in irons than anything else.'

'True enough,' she said. 'I suppose the next thing you'll tell me is that you can't afford to lose precious time. That it's all for Max.'

I was surprised, not really understanding what she was driving at. 'What else?'

'Oh, no, Ellis, not that. Not the lie in the soul at this stage in the game. You want to do this for Ellis Jackson and nobody else. They put the boot into you, whoever they are—isn't that the phrase? Now you want to put it into them, only harder. Your primary response to almost every situation is a violent one.'

'Thank you, Dr. Kildare,' I told her, but there was a certain truth in what she said. Enough to make me feel uneasy. It was as if one had looked into the mirror and had no liking for what was there.

She said coolly, 'This place Sidbury—where is it?'

'Edge of the Mendips near Wells.'

'I don't know that part of the country.'

'Seventy miles or so from here. An hour and a half in the Alfa.'

'All right,' she said. 'On one condition.'

'What's that?'

'That I drive. Your reflexes aren't up to it, not in the state you're in.'

I could have argued about that, but it wouldn't have done any good and in any case, as I turned and went back into the kitchen, there was another of those clicks inside my head and the light shade mushroomed above my head.

'Wait for me in the car,' she said. 'I won't be long.'

We were back in that echo chamber again and as the walls started to undulate, I went out into the rain, got into the front passenger seat and strapped myself in.

I closed my eyes, breathed slowly and regularly and tried to remember everything Black Max had ever taught me about relaxation because nothing was going to stop me now. I was going to get to Sidbury and squeeze the truth of things out of friend Pendlebury if it was the last thing I did.

6 *The Temple of Truth*

I had expected her to say something about St. Claire, to make some kind of comment on the situation, but she didn't. Perhaps that was the true reason she had insisted on driving—to occupy herself fully and crowd thought out, for brother-sister relationships when they are close, are confused affairs at best, strange currents pulling every which-way just beneath the surface.

She worshipped St. Claire, always had, which was understandable enough. She was a different person when he was around, smiling slightly anxiously, always to hand with anything from an ashtray to a Bloody Mary at the snap of his fingers.

It wasn't the kind of night for much traffic, heavy relentless rain clearing the road from Newbury on. Some of the most beautiful country in England all around and it might as well not have existed for all we could see of it.

She drove with all the fierce, dedicated concentration of the professional Grand Prix driver, using the gears constantly, she and that magnificent car against the darkness and the torrential rain.

None of which left much time for conversation which suited me admirably. By the time we reached Marlborough, I was feeling reasonably myself again or at least, confident of retaining some sort of control. We moved on through Chippenham, dropping down into Bath in just on the hour.

About a mile out of Bath on the A39 as we were passing through Corston, she pulled in to the kerb at a public telephone box without warning and switched off the engine.

'I'm going to phone Sean O'Hara. He should be home by now.'

She was out of the Alfa before I could reply, taking the keys with her, probably because of some basic fear that I might run out on her. Not that I hadn't thought of it, but circumstances were against me. I helped myself to a cigarette from her handbag, got out and half-opened the booth door so that I could hear what was going on.

She was talking fast and looking frustrated. 'But surely you have another number at which he can be reached?'

From the look on her face, she obviously wasn't getting anywhere so I reached in and took the receiver from her hand. 'Who's speaking?'

The voice was solid like a rock, but perfectly polite. 'The porter at Carley Mansions. Dr. O'Hara has an apartment here, sir.'

'Has he been in this evening?'

'About half an hour ago, sir, and left again within ten minutes. All his professional calls tonight are being handled by Dr. Meyer Goldberg at Sloane 8235.'

'This is a private call.'

'Then I'm sorry, but I can't help you, sir. Dr. O'Hara didn't say where he could be reached. Never does on his night off, sir.'

'Wise man,' I said. 'When he does come in, tell him Ellis Jackson phoned and will phone again, probably in the morning. It's most urgent.'

I replaced the receiver and eased Helen out into the rain. 'If I know my Sean he'll be hard at it in some other bed than his own till the small hours. He has one great weakness—anything female between the ages of eighteen and twenty-five. He should consult an analyst.'

She actually managed to laugh. 'Ellis Jackson, you're a complete and unmitigated bastard.'

'Now don't go all clinical on me,' I told her. 'We want to be on the other side of Chewton Mendip which is a good ten miles from here so let's get going.'

We moved on through the quiet hills, reaching Sidbury just after ten, a couple of narrow streets flanked by fifteenth century houses, deserted in the heavy rain. We slowed as an inn loomed out of the shadows on our left, a dozen or so cars parked outside and then I noticed a garage on the corner opposite and the lights were still on above the pumps.

'Try there.' I said and she nodded and pulled over.

A middle-aged man in an old raincoat and tweed cap was standing in a small glass booth at the entrance, coins and notes stacked on the shelf before him in neat piles. He looked up in some surprise when Helen touched the horn, but came out at once. She asked for eight gallons and I got out and moved round to stand at his side.

'A dirty night.'

'That it is,' he said. 'I was just closing.'

'I'm looking for a place called Sargon House,' I said. 'Owned by a chap called Pendlebury.'

He seemed surprised. 'Come far, have you?'

'London,' I said. 'Why?'

He put the filler cap back on. 'Long way for nothing. They usually finish up there around ten o'clock.'

'Finish what?' I asked him.

'Why, the services. That's what you've come for, ain't it? That's what they all come for.'

It was Helen who cut in smoothly, producing a five pound note from her bag and holding it out to him through the window. 'I know, it's very annoying. We broke down in Newbury, then I took a wrong turning on the way out of Bath and we ended up miles out of the way.'

He glanced down, really noticing her for the first time and his expression changed as most men's did when confronted with that extraordinary face.

'Can't read the signs properly on a night like this,' he said as if wishing to assure her that it wasn't her fault.

He went into the booth and I got back into the Alfa. 'Quick thinking.'

She didn't get a chance to reply for he was already back with the change. 'Straight on to the edge of the village, over the bridge and sharp right. Keep on that road through the woods for another quarter of a mile. You can't miss it. He has a board by the gate listing all the service times, just like church.'

He didn't sound as if he approved but she thanked him and drove away.

'All very mysterious,' she said as we went over the bridge. 'What do you think our Mr. Pendlebury's up to?'

'God knows,' I said. 'We'll just have to wait and see.'

We moved on along a dark tunnel through trees beside a high stone wall, towards a patch of light on the left that finally blossomed into a couple of lamps suspended from a wrought iron frame above high gates which stood wide.

There was a board beside the gate handsomely painted in gold and blue. It carried the legend *Temple of Truth* and listed various activities underneath, including week-long retreats and the times of services. Saturday night was eight till ten. Pendlebury's name appeared at the bottom of the list, naked and unadorned.

'Well, at least he hasn't called himself bishop,' I said. 'Let's get on up to the house and see what it's all about.'

The drive moved on through pine trees emptying into about a couple of acres of terraced gardens containing the house. It was Georgian and not all that large. A couple of dozen cars were parked in the gravelled circle in front of the entrance and most of them seemed to be in the Jaguar-Bentley bracket.

Helen pulled in at the end of the line and I got out and moved towards the porch. The front door stood open and I paused by the steps and waited for her to join me.

'It looks as if they're still at it,' she said. 'What do we do now?'

'Assume a suitably devout expression and join the party.'

As I paused in the porch, she put a hand on my arm. 'I'm not so sure this is a good idea.'

I said, 'You want Max back, don't you?'

I didn't give her a chance to discuss it any further and went through into the wide hall beyond. It was illuminated by candlelight, half a dozen of them burning in a many-branched silver holder standing on a small table and there was the heavy, all-pervading scent of incense everywhere.

There was a murmur of voices from a large double door to one side by the stairs. It was slightly ajar and I pushed it open a little so that we could look inside.

The room was long and rather narrow, curtains drawn across the windows at one side, Chinese tapestries covering the wall on the other. Thirty or forty people sat crosslegged on the floor in the half-darkness for, like the hall, the only illumination came from candles, in this case positioned in front of a kind of altar on which stood a gold-painted figure of Buddha.

There was the usual small fire burning in a bowl before it and a man prayed there, stretched out on the floor like a penitent, arms out on either side in the shape of a cross. He was wearing a saffron robe which left one shoulder bare and his head was shaved.

When he stood up and turned, I saw that he was a European with a rather fine face and calm, wise eyes.

'Pendlebury?' Helen breathed in my ear.

I don't know why, but I was inclined to think it was, purely on hunch.

His voice when he spoke was as calm as the eyes and melodious in the extreme. I think it was that which struck the first really jarring note for it occurred to me suddenly that it was as if he were not a truly real person, but some-one playing a part.

He said, 'And so I give you a text on which to meditate, sisters and brothers all. To do good—this is too easy. To be good—this is all there is. This is the golden key.'

He blessed them, hand high, then moved off to one side. It was only after he had gone that his audience started to rise.

It was then that I noticed the monks—two of them. Saffron robes, shaven heads just like Pendlebury—only these were Chinese. The most surprising thing was the collecting bags. They carried one each and as the audience started to file out, people paused to make their contributions. No silver collection this. Only the rustle of paper money. I stepped back, taking Helen by the arm and moved into the shadows by the stairs.

'What now?' she demanded.

'We'll see if his holiness will grant us an audience. Give me a couple of fivers and leave me to do the talking.'

As she got the money out of her bag the audience started to emerge, mainly women from what I could see. Affluent, middle-aged and anxious. The kind who, having everything, end up by finding they have nothing and search ceaselessly for some means of filling the vacuum.

They moved out through the front door shepherded by the two monks, one of whom moved off almost immediately. As the other eased the last couple of visitors out and closed the door, I stepped from the shadows by the stairs and stood waiting, Helen at my shoulder.

When he turned and found us there his actions were extremely interesting. His right foot eased forward, his body dropping into the basic defence pose common to all the martial arts. Nothing too obvious to the uninitiated, but it was there.

I said brightly. 'We were wondering if Mr. Pendlebury could possibly spare us a few minutes.'

He relaxed completely and actually managed a smile of sorts. 'The *guru* is always extremely tired after a service,' he said in excellent English. 'You must understand this. The mental strain is so intense. He is always available to help those in need or genuine seekers after self-knowledge, but by arrangement in advance.'

I produced the two five pound notes Helen had given me and offered them to him. 'I didn't get a chance to contribute earlier. The service was an inspiration.'

'Wasn't it?' he said simply, taking the two notes and stuffing them into the already bulging collection bag which he held in his left hand. 'I will see if the *guru* will see you.'

He opened a door to the left of the stairs and moved inside. Helen said quietly. 'I didn't like him.'

'Any particular reason?'

'It was the eyes. They didn't smile when his mouth did. A funny kind of monk.'

'Not really.' I said softly. 'Judo, Karate—all the martial arts are just a Japanese development of the ancient Chinese art of Shaolin Temple Boxing which first came from India with Zen Buddhism in the sixth century and was improved on by the monks of Shaolin Temple in Honan Province.'

'That sounds like a pretty wild sort of scene for priests.'

'They were hard times,' I said. 'You didn't get far by turning the other cheek.'

The door opened, the monk emerged and stood to one side, motioning us in. 'The *guru* can spare you five minutes, but he is very tired. It would be appreciated if you do not stay beyond the stated time. Any further meeting will have to be by appointment.'

I moved inside, Helen behind me a little reluctantly and I looked around quickly. The room was large, the wall draped with superb Chinese tapestries, collector's items without a doubt and the floor was covered with hand-woven silken rugs of equal magnificence.

Pendlebury was on his knees in front of a small figurine of Buddha set in a small alcove and the monk whispered in my ear, 'He will not keep you long.' He went out closing the door softly behind him.

There was a log fire in a wrought iron basket on the hearth, a very English touch, but the ebony desk was Chinese as were the ceramics on the shelves in the large alcove beside the fireplace. Several figurines, a selection of bowls and four or five quite exquisite vases. I moved across casually to examine them.

The golden voice said, 'I see you are admiring my little collection.'

He was older than I had at first thought, the skin pouched beneath the eyes and tight over the cheekbones. In the candle-light out there he had looked good. Somehow ageless, but I realised now that he was just an old pro, at his best on stage and looking about a hundred years old off.

There was a kind of warmth there when he reached out to touch one of the figurines, a woman on horseback in wimple and conical hat.

'An example of Ming Dynasty work at its best.'

Helen said, 'These things must be worth a great deal of money.'

'How can one put a price on beauty?' At that he was back playing a part again moving to the desk and seating himself. 'In what way can I serve you? You need guidance, perhaps?'

'You could put it like that.' I took Helen by the elbow and led her to the chair on the opposite side of the desk. 'My name's Ellis Jackson. Does that mean anything to you?'

It had roughly the same effect as a good, solid kick between the legs. He suddenly looked older than it was humanly possible to be, a walking corpse, the skin of his face drying before my eyes.

He tried hard and failed miserably. 'I—I'm afraid not.'

'Now that I really do find surprising,' I told him. 'When we consider the fact that only last night, you offered someone a thousand pounds to see me dead.'

But by now, he'd managed to regain some kind of control. 'I'm afraid I don't know what you're talking about. Here, we are concerned only with the conquest of self. How could we reconcile this with attempts to bring about the destruction of a fellow human being?'

'You can keep that stuff for the paying customers,' I said. 'But my friend here has a problem you might be able to help us with. She's lost her brother and for some odd reason I've got complete faith in your ability to tell us where he is.'

Pendlebury looked uncertainly at Helen. 'Your brother? I'm afraid I don't quite understand.'

'Brigadier-General James Maxwell St. Claire,' I put in.

He started to his feet and at the same moment an arm slid across my throat. I suppose he must have been standing behind one of the tapestries or—more probably—there was a concealed door.

In any event, I put my heel down hard enough into the bare instep to crack bone and brought both elbows backwards, striking beneath the ribs on either side. But he was good—damn good. He hung on with everything he had because that's what he'd dedicated his whole life to learning to do, but his arm slackened. Not much, but enough for me to get my fingers to his wrists. I tore them free, dropped to one knee and threw him across the room. He knocked Pendlebury out of his chair into those shelves in the alcove and several thousand pounds' worth of rare pottery was scattered across the floor. Some of the pieces actually bounced and others simply disintegrated.

Pendlebury was on his knees, howling in anguish like a hurt dog, but I had other things to think about because just then, the other monk burst in through the door.

They're all the same, most of the really expert exponents of the martial arts. They think technique all the time. They spend about twenty years of their life mastering *karate* or *judo* or *aikido* and in the end, their own excellence is against them because they operate best when they get the same standard in return from their opponents.

This one gave the usual terrible cry to frighten me and struck a typical *karate* stance, assuming he'd get it back. So I dropped in a prizefighter's crouch, just to confuse him. He hesitated and was lost because as I led with the right, I switched techniques and pulled the rug out from under him.

In other circumstances it might have seemed amusing, but I was beginning to lose my sense of humour fast. As he

303

started to get up, I gave him a boot in the face, real old English back alley variety and he went against the wall hard, slid to the floor and didn't get up.

As I turned, Helen cried a warning. The black Red Dragon tapesty on the rear wall ballooned out like a sail in the wind and three more Chinese burst through, conventionally attired in neat, dark suits, but yelling loud enough to blow the place apart. There wasn't much I could do, particularly as someone tripped me neatly from the rear around then, sending me headlong amongst those flying feet.

I was on my face trying to crawl, head singing and then the walls started to undulate again and I closed my eyes hard and tried to stop myself from drifting off. My arms were behind my back now and Helen screamed again and there was a voice calling my name insistently.

'Ellis—Ellis. Look at me.'

A hand slapped my face gently so I opened my eyes and looked straight into the pleasant concerned face of Colonel Chen-Kuen.

7 Down among the dead men

Another aspect of that privileged nightmare I had been living, but this time I was conscious of a kind of relief for now, beyond any possibility of doubt, I knew that I had been right from the beginning. That things had truly been as I had imagined. This man was no figment of some disordered mind. This man was flesh and blood.

I lay there, half-conscious, my face against the floor as

someone held my hands behind my back and I listened to him as he spoke briefly to the others in Chinese.

There was no sign of Helen, she had presumably already been moved, and I watched as Pendlebury's two assistants were helped out of the room, both of them looking decidedly the worse for wear.

Pendlebury sat huddled in the chair behind his desk, head in hands, occasionally looking up to stare hopelessly around the room, an expression of utter despair on his face, completely unable to cope with things as they had developed.

Chen-Kuen went to the desk and leaned across, one hand on his shoulder, talking earnestly in a low voice. Whatever he was saying, Pendlebury didn't like for he shook his head helplessly from side-to-side.

Chen-Kuen raised his voice, as if to impress the seriousness of things on him and said firmly in English, 'But my dear Pendlebury, it must be done. I'll leave Pai-Chang to handle it. All you have to do is give him whatever assistance he requires. You can both follow later.'

Pendlebury nodded, stood up and went out in a kind of daze. Chen-Kuen watched him go, frowning slightly. He helped himself to a cigarette from a box on the desk and one of the Chinese, a small, vital looking man in a well-tailored suit of dark worsted, offered him a light. This was presumably the Pai-Chang referred to and they spoke together briefly in Chinese.

'We must leave at once,' Chen-Kuen said. 'I'm already considerably later than I had intended. I leave things here in your hands with every confidence. You know what to do. I shall look for you tomorrow.'

'And the old man?' Pai-Chang said. 'Shall I bring him with me or does he carry on here?'

Chen-Kuen shook his head. 'This place is of no further

use to us. As for Pendlebury . . .' He sighed and looked as if he genuinely meant it. 'A broken man. He has lost his faith and that is always dangerous.'

'The same way as the other?' Pai-Chang asked.

'I think it would be the sensible thing.'

We were alone now, the three of us and I made some sort of movement which immediately caught his eye. He nodded to Pai-Chang who crossed the room quickly and heaved me to my feet with no apparent effort.

'My dear Ellis, you must sit down,' Chen-Kuen said. 'You don't look at all well.'

Pai-Chang shoved me into a chair and Chen-Kuen sat on the edge of the desk. 'Still the same old Ellis—as violent and unpredictable as ever. How many dead men did you leave behind at Marsworth Hall?'

'Only one,' I said. 'The bastard your friend Pendlebury bribed to see me off. Surely you could have done better than him? He's a joke. Nobody could believe in him for more than five minutes together at any one time.'

He sighed. 'One must use the tools which come to hand in my kind of work, Ellis, and Pendlebury had his uses. I wouldn't underestimate him, by the way. Hundreds of people, those who have visited him here, think of him as a new Messiah.'

I let that one go. 'What have you done with St. Claire?'

He didn't attempt to prevaricate although I suppose there wouldn't have been much point. He simply said, 'All right, Ellis, cards on the table. Just tell me how things stand.'

'Gladly,' I said. 'You've had it. The right people know all about you, thank God. You're on borrowed time.'

He didn't seem in the least put out, stood up and walked out quickly leaving Pai-Chang in charge. I tried to ease my wrists without much success for they had been tied very

306

securely with a rather thin cord which bit into the flesh painfully. Pai-Chang came across at the first sign of movement and examined them.

He moved back to the desk satisfied and helped himself to a cigarette, leaving me to my own dark thoughts. God knows, but it was a mess whichever way you looked at it.

A moment later Chen-Kuen returned, walking briskly across to the desk and sitting on the edge again. He smiled amicably. 'All is revealed, Ellis, as they used to say in those old melodramas.'

'What are you driving at?'

'I now know exactly what the situation is. Very simple really. I had a quiet word with Dr. St. Claire. Explained how unpleasant the consequences would be for you if she didn't tell me the truth.' He shook his head. 'You two are the only ones who know about Pendlebury and this place, Ellis. You weren't being very honest with me.'

He sounded exactly like some fatherly headmaster reproving a recalcitrant schoolboy. I could have called him a name or two, but there didn't seem any point.

'What happens now?'

'The girl can leave with me. A nice surprise for her brother. But you, Ellis.' He gave another of those sighs of his. 'This time we really must finish what was started.'

'It was a rotten idea from the first,' I said. 'You never stood more than a fifty-fifty chance of getting away with it.'

'But still worth it,' he said. 'So much neater to have St. Claire officially dead and beneath the sod, as the Irish say. Things were rushed, that was the trouble. Certain pressures built up and we were forced to move a little too quickly for comfort, but that, as they say, is another story and of little interest to you now.'

'Just tell me one thing. Who was the substitute you provided?'

307

'I believe he was bosun on a Panamanian timber boat. Brought in from Antwerp as an illegal immigrant. He will not be missed because he was never here.'

'And Sheila Ward?' It hurt to ask that one.

'Had worked for us for four years.'

'And you killed her.'

'She was what you would term expendable or if you would prefer it another way, more use to us dead than alive.'

'You bastard,' I said. 'And what good has it done you at the end of things? Your bloody plan didn't work.'

'But I still have General St. Claire which is all that counts,' he said. 'War is war. Your side and mine are engaged in one whether you like to admit it or not; in war, people die and how they die is immaterial. It is all one in the end. We will win and you will lose because history is on our side.'

Strange, but those words were words I'd heard before from Madame Ny. The same sentiments, the same phrases, the same absolutely implacable belief in the rightness of the cause.

He stood up, stubbed out his cigarette and said rather formally, 'And now I must leave you and with a certain regret. We might have been friends you and I in other circumstances, but there it is.'

He walked out quickly and Pai-Chang went with him. I sat there in the chair, straining hopelessly at my wrists and a moment later, Pendlebury came in. He was wearing slacks and a polo neck sweater and when he reached into the box for a cigarette, his hand was shaking.

'You shouldn't have come here,' he said. 'It was a stupid thing to do.'

'What are they going to do with me?'

He managed to light the cigarette with some difficulty

and stood looking at me, a kind of helpless horror on his face.

'Oh, for God's sake, man,' I said. 'Pull yourself together and tell me the worst.'

'All right,' he said. 'There's an ornamental lake on the other side of the trees from the house, sixty feet deep at one end where the old quarry used to be.'

'Don't tell me any more,' I said. 'Let me guess. You and Pai-Chang take me out in some convenient boat and put me over the side with fifty pounds of chain round my ankles.' I laughed in his face. 'You poor bloody booby. When I go, you go. I heard Chen-Kuen give the order.'

His face turned very pale. 'It's a lie.'

'Have it your own way.' I shrugged. 'I'd say it was the logical thing to do. You know too much.'

He said slowly, 'I won't believe it. It can't be true.' And then as the thought struck him, a new light came into his eyes. 'You *are* lying. I know you are. If they spoke together at all, they'd have spoken in Chinese. They always do.'

'One of the few useful accomplishments I picked up in North Vietnam,' I said in Cantonese. 'Or hadn't you heard?'

He stared at me in horror, mouth gaping, but was unable to take things further for at that moment, Pai-Chang returned. He heaved me from the chair and pushed me ahead of him into the hall. We went along a narrow passage towards the rear of the building, opened one of several doors and he shoved me inside. I caught a brief glimpse of a small, narrow storeroom and then the door closed leaving me in total darkness. I waited a couples of minutes for my eyes to get adjusted and then started a cautious reconnaissance, following the wall, one foot extended. The cupboard was quite bare so I slid down to the ground and started to strain at my bonds.

* * *

It was perhaps an hour later when the door was flung open and Pai-Chang appeared. He was wearing a navy blue anorak and looked tough and very competent as he pulled me out into the corridor and shoved me along in front of him.

Pendlebury was waiting for us in the entrance hall. He was obviously under considerable strain and looked faintly ridiculous in an old oilskin coat a size too large for him.

He glanced at me nervously, then dropped his gaze as Pai-Chang pushed me out of the front door and down the steps into the rain. Pendlebury stumbled along behind and the Chinese waited for him, face impassive before starting across the lawn.

The rain fell without pause, there was the heavy rank smell of rotting vegetation as we neared the lake and then the dark shape of an old boathouse loomed out of the night. Pai-Chang unbolted the heavy wooden doors and pulled one of them open. He moved inside ahead of us, there was a click and a light came on over the door.

The boathouse ran out into the lake itself and a narrow wooden jetty extended even further, a single light burning at the far end, presumably turned on by the same switch as the other.

There were several old rowing skiffs on view plus the accumulated junk of years, but Pai-Chang took me by the arm and pushed me along the jetty towards the light.

A boat was moored there, a medium size rowing boat with oars inside, half-full of water as far as I could judge. The rain bounced from the wet planking and our feet made a hollow booming sound.

Pai-Chang pushed me down on a pile of old, rotting canvas and said to Pendlebury, 'Watch him. I'll get the boat.'

As he moved away I said to Pendlebury in a low voice,

'You'll never get by on your own, can't you see that? I'm the only person who can help you now.'

In the sickly, yellow light of the lamp he looked terrible. As if he might die of fright at any moment and his hands were shaking again.

'What am I going to do?' he whispered in a hoarse voice.

'You've got about half a minute to make up your mind,' I said urgently. 'So make the most of it.'

Pai-Chang had descended the ladder to the boat some six feet below and now he was coming up again, his feet rattling the rungs. Pendlebury dropped to one knee behind me. There was the click of a knife-blade opening, a few quick movements and my bonds parted.

Pai-Chang came forward quickly, 'What's going on?'

He leaned down to peer closer in the dim light and I reached for his throat as I came up, which was a bad mistake for my hands were still numb and I couldn't exert any real strength. A grab at the throat is never to be advised if anything else will do as Pai-Chang demonstrated by clutching the lapels of my old Burberry, sticking a foot in my belly and tossing me over his head.

I went into the lake head first and had enough sense to stay under, turning and swimming beneath the jetty, surfacing cautiously on the other side. There was another ladder close to hand and I pulled myself out of the water very carefully and peered over the edge of the jetty.

Pendlebury was crouched on one knee on the left, a look of complete terror on his face and Pai-Chang stood on the other side of the jetty peering into the dark waters, an automatic in one hand.

There was a boat hook hanging on a nail beside the ladder. I got one hand on it quickly and went over the edge of the jetty in a kind of rush. I went down on one knee, my foot slipping on the wet planking. He whirled

311

round, gun ready. I lunged awkwardly at him with the boat hook, the only thing I could do, and caught him in the throat under the chin. He gave a short, stifled cry and went back into the water.

I poked around in the darkness with the end of the boat-hook for a while, but it soon became obvious that he wasn't going to come up again. Pendlebury had slumped down to the wet planking and seemed to be crying, his face buried in his hands, shoulders heaving. I hauled him to his feet and gave him a shake.

'You can cut that out for a start. Where have they gone?' He hesitated rather obviously so I grabbed him by the throat. 'Suit yourself. I'd just as soon put you over the side to join your friend.'

'No, for God's sake, Jackson,' he gabbled. 'I'll tell you anything you want to know if only you'll promise to let me go.'

'All right,' I said. 'Start talking.'

'There's an island called Skerry about seven or eight miles off the Devon coast not far from Lundy. A group of Buddhist monks took the place over about four years ago. They were supposed to be refugees from Tibet, but they're part of Chen-Kuen's intelligence operations in Western Europe.'

'You're sure about this?'

He nodded vigorously. 'I've been there several times.'

'And that's where Chen-Kuen has gone now?'

'That's right. Connors Quay near Hartland Point is where he's making for.'

I thought about it all for a while standing there in the yellow light on the jetty with the rain falling. 'Did they leave the car I came in?'

'It's in the garage. Pai-Chang and I were supposed to leave in it after disposing of you.'

312

'Excellent.' I said. 'Let's get moving then.'

He backed away from me fearfully. 'You said I could go. You promised.'

'I know,' I said grimly, 'but then I'm a terrible liar. I intend to be at this place Connors Quay by morning and I've decided to take you with me, just to make sure you're telling the truth.'

There was nothing left in him at all after that and he collapsed completely, a broken man whose main difficulty was finding enough strength to place one foot in front of the other.

We were in the house for as long as it took me to help myself to dry clothes from his room and were on our way within a quarter of an hour.

8 Connors Quay

I had some sort of wild notion that it might be possible to catch Chen-Kuen and his party before they reached their destination, but that was an utter impossibility as any sober examination of the facts indicated.

Connors Quay was the best part of a hundred miles from Sidbury, but in spite of the night and the weather, it was unlikely to take more than two and a half hours to get there and they had been on the way at least an hour and a half already.

It occurred to me that there might very well be some delay before they actually put to sea and suggested as much to Pendlebury.

313

'I'm not sure,' he said, 'but it's certainly a possibility. It would depend on the tide.'

'Why should that be?'

'It's the harbour on the island itself that's the trouble. You can only get in and out at high tide. It's the reefs, you see. The whole place is surrounded by them.'

'I see—and how many are there on this place at any one time?'

He seemed to come to life at that, turning sharply to look at me. 'Between forty and fifty, but I don't think you understand. They really are what they seem to be. Zen Buddhists. They lead a scrupulously religious life against a background of strict military training, just as in the old days. A man must be ready for all things, this is their philosophy.'

'A bloody fine way of peace they seem to enjoy.'

'But that's the conventional mistake of the Westerner. You entirely misconceive the whole philosophy. There is nothing wrong in fighting for what is good and desirable. In Japan, for example, most of the samurai were Zen disciples. The Zen way was the way for the warrior.'

'Communist-Buddhist monks,' I said. 'That's a new one.'

'Even Catholic priests fight the people's war in some South American countries,' he retorted. 'What about the Dominicans, for instance? More Marxist than the Marxists themselves. Isn't that what some people say?'

'All right,' I said. 'Roll on the day, only I'll make damn certain I'm not here to see it. I've had a bellyful of your lot and their philosophy. How in the hell did you get mixed up with them, anyway? I wouldn't have thought it was your life-style.'

'I first met Master Chen-Kuen many years ago when he was a student at the London School of Economics. I was lecturing in Fine Arts at the time and studying Zen as a

314

disciple of an old Japanese master who had been living in London for some time. He introduced me to Chen-Kuen who helped me a great deal in the years that followed. I wrote several books and gained something of a reputation in the field.'

'And then he reappeared and offered you the chance to run your own show at Sidbury?'

'How did you know that?' He seemed surprised, but didn't wait for an answer and simply carried straight on. 'The trouble is I'm weak.' There was real pathos in his voice when he said that. 'My convictions have never gone very deep. I didn't like some of the things that I was drawn into, but by then it was too late. I had to do as I was told.'

'What particular piece of nastiness was he holding over your head? Young boys or public lavatories?'

I suppose I was being unnecessarily brutal under the circumstances for he flinched as if I had struck him and lapsed into silence. I suspect I was closer to the truth than I had realised.

* * *

Through Bridgwater and on to Taunton, I followed the narrow tunnel of light, darkness crowding in on either side. I drove alone with my thoughts for Pendlebury might as well have ceased to exist.

I went through it all then, starting with Tay Son and my first meeting with St. Claire, Chen-Kuen, Madame Ny—it all came crowding back in extraordinary detail, clearer even than the events of the past few days.

Then there was Helen. It occurred to me with something approaching guilt, that I hadn't really given her a great deal of thought. Hadn't even bothered to ask myself why Chen-

315

Kuen had decided to take her with him unless she was to prove some sort of sop for her brother.

And what about St. Claire? Had they passed him on already along the pipeline or was he still on the island? I think it was then that it occurred to me for the first time that if he was already on the high seas it would prove practically impossible to get him back.

*   *   *

Dawn seemed a long time in coming—grey and sombre, simply a lightening of the darkness and, in its place, a curtain of heavy rain so that when we drove through Bideford and took the coast road towards Hartland Point, it was impossible to see Lundy Island, so poor was the visibility.

Pendlebury had made no attempt to speak for some considerable time. In that grey light, his face was like a death mask, a look of complete desolation that in other circumstances might have made me feel sorry for him. He'd got into dark waters perhaps—gone in over his head and yet the cold, hard fact was that he had been prepared to act as agent in the small matter of my attempted murder. Five o'clock in the morning on the North Devon coast with the rain sweeping in from the Atlantic was no place for pity.

I found the sign for Connors Quay, turned into a narrow, winding road with hedges so high it was impossible to see over them and pulled into a small layby, cutting the engine. I lowered the window and breathed in the cold, morning air.

It was Pendlebury who spoke first, his voice as sombre as the morning. 'Mr. Jackson, are you familiar with the Chinese expression *wu*?'

I nodded, 'The whole basis of Zen Philosophy. It roughly means acquiring a new viewpoint.'

316

He said, 'Or insight, if you like. What the Japanese term *satori*.'

'So what?'

'Sitting here at the tail-end of things for the past couple of hours with nothing to do except think, it has come to me, rather forcibly, that I have been wrong all these years. These are evil people and I have been part of that evil.'

'A little late in the day for that kind of talk.'

'Perhaps.' He smiled faintly. 'But not too late for me to offer my help.'

'And I'm supposed to believe that?'

'I hope you will, but any other attitude would be perfectly understandable.'

It was the voice that was the most impressive thing. Grave, serious and very calm, certainly nothing like the play-actor I had heard addressing the audience at the end of the service at the temple. None of which meant that I wasn't going to treat him with every caution.

I said, 'All right, outline the situation for me at Connors Quay for a start.'

'There was a quarry there years ago. They used to take the stone away by sea so there's quite a substantial pier. The whole place went into a decline at the turn of the century. It's private land now. Owned by the monks.'

'Do any of them live there?'

'No, there's only one habitable house left in the place. What used to be the village inn years ago. Davo lives there.'

'Who's he?'

'The rather unpleasant individual they employ to look after things at this end. I think he's a Hungarian refugee. Came over after the rising in 1956. He runs their supplies across in a thirty foot launch and sees that trespassers aren't made welcome.'

317

'Is there a telephone?'

'Yes, at the pub, but not to the island.'

'All right,' I said. 'Let's pay him a call, shall we?'

I took the Alfa down through that winding lane for another couple of miles and finally rolled to a halt at a five-barred gate which effectively cut off further progress. A large sign said *Private—keep out* and another *Warning —Guard Dogs Loose.* The gate itself had been secured with a heavy chain and two large padlocks.

'It's another quarter of a mile from here,' he said. 'We'll have to walk.'

'So it would appear. What about the dogs?'

'An empty threat. They don't exist in fact, but it keeps the holidaymakers away in the season.'

I decided on balance to believe him for he was, after all, going with me. We climbed over the gate and started downhill along a narrow, rutted track that followed a high hedge which to a certain extent broke the impact of the rain which was being driven in from the sea by the wind with some force now.

Pendlebury said nothing for a while and then caught my arm. 'From the next hedge you can see everything.'

Another five-barred gate which this time stood open and beyond, a hillside dropping steeply towards the inlet below. Half-a-dozen ruined cottages as he had said and the old pub, smoke rising from the chimney. Beyond, the pier running well out to sea into deep water, a tangle of rusting girders. There was a thirty-foot launch moored at the far end, but no sign of life as far as I could see. At least, not on deck, although it was difficult to be certain with the heavy rain and slight sea mist.

'There's a small stream about a hundred yards to the left,' Pendlebury said. 'It drops down to the back of the pub. We could approach unseen that way.'

Which seemed sensible enough and I followed him along the line of the hedge. He was limping heavily and his breathing wasn't all that it might have been, especially when we scrambled down into a gully and followed the stream where the going was considerably rougher.

His face was damp and not only from the rain when we climbed over the bank at the bottom and crouched behind a crumbling slate wall a few yards away from the back of the pub. There was a door to the yard, four windows at ground and first floor level, staring blindly into the grey morning, the smoke from the chimney the only sign of life.

I followed the wall round the side of the pub and peered over. A man was coming along the pier, perhaps a hundred yards away carrying a sack over his shoulder. He was dressed in sea boots, an old reefer jacket and cloth cap. I couldn't see his face for he had his head bowed against the rain.

Pendlebury said, 'That's Davo. Probably just returning from running them out to the island.'

'All right,' I said. 'Let's see if we can get inside before he arrives.'

We went through a small gate in the wall, crossed the yard and tried the back door. It was locked, in fact, looked as if it hadn't been opened in years. By then, it was too late to try anything else for Davo's voice was loud and clear now and not unpleasant. A slow, sad song to go with the weather and certainly not English although whether or not it was Hungarian I wasn't qualified to say.

'We'll let him get in, then we go round to the front and you knock on the door,' I told Pendlebury. 'Then get out of the way and leave the rest to me.'

His face sagged a little, but he didn't attempt to argue. We waited until the door banged and then made our move, following the wall round the side of the pub to the front.

There was still an old wooden sign swinging from a bar above the door, the colours vivid in the morning light. Scarlet and black mainly as befitted the subject. Death himself on a throne of corpses, the fleshless face beneath the crown, a cape of ermine falling from bony shoulders. *The Death of Kings* it was called.

I nodded to Pendlebury who was looking worried. He took a deep breath and started forward and I went after him, crouching to stay beneath the level of the windows. He glanced at me hesitantly, then knocked on the door.

There was a movement inside and then the door was opened cautiously.

Pendlebury forced a smile. 'Good morning, Davo.'

There was a grunt, surprise I suppose, and then the reply came. 'You? But I don't understand.'

For once, the lesser gods smiled on me for he stepped into the open and I saw that he was holding a Luger flat against his right thigh. He sensed my presence, started to turn as I booted him in the pit of the stomach. I gave him my knee in the face for good measure and put him flat on his back.

I picked up the Luger and put it in my pocket. Pendlebury was looking at me with something close to fear on his face. 'You never do things by halves, do you, Mr. Jackson.'

'I could never see the point,' I said. 'Now let's get him inside.'

*   *   *

Davo's face was his most remarkable feature. Judas Iscariot to the life, one eye turned into the corner, the mouth like a knife slash. A face as repulsively fascinating as a mediaeval gargoyle.

We got him into a wooden chair by a deal table and I told Pendlebury to find me something to tie him with. He went out to the kitchen and returned with a length of clothes line. I lashed the Hungarian's wrists together behind the chair, then sat back and waited for him to recover.

This must have been the main room of the inn at one time. The floor was stone-flagged, the low ceiling supported by black oak beams and the stone fireplace was so large that there was an ingle-nook with a bench on either side.

There was a great driftwood fire burning there, warm and comfortable after the rawness outside, but even more interesting, a bottle of White Horse whisky on the table amongst the debris of what had presumably been last night's meal.

I poured some into a relatively clean cup, passed the bottle to Pendlebury and moved to the window to look outside. There was a telephone on the sill, Pendlebury had been telling the truth about that anyway. I swallowed some of my whisky and Davo groaned behind me.

He still didn't look too good so I went into the kitchen, filled a jug with cold water and threw it in his face. That brought him back to life with a jolt and he sat there cursing freely.

I slapped him back-handed just to get things off on the right foot which at least shut him up for a moment.

'That's better,' I said cheerfully. 'Now let's have a few answers. You've just taken Chen-Kuen and a party that included a young coloured woman across to Skerry. Am I right?'

Davo's bad eye rolled wildly as he turned his head to glare at Pendlebury. 'You're a dead man walking for this.'

I slapped him again, a little harder this time. 'I asked you a question.'

He spat in my face, hardly a pleasant sensation and certainly calculated to bring out the worst in me. There was an old three-foot iron poker standing in the hearth. I picked it up and shoved it into the flames. The abuse stopped with dramatic suddenness.

I said, 'During the past three days, I've been beaten up, drugged, committed to an institution for the criminally insane. We'll forget about the attempts on my life, they've become routine. I think you could say my patience has finally run out. I was trained in a hard school, my friend. Harder than you'll ever know. I'm going to wash my face and have another whisky, then I'll try some more conversation. The poker should be white-hot by then. Think about it.'

Pendlebury looked absolutely terrified and Davo's eyes rolled frantically as he strained against the chair. I went into the kitchen, ran the cold tap and splashed my face, then I returned to the living-room and poured another whisky. I took my time, rolling it around my mouth, more for effect than anything else for it was hardly the time of day to appreciate good Scotch.

I put down the cup and said calmly, 'Right, let's start again. You've just returned from delivering Chen-Kuen and a party that included a young coloured woman to Skerry. Am I right?'

He strained against his bonds with all his strength, face contorted with the effort and the chair suddenly went over backwards. It must have been painful for his arms were pinned underneath and he stayed there, his body still tied to the chair in a sitting position. I walked to the fire, pulled out the poker and examined it. The end foot or so glowed white-hot, incandescent. I stood over him for a moment then touched it to the chair back. The wood actually burst into flame, paint sizzled, the smell immediately apparent.

He was tough but not that tough. He let out a yell that rattled the window frames. 'Yes, yes, you're right.'

'General St. Claire—is he out there?' He frowned, fear and bewilderment mixed in his expression. 'A big man—a Negro. Quite unmistakable.'

He nodded frantically, his expression clearing. 'Yes, he came through the night before last.'

The relief was fantastic—so much so that I lowered my arm unthinkingly and the end of the poker touched the front of his jacket which flared at once.

'It's the truth,' he screamed. 'I swear it.'

I pursued my advantage. 'All right, what are they up to at the moment?'

'They're getting ready to leave.'

'Leave?' Pendlebury cut in. 'Who's leaving?'

'Everyone,' Davo said, 'I'm supposed to clear up here, then return to the island as soon as possible. We've got till nine-fifteen. They're getting the *Leopard* ready for sea now.'

I glanced at Pendlebury who said, 'The *Leopard*'s a sixty-foot ocean-going motor yacht. Panamanian registration.'

I turned back to Davo. 'What's her range?'

'Two thousand one hundred miles on full tanks at a cruising speed of twenty knots. She'll do thirty.'

Which made the whole thing about as bad as it could be. 'You said you'd got until nine-fifteen. What did you mean?'

'The tide drops like hell after that,' he said wearily. 'She'd never get over the reefs at the entrance. It's an excuse for a harbour at the best of times. The passage in through the rocks is only thirty feet wide.'

I tossed the poker into the fire, nodded to Pendlebury and we lifted him upright again, still strapped into his chair.

323

Pendlebury said. 'What are you going to do? You can't stop them. It's too late.'

'Watch him,' I said and crossed to the telephone on the window sill.

* * *

He must have been sitting beside that phone biting his nails for I only got the ringing tone for a second and then the receiver was lifted.

'Morning, Sean,' I said. 'Was it worth it?'

'Ellis, for God's sake where are you? I came home at 3 a.m. to find all hell had broken loose at Marsworth Hall. You missing and Flattery, the night nurse, gone. I'd have been down there myself by now if it hadn't been for the message you left with the porter.'

So they still hadn't found Flattery and I wondered how many times that lift had been used since I left. There was a certain grim humour in the thought but it was hardly the time to go into it.

'Now listen carefully,' I said. 'Because I'm running out of time. Get in touch with Vaughan. He's due in from Paris first thing. Tell him I've found St. Claire.'

'You've what!'

'I'm phoning from a place called Connors Quay in North Devon, near Hartland Point. There's an island about eight miles offshore called Skerry. The place is inhabited by a colony of forty or fifty Zen Buddhist monks who are supposed to be Tibetan refugees and aren't.'

'And you say St. Claire's there?'

'And his sister, only don't ask me to explain that one. I haven't got time. Tell Vaughan the man in charge is our old friend Colonel Chen-Kuen. He'll like that.'

There was a heavy silence. 'Look, are you getting all this down?'

'I don't need to. All my calls are tape recorded automatically.'

I said, 'Sean, I'm saner than I've been in months if that's what's worrying you and I haven't got time to argue the point. Chen-Kuen and his whole crowd intend to cut and run in a sixty-foot motor yacht called *Leopard*—Panamanian registration. They've only got till nine-fifteen. After that they lose the tide. You call Vaughan and tell him I'm going to hold the whole bloody crowd of them on that island till he gets there.'

'But how on earth can he manage in time?'

'Well, in Vietnam, we had a little item called the helicopter. I would have thought that the British Army, even allowing for its present depressed state, could run to two or three. And if the rest of these so-called monks are anything like the ones I've come across already, he'll need about half a company of the best assault troops he can lay his hands on. Over and out.'

I heard a final, urgent cry as I slammed down the receiver. When I turned, both Pendlebury and Davo were staring at me.

Pendlebury said, 'But this is madness. How can you hope to stop them on your own?'

'All I have to do is to prevent the *Leopard* from sailing until my friend Vaughan arrives with the cavalry.'

'And how can you possibly do that?'

'To use an apt, but rather inelegant English phrase, I'm going to block her passage.'

Out of the silence which followed, Davo said hoarsely, 'You're crazy.'

'I don't see why. We have a thirty foot wide outlet from that harbour from what you tell me and you have a thirty-foot launch at the end of the pier. The one should fit very nicely into the other, especially if we sink her in position.'

'You keep saying we,' Pendlebury said.

'I wouldn't dream of leaving you behind.' I produced the Luger and thumbed off the safety catch. 'All for one and one for all. That's my motto.'

Poor devil, he looked as if he might burst into tears at any moment, but not Davo. His face had hardened again, the eyes never left me. Now him, I would have to watch every step of the way.

9 *The run to the island*

The sea was choppy, rain squalls driven in towards the coast by a wind from the north-west and the old motor launch at the end of the pier bounced around at her moorings in a manner calculated to alarm all but the most experienced sailor.

We went down an iron staircase to the lower landing and down there, every sound seemed magnified, the waves booming beneath the lattice of rusting iron and receding again with great sucking sounds, reluctant and angry.

Pendlebury fell going over the rail, sprawling across a pile of stinking fishing nets. He staggered to his feet and looked across the inlet to the sea beyond where the waves were lifting into whitecaps, line upon line of them marching out of the mist and rain.

'You don't like it, eh?' Davo laughed hoarsely. 'Better get used to it. Likely to get worse before it gets better.'

I gave him a shove towards the wheelhouse. 'Get this thing moving. Try anything funny and I'll put a bullet through your knee-cap just for starters.'

There didn't seem much point in asking Pendlebury to help for he already looked about as ill as it was possible to be and squatted by the stern rail. I cast off from the deck for it suddenly occurred to me that the lines wouldn't be needed any more anyway.

The engines coughed into life at the same moment and as we left the shelter of the pier, waves started to slap against the hull and I could feel the vibration beneath my feet in the deck itself.

We heeled over as Davo increased speed and ploughed through that carpet of white water towards the mouth of the inlet. It was only when we actually moved out into open waters that the force of the wind was felt as great rain squalls thundered in towards the cliffs. The launch almost came to a dead halt, faltered, then started forward again as Davo increased power and the engine note deepened.

We ploughed on, bouncing across a continuous pattern of steep waves, water cascading across the deck. The wheelhouse was completely open to the stern deck and I stood to one side and hung on to a rail, the Luger ready in the other hand, close enough to Davo to watch what he was up to, but too far away to be rushed.

Pendlebury was sick over the rail a couple of times and finally staggered towards me. 'I think I'd better go low.'

'Nothing doing.' I gave him a push that sent him to the pile of fishing nets. 'You stay there where I ca an eye on you.'

Davo could handle a boat all right, I'll say that for him, for he varied his engine speed frequently to meet the constantly changing conditions in a way that showed he knew his business.

We were three miles out before we could see Skerry and the island was constantly obscured by rain as squall after

327

squall raced in. Gradually things jumped into focus as we drew nearer. Black cliffs streaked with guano, breakers pounding in at their base.

Davo altered course and the other side of the island drifted into view, a great, rambling house standing in beech trees just below the rim of a hill, a Gothic monstrosity with mock turrets and so many chimneys it was impossible to count them. It had been built on the high tide of Victorian prosperity and a considerable amount of planting had been done at the same time, pine trees flooding up out of every gully and hollow.

The boat was rolling badly, so turbulent was the water. Davo hung on to the wheel, playing every trick of the current, but Pendlebury was in acute distress, sprawled across the nets, hanging on for dear life.

That particular squall raced past us and as we turned in towards the inlet below the house we were momentarily in quieter water.

Davo altered course another point. 'All right, what happens when we get there?'

I knew enough about small boat sailing to be on reasonably firm ground. I said, 'We take her in nice and easy. As soon as we're into the passage, cut the engine and I'll put anchor over. Then we open the sea-cocks.'

'It won't work,' he said. There'll be one hell of a swell in there.'

'It better,' I said firmly. 'If she breaks through into the harbour there'll be a dead man at the wheel.'

He glanced sideways, that eye of his rolling again and saw from my face, I suppose, that I meant it.

'And what happens to us?'

'We swim for it.'

He shook his head. 'Not a chance without life-jackets.'

328

Which was reasonable enough. 'All right, where are they?'

'The locker behind you.'

I opened it, keeping a close eye on him, pulled three or four out and got one over my head, one-handed. When Pendlebury reached for another I stamped on his hand.

'Not yet—you two get yours at the right moment and only if you behave yourself.'

Davo's jaw tightened, but it was Pendlebury who reacted most strongly. 'But I can't swim, Jackson.'

His words were taken away as another squall swept over the waves, rain bouncing across the deck like bullets. The boat yawed, almost turning broadside on. Davo fought to control her as a curtain of green water washed over us, sending Pendlebury across the deck into the starboard rail.

We were very close now, those black cliffs towering above us, birds wheeling in great clouds, razorbills, gulls, shags and a storm petrel swept low over the wheelhouse and up through the spray.

The sea was running in towards the inlet like a river in spate, turning over on itself constantly, washing over green-black rocks and I could see what he meant about the passage. A breakwater of giant blocks of masonry curved round on either side over the reef. The gap between was narrow enough to take the breath away.

But there was no time for qualms now—only action. He dropped his speed for the final run in and the sea caught us in its grip relentlessly.

Davo cried above the roaring, 'No good. I need more speed to control her.'

I held on tight with my left hand and raised the Luger, taking deliberate aim. 'I meant what I said. Do exactly as I told you or I'll blow your head off.'

'But we'll all be killed,' Pendlebury screamed and then, as the boat rolled wildly and plunged in towards the passage he flung himself at me.

He clawed at my left arm and as I flung him away, Davo made his move, turning to grab at the Luger. I shot him twice in the body at point blank range, the force lifting him back against the side of the wheelhouse.

The wheel spun like a mad thing, the boat turned broadside on and the sea simply took us in its giant hand and tossed us into that narrow opening. I grabbed hard at the nearest rail with both hands out of sheer self-preservation, the Luger going its own way and a second later the launch smashed into the end of one of the piers.

The hull splintered like matchwood, the sea pulled us out again with a dreadful sucking sound the launch almost standing up on end and I rolled helplessly down the steeply inclined deck and went over the stern into the sea.

It was the life-jacket which saved me. I surfaced in time to see the launch swept in again, high on a crest that smashed it down hard across the rocks at the foot of the sea wall, the stern jutting out across the entrance to the harbour.

Not quite what I had intended, but just as effective. Men were running along the wall now, saffron robes vivid against the grey. They weren't going to be pleased with what they found, but that didn't concern me. I had other things to think about.

I was caught in a current of considerable strength that took me away from the harbour in a great curve, bearing me out beyond the point and round to the other side parallel to the shore and perhaps fifty yards out.

On such a course, I could inevitably drift past the island altogether into the wide Atlantic, America next stop, but it was not to be for with something of an anti-climax, the current changed course abruptly, swinging in towards a wide bay at the foot of the cliffs.

Not that I was to be let off too lightly. A wall of water, green as bottle glass, smashed down on me, driving me under the surface. I went deep, too deep, fighting for life like a fish on a hook.

I surfaced in a sea of white water, gasping for air and went under again as another wall of water rushed in. My foot kicked sand or shingle, something solid at any rate and I found myself sprawling across a great, round boulder streaming with water, seaweed all around.

Another wave bowled me over. My hands found a jagged edge of rock, held on fast. As the sea receded again, I lurched forward across the rocks, stumbling like a drunken man and fell on my face on a strip of the softest, purest, whitest sand I have ever known at the base of the cliffs.

* * *

The sea still roared inside my head when I stood up, the earth moved beneath my feet which was hardly surprising. I got the life-jacket off, pushed it down out of sight behind some stones, then examined the cliffs.

They were nothing like as perpendicular as they had seemed from the sea, sloping gently backwards at one point, cracked and fissured by great gullies. It was an easy enough climb and I emerged on a round shoulder of rock about a hundred feet above the beach within five or six minutes. From there it was no more than a strenuous scramble over grass and tilted slabs of black stone. I slowed to approach the edge with caution perhaps ten minutes after leaving the beach.

I found myself twenty or thirty yards from the edge of a stand of pines. There didn't seem to be anyone about so I put down my head and ran for cover.

It was quiet in there as pine woods often are, the trees crowding closely together, their branches intermingled so that not much of the rain was managing to get through. I paused to catch my breath, then started to move in the general direction of the harbour.

Within a couple of minutes I was able to see the house and then the trees started to peter out which made things awkward for there was a good fifty yards of clear ground to the nearest point from which I would be able to see down into the inlet, and yet I had to know what was going on down there.

A slight fold in the ground provided me with some sort of cover and took me half-way. I crawled from that point through the wet grass, not that it made much difference for I was soaked to the skin already.

The view from the edge was more than interesting. The launch was hard on the rocks at the base of the breakwater, her stern partially under the water, but virtually blocking the entrance. There were at least two dozen monks down there and others running down the twisting road from the house to join them.

Several were at the edge of the breakwater directly above the boat, obviously making an attempt to assess the situation. The *Leopard* was tied up to a jetty well inside the harbour where the water was comparatively calm, a beautiful boat in blue and white that looked capable of crossing the Atlantic if necessary.

There was a sudden commotion amongst the monks, voices drifted up, blown by the wind. They clustered at the edge of the breakwater above the rocks, someone produced a rope. I saw it snake out over the edge, presumably to the rocks to one side of the launch which were out of my sight.

One of the monks went over himself. There was a short pause, then several laid hands on the line. After a while, Rafe Pendlebury appeared.

They had him on his back for some time, working in relays, obviously pumping the water out of him and then a rather startling thing happened. There was a clattering of hooves and I glanced up to see three or four monks riding down from the house, mounted on what looked like sturdy Welsh mountain ponies. The most interesting thing was that Chen-Kuen was in the lead.

As the crowd parted on the breakwater to let him through, the men working over Pendlebury hauled him into a sitting position and one of them started to thump him vigorously in the back. Chen-Kuen dismounted and crouched beside him.

None of this, of course, made the future any too bright as far as I was concerned, for whichever way you looked at it, once he'd heard Pendlebury's story, he'd come looking for me, hoping with all his heart that I had survived to reach the shore so that he could see to me himself.

It was time to get moving, but to where? It was obvious that they'd be starting to scour the island within minutes, particularly this section of the cliff. I think it was then, as I started back towards the line of trees, that it occurred to me that the safest place to be during the next couple of hours might be the house itself, or at least within its grounds. Certainly the last place they would consider looking for a while.

Which meant getting there while most of them were still down on the breakwater. I ran into the shelter of the trees, pushing my way through the close knit branches towards the far side for it had become apparent to me that this particular section stretched on a course parallel with the shape of the cliffs above the inlet, dropping down behind the house itself. If I kept to the trees all the way, it would take forever, but once through to clear ground on the other side and using them as a shield, I could make much faster progress.

God, but it was a tangle and I pushed through, head down, branches tearing at my head. As I neared the edge, I heard a horse whinny, the stamp of hooves and paused, going on with extreme caution. It was only a herd of twenty or thirty of those shaggy mountain ponies, grazing together in a tight group—or so I thought.

As I moved into the open, two or three of the ponies nearest to me shied, setting the whole herd stamping nervously. I started to run along the edge of the trees and immediately became aware of the drumming of hooves in the rear.

Presumably he'd been acting as some sort of herdsman, though God knows where he'd been hiding—probably sheltering from the rain in the trees at the edge of the wood. He certainly looked the part for he was wearing a great sheepskin *shuba* belted at the waist, a garment habitually worn by Tibetan monks in cold weather and a conical sheepskin hat with ear flaps.

I made it into the trees with a final lung-bursting rush. He almost had me, but amongst those closely packed pines, he was at something of a disadvantage. The strange thing was that he didn't seem to be carrying a gun, only a sword with an ivory handle which hung under his left armpit, suspended by a sling from around his neck. He drew it suddenly, urging the pony on, slashing at the branches before him to clear his way.

He was perhaps three or four yards to my rear and I turned suddenly, doubled back to the left of him, ran in from the side, grabbed his foot and heaved him from the saddle.

334

There was a certain amount of confusion for a few moments after that. I flung myself under the pony's belly, one hand reaching for the herdsman's throat, the other for his sword-hand for he'd hung on to that tight enough.

Not that he could do much damage with it in those circumstances for it was a good three feet long, curving wickedly—an excellent specimen of the ancient Chinese blade of which the Japanese *samurai* sword is a copy. A terrifying weapon in the hands of a trained *kendo* swordsman, but not much use when threshing about on the ground at close quarters.

In any case, I chopped him across the throat with the edge of my hand the moment I got close which quietened him effectively enough.

The pony was certainly well trained for he had stopped dead a yard or two away and stood waiting, pawing the ground nervously with one hoof. I thought about it for at least one full second, then did what seemed the obvious thing and started to undress my friend on the floor.

The sheepskin *shuba* and the hat with the ear flaps were all that I needed for, although they both stank abominably, they would provide me with as effective a disguise as I could wish for, at least at a distance.

I took his sword, sheathed it and slipped the sling over my neck. He was still alive when I left him although I must admit he didn't look good. But I had other things on my mind as I grabbed the pony's bridle and pushed him on through the trees into the open.

I urged him up the slope on a course diagonal to the line of the trees. Immediately, the whole herd of ponies came after me, several streaking past, heads down. The rain blew in from the sea in great gusting clouds. Cutting visibility, so that it was something of a shock when a number of horsemen streamed over the crest of the hill and galloped along the skyline.

They were half-obscured by the rain, yellow robes vivid against the grey like something out of an old Chinese water colour painting. I raised one hand in a half-salute and kept on going, thankful that the ponies had chosen to follow me. The riders faded to the left and I went over the crest and plunged down towards the trees at the back of the house.

The ponies milled around me, pushing and snorting, the smell of them heavy on the damp air as I jumped to the ground. I smacked my mount hard across the rump sending it cantering back the way we had come. The others followed and I moved into the trees.

A grey stone wall about five feet in height divided the woods from the gardens surrounding the house. I scrambled over and dropped into the clump of rhododendrons. Everything was in excellent order, leaves raked into symmetrical piles, paths tidied, grass neatly trimmed. All as I would have expected in a place run by people who looked upon work of any description as being not only a moral obligation, but an act of worship.

I worked my way closer to the house which was not particularly difficult for the banks of rhododendrons gave excellent cover. I finally halted in the shelter of an old summer house. It had the general air of decay common to such places long disused. Rain drifted in through a broken pane of glass, cobwebs glistened in each dark corner. A faint uneasy stirring, a memory of childhood perhaps as I crouched there.

Poor little Ellis Jackson taking on the whole world again. I managed some sort of a smile at that one and got to my feet. I could stay where I was, keep under cover till Vaughan and his men arrived or try the house, which was certainly the most interesting prospect.

It seemed to be waiting for me, crouched there in the rain. If I was going to make a move, it would have to be a bold one, so I stood up, walked briskly along the path till I came to the courtyard at the rear of the building. I pulled the sheepskin cap down as far as it would go and started across.

When I was half-way there, the door opened, I veered sharply to my left, walking at exactly the same pace towards what looked like the stable block. I was aware of two monks emerging from the door. I kept on going. The entrance to the stable block was a great iron-bound door, obviously large enough to allow a carriage through, but there was the usual judas gate set in it and I stepped inside.

There were entrances off the tunnel to left and right containing rows of stalls. I could smell the ponies, hear the odd stamp as an animal moved nervously. The tunnel emptied into a large central hall with a domed roof which had presumably been either a carriage-house or, more probably, an indoor riding school at one time.

That it was now used for a different purpose was perfectly obvious. There were rifle racks along one wall containing not only AK47s but several MI6s, ammunition belts complete with bayonets in scabbard and a couple of M79 grenade launchers which I presumed were just for show until I noticed the belts of grenades hanging from pegs above them.

Even more interesting was the row of life-sized dummies hanging in a line parallel with the rear wall, each one a replica of an American G.I. right down to his jungle green fatigues. They had all been bayoneted dozens of times.

I helped myself to an AK47, loaded it and buckled an

ammunition belt about my waist, then moved back along the tunnel to the main entrance and opened the door cautiously. The courtyard was deserted, so I stepped out and crossed to the house again.

The rear door opened into a dark, stone-flagged corridor of the type usually found in a house of that sort leading from the kitchens to the residential area.

I moved along it cautiously, pausing at a green baize door at the far end, the kind you find only in England and nowhere else. It went with weekend house parties, tinkling ice in tall glasses, people seeking a fourth for bridge. I stifled an insane desire to laugh as I put my ear to that door and listened.

I tried it carefully, peering out through the crack and looked into a fairly large hall floored with black and white Dutch tiles, a wide oak staircase giving access to the second floor.

But at that, the resemblance to any other English country house faded. The walls were hung with dragon tapestries and the niche which had probably been originally intended for an Italian marble statue now contained the usual gold-painted figure of Buddha and the air was heavy with the smell of the incense that burned in the brass bowl in front of it.

I hesitated, debating whether to carry straight on or not when an astonishing thing happened. A door opened in the gloom of the corridor on the far side and Helen St. Claire appeared.

She was dressed exactly as I had last seen her in slacks and sweater. She looked tired, very tired, and clenched and unclenched her hands nervously. I noticed that particularly.

The two Chinese with her wore dark trousers and Guernsey sweaters and each had an ammunition belt, twin to my own, strapped about his waist and carried an assault rifle. They went up the main staircase. I waited until they reached the landing and went after them.

The main corridor was deserted when I got up there myself, but there were voices talking in Chinese at the other end. A moment later, I heard someone coming and barely had time to dodge into a small dead-end corridor out of sight. One of the two guards went past and descended the stairs quickly. I gave him a moment or so to get out of the way, then started along the corridor in search of Helen.

When I peered round the corner at the end, I found the other guard standing outside a mahogany door. I didn't really get much chance to consider what to do next—it was decided for me by the man himself turning his back to peer out of a nearby window. Such a chance was obviously not to be misused so I stepped close behind him and tried a simple *shime-waza*, a strangle hold which clamped across his carotid artery and had him unconscious in seconds.

I left him there on the floor for the moment for there wasn't much else I could do and tried the door handle, the AK ready for action under one arm, finger on the trigger. The door opened gently and I slipped inside.

It was an airy, rather pleasant room with pale yellow wallpaper, white curtains billowing in the breeze from the open window. There was a bed in one corner and a desk over by the window. Helen St. Claire stood in front of it —her brother sat behind.

*   *   *

In a way, it was as if she ceased to exist for a moment. He sat there staring at me dressed in the same kind of Guernsey sweater as the guards only a size too small, a look of utter astonishment on his face.

'Oh, no, Ellis,' I heard Helen say.

And then he smiled, that famous St. Claire smile that made him unique, himself alone and like no other man on top of the earth—and jumped to his feet, the chair falling backwards.

'Well, damn me, boy, but it's about time.'

'I'd have thought you long gone by now,' I said. 'They must have put something in your tea.'

But they hadn't if the way he came round that desk in a rush was anything to go by. It was Tay Son all over again and I was more pleased to see him than I would have thought possible.

I put out my hand to meet his and, when he was close enough, he kicked me in the stomach with everything he had and I went down like a tree falling.

10 Black Max

I didn't lose consciousness—simply fought for air as I writhed on the floor, the centre of a dark agony, eyes tight shut. Helen was on her knees beside me, I was aware of that because I could smell her perfume, recognise that cool hand. As for St. Claire, there was no answer to that—not for the moment—none that made sense.

When I opened my eyes, the faces above me were a meaningless blur. I closed them again, felt myself being picked up and carried across the room to be dumped in a chair.

After a while my mouth was forced open and brandy poured down my throat. Only a little, but it burned and I started to cough. A hand pounded me between the shoulder blades and St. Claire laughed.

'Keep going, boy, you'll make it.'

I surfaced again and found him sitting on the edge of the desk. He grinned, a kind of admiration on his face and shook his head. 'Christ, Ellis, but you're indestructible.'

I ignored him and turned to Helen who was standing at the other end of the desk, nothing but despair on her face. 'Are you all right?' I asked her.

She simply dissolved into tears, something I had never known her do before, sobbing helplessly, her whole body shaking. St. Claire went to her at once, gathered her into those great arms, stroked her hair and spoke in a low, soothing voice, words that I could not hear.

I threw a quick glance over my shoulder to discover the other guard standing there, clutching a machine pistol, so any ideas I might have had about making a run for it were smartly nipped in the bud. In any event, at the same moment, the door opened and Chen-Kuen entered. He wore untanned leather riding boots, a saffron robe that fell just below his knee and a quilted, wide-sleeved *shuba* over it in black. Completely mediaeval, imposing, vital looking, he dominated the room instantly.

He nodded to St. Claire. 'Take her next door, Max. I'll send for you when I want you.'

St. Claire did exactly as he was told, going out instantly, one arm about his sister's shoulders.

Chen-Kuen told the guard to wait outside, speaking in Chinese this time, then sat on the edge of the desk and looked at me, a slight frown on his face, of concern more

341

than anything else. His right hand, I noticed, was inside his robe.

'Are you all right?'

'I'll survive.'

He smiled at that. 'One must admit you seem to have a flair for doing just that. There is a Zen saying: When a lioness gives birth to cubs, after three days she pushes them over a cliff to see if they can get back.'

'To hell with that kind of talk,' I said. 'Let's have some facts. I'd say I've earned them. As St. Claire obviously isn't here under any kind of duress, I presume he's been working for you?'

'Exactly.' He sat down behind the desk and helped himself to a cigarette from an ivory box, his right hand still inside the robe.

There was a kind of iron band around my head that seemed to be squeezing tighter by the second. The pain was quite intense so that thinking, clear, rational thinking at any rate, which was what I needed now, was extraordinarily difficult.

I said, 'So that's why he had to die? Presumably because they were finally on to him?'

He nodded. 'And dead, or at least supposed dead, he would have been rather more use to us, as I'm sure you will understand.'

'Are you trying to tell me he broke out there in Tay Son? That you had your way with him?' I shook my head. 'No, that isn't possible. I was there. I was with him. I knew what was happening.'

'My dear Ellis, if you mean did I succeed in brainwashing him into becoming a dedicated Marxist, the answer is no. It was not possible with his psychological type and there was no need.'

'I don't understand.'

'It's simple enough. To use a popular American phrase, St. Claire's one great need is to be where the action is. To hold the centre of the stage. To perform violent, spectacular deeds, to live dangerously. Call it what you will. Strangely enough in view of his past—I refer mainly to his military record now—he does not need an audience, but he does have an obsessional need for danger and excitement. Obsession, as you know, may take many forms. Various kinds of sexual aberration, for example, strange needs which simply cannot be denied by the subject.'

'And you're trying to tell me that St. Claire has just as total an obsession for action, violence and so on?'

'It explains his whole life. There is, of course, an element of self-destruction involved, suicidal, if you like, which he fails to recognise himself. I discovered all this quite early in our relationship at Tay Son. The rest was easy.'

The whole had been delivered in a careful academic tone as if he were back at university holding a tutorial or seminar.

I said, 'You'll have to spell it all out for me.'

'He was dead, Ellis. To the world outside, he had been killed in action. I pointed this out to him. Told him he would be sent to China and held in solitary confinement for the rest of his days.'

'And the alternative was to agree to work for you?'

'Exactly—to go back to the outside world, a hero if possible and work for us.'

'But he didn't need to do it,' I said. 'How could you possibly guarantee that he would play the game your way once he was free?'

'It was worth the chance. To discredit him would have been simplicity itself.' He shrugged. 'We could have released tape recordings of various conversations, signed

343

documents, that sort of thing. Even if all these had been dismissed as a communist plot, the mud would have stuck. He would have been finished in real terms. Still employed by the army perhaps for the sake of appearances, but in some backwater job of that type that would have driven a man like him out of his mind. In any case, there was no need for threats. He began to enjoy it, Ellis. He discovered that it was, as you English say, just his cup of tea. A new thrill, if you like, for a man who had tried everything else there was to try. To pit his wits against the intelligence departments of every country in the NATO alliance, which was what he was eventually doing. To make fools of them all.'

'Only some of the time presumably.'

He shook his head. 'No, he was quite brilliant, I must give him that although I have always detested the man. In the end he was betrayed by a defector from our own side. Even then, both the CIA and British intelligence discounted the suggestion as a fabrication at first.'

So even Vaughan had been less than honest with me? Poor little Ellis Jackson indeed. I was beginning to feel rather angry, but there was one thing I still had to know. In a way, the most important item of all.

I said, 'Where did I fit in to all this? Way back, I mean?'

'In Vietnam?' He nodded. 'I wondered when you would get round to that. You were used from the beginning, I should imagine that must have got through to you by now. Frankly, Ellis, you were something of a godsend to us. Exactly the right man at the right time. We were doubly lucky in that your psychological pattern, which I'm sure you'll be the first to agree is hardly normal, was just right. Black Max was exactly what you needed and you, in turn, were exactly the right companion for his spectacular escape. You confirmed to the world so beautifully what a

344

hero he'd been—how he had stood firm against everything they'd done to him.'

I was surprised I could still talk. 'And later, when he found me in London again?'

'By design—all arranged. He always thought you might be useful so he persuaded me to provide you with just what you needed—Sheila Ward.'

'Another Madame Ny?'

'If you like. She was killed in Hanoi in an air raid six months ago, by the way, if you're still interested.'

'She can rot in hell for all I care.'

I shouted at him, hands clenched, taking a quick step forward. His hand came out of the robe holding some sort of automatic pistol.

I said, 'Do you want to know something rather funny? I always rather liked you.'

'And I you. Nothing personal, Ellis, you understand that. I have my duty. I serve a great cause. The greatest in the world. The people's cause.'

'Always your bloody cause,' I said. 'You're all the same, both sides of the bloody fence, nothing to choose between you.' I laughed in his face. 'You've lost out this time, by God, at least I'll have that consolation.'

'I don't think so. Friend Pendlebury came ashore on the rocks by the breakwater so I know all about your telephone call to London—the time element involved.' He got to his feet and walked to the window. 'You tried, Ellis, and you lost. See for yourself.'

There were about forty of them down there heaving on a double line which snaked over the breakwater and was presumably attached to the wrecked launch and the *Leopard* was manœuvring her way into the outlet channel, obviously with the idea of trying a little pushing.

'We'll be on our way within half-an-hour, all of us.' He

345

patted me on the shoulder. 'You'll go with us, of course. I was foolish to leave you behind at Sidbury. Your particular virtues are hard to come by. We'll find a use for you, never fear. And now I must go down to the harbour to hurry them along.'

I really did think that I was going crazy then. I suppose it was his calmness, the cool assumption that having realised I had lost, I would be a good boy from now on and do the sensible thing.

He opened the door and as he went out, the guard stepped back in. The door closed and I returned to the window and looked down at the harbour. As I watched, the launch actually moved, the stern lifting out of the water and the *Leopard* started to inch forward.

Behind me, the door opened and, when I turned, St. Claire stood there, Helen at his shoulder.

* * * *

In that first moment, in that one fixed point in time I could have killed him—would have done if a gun had come to hand and Chen-Kuen's words returned to haunt me. *Black Max* was exactly what I had needed, wasn't that what he had said? Not Brigadier-General James Maxwell St. Claire, but Black Max, every boy's fantasy figure. The father I'd never known. There, it was out.

And I think he knew something had broken deep inside for his face, when he came forward, was deadly serious.

He raised a hand as if he thought I would rush him. 'Let's get one thing straight, Ellis. Helen knew nothing about it. Okay?'

'I loved you, do you know that?' It was a howl of agony straight up from my guts. 'You were everything I never had. A god on earth. And you used me. You never gave a

346

damn from the first to the last. You stood by while they set me up for a criminal lunatic—tried to drive me clean out of my wits.'

His eyes widened in utter astonishment and in that single tiny moment of truth, I saw into the heart of the man. The tremendous ego that made him incapable of seeing anything in any other terms except those of self. No love here, not for anyone, even Helen, certainly not for me and perhaps not even for himself in the final analysis.

And now came the attempt at self-justification. 'You know what happens when you get the Congressional? Well, I'll tell you, boy. That's it.' He made a cutting motion through the air between us. 'Finish. All washed-up. I'd rather be you than me, says the President. Your country loves you. No more action for you, boy. No, not ever.'

'What's this supposed to be, an excuse?' I yelled.

'I sat on my arse in the Pentagon for five years after Korea. Five more at Staff College, instructing. When that chance came to go to Vietnam as a member of the President's own commission. To smell a little powder again . . .'

I punched him in the mouth with all my strength, hard enough to rock even him, sending him staggering back into the guard at the door.

The whole thing had been quite unpremeditated, a completely spontaneous gesture of rage and frustration, but the results were more than I could have hoped if the whole thing had been by design.

St. Claire lost his footing and cannoned into the guard who grabbed frantically at the wall in an effort to keep his balance and succeeded in dropping his rifle in the process. A hound dog couldn't have descended on a rabbit any faster than I snapped up that AK. I drove the butt into the side of the guard's skull and rammed the muzzle into

St. Claire's face as he scrambled on to one knee.

Helen gave a terrible cry, a hand to her mouth, imagining I suppose, that I would kill him there and then. She rushed in at me and I sent her back against the wall with a stiff right arm.

'I'm leaving now,' I told St. Claire, 'And I'm taking her with me. If you want me and I think I can assure you you will, I'll be waiting out there in the woods somewhere. When you come looking, we'll see just how good you really are.'

He opened his mouth to speak and I reversed the rifle and struck him a heavy blow in the side of the neck with the butt.

Helen opened her mouth to cry and as he slumped to the floor, I slapped her heavily across the face. 'None of that. You do exactly as you're told from now on, understand me?'

I shoved her out into the corridor ahead of me and closed the door.

I think that was the beginning of a kind of madness, a black, killing rage. Utter humiliation was the root cause, I suppose. All my life I had never known what it was to have a real relationship with anyone. Sold down the river at every turn. Madame Ny, Sheila Ward, and now Black Max St. Claire. Poor little Ellis Jackson indeed. Well, we'd bloody well see about that.

If anyone had tried to stop me, I'd simply have shot my way through, but the house was quiet as we went down the stairs, everyone, I suppose, being down at the breakwater helping with the launch. I ran across the yard to the stable block, dragging her behind me by the hand. As I shoved her ahead of me, she was sobbing hysterically.

I went straight to the weapon racks and helped myself to an ammunition belt complete with bayonet which I

348

buckled about my waist after checking that I'd got the right one. Next I draped two belts of grenades around my neck and slung one of the M79 grenade launchers over my shoulder.

Helen had sunk down on the floor against the wall apparently exhausted. I hauled her to her feet and shook her. 'Come on, let's get moving.'

She seemed completely bewildered. 'But I don't understand. What can you possibly hope to do on your own?'

'Show these bastards how to fight a war,' I said and I picked up an AK assault rifle and pushed her towards the door.

I followed the same route out as I had used on the way in, through the rhododendron bushes and over the stone wall to the meadow beyond.

From then on, something happened that can't be explained in purely physical terms. It was as if I had forgotten what fatigue was and was possessed of limitless energy. I ran across that meadow towards the pine trees without flagging, dragging her behind me and when we reached their shelter, it was Helen who sobbed for breath.

I suppose I'd gone *berserk* in a way, just like the old Norsemen and a furious energy bubbled up inside me, God knows from where.

I pushed Helen along in front of me through the trees and she cried out in pain as branches flailed at her face, but I had no time for pity. When we came out on the other side, there was the usual twenty or thirty yards of open ground to the edge of the cliff. I dragged her down on her hands and knees and made her crawl like an animal, great sobs tearing at her throat, towards an outcrop of rock on a small point a few yards away.

It sloped upwards, no more than three feet off the

ground at the highest point, forming a natural breastwork and beyond was the inlet.

I laid out the AK and several clips of ammunition. Next came the M79 and lastly, the two pouches of six grenades each. I pushed Helen down flat and peered over the edge of the rock.

I wasn't a moment too soon. The combined efforts of the monks hauling on the lines and the *Leopard* using her prow as a ram had almost succeeded in their object. The launch had been pushed partially away from the gap between the two breakwaters. The *Leopard* was almost through although she was being thrown about in the heavy swell.

I slithered back down the rock and extracted the first grenade from its pouch. To my horror, it was a smoke grenade designed to be fired by the M79, but no earthly use for my purpose. The other belt contained what I was seeking, which was something, although I was now reduced to six instead of the twelve I had intended.

The M79 grenade launcher is breech-loading and in a way, resembles a sawn-off shot-gun. It fires a rather lethal cartridge-type grenade with high fragmentation on impact. I wasn't too sure about the range from here, but the height I was firing from would help considerably. I shoved one up the spout, aimed for the *Leopard*, resting the barrel on the edge of the rock and fired.

I could actually follow the progress of the grenade through the air. It overshot the *Leopard* and landed on the rocks behind the launch. The effect was all that I could have wished for. A couple of monks fell over the edge of the breakwater and pieces of the launch's hull lifted lazily into the air.

But it was the *Leopard* I was after and I had missed. I remembered the old deer-stalking maxim from boyhood, the general at his best and teaching me to shoot. *Always aim high when firing downhill.*

The second grenade landed between the breakwater and the *Leopard*, the explosion putting a hole in her hull the size of a house door. The third bounced on the stern and the deck disintegrated in a great scarlet mushroom as the fuel tank exploded.

She sank like a stone a few seconds later.

*   *   *

It had all happened so quickly, this thunderbolt descending, that those on the breakwater were still in utter confusion. I had no time to look for Chen-Kuen personally, just hoped that he was down there as I aimed another grenade on the breakwater itself.

It took out six or seven monks at one fell swoop, bodies hurtling backwards into the harbour. They certainly scattered after that. The fifth grenade did nothing like as much damage. It was round about then that shots started to come back in our direction so I dropped the M79 and tried the AK47.

Most of the monks were running up the hill towards the house. I picked off a couple who were well up in front and that really did it. Men scattered in all directions. Within a couple of minutes, there didn't really seem to be anyone left on view at all.

After that, the bullets started to fly thick and fast. I think I knew from the beginning that such a position would not really be tenable for very long. What really decided me was Helen. She had been lying crouched close to the earth, her face turned towards me, absolutely terrified.

Now, she gave a sudden sharp cry and clapped a hand to her cheek. It was either a ricochet or perhaps a splinter

351

of rock, but in any event, she had a nasty gash, bone-deep, blood pouring through her fingers.

I slung the grenade launcher over my shoulder, the pouches around my neck, grabbed her by the arm and ran for the cover of the woods.

11 Seek and destroy

Helen was in no condition to go anywhere, but I urged her on, following the line of the woods for a couple of hundred yards or so, but it was no good. She just didn't have the strength and constantly stumbled so that it was a physical effort to keep her upright.

We cut through the trees and paused beside a low stone wall. Somewhere not too far away, I heard voices calling, the sound of hoofbeats.

The game was afoot with a vengeance for they were hopelessly trapped on this island till Vaughan got here. Nowhere to run. Nothing to do except run Ellis Jackson into the ground. Well, if that's what they wanted, they could have it. I'd been in worse places and survived.

With a sudden rush, a dozen or so horsemen cantered over the hill to the right and crossed our field of vision. They were all wearing monk's robes except for St. Claire who was in the lead, mounted on a pony like the rest although it seemed ridiculously small for him.

Helen moaned as if about to cry out and I got a hand to her mouth to close it. The hoofbeats faded into the rain and I released her.

The blood on her cheek was congealing now. She

fumbled in her pocket and found a handkerchief which she rolled into a pad and held against the wound.

'All right,' I said. 'Let's move out.'

She said weakly, 'Even now, here at the final end of things, you can't tell the difference between fantasy and reality. You still believe you can take on the whole world and win.'

'It's all I've had to hang on to since I was eight years old. Now get on your bloody feet and move.'

I pulled her up and shoved her in front of me, pushing her into a stumbling run, out into the open across the meadow for that fringe of pine wood at the edge of the cliff above the inlet was one place they would turn inside out. To venture into open country would be unlooked for and it is the unexpected that succeeds in war. We laboured up to the crest of the hill and I pushed her down into a small hollow and crouched beside her.

They were calling now on every side down there in the hollow, beating through the trees to flush me out like a shooting party out for a morning's sport.

Beyond the crest of the slope on which we lay there was a long, sloping hillside of sparse grass, no cover anywhere, but on top was a circle of stones, one of those legacies of the Bronze Age so common in the west country. It was obvious standing out there for the whole world to see on top of that mound and therefore the last place they would think of looking, or so it seemed to me then.

I said to Helen, 'Take a deep breath and get ready to run. We've got about three hundred yards to go. I don't want to end up by dragging you by your hair, but I will if I have to.'

She made no comment, simply got to her feet and stumbled forward, clutching the handkerchief to her cheek. We were in maximum danger all the way of course—completely in the open—no place to hide if anyone should appear. It needed luck and we got it, for suddenly the wind started to drive the rain in across the cliffs again in great solid sheets, cutting down visibility considerably.

We made it into the standing circle and dropped down into cover and, below, the wind ripped rain and mist away to disclose more horsemen on the fringe of the woods.

'That's what I call timing,' I told her.

She crouched against one of the standing stones, the pad to her face, the eyes very wide and filled with pain. 'You could have killed Max down there—picked him off as he rode past. Why didn't you?'

'I'm saving him for later.'

I rammed a full clip into the AK. She said in a hoarse voice, 'What kind of man are you to kill so easily—so terribly?'

'Ask him,' I said. 'Ask Black Max. He made me what I am if anyone did.'

She shook her head. 'No, I can't accept that. Each man is responsible for his own destiny.'

'I bet that sounds good in those lectures you give at the Sorbonne. Does it excuse your brother's conduct, by the way? Murderer, renegade, traitor. Or didn't he tell you?'

She broke down completely then and slid to the ground, her face pillowed in the wet grass. She would never be able to condemn him, I saw that now—had always known, I suppose. She loved the man—worshipped him with every fibre of her being. To have suggested that love was possibly incestuous would have been to make it entirely too superficial. This thing went far beyond that.

And yet I could feel no pity. I was long past that. I wanted to see them all in hell—to suffer as I had suffered. As for St. Claire, it seemed to me then that thirty years of some kind of penal servitude or other would do very well

—the least they'd give him. A bullet would be much too easy.

I wanted all these things so much that I could taste them and as I have said, I think that by then, I was more than a little mad—hardly surprising in view of what had happened. I gazed up into the grey morning praying for Vaughan and somewhere a pony whinnied.

There was a group of them crossing the curve of the hill half-way down, their voices clear. I slid the AK forward, ready for action, motioning Helen to silence.

They kept on going at a fast trot and then it happened. One man at the rear wheeled his pony out of line and cantered up towards the standing circle.

* * *

Even then, at the end of things, I held off, waiting, hoping that he might turn away. He reined-in a yard or two away, a young man, rain beading his face, a black and scarlet band tied firmly around his forehead, the ends hanging down a couple of feet at the rear. His only weapon was one of those three foot swords slung under his arm in an ivory sheath.

I think it was then that I realised what was happening—saw the affinities with the *samurai* code. He was a warrior, ready to die with honour in the old way, the only way for a man—sword in hand. The band around his head was obviously similar to the *samurai* death band, worn by those who seek to die in the face of the enemy.

It may seem crazy, all this, yet subsequent events proved me to be entirely right. It was as if this was all they had left—to seek and destroy the man who had destroyed them —to hunt him down in their own way.

He started to turn his pony, then wheeled suddenly. I

355

don't know what it was he had seen, but it was enough. His mouth opened in a terrible cry to fill his limbs with courage, to bring the *ch'i* up from his belly, the sword flashed and he jumped the pony over the crest of the slope into the circle.

I rolled on my back as Helen screamed and lifted him out of the saddle with a quick burst. He rolled over twice and lay still. The pony cantered away and there was only the silence.

* * *

They had stopped in a tight group, gazing up towards the circle, but broke almost at once, peeling away to the left and the right to encircle the hill. There didn't seem to be any point in wasting time about opening hostilities, so I tried a snap shot that knocked one out of the saddle immediately.

And then my luck deserted me, or so it seemed, for that wind started to blow again, driving in from the sea, great, heavy rain squalls that dropped a grey curtain over everything.

There was a flash of yellow, a pony coming in from my left, stretched to the limit, the rider low over its neck. I had only time for a short burst and swung as hooves drummed in from directly behind. That one almost made it, riding in at full tilt, sword raised and I emptied the AK into him and jumped out of the way. The pony carried straight on through the circle and out the other side, the rider still upright in the saddle.

I got another clip out of the pouch at my belt and rammed it home as hooves drummed again—so many different directions that I didn't know what to expect next. I compromised by emptying the AK blindly into the mist and rain in several short bursts, taking care of as many points of the compass as I could.

That seemed to cool them off for a while and I feverishly reloaded and slumped down against one of the stones to get my breath.

Helen was watching me, eyes wide, staring. 'They're going to kill you,' she said dully. 'You don't have a chance.'

'As good a way to go as any,' I said. 'Toll for the brave.' I patted the stone I was leaning against. 'This thing's seen it all for the past three or four thousand years. I won't be the first.'

But if I were to go, they would have a hard time of it, I promised myself that. I loaded the M79 with the last grenade and took the smoke grenades out of their pouches, laying them ready in a neat row. At least they might frighten the ponies.

It was then that the first firing started, neatly disposing of my theory about honour and the way of the sword and dying according to the old ritual.

Bullets ricocheted from the stones, whined away into space for perhaps a minute. Then there was silence and in that silence the drum of hooves from several directions at once.

The strategy was plain, but by then, death had become a matter of indifference to me. I jumped to my feet, emptied the AK in a wide arc into the rain on full automatic, shoved in a second clip instantly and repeated the performance in another direction.

I certainly hit something to judge from the disturbance and rammed another clip home and swung as two of them charged out of the greyness, shoulder-to-shoulder from the other side, sword in hand. I gave them the whole magazine, one of them bouncing across the ground, coming to rest across Helen's legs. I shoved him away with my foot, but he was already dead.

The wind changed again, ripping the curtain away, exposing the shambles on the hillside, at least seven or eight bodies sprawled out there, some still alive, voices calling for aid, ponies wandering aimlessly.

They were strung out at the bottom of the hill—at least twenty of them. Some on ponies and some dismounted. At that distance it was not possible to see if St. Claire or Chen-Kuen were there, but it was certainly too good a chance to miss.

I raised the M79 to my shoulder, aiming high, remembering it was down hill and fired the last grenade. It landed in the exact centre of the line and I followed it with a smoke grenade for good measure.

It was only then, at the sight of that thick, grey-black cloud rising into the rain like a living thing that it occurred to me that it might still be possible to get out of there. I had two spare clips of ammunition left in the pouch which wasn't going to last me for long, especially if they decided to repeat the earlier performance. I pulled out the bayonet from its sheath at my belt and clipped it in place.

Helen said weakly, 'Still taking on the whole world, Ellis?'

'Something like that. I'm moving out. You just lie low and wait. Whatever happens, you win. Neither side's going to harm you.'

I dropped to one knee and fired off the smoke grenades one after the other in a neat pattern to cover the entire hillside and allowing for the wind.

There was bound to be confusion down there now and I intended to take full advantage of it. I fixed my bayonet on the end of the AK and port ready for action, just like the drill book. I could hear voices, ran past a couple of the wounded or dying, then came across exactly what I was looking for—one of the riderless ponies.

I swung into the saddle and urged it forward, taking my direction from the slope of the hill, trying to move away from the carnage below. So thick was the smoke by now that I almost defeated my own purpose.

I was aware of movement on either side, voices calling, ponies neighing and my own mount was proving difficult to control one-handed for he was obviously terrified in the smoke.

But I see now that it was all a nightmare from the beginning, no meaning to any of it, no sense and this was just another scene from hell.

Perhaps, because of that, it seemed entirely appropriate when Brigadier-General James Maxwell St. Claire rode out of the fog to confront me.

* * *

By then, I had come to expect such turns and it was St. Claire who was the most astonished of the two. I could have killed him then for although he wore a cartridge belt and bayonet at the waist like my own, his MI6 rifle was slung behind his back and I already had him covered with the AK.

He brushed it aside as if it did not exist, a patina of sweat on his face. 'Where's Helen? What have you done with her?'

'Back there on the hill. A scratch on the face, that's all. She'll survive. Is anyone left down there?'

'Enough to see you off, boy. They'll run you into the ground now.' He shook his head, a kind of awe in his voice. 'You are hell on wheels, boy. I should have remembered that.' And then, as if an afterthought, 'Aren't you going to kill me?'

I shook my head. 'Thirty years, Max, that's what they'll give you. I only wish it could be on Devil's Island.'

I got through to him with that all right. Hurt him, I think in some personal way and it is hard to escape the thought that in the end, after all that had happened, my opinion of him was still something he regarded as important.

I put my heels into the pony and galloped away along the hillside, away from the cries of the dying, the confused stamping of the horses. A moment later, I burst out of the smoke into the freshness of the rain, the green hillside, woods to the left of me, a carpet of tussocky grass stretching down to a scattering of pine trees that dropped into a gully which presumably sloped to a beach below.

I reined in to take my bearings, there was a single shot and the pony seemed to leap into the air, then started to go down. I managed to roll clear, still clutching the AK, turned and saw seven or eight horsemen on the brow of the hill below the smoke, saw something else in the same moment, coming in low over the sea out of the rain—three Siebe Martin assault helicopters.

Hilary Vaughan and the cavalry arriving at the end of things, but too late for Ellis Jackson. The horsemen fanned out and started to charge on. I emptied most of my magazine at them wildly as I sprawled there on the ground, kicking up earth in great fountains. At least it scattered the ponies for a moment and I scrambled to my feet. If I could reach the wood there might still be hope and I ran for all I was worth, blood in my mouth, not that I stood any kind of chance.

One rider curved in between me and the trees. I fired from the waist on the run and caught him somewhere or other for he swayed in the saddle. I veered sharply to the left, firing again at point-blank range as another cut across my line of vision.

There were still a few rounds left in the magazine and I decided to hang on to them for as the six remaining riders herded me back towards the cliff edge, I saw that only one of them was armed, presumably the man who had shot my pony.

The rest had only the long ivory-handled swords slung beneath the left armpit, each man in wide sleeved yellow robe and wearing a death band round the head.

The man with the rifle tossed it to one side, vaulted from the saddle and drew his sword. He raised it high above his head in true *kendo* style.

I had first handled a rifle and bayonet at the tender age of fourteen in the officer's training corps at school. The Academy, Benning, hand-to-hand fighting in the trenches at Do San—you might say we'd been together a long time.

At any rate, I knew my business. He turned his back and posed—all the showy technique in the world—then swung with one hell of a cry and delivered a basic *do* cut to the right side of the chest. I parried with ease and pointed. He retreated, trapped by his training, the technique hard-learned over the years, turned his back on me and posed again, so I gave him the bayonet below the shoulder blades and slightly to the left, penetrating the heart and killing him instantly. Then I blew him off the end with a quick burst which proved to be the last of my magazine.

There was no time to reload, a moment only in which his companions sat their mounts in stunned silence and then they were out of the saddle, swords unsheathed, gleaming dully in the grey morning.

Five against one. Big odds, even for little Ellis Jackson, although this lot were so crazy I suspected they might come in one at a time. I never found out, for a sudden cry tore the morning in two and St. Claire galloped down the hill and reined-in beside the other ponies.

* * *

The monks hesitated, turning towards him as if expecting orders. What happened then was the most surprising thing of all, yet not surprising in the final analysis, for he ran through them, unslinging his rifle and fixing bayonet, taking up his position beside me.

He smiled at me once, that famous St. Claire smile, then turned to face them. 'Who dies first?' he called in Chinese.

12 The last 'banzai'

I know now that he was seeking his death. A warrior's end, the best way out, when all was said and done, for a man like him.

But there was no time to consider the implications of his act for with a concerted cry that would have done credit to the Imperial Japanese Guard's last *banzai* in their final battle of the Second World War, the five of them came in like one man.

Two chose me and three, not unnaturally, settled for St. Claire. As I parried the first cut, I was aware in a detached sort of way of one of the helicopters dropping down behind the rim of the hill, presumably to the scene of the battle where smoke curled thickly into the air, but that wasn't going to help us here.

362

The tip of a blade nicked my right arm, I twisted, gave my opponent the butt under the chin and flung myself to one side as the other's blade sliced at my head.

St. Claire had put one man down, was backed up against the ultimate edge of the cliff now, blood on his face, holding off the other two.

I slipped on the wet grass and rolled wildly to avoid the slashing blade that hacked at my head. It missed by a matter of inches, biting deep into the turf and I gave him the bayonet up under the breastbone with both hands.

As I turned to scramble up, one of St. Claire's assailants managed to get in close, clutching him by the left arm, smothering the rifle, leaving the way clear for his companion to deliver the death blow.

Strange, but in that moment he was my dearest friend again and my only thought was to aid him. I gave a terrible cry, jumped in and bayoneted the one with the sword in the back.

Not that it did St. Claire much good in the end for the other, sensing, I suppose, that all was lost, suddenly pushed with all his strength and they both went over the edge.

* * *

It was a drop of a hundred feet at least to where the sea sprawled in across jagged black rocks in a carpet of white foam, boiling ceaselessly. That anyone could survive such a fall didn't seem possible except for the uncertain chance of dropping into a patch of deep water between the rocks, but as I looked down, St. Claire appeared miraculously like some great dark seal.

And yet he was badly injured—had to be for he was unable to help himself and the current took him out across the rocks in a sudden swirl, leaving him sprawled face-down across a mattress of seaweed.

To the right of me, the ground sloped steeply to the start of a reasonably large gully. I skidded along the slope on the wet grass and found the gully to be a wide funnel partially choked with sand and clay, probably a natural outfall for rainwater.

I went down without pause in a shower of earth and sand, still clutching my rifle in one hand. The last twenty or thirty feet or so were virtually perpendicular, but the sand on the beach at that spot was soft and white and broke my fall very effectively.

I could see him clearly now out there on a kind of peninsula of rock which jutted into the sea. As another wave broke over him, I dropped the rifle, ran across the beach and waded through the shallows towards the rocks.

I seemed to hear my name, thought at first it was perhaps St. Claire, but this was from another direction. I turned, waist-deep in water. Further along the cliffs, the pine trees flooded down in a great fold, spreading into a gently sloping hillside of grass merging into sand that gave easy access to the beach.

A horseman had paused half-way down—Colonel Chen-Kuen in yellow robes, black quilted *shuba* and death band, scarlet tails fluttering behind. He came down the rest of the bank in a great sliding apron of sand, put spurs to the pony and was across the beach and into the shallows like a thunderbolt, the sword streaking from its scabbard.

And I had nothing, but empty hands and waited there for him, waited for the steel to descend. But in the last moment, he was victim of his own peculiar notions of honour, realised my weaponless state, reined in his mount and sheathed the sword.

He sat there looking at me gravely, holding the pony in tightly as it moved nervously from side to side, an unforgettable picture in those mediaeval robes, vivid against the grey sky.

'I always underestimated you, Ellis,' he said and then leapt at me from the saddle, arms outstretched.

I went down under his weight, but at the same moment a wave swept in and turned the world upside down. When I surfaced again he was three or four yards away.

He ploughed towards me, assuming a martial stance. It was all to be according to the book, I realised this now. A solemn ritual between equal adversaries. Almost a religious rite.

He gave the usual courage shout, then threw a reverse punch which takes the uninitiated unawares as it is delivered with the hand on the same side as the rear foot.

I evaded it with a right block, pivoted and delivered a reverse elbow strike that caught him full in the mouth, breaking teeth. Another wave washed us apart and as the swell subsided, he came in with a rush, delivering one blow after another at my head with the edge of his hands. I countered with the *juji-uke*, the X-block and got another elbow strike into his face.

A second wave swept in, much larger this time, driving me back towards the rocks in a welter of dirty brown foam. He was on his feet before I was that time, catching me in the left ribs with with a reverse punch, screwing it in with all his force, all his energy focussed on that one place.

I could feel at least two ribs go and dropped to one side and delivered a roundhouse kick to his groin, awkwardly because of the water. He went down and I gave him an old-fashioned punch in the stomach at close quarters and moved in close as he keeled over. It was a mistake for he erupted from the water with incredible speed and energy, the edge of his hand striking with all the cutting force of that sword of his.

He broke my left arm with that single, devastating blow, would have had me cold a second later if another great wave had not smashed in across us. I went deep in a maelstrom of green water and surfaced to find him floundering a good fifteen yards away. It was all I needed and I plunged towards the shore.

As I staggered up on to the beach, I glanced over my shoulder and saw him wading towards his pony. After that, I put down my head and ran like hell towards that narrow funnel in the cliff where I had descended.

The hooves were already drumming as I dropped to one knee beside the AK. I didn't bother looking over my shoulder, simply concentrated on getting the final clip out of the ammunition belt at my waist and into the rifle and I had only one usable hand, remember.

He cried my name out loud once, perhaps recognising his executioner and greeting me, or perhaps an appeal for me to play the game his way and with honour, man-to-man to the end.

I turned, dropped to one knee, poked the AK out in front of me one-handed and shot him in the head. It was only then, as he tumbled backwards out of the saddle, that I realised that he hadn't even bothered to draw his sword.

* * *

A helicopter soared in over the cliffs, moving out to sea, turned and came closer, seeking a safe place to land, a difficult thing to do on that narrow beach with the down-draughts always to be found in such an area.

I had more important things on my mind and ran back across the sand, one arm dangling uselessly and ploughed through the shallows to the rocks.

By some miracle he was still in sight, a little further out now on a ledge of rock jutting over deep water to one side. By rights he should already have been dead, but presumably a chance wave had left him there. It would only take one more to finish him, to wipe him from the face of memory forever.

It was necessary to climb down to get to that particular point and the boulders were slippery and treacherous, covered with seaweed and green slime that would have made the going hard in normal circumstances, but with my broken arm, almost impossible.

I made it—had to and nothing above this earth or beneath it could have stopped me. Water boiled in again, sending me back against a boulder, spraying knee-deep and somewhere my name was called. When I turned, there were men up there on the rocks by the shore in camouflage jump jackets and red berets.

I floundered on, knee-deep, convinced that he must have gone, fell forward on the edge at last and looked over to the ledge below.

He was still there, eyes tight shut as if in pain and when he opened them and saw me, there was immediate recognition. He raised his left arm, I reached out my right, found his hand and held on tight.

'Now then you old bastard.'

'Did you sort them out, boy? Did you dust them up good?'

'Right down the line.'

'I always did say you had qualities. I'm not going to say I'm sorry. No point. You should have learned the truth of life by now.'

'Who's asking you?'

A wave washed in across us. Those paratroopers were

very close now. He said, 'Okay, Ellis, let go.'

'Like hell I will.'

'Thirty years, boy, and a cripple at that. Is that what you want? Will that mean it never happened?'

He smiled, that famous St. Claire smile and something like bile rose in my throat to choke me, I sobbed out loud, at the end of something at last, holding him tight till the next wave came, then letting it take him with it as it receded.

I saw him once more, the face dark against the white foam out there and then he was gone.

It was perhaps a minute later, not more, that a largish individual in a camouflaged uniform, ploughed through the foam and got a grip on me. I turned, clutching at his leg with my one good hand and looked up at Hilary Vaughan.

He pulled me up and we stood there, water ebbing about our knees and he waved his men back. I said, 'I let him go.'

He nodded. 'Best thing under the circumstances.'

'For whom?'

But he had no answer to that one. Simply took me by the arm with surprising strength and helped me up to where his men waited.

* * *

The helicopter was not too far away, but I sat down on a rock and Vaughan pushed a cigarette into my mouth. 'You cut it rather fine,' I told him.

'I would have thought the boot was on the other foot, old lad,' he said gravely.

'You got what you wanted, didn't you? Are your men having any trouble with the rest of them?'

'I'm using the Guards Parachute Company,' he said. 'Those lads just don't have trouble—not with anybody.'

In the middle distance a familiar figure was running towards us from the helicopter—Helen St. Claire, a field dressing taped to her face.

Vaughan glanced over his shoulder and said, 'We picked her up on top—quite hysterical. This might not be pleasant, I warn you.'

She stopped three or four yards away, staring at me uncertainly. 'Max?' she demanded in a strangely querulous way. 'What have you done with Max?'

'Max is dead, Helen,' I said tonelessly.

She might have been carved from stone, so still was she as she stood there and then she moved very close to me, staring into my face.

'You killed him, didn't you? You killed my brother, you white bastard. You killed my brother.'

She struck me across the face again and again, sobbing hysterically until Vaughan dragged her off. He held her for a moment until she seemed quieter, then released her. She turned and ran back along the shore towards the helicopter.

I don't suppose I was capable of rational thought then. I said to him, 'You lied to me, didn't you? You knew all about St. Claire from the beginning.'

He nodded. 'The way it had to be, Ellis.'

Like St. Claire, he saw no reason to say he was sorry. I watched Helen go, head down, following the shoreline and he said quietly, 'You've lost her, Ellis. You realise that?'

'I never had her,' I turned to look out to sea. 'I never really had anything worth the having.'

'Oh, I don't know. You've done well, Ellis. Exceptionally well. We could use you—in the future, I mean, when you've got over all this.'

369

I found that so funny, I could have laughed out loud. Instead, I simply shook my head. 'I don't think so.'

'I wouldn't be too sure. Give yourself time. After all, what will you do now? It would be some kind of solution. A damned sight better than going back to that cottage in the marshes.'

He could have been right, very probably was, but not then—not by any stretch of the imagination. I stood up and stared out at the grey waters, looking for St. Claire, listening for his voice, the slightest indication that he had ever existed, and failed. Then I turned and infinitely slowly, because I was suddenly very tired, walked away along the shore.

The Valhalla
Exchange

For my mother and father, who
helped more than a little with
this one

Whether Martin Bormann survived the holocaust that was Berlin at the end of the Second World War may be arguable, but it is a matter of record that Russian radar reported a light aircraft leaving the vicinity of the Tiergarten in Berlin on the morning of 30 April, the very day on which Adolf Hitler committed suicide. As for the remainder of this story, only the more astonishing parts are true – the rest is fiction.

I

On the Day of the Dead in Bolivia children take food and presents to the cemetery to leave on the graves of the departed. An interesting blend of the pagan and Christian traditions and highly appropriate the way things turned out. But even the most superstitious of Bolivian peasants would hardly expect the dead to get up and walk on such an occasion. I did.

La Huerta was a mining town of five or six thousand people, lost in the peaks of the high Andes. The back of beyond. There was no direct passenger flight from Peru, so I'd flown in from Lima in an old DC3 that was doing some kind of cargo run to an American mining company.

It was raining hard when I arrived, but by some dispensation or other there was a cab standing outside the small terminal building. The driver was a cheerful Indian with a heavy moustache. He wore a yellow oilskin coat and a straw hat and seemed surprised and gratified at the sight of a customer.

'The hotel, señor?' he asked, as he seized my valise.

'The Excelsior,' I said.

'But that is the hotel, señor.' His teeth gleamed in the lamplight. 'The only one.'

The interior of the cab stank, the roof leaked, and as we started down the hill to the lights of the town I felt unaccountably depressed. Why in the hell was I here, doing the same thing I'd done so many times before? Chasing my tail for a story that probably didn't exist in the first place. And La Huerta itself didn't help as we turned into a maze of narrow streets, each one with the usual open sewer running down the centre, decaying, flat-roofed houses crowding in, poverty and squalor on every side.

We emerged into a central plaza a few minutes later. There was a large and rather interesting baroque fountain in the centre, some relic of colonial days, water gushing forth from the mouths and nostrils of a score of nymphs and dryads. The fact that it was working at all seemed a small miracle. The hotel was on the far side. As I got out I noticed a number of people sheltering under a colonnade to my right. Some of them were in carnival costume and there was the smell of smoke on the damp air.

'What's all that?' I asked.

'All Saints' Day, señor. A time of festival.'

'They don't look as if they're enjoying themselves too much.'

'The rain.' He shrugged. 'It makes it difficult for the fireworks. But then this is a solemn occasion with us. Soon they will go in procession to the cemetery to greet their loved ones. The Day of the Dead, we call it. You have heard of this, señor?'

'They have the same thing in Mexico.'

I paid him off, went up the steps and entered the hotel. Like everything else in La Huerta, it had seen better days, but now its pink, stucco walls were peeling and there were damp patches in the ceiling. The desk clerk put down his newspaper hurriedly, as amazed as the cab driver had been at the prospect of custom.

'I'd like a room.'

'But of course, señor. For how long?'

'One night. I'm flying back to Peru in the morning.'

I passed my papers across so that he could go through the usual rigmarole the government insists on where foreigners are concerned.

As he filled in the register he said, 'You have business here, señor? With the mining company, perhaps?'

378

I opened my wallet and extracted a ten-dollar American bill which I placed carefully on the counter beside the register. He stopped writing, the eyes dark, watchful.

'It was reported in one of the Lima newspapers that a man died here Monday. Dropped dead in the plaza, right outside your front door. It rated a mention because the police found 50,000 dollars in cash in his suitcase and passports in three different names.'

'Ah, yes, Señor Bauer. You are a friend of his, señor?'

'No, but I might know him if I see him.'

'He is with the local undertaker. In such cases they keep the body for a week while relatives are sought.'

'So I was informed.'

'Lieutenant Gómez is Chief of Police in charge of the affair and police headquarters are on the other side of the plaza.'

'I never find the police too helpful in these affairs.' I laid another ten-dollar bill beside the first. 'I'm a journalist. There could be a story in this for me. It's as simple as that.'

'Ah, I see now. A newspaperman.' His eyes lightened. 'How may I help you?'

'Bauer – what can you tell me about him?'

'Very little, señor. He arrived last week from Sucre. Said he expected a friend to join him.'

'And did anyone?'

'Not that I know of.'

'What did he look like? Describe him.'

'Sixty-five, maybe older. Yes, he could have been older, but it's difficult to say. He was one of those men who give an impression of vitality at all times. A bull of a man.'

'Why do you say that?'

'Powerfully built. Not tall, you understand me, but with broad shoulders.' He stretched his arms. 'A thick, powerful neck.'

'A fat man?'

'No, I don't remember him that way. More the power

of the man, an impression of strength. He spoke good Spanish, with a German accent.'

'You can recognize it?'

'Oh, yes, señor. Many German engineers come here.'

'Can I see the entry in the register?'

He turned it round to show me. It was on the line above mine. There were the details from his passport entered by the clerk, and beside it Bauer's signature, a trifle spidery, but firm, and the date beside it, using a crossed seven, continental style.

I nodded and pushed the two bills across. 'Thank you.'

'Señor.' He snapped up the twenty dollars and tucked them into his breast pocket. 'I'll show you your room.'

I glanced at my watch. It was just after eleven. 'Too late to visit the undertaker now.'

'Oh, no, señor, there is a porter on duty all night. It is the custom here for the dead to be in waiting for three days, during which time they are watched over both night and day in case . . .' Here, he hesitated.

'. . . of a mistake?' I suggested.

'Exactly, señor.' He smiled sadly. 'Death is a very final affair, so one wants to be sure. Take the first street on the left. You will find the undertaker's at the far end. You can't miss it. There's a blue light above the door. The watchman's name is Hugo. Tell him Rafael Mareno sent you.'

'My thanks,' I said formally.

'At your orders, señor. And if you would care to eat on your return, something could be managed. I am on duty all night.'

He picked up his newspaper and I retraced my steps across the hall and went outside. The procession had formed up and started across the square as I paused at the top of the steps. It was much as I had seen in Mexico. There were a couple of characters in front, blazing torches in hand, dressed to represent the Lords of Death and Hell. Next came the children, clutching guttering candles, some already extinguished in the heavy rain, the adults following on behind with baskets of bread and fruit. Someone started to play a flute, low and plaintive, and a finger drum joined in. Otherwise, they moved in complete silence.

We seemed to be going the same way and I joined on at the tail of the procession, turning up the collar of my trenchcoat against the heavy rain. The undertaker's was plain enough, the blue light subdued above the door as Mareno had indicated. I paused, watching the procession continue, the sound of that flute and drum strangely haunting, and only when they had turned into another alley and moved out of sight did I pull the bell chain.

There was silence for quite some time, only the rain. I was about to reach for the chain again when I became aware of a movement inside, dragging footsteps approaching. A grill opened at eye-level, a face peered out, pale in the darkness.

'Hugo?'

'What is it you want, señor?' The voice was the merest whisper.

'I would like to see the body of Señor Ricardo Bauer.'

'Perhaps in the morning, señor.'

'Rafael Mareno sent me.'

There was a pause, then the grill was closed. There was the sound of bolts being withdrawn, the door creaked open. He stood there, an oil lamp in one hand, very old, very frail, almost as if one of his own charges had decided to get up and walk. I slipped inside, he closed the door.

'You will follow me, please?'

He led the way along a short passage and opened an oaken door and I could smell death instantly, the cloying sweetness of it heavy on the cold air. I hesitated, then followed him through.

The room into which I entered was a place of shadows, a single oil lamp suspended from a chain in the centre supplying the only light. It was a waiting mortuary of a type I had seen a couple of times before in Palermo and

Vienna, although the Viennese version had been considerably more elaborate. There were perhaps a dozen coffins on the other side of the room, but first he led me up some steps to a small platform on which stood a desk and chair.

I gazed down into the shadows in fascination. Each coffin was open, a corpse clearly visible inside, the stiff fingers firmly entwined in one end of a string that went up over a pulley arrangement, across to the desk where the other end was fastened to an old-fashioned bell that hung from a wall bracket.

He put down his lamp. I said, 'Has anyone ever rung that thing?'

'The bell.' I saw now that he was very old, eighty at least, the face desiccated, the eyes moist. 'Once, señor, ten years ago. A young girl. But she died again three days later. Her father refused to acknowledge the fact. He kept her with him for a month. Finally the police had to intervene.'

'I can see how they would have to.'

He opened a ledger and dipped a pen in an inkwell. 'Your relationship to Señor Bauer, señor. I must enter it in the official record.'

I took out my wallet and produced another of those ten-dollar bills. 'Nothing so formal, my friend. I'm just a newspaperman, passing through. I heard the story and thought I might recognize him.'

He hesitated, then laid down the pen. 'As you say, señor.' He picked up the lamp. 'This way.'

It was the end coffin on the back row and I received something of a shock as the old man raised his lamp to reveal red lips, a gleam of teeth, full, rounded cheeks. And then I realized, of course, that the undertaker had been going to work on him. It was as if a wax tailor's dummy had been laid out for my inspection, a totally unreal face heavy with make-up, resembling no photo that I had ever seen. But how could he hope to, thirty years

382

on? A big, big difference between forty-five and seventy-five.

When the bell jangled, I almost jumped out of my skin and then realized it had sounded from outside. Hugo said, 'You will excuse me, señor. There is someone at the door.'

He shuffled off, leaving me there beside Bauer's coffin. If there had been rings, they'd taken them off, and the powerful fingers were intertwined on his chest, the string between them. They'd dressed him in a neat blue suit, white collar, dark tie. It really was rather remarkable.

I became aware of the voices outside in the corridor, one unmistakably American. 'You speak English? No?'

Then the same voice continuing in bad Spanish, 'I must see the body of the man Bauer. I've come a long way and my time is limited.'

Hugo tried to protest. 'Señor – it is late,' but he was obviously brushed aside.

'Where is the body? In here?'

For some reason, some sixth sense operating if you like, I moved back into the darkness of the corner. A moment later I was glad that I had.

He stepped into the room and paused, white hair gleaming in the lamplight, rain glistening on his military raincoat, shoulders firm, the figure still militarily erect, only the whiteness of the hair and the clipped moustache hinting at his seventy-five years.

I don't think I've ever been so totally astonished, for I was looking at a legend in his own time, General Hamilton Canning, Congressional Medal of Honour, DSC, Silver Star, Médaille Militaire, the Philippines, D-Day, Korea, even Vietnam in the early days. A piece of walking history, one of the most respected of living Americans.

He had a harsh distinctive voice, not unpleasant, but it carried with it the authority of a man who'd been used to getting his own way for most of his life.

'Which one?'

Hugo limped past him, lamp held high, and I crouched back in the corner. 'Here, señor.'

Canning's face seemed calm enough, but it was in the eyes that I saw the turbulence, a blazing intensity, but also a kind of hope as he stood at the end of the coffin and looked down at the waxen face. And then hope died, the light went out in the eyes – something. The shoulders sagged and for the first time he looked his age.

He turned wearily and nodded to Hugo. 'I won't trouble you any further.'

'This was not the person you were seeking, señor?'

Canning shook his head. 'No, my friend, I don't think so. Good night to you.'

He seemed to take a deep breath, all the old vigour returning, and strode from the room. I came out of the shadows quickly.

'Señor.' Hugo started to speak.

I motioned him to silence and moved to the entrance. As Canning opened the door, I saw the cab from the airstrip outside, the driver waiting in the rain.

The general said, 'You can take me to the hotel now,' and closed the door behind him.

Hugo tugged at my sleeve. 'Señor, what passes here?'

'Exactly what I was wondering, Hugo,' I said softly, and I went along the passage quickly and let myself out.

The cab was parked outside the hotel. As I approached, a man in a leather flying jacket and peaked cap hurried down the steps and got in. The cab drove away through the rain. I watched it go for a moment, unable to see if Canning was inside.

Rafael wasn't behind the desk, but as I paused, shaking the rain from my coat, a door on my left opened and he emerged.

He smiled. 'Were you successful, señor?'

'Not really,' I said. 'Did I see the cab driving away just now?'

'Ah, yes, that was the pilot of Mr Smith, an American gentleman who has just booked in. He was on his way to La Paz in his private aeroplane, but they had to put down here because of the weather.'

'I see. Mr Smith, you say?'

'That is correct, señor. I've just given him a drink in the bar. Could I perhaps get you something?'

'Well, now,' I said. 'A large brandy might be a sensible idea, considering the state I'm in.'

I followed him, unbuttoning my trenchcoat. It was a pleasant enough room, rough stone walls, a well-stocked bar at one side. Canning was seated in an armchair in front of a blazing log fire, a glass in one hand. He looked up sharply.

'Company, señor,' Rafael said cheerfully. 'A fellow guest. Señor O'Hagan – Señor Smith. I'll just get your brandy now,' he added and moved away.

'Not a night for even an old tomcat to be out,' I said, throwing my coat over a chair. 'As my old grannie used to say.'

He smiled up at me, the famous Canning charm well in evidence, and stuck out his hand. 'English, Mr O'Hagan?'

'By way of Ulster,' I said. 'But we won't go into that, General.'

The smile stayed firmly in place, only the eyes changed, cold, hard, and the hand tightened on mine with a grip of surprising strength considering his age.

It was Rafael who broke the spell, arriving with my brandy on a tray. 'Can I get you another one, señor?' he asked.

Canning smiled, all charm again. 'Later, my friend. Later.'

'Señores.'

Rafael departed. Canning leaned back, watching me,

then swallowed a little Scotch. He didn't waste time trying to tell me how mistaken I was, but said simply, 'We've met before presumably?'

'About fifteen minutes ago up the street at the mortuary,' I said. 'I was standing in the shadows, I should explain, so I had you at something of a disadvantage. Oh, I've seen you before at press conferences over the years, that sort of thing, but then one couldn't really specialize in writing about politics and military affairs without knowing Hamilton Canning.'

'O'Hagan,' he said. 'The one who writes for *The Times*?'

'I'm afraid so, General.'

'You've a good mind, son, but remind me to put you straight on China. You've been way out of line in that area lately.'

'You're the expert.' I took out a cigarette. 'What about Bauer, General?'

'What about him?' He leaned back, legs sprawled, all negligent ease.

I laughed. 'All right, let's try it another way. You ask *me* why a reasonably well-known correspondent for the London *Times* takes the trouble to haul himself all the way from Lima to a pesthole like this, just to look at the body of a man called Ricardo Bauer who dropped dead in the street here on Monday.'

'All right, son,' he said lazily. 'You tell me. I'm all ears.'

'Ricardo Bauer,' I said, 'as more than one expert will tell you, is one of the aliases used by Martin Bormann in Brazil, the Argentine, Chile and Paraguay on many occasions during the past thirty years.'

'Martin Bormann?' he said.

'Oh, come off it, General. Reichsleiter Martin Bormann, Head of the Nazi Party Chancellery and Secretary to the Führer. The one member of Hitler's top table unaccounted for since the war.'

'Bormann's dead,' he said softly. 'He was killed attempting to break out of Berlin. Blown up crossing the Weidendammer Bridge on the night of May 1st, 1945.'

'Early hours of May 2nd, General,' I said. 'Let's get it right. Bormann left the bunker at 1.30 a.m. It was Erich Kempka, Hitler's chauffeur, who saw him come under artillery fire on that bridge. Unfortunately for that story, the Hitler Youth Leader, Artur Axmann, crossed the Spree River on a railway bridge, as part of a group led by Bormann, and that was considerably later.'

He nodded. 'But Axmann asserted also that he'd seen Bormann and Hitler's doctor, Stumpfegger, lying dead near Lehrter Station.'

'And no one else to confirm the story,' I said. 'Very convenient.'

He put down his glass, took out a pipe and started to fill it from a leather pouch. 'So, you believe he's alive. Wouldn't you say that's kind of crazy?'

'It would certainly put me in pretty mixed company,' I said. 'Starting with Stalin and lesser mortals like Jacob Glas, Bormann's chauffeur, who saw him in Munich after the war. Then there was Eichmann – when the Israelis picked him up in 1960 he told them Bormann was alive. Now why would he do that if it wasn't true?'

'A neat point. Go on.'

'Simon Wiestenthal, the Nazi hunter, always insisted he was alive, maintained he had regular reports on him. Ladislas Farago said he actually interviewed him. Since 1964 the West German authorities have had 100,000 marks on his head and he was found guilty of war crimes at Nuremburg and sentenced to death in his absence.' I leaned forward. 'What more do you want, General? Would you like to hear the one about the Spaniard who maintains he travelled to Argentine from Spain with Bormann in a U-boat in 1945?'

He smiled, leaning over to put another log on the fire. 'Yes, I interviewed him soon after he came out with that story. But if Bormann's been alive all these years, what's he been doing?'

'The Kameradenwerk,' I said. 'Action for comrades. The organization they set up to take care of the movement after the war, with hundreds of millions of gold salted away to pay for it.'

'Possible.' He nodded, staring into the fire. 'Possible.'

'One thing *is* sure,' I said. 'That isn't him lying up there at the mortuary. At least, you don't think so.'

He glanced up at me. 'Why do you say that?'

'I saw your face.'

He nodded. 'No, it wasn't Bormann.'

'How did you know about him? Bauer, I mean. Events in La Huerta hardly make front-page news in the *New York Times*.'

'I employ an agent in Brazil who has a list of certain names. Any mention of any of them anywhere in South America and he informs me. I flew straight down.'

'Now that I find truly remarkable.'

'What do you want to know, son? What he looked like? Will that do? Five foot six inches, bull neck, prominent cheekbones, broad, rather brutal face. You could lose him in any crowd because he looked so damned ordinary. Just another working stiff off the waterfront or whatever. He was virtually unknown to the German public and press. Honours, medals meant nothing to him. Power was all.' It was as if he was talking to himself as he sat there, staring into the fire. 'He was the most powerful man in Germany and nobody appreciated it until after the war.'

'A butcher,' I said, 'who condoned the final solution and the deaths of millions of Jews.'

'Who also sent war orphans to his wife in Bavaria to look after,' Canning said. 'You know what Göring said at Nuremberg when they asked him if he knew where Bormann was? He said, "I hope he's frying in hell, but I don't know."'

He heaved himself out of the chair, went behind the

bar and reached for a bottle of Scotch. 'Can I get you another?'

'Why not?' I got up and sat on one of the bar stools. 'Brandy.'

As he poured some into my glass he said, 'I was once a prisoner-of-war, did you know that?'

'That's a reasonably well-known fact, General,' I said. 'You were captured in Korea. The Chinese had you for two years in Manchuria. Isn't that why Nixon hauled you out of retirement the other year to go to Peking with him?'

'No, I mean way, way back. I was a prisoner once before. Towards the end of the Second World War, the Germans had me. At Schloss Arlberg in Bavaria. A special set-up for prominent prisoners.'

And I genuinely hadn't known, although it was so far back it was hardly surprising, and then his real, enduring fame had been gained in Korea, after all.

I said, 'I didn't know that, General.'

He dropped ice into his glass and a very large measure of whisky. 'Yes, I was there right to the bitter end. In the area erroneously known as the Alpine Fortress. One of Dr Goebbels's smarter pieces of propaganda. He actually had the Allies believing there was such a place. It meant the troops were very cautious about probing into that area at first, which made it a safe resting place for big Nazis on the run from Berlin in those last few days.'

'Hitler could have gone, but didn't.'

'That's right.'

'And Bormann?'

'What do you mean?'

'The one thing that's never made any sense to me,' I said. 'He was a brilliant man. Too clever by half to leave his chances of survival to a mad scramble at the final end of things. If he'd really wanted to escape he'd have gone to Berchtesgaden when he had the chance instead of staying in the bunker till the end. He'd have had a plan.'

'Oh, but he did, son.' Canning nodded slowly. 'You can bet your sweet life on that.'

'And how would you know, General?' I asked softly. And at that he exploded, came apart at the seams.

'Because I saw him, damn you,' he cried harshly. 'Because I stood as close to him as I am to you, traded shots with him, had my hands on his throat, do you understand?' He paused, hands held out, looking at them in a kind of wonder. 'And lost him,' he whispered.

He leaned on the bar, head down. There was a long, long moment in which I couldn't think of a thing to say, but waited, my stomach hollow with excitement. When he finally raised his head, he was calm again.

'You know what's so strange, O'Hagan? So bloody incredible? I kept it to myself all these years. Never mentioned it to a soul until now.'

2

It began, if it may be said to have begun anywhere, on the morning of Wednesday, 25 April 1945, a few miles north of Innsbruck.

When Jack Howard emerged from the truck at the rear of the column just after first light, it was bitterly cold, a powdering of dry snow on the ground, for the valley in which they had halted for the night was high in the Bavarian Alps, although he couldn't see much of the mountains because of the heavy clinging mist which had settled among the trees. It reminded him too much of the Ardennes for comfort. He stamped his feet to induce a little warmth and lit a cigarette.

Sergeant Hoover had started a wood fire, and the men, only five of them now, crouched beside it. Anderson, O'Grady, Garland and Finebaum who'd once played clarinet with Glenn Miller and never let anyone forget it. Just now he was on his face trying to blow fresh life into the flames. He was the first to notice Howard.

'Heh, the captain's up and he don't look too good.'

'Why don't you try a mirror?' Garland inquired. 'You think you look like a daisy or something?'

'Stinkweed – that's the only flower he ever resembled,' O'Grady said.

'That's it, hotshot,' Finebaum told him. 'You're out. From here on in you find your own beans.' He turned to Hoover. 'I ask you, Sarge. I appeal to your better nature. Is that the best these mothers can offer after all I've done for them?'

'That's a truly lousy act, Finebaum, did I ever tell you

that?' Hoover poured coffee into an aluminium cup. 'You're going to need plenty of practice, boy, if you're ever going to get back into vaudeville.'

'Well, I'll tell you,' Finebaum said. 'I've had kind of a special problem lately. I ran out of audience. Most of them died on me.'

Hoover took the coffee across to the truck and gave it to Howard without a word. Somewhere thunder rumbled on the horizon.

'Eighty-eights?' the captain said.

Hoover nodded. 'Don't they ever give up? It don't make any kind of sense to me. Every time we turn on the radio they tell us this war's as good as finished.'

'Maybe they forgot to tell the Germans.'

'That makes sense. Any chance of submitting it through channels?'

Howard shook his head. 'It wouldn't do any good, Harry. Those krauts don't intend to give in until they get you. That's what it's all about.'

Hoover grunted. 'Those mothers better be quick or they're going to miss out, that's all I can say. You want to eat now? We still got plenty of K-rations and Finebaum traded some smokes last night for half a dozen cans of beans from some of those Limey tank guys up the column.'

'The coffee's just fine, Harry,' Howard said. 'Maybe later.'

The sergeant moved back to the fire and Howard paced up and down beside the truck, stamping his feet and clutching the hot cup tightly in mittened fingers. He was twenty-three years of age, young to be a captain of Rangers, but that was the circumstance of war. He wore a crumpled Mackinaw coat, wool-knit muffler at his throat and a knitted cap. There were times when he could have passed for nineteen, but this was not one of them, not with the four-day growth of dark beard on his chin, the sunken eyes.

But once he had been nineteen, an Ohio farmer's son with some pretensions to being a poet and the desire to write for a living which had sent him to Columbia to study journalism. That was a long time ago – before the flood. Before the further circumstances of war which had brought him to his present situation in charge of the reconnaissance element for a column of the British 7th Armoured Division, probing into Bavaria towards Berchtesgaden.

Hoover squatted beside the fire. Finebaum passed him a plate of beans. 'The captain not eating?'

'Not right now.'

'Jesus,' Finebaum said. 'What kind of way is that to carry on?'

'Respect, Finebaum.' Hoover prodded him with his knife. 'Just a little more respect when you speak about him.'

'Sure, I respect him,' Finebaum said. 'I respect him like crazy and I know how you and he went in at Salerno together and how those krauts jumped you outside Anzio with those machine guns flat zeroed in and took out three-quarters of the battalion and how our gracious captain saved the rest. So he's God's gift to soldiery; so he should eat occasionally. He ain't swallowed more than a couple of mouthfuls since Sunday.'

'Sunday he lost nine men,' Hoover said. 'Maybe you're forgetting.'

'Those guys are dead – so they're dead – right? He don't keep his strength up, he might lose a few more, including me. I mean, look at him! He's got so skinny, that stinking coat he wears is two sizes too big for him. He looks like some fresh kid in his first year at college.'

'I know,' Hoover said. 'The kind they give the Silver Star with Oak Leaf Cluster to.'

The others laughed and Finebaum managed to look injured. 'Okay – okay. I've come this far. I just figure it would look kind of silly to die now.'

'Everybody dies,' Hoover said. 'Sooner or later. Even you.'

'Okay – but not here. Not now. I mean, after surviving D-Day, Omaha, St-Lo, the Ardennes and a few interesting stop-offs in between, it would look kind of stupid to buy it here, playing wet-nurse to a bunch of limeys.'

'We've been on the same side for nearly four years now,' Hoover said. 'Or hadn't you noticed?'

'How can I help it with guys going around dressed like that?' Finebaum nodded to where the commanding officer of the column, a lieutenant-colonel named Denning, was approaching, his adjutant at his side. They were Highlanders and wore rather dashing Glengarry bonnets.

'Morning, Howard,' Denning said as he got close. 'Damn cold night. Winter's hung on late up here this year.'

'I guess so, Colonel.'

'Let's have a look at the map, Miller.' The adjutant spread it against the side of the truck and the colonel ran a finger along the centre. 'Here's Innsbruck and here we are. Another five miles to the head of this valley and we hit a junction with the main road to Salzburg. We could have trouble there, wouldn't you say so?'

'Very possibly, Colonel.'

'Good. We'll move out in thirty minutes. I suggest you take the lead and send your other jeep on ahead to scout out the land.'

'As you say, sir.'

Denning and the adjutant moved away and Howard turned to Hoover and the rest of the men who had all edged in close enough to hear. 'You got that, Harry?'

'I think so, sir.'

'Good. You take Finebaum and O'Grady. Garland and Anderson stay with me. Report in over your radio every five minutes without fail. Now get moving.'

As they swung into action, Finebaum said plaintively, 'Holy Mary, Mother of God, I'm only a Jewish boy, but pray for us sinners in the hour of our need.'

On the radio, the news was good. The Russians had finally encircled Berlin and had made contact with American troops on the Elbe River seventy-five miles south of the capital, cutting Germany in half.

'The only way in and out of Berlin now is by air, sir,' Anderson said to Howard 'They can't keep going any longer – they've got to give in It's the only logical thing to do '

'Oh, I don't know,' Howard said. 'I'd say that if your name was Hitler or Goebbels or Himmler and the only prospect offered was a short trial and a long rope, you might think it worth while to go down, taking as many of the other side with you as you possibly could.'

Anderson, who had the wheel, looked worried, as well he might, for unlike Garland he was married with two children, a girl of five and a boy aged six. He gripped the wheel so tightly that the knuckles on his hands turned white.

You shouldn't have joined, old buddy, Howard thought. *You should have found an easier way. Plenty did.*

Strange how callous he had become where the suffering of others was concerned, but that was the war. It had left him indifferent where death was concerned, even to its uglier aspects. The time when a body had an emotional effect was long since gone. He had seen too many of them. The fact of death was all that mattered.

The radio crackled into life. Hoover's voice sounded clearly. 'Sugar Nan Two to Sugar Nan One. Are you receiving me?'

'Strength nine,' Howard said. 'Where are you, Harry?'

'We've reached the road junction, sir. Not a kraut in sight. What do we do now?'

Howard checked his watch. 'Stay there. We'll be with you in twenty minutes. Over and out.'

He replaced the handmike and turned to Garland. 'Strange – I would have expected something from them up there. A good place to put up a fight. Still . . .'

There was a sudden roaring in his ears and a great wind seemed to pick him up and carry him away. The world moved in and out and then somehow he was lying in a ditch, Garland beside him, minus his helmet and most of the top of his skull. The jeep, or what was left of it, was on its side. The Cromwell tank behind was blazing furiously, its ammunition exploding like a firework display. One of the crew scrambled out of the turret, his uniform on fire, and fell to the ground.

There was no reality to it at all – none. And then Howard realized why. He couldn't hear a damn thing. Something to do with the explosion probably. Things seemed to be happening in slow motion, as if under water, no noise, not even the whisper of a sound. There was blood on his hands, but he got his field-glasses up to his eyes and traversed the trees on the hillside on the other side of the road. Almost immediately a Tiger Tank jumped into view, a young man with pale face in the black uniform of a Sturmbannführer of SS-Panzer Troops, standing in the gun turret, quite exposed. As Howard watched helplessly he saw the microphone raised. The lips moved and then the Tiger's 88 belched flame and smoke.

The man whom Howard had seen in the turret of the lead Tiger was SS-Major Karl Ritter of the 3rd Company, 502nd SS Heavy Tank Battalion, and what was to take place during the ensuing five minutes was probably the single most devastating Tiger action of the Second World War.

Ritter was a Tiger ace with 120 claimed victories on the Russian Front, a man who had learned his business the hard way and knew exactly what he was doing. With only two operational Tigers on the hillside with him, he was hopelessly outnumbered, a fact which a reconnaissance on foot had indicated to him that morning and it was obvious that Denning would expect trouble at the junction with the Salzburg road. Therefore an earlier attack had seemed essential – indeed there was no alternative.

It succeeded magnificently, for on the particular stretch of forest track he had chosen there was no room for any vehicle to reverse or change direction. The first shell from his Tiger's 88 narrowly missed direct contact with the lead jeep, turning it over and putting Howard and his men into the ditch. The second shell, seconds later, brewed up the leading Cromwell tank. Ritter was already transmitting orders to his gunner, Sergeant-Major Erich Hoffer. The 88 traversed again and, a moment later, scored a direct hit on a Bren-gun carrier bringing up the rear.

The entire column was now at a standstill, hopelessly trapped, unable to move forward or back. Ritter made a hand signal, the other two Tigers moved out of the woods on either side and the carnage began.

In the five minutes which followed their three 88s and six machine guns left thirty armoured vehicles, including eight Cromwell tanks, ablaze.

The front reconnaissance jeep was out of sight among the trees at the junction with the road to Salzburg. O'Grady was sitting behind the wheel, with Hoover beside him lighting a cigarette. Finebaum was a few yards away, directly above the road, squatting against a tree, his M1 across his knees, eating beans from a can with a knife.

O'Grady was eighteen and a replacement of only a few weeks' standing. He said, 'He's disgusting, you know that, Sarge? He not only acts like a pig, he eats like one.

And the way he goes on, never stopping talking – making out everything's some kind of bad joke.'

'Maybe it is as far as he's concerned,' Hoover said. 'When we landed at Omaha there were 123 guys in the outfit. Now there are six including you, and you don't count worth a shit. And don't ever let Finebaum fool you. He's got a pocket full of medals somewhere, just for the dead men he's left around.'

There was the sudden dull thunder of heavy gunfire down in the valley below, the rattle of a machine gun.

Finebaum hurried towards the jeep, rifle in hand. 'Hey, Harry, that don't sound too good to me. What you make of it?'

'I think maybe somebody just made a bad mistake.' Hoover slapped O'Grady on the shoulder. 'Okay, kid, let's get the hell out of here.'

Finebaum scrambled into the rear and positioned himself behind the Browning heavy machine gun as O'Grady reversed quickly and started back down the track to the valley road. The sound of firing was continuous now, interspersed with one heavy explosion after another, and then they rounded a bend and found a Tiger tank moving up the road towards them.

Finebaum's hands tightened on the handles of the machine gun, but they were too close for any positive action and there was nowhere to run, the pine trees pressing in on either side of the road at that point.

O'Grady screamed at the last moment, releasing the wheel and flinging up his arms as if to protect himself, and then they were close enough for Finebaum to see the death's-head badge in the cap of the SS-major in the turret of the Tiger. A moment later, the collision took place and he was thrown head-first into the brush. The Tiger moved on relentlessly, crushing the jeep beneath it, and disappeared round the bend in the road.

Howard had lost consciousness for a while and came back to life to the sound of repeated explosions from the ammunition in another burning Cromwell. It was a scene from hell, smoke everywhere, the cries of the dying, the stench of burning flesh. He could see Colonel Denning lying in the middle of the road on his back a few yards away, revolver still clutched firmly in one hand, and beyond him a Bren-gun carrier was tilted on its side against a tree, bodies spilling out, tumbled one on top of another.

Howard tried to get to his feet, started to fall and was caught as he went down. Hoover said, 'Easy, sir. I've got you.'

Howard turned in a daze and found Finebaum there also. 'You all right, Harry?'

'We lost O'Grady. Ran head-on into a Tiger up the road. Where are you hit?'

'Nothing serious. Most of the blood's Garland's. He and Anderson bought it.'

Finebaum stood, holding his M1 ready. 'Heh, this must have been a real turkey shoot.'

'I just met Death,' Howard said dully. 'A nice-looking guy in a black uniform, with a silver skull and cross-bones in his cap.'

'Is that so?' Finebaum said. 'I think maybe we had a brush with the same guy.' He stuck a cigarette in his mouth and shook his head. 'This is bad. Bad. I mean to say, the way I had it figured, this stinking war was over and here some bastards are still trying to get me.'

The 502nd SS Heavy Tank Battalion, or what was left of it had temporary headquarters in the village of Lindorf, just off the main Salzburg Road, and the battalion commander, Standartenführer Max Jäger, had set up his command post in the local inn.

Karl Ritter had been lucky enough to get possession

of one of the first-floor bedrooms and was sleeping, for the first time in thirty-six hours, the sleep of total exhaustion. He lay on top of the bed in full uniform, having been too tired even to remove his boots.

At three o'clock in the afternoon he came awake to a hand on his shoulder and found Hoffer bending over him. Ritter sat up instantly. 'Yes, what is it?'

'The colonel wants you, sir. They say it's urgent.'

'More work for the undertakers.' Ritter ran his hands over his fair hair and stood up. 'So – did you manage to snatch a little sleep, Erich?'

Hoffer, a thin wiry young man of twenty-seven, wore a black Panzer sidecap and a one-piece overall suit in autumn-pattern camouflage. He was an inn-keeper's son from the Harz Mountains, had been with Ritter for four years and was totally devoted to him.

'A couple of hours.'

Ritter pulled on his service cap and adjusted the angle to his liking. 'You're a terrible liar, you know that, don't you, Erich? There's oil on your hands. You've been at those engines again.'

'Somebody has to,' Hoffer said. 'No more spares.'

'Not even for the SS.' Ritter smiled sardonically. 'Things really must be in a mess. Look, see if you can rustle up a little coffee and something to eat. And a glass of schnapps wouldn't come amiss. I shouldn't imagine this will take long.'

He went downstairs quickly and was directed, by an orderly, to a room at the back of the inn where he found Colonel Jäger and two of the other company commanders examining a map which lay open on the table.

Jäger turned and came forward, hand outstretched. 'My dear Karl, I can't tell you how delighted I am. A great, great honour, not only for you, but for the entire battalion.'

Ritter looked bewildered. 'I'm afraid I don't understand.'

'But of course. How could you?' Jäger picked up a

signal flimsy. 'I naturally passed full details of this morning's astonishing exploit straight to division. It appears they radioed Berlin. I've just received this. Special orders, Karl, for you and Sturmscharführer Hoffer. As you can see, you're to leave at once.'

Hoffer had indeed managed to obtain a little coffee – the real stuff, too – and some cold meat and black bread. He was just arranging it on the small sidetable in the bedroom when the door opened and Ritter entered.

Hoffer knew something was up at once, for he had never seen the major look so pale, a remarkable fact when one considered that he usually had no colour to him at all.

Ritter tossed his service cap on to the bed and adjusted the Knight's Cross with Oak Leaves that hung at the neck of his black tunic. 'Is that coffee, I smell, Erich? Real coffee? Who did you have to kill? Schnapps, too?'

'Steinhager, Major.' Hoffer picked up the stone bottle. 'Best I could do.'

'Well, then, you'd better find a couple of glasses, hadn't you. They tell me we've got something to celebrate.'

'Celebrate, sir?'

'Yes, Erich. How would you like a trip to Berlin?'

'Berlin, Major?' Hoffer looked bewildered. 'But Berlin is surrounded. It was on the radio.'

'Still possible to fly to Templehof or Gatow if you're important enough – and we are, Erich. Come on, man, fill the glasses.'

And suddenly Ritter was angry, the face paler than ever, the hand shaking as he held out a glass to the sergeant-major.

'Important, sir? Us?'

'My dear Erich, you've just been awarded the Knight's Cross, long overdue, I might add. And I am to receive the Swords, but now comes the best part. From the Führer himself, Erich. Isn't it rich? Germany on the brink of total disaster and he can find a plane to fly us in specially, with Luftwaffe fighter escort, if you please.' He laughed wildly. 'The poor sod must think we've just won the war for him or something.'

3

On the morning of 26 April, two Junker 52s loaded with tank ammunition managed to land in the centre of Berlin in the vicinity of the Siegessäule on a runway hastily constructed from a road in that area.

Karl Ritter and Erich Hoffer were the only two passengers, and they clambered out of the hatch into a scene of indescribable confusion, followed by their pilot, a young Luftwaffe captain named Rösch.

There was considerable panic among the soldiers who immediately started to unload the ammunition. Hardly surprising, for Russian heavy artillery was pounding the city hard and periodically a shell whistled overhead to explode in the ruined buildings to the rear of them. The air was filled with sulphur smoke and dust and a heavy pall blanketed everything.

Rösch, Ritter and Hoffer ran to the shelter of a nearby wall and crouched. The young pilot offered them cigarettes. 'Welcome to the City of the Dead,' he said. 'Dante's new Inferno.'

'You've done this before?' Ritter asked.

'No, this is a new development. We can still get in to Templehof and Gatow by air, but it's impossible to get from there to here on the ground. The Ivans have infiltrated all over the place.' He smiled sardonically. 'Still, we'll throw them back given time, needless to say. After all, there's an army of veterans to call on. Volkssturm units, average age sixty. And a few thousand Hitler Youth at the other end, mostly around fourteen. Nothing much in between, except the Führer, whom God preserve, natur-

403

ally. He should be worth a few divisions, wouldn't you say?'

An uncomfortable conversation which was cut short by the sudden arrival of a field car with an SS military police driver and sergeant. The sergeant's uniform was immaculate, the feldgendarmerie gorget around his neck sparkling.

'Sturmbannführer Ritter?'

'That's right.'

The sergeant's heels clicked together, his arm flashed briefly in a perfect party salute. 'General Fegelein's compliments. We're here to escort you to the Führer's headquarters.'

'We'll be with you in a minute.' The sergeant doubled away and Ritter turned to Rösch. 'A strange game we play.'

'Here at the end of things, you mean?' Rösch smiled. 'At least I'm getting out. My orders are to turn round as soon as possible and take fifty wounded with me from the Charité Hospital, but you, my friend. You, I fear, will find it rather more difficult to leave Berlin.'

'My grandmother was a good Catholic. She taught me to believe in miracles.' Ritter held out his hand. 'Good luck.'

'And to you.' Rösch ducked instinctively as another of the heavy 17·5 shells screamed overhead. 'You'll need it.'

The field car turned out of the Wilhelmplatz and into Vosstrasse and the bulk of the Reich Chancellery rose before them. It was a sorry sight, battered and defaced by the bombardment, and every so often another shell screamed in to further the work of destruction. The streets were deserted, piled high with rubble so that the driver had to pick his way with care.

'Good God,' Hoffer said. 'No one could function in such a shambles. It's impossible.'

'Underneath,' the police sergeant told him. 'Thirty metres of concrete between those Russian shells and the Führer's bunker. Nothing can reach him down there.'

'Nothing?' Ritter thought. 'Can it be truly possible this clown realizes what he is saying or is he as touched by madness as his masters?'

The car ramp was wrecked, but there was still room to take the field car inside. As they stopped, an SS sentry moved out of the gloom. The sergeant waved him away and turned to Ritter. 'If you will follow me, please. First, we must report to Major-General Mohnke.'

Ritter removed his leather military greatcoat and handed it to Hoffer. Underneath, the black Panzer uniform was immaculate, the decorations gleamed. He adjusted his gloves. The sergeant was considerably impressed and drew himself stiffly to attention as if aware that this was a game they shared and eager to play his part.

'If the Sturmbannführer is ready?'

Ritter nodded, the sergeant moved off briskly and they followed him down through a dark passage with concrete walls that sweated moisture in the dim light. Soldiers crouched in every available inch of space, many of them sleeping, mainly SS from the looks of things. Some glanced up with weary, lacklustre eyes that showed no surprise, even at Ritter's bandbox appearance.

When they talked, their voices were low and subdued and the main sound seemed to be the monotonous hum of the dynamos and the whirring of the electric fans in the ventilation system. Occasionally, there was the faintest of tremors as the earth shook high above them and the air was musty and unpleasant, tainted with sulphur.

Major-General Mohnke's office was as uninviting as everything else Ritter had seen on his way down through the labyrinth of passageways. Small and spartan with the usual concrete walls, too small even for the desk and chair and the half a dozen officers it contained when they arrived. Mohnke was an SS Brigadeführer who was now commander of the Adolf Hitler Volunteer Corps, a force of 2,000 supposedly handpicked men who were to form the final ring of defence around the Chancellery.

He paused in full flight as the immaculate Ritter entered the room. Everyone turned, the sergeant saluted and placed Ritter's orders on the desk. Mohnke looked at them briefly, his eyes lit up and he leaned across the table, hand outstretched.

'My dear Ritter, what a pleasure to meet you.' He reached for the telephone and said to the others, 'Sturmbannführer Ritter, gentlemen, hero of that incredible exploit near Innsbruck that I was telling you about.'

Most of them made appropriate noises, one or two shook hands, others reached out to touch him as if for good luck. It was a slightly unnerving experience and he was glad when Mohnke replaced the receiver and said, 'General Fegelein tells me the Führer wishes to see you without delay.' His arm swung up dramatically in a full party salute. 'Your comrades of the SS are proud of you, Sturmbannführer. Your victory is ours.'

'Am I mad or they, Erich?' Ritter whispered as they followed the sergeant ever deeper into the bunker.

'For God's sake, Major.' Hoffer put a hand briefly on his arm. 'If someone overhears that kind of remark . . .'

'All right, I'll be good,' Ritter said soothingly. 'Lead on, Erich. I can't wait to see what happens in the next act.'

They descended now to the lower levels of the Führerbunker itself. A section which, although Ritter did not know it then, housed most of the Führer's personal staff as well as Goebbels and his family, Bormann and Dr Ludwig Stumpfegger, the Führer's personal physician. General Fegelein had a room adjacent to Bormann's.

It was similar to Mohnke's – small with damp, concrete walls and furnished with a desk, a couple of chairs and a filing cabinet. The desk was covered with military maps which he was studying closely when the sergeant opened the door and stood to one side.

Fegelein looked up, his face serious, but when he saw Ritter, laughed excitedly and rushed round the desk to greet him. 'My dear Ritter, what an honour – for all of us. The Führer can't wait, I assure you.'

Such enthusiasm was a little too much, considering that Ritter had never clapped eyes on the man before. Fegelein was a one-time commander of SS cavalry, he knew that, awarded the Knight's Cross, so he was no coward – but the handshake lacked firmness and there was sweat on the brow, particularly along the thinning hairline. This was a badly frightened man, a breed with which Ritter had become only too familiar over the past few months.

'An exaggeration, I'm sure, General.'

'And you, too, Sturmscharführer.' Fegelein did not take Hoffer's hand but nodded briefly. 'A magnificent performance.'

'Indeed,' Ritter said dryly. 'He was, after all, the finger on the trigger.'

'Of course, my dear Ritter, we all acknowledge that fact. On the other hand . . .'

Before he could take the conversation any further the door opened and a broad, rather squat man entered the room. He wore a nondescript uniform. His only decoration was the Order of Blood, a much-coveted Nazi medal specially struck for those who had served prison sentences for political crimes in the old Weimar Republic. He carried a sheaf of papers in one hand.

'Ah, Martin,' Fegelein said. 'Was it important? I have the Führer's orders to escort this gentleman to him the instant he arrived. Sturmbannführer Ritter, hero of Wednesday's incredible exploit on the Innsbruck road. Reichsleiter Bormann you of course know, Major.'

But Ritter did not, for Martin Bormann was only a

name to him, as he was to most Germans – a face occasionally to be found in a group photo of party dignitaries, but nothing memorable about it. Not a Goebbels or a Himmler – once seen, never forgotten.

And yet here he was, the most powerful man in Germany, particularly now that Himmler had absconded. Reichsleiter Martin Bormann, head of the Nazi Party Chancellery and Secretary to the Führer.

'A great pleasure, Major.' His handshake was firm with a hint of even greater strength there if necessary.

He had a harsh, yet strangely soft voice, a broad, brutal face with Slavic cheekbones, a prominent nose. The impression was of a big man, although Ritter found he had to look down on him.

'Reichsleiter.'

'And this is your gunner, Hoffer.' Bormann turned to the sergeant-major. 'Quite a marksman, but then I sometimes think you Harz mountain men cut your teeth on a shotgun barrel.'

It was the first sign from anyone that Hoffer was more than a cypher, an acknowledgement of his existence as a human being, and it could not fail to impress Ritter, however reluctantly.

Bormann opened the door and turned to Fegelein. 'My business can wait. I'll see you downstairs anyway. I, too, have business with the Führer.'

He went out and Fegelein turned to the two men. Ritter magnificent in the black uniform, Hoffer somehow complementing the show with his one-piece camouflage suit, sleeves rolled up to the elbow. It couldn't be better. Just the sort of fillip the Führer needed.

Bormann's sleeping quarters were in the Party Chancellery Bunker, but his office, close to Fegelein's, was strategically situated so that he was able to keep the closest of contacts with Hitler. One door opened into the telephone exchange and general communication centre, the other to Goebbel's personal office. Nothing, therefore, could go in to the Führer or out again without the Reichsleiter's knowledge, which was exactly as he had arranged the situation.

When he entered his office directly after leaving Fegelein, he found SS-Colonel Willi Rattenhuber, whose services he had utilized as an additional aide to Zander since 30 March, leaning over a map on the desk.

'Any further word on Himmler?' Bormann asked.

'Not as yet, Reichsleiter.'

'The bastard is up to something, you may depend on it, and so is Fegelein. Watch him, Willi – watch him closely.'

'Yes, Reichsleiter.'

'And there's something else I want you to do, Willi. There's a Sturmbannführer named Ritter of the 502nd SS Heavy Tank Battalion on his way down now to receive the Swords from the Führer. When you get a moment, I want his records – everything you can find on him.'

'Reichsleiter.'

'That's what I like about you, Willi, you never ask questions.' Bormann clapped him on the arm. 'And now, we'll go down to the garden bunker and I'll show him to you. I think you'll approve. In fact I have a happy feeling that he may serve my purpose very well indeed.'

In the garden bunker was the Führer's study, a bedroom, two living rooms and a bathroom. Close by was the map room used for all high-level conferences. The hall outside served as an anteroom, and it was there that Ritter and Hoffer waited.

Bormann paused at the bottom of the steps and held Rattenhuber back in the shadows. 'He looks well, Willi, don't you agree? Quite magnificent in that pretty uniform with the medals gleaming, the pale face, the blond hair. Uncle Heini would have been proud of him: all that's fairest in the Aryan race. Not like us at all, Willi. He will undoubtedly prove a shot in the arm for the Führer. And notice the slight, sardonic smile on his mouth. I tell you there's hope for this boy, Willi. A young man of parts.'

Rattenhuber said hastily, 'The Führer comes now, Reichsleiter.'

Ritter, standing there at the end of a line of half a dozen young boys in the uniform of the Hitler Youth, felt curiously detached. It was rather like one of those dreams in which everything has an appearance of reality, yet events are past belief. The children on his right hand, for instance. Twelve or thirteen, here to be decorated for bravery. The boy next to him had a bandage round his forehead, under the heavy man's helmet. Blood seeped through steadily, and occasionally the child shifted his feet as if to prevent himself falling.

'Shoulders back,' Ritter said softly. 'Not long now.' And then the door opened. Hitler moved out flanked by Fegelein, Jodl, Keitel and Krebs, the new Chief of the Army General Staff.

Ritter had seen the Führer on several occasions in his life. Speaking at Nuremburg rallies, Paris in 1940, on a visit to the Eastern Front in 1942. His recollection of Hitler had been of an inspired leader of men, a man of magical rhetoric whose spell could not fail to touch anyone within hearing distance.

But the man who shuffled into the anteroom now might have been a totally different person. This was a sick old man, shoulders hunched under the uniform jacket that seemed a size too large, pale, hollow-cheeked, no sparkle in the lack-lustre eyes, and when he turned to take from the box Jodl held the first Iron Cross Second Class, his hand trembled.

He worked his way along the line, muttering a word or two of some sort of encouragement here and there, patting an occasional cheek, and then reached Ritter and Hoffner.

410

Fegelein said, 'Sturmbannführer Karl Ritter and Sturmscharführer Erich Hoffer of the 502nd SS Heavy Tank Battalion.' He started to read the citation. 'Shortly after dawn on the morning of Wednesday, April 25th . . .' but the Führer cut him off with a chopping motion of one hand.

There was fire in the dark eyes now, a sudden energy as he snapped his fingers impatiently for Jodl to pass the decoration. Ritter stared impassively ahead, aware of the hands touching him lightly, and then, for the briefest of moments, they tightened on his arm.

He looked directly into the eyes, aware of the power, the burning intensity, there again if only for a moment. the hoarse voice saying, 'Your Führer thanks you, on behalf of the German people.'

Hitler turned. 'Are you aware of this officer's achievement, gentlemen? Assisted by only two other tanks, he wiped out an entire British column of the 7th Armoured Division. Thirty armoured vehicles left blazing. Can you hear that and still tell me that we cannot win this war? If one man can do so much what could fifty like him accomplish?'

They all shifted uncomfortably. Krebs said, 'But of course, my Führer. Under your inspired leadership anything is possible.'

'Goebbels must have written that line for him,' Bormann whispered to Rattenhuber. 'You know, Willi, I'm enjoying this, and look at our proud young Sturmbannführer. He looks like Death himself with that pale face and black uniform, come to remind us all of what waits outside these walls. Have you ever read "Masque of the Red Death" by the American writer Poe?'

'No, I can't say that I have, Reichsleiter.'

'You should, Willi. An interesting parallel on the impossibility of locking out reality for long.'

An orderly clattered down the steps, brushed past Bormann and Rattenhuber and hesitated on seeing what was taking place. Krebs, who obviously recognized the man, moved to one side and snapped his fingers. The orderly passed him a signal flimsy which Krebs quickly scanned.

Hitler moved forward eagerly. 'Is it news of Wenck?' he demanded.

He was still convinced that the 12th Army under General Wenck was going to break through to the relief of Berlin at any moment.

Krebs hesitated and the Führer said, 'Read it, man! Read it!'

Krebs swallowed hard, then said, 'No possibility of Wenck and the 9th Army joining. Await further instruction.'

The Führer exploded with rage. 'The same story as Sunday. I gave the 11th Panzer Army to SS-General Steiner and all available personnel in his area with orders to attack. And what happened?'

The fact that the army in question had existed on paper only, a figment of someone's imagination, was not the point, for no one would have had the courage to tell him.

'So, even my SS let me down – betray me in my hour of need. Well, it won't do, gentlemen.' He was almost hysterical now. 'I have a way of dealing with traitors. Remember the July plot? Remember the films of the executions I ordered you to watch?'

He turned, stumbled back into the map room followed by Jodl, Keitel and Krebs. The door closed. Fegelein, moving as a man in a dream, signalled to one of the SS orderlies, who took the children away.

There was silence, then Ritter said, 'What now, General?'

Fegelein started. 'What did you say?'

'What do we do now?'

'Oh, go to the canteen. Food will be provided. Have a drink. Relax.' He forced a smile and clapped Ritter on the shoulder. 'Take it easy for a while, Major. I'll send for you soon. Fresh fields to conquer, I promise.'

He nodded to an orderly, who led the way. Ritter and Hoffer followed him, up the steps. Bormann and Ratten-huber were no longer there.

At the top, Ritter said softly, 'What do you think of that, then, Erich? Little children and old men led by a raving madman. So, now we start paying the bill, I think – all of us.'

When he reached his office, Fegelein closed the door, went behind his desk and sat down. He opened a cupboard, took out a bottle of brandy, removed the cork and swallow-ed deeply. He had been a frightened man for some time, but this latest display had finished him off.

He was exactly the same as dozens of other men who had risen to power in the Nazi party. A man of no background and little education. A one-time groom and jockey who had risen through the ranks of the SS and after being appointed Himmler's aide at Führer head-quarters, had consolidated his position by marrying Eva Braun's sister, Gretl.

But now even Himmler had cleared off, had refused every attempt aimed at returning him to the death-trap which Berlin had become. It occurred to Fegelein that perhaps the time had come for some definite action on his own part. He took another quick pull on the brandy bottle, got up, took down his cap from behind the door and went out.

It was seven o'clock that evening and Ritter and Hoffer were sitting together in the canteen, talking softly, a bottle of Moselle between them, when a sudden hubbub broke out. There were cries outside in the corridor, laughter and then the door burst open and two young officers ran in.

Ritter grabbed at one of them as he went by. 'Hey, what's all the excitement?'

'Luftwaffe General Ritter von Greim has just arrived from Munich with the air-ace, Hannah Reitsch. They landed at Gatow and came on in a Fieseler Storch.'

'The general flew himself,' the other young officer said. 'When he was hit, she took over the controls and landed the aircraft in the street near the Brandenburger Tor. What a woman.'

They moved away. Another voice said, 'A day for heroes, it would seem.'

Ritter looked up and found Bormann standing there. 'Reichsleiter.' He started to rise.

Bormann pushed him down. 'Yes, a remarkable business. What they omitted to tell you was that they were escorted by fifty fighter planes from Munich. Apparently over forty were shot down. On the other hand, it was essential General von Greim got here. You see, the Führer intends to promote him to Commander-in-Chief of the Luftwaffe with the rank of Feldmarschall, Göring having finally proved a broken reed. Naturally he wished to tell General Greim of this himself. Signal flimsies are so impersonal, don't you think?'

He moved away. Hoffer said in a kind of awe, 'Over forty planes – forty, and for what?'

'To tell him in person what he could have told him over the telephone,' Ritter said. 'A remarkable man, our Führer, Erich.'

'For God's sake, Major.' Hoffer put out a hand, for the first time real anger showing through. 'Keep talking like that and they might take you out and hang you. Me, too. Is that what you want?'

When Bormann went into his office, Rattenhuber was waiting for him.

'Did you find General Fegelein?' the Reichsleiter inquired.

'He left the bunker five hours ago.' Rattenhuber checked his notes. 'According to my information, he is at present at his home in Charlottenburg – wearing civilian clothes, I might add.'

Bormann nodded calmly. 'How very interesting.'

'Do we inform the Führer?'

'I don't think so, Willi. Give a man enough rope, you know the old saying. I'll ask where Fegelein is in the Führer's hearing later on tonight. Allow him to make this very unpleasant discovery for himself. Now, Willi, we have something far more important to discuss. The question of the prominent prisoners in our hands. You have the files I asked for?'

'Certainly, Reichsleiter.' Rattenhuber placed several manilla folders on the desk. 'There is a problem here. The Führer has very pronounced ideas on what should happen to the prominenti. It seems that he was visited by Obergruppenführer Berger, Head of Prisoner of War Administration. Berger tried to discuss the fate of several important British, French and American prisoners as well as the Austrian Chancellor, Schuschnigg, and Halder and Schacht. It seems the Führer told him to shoot them all.'

'Conspicuous consumption, I would have thought, Willi. In other words, a great waste.' Bormann tapped the files. 'But it's these ladies and gentlemen who interest me. The prisoners of Arlberg.'

'I'm afraid several have already been moved since my visit, on your instructions, two months ago. Orders of the Reichsführer,' Rattenhuber told him.

'Yes, for once Uncle Heini moved a little faster than I had expected,' Bormann said dryly. 'What are we left with?'

'Just five. Three men, two women.'

'Good,' Bormann said. 'A nice round number. We'll start with the ladies first, shall we? Refresh my memory.'

'Madame Claire de Beauville, Reichsleiter. Age thirty. Nationality, French. Her father made a great deal of money in canned foods. She married Étienne de Beauville. A fine old family. They were thought to be typical socialites flirting with their new masters. In fact her husband was working with French Resistance units in Paris. He was picked up in June last year on information received and taken to Sicherheitdienst headquarters at Avénue Foch in Paris. He was shot trying to escape.'

'The French,' Bormann said. 'So romantic.'

'The wife was thought to be involved. There was a radio at the house. She insisted she knew nothing about it, but Security was convinced she could well have been working as a – pianist?'

He looked up, bewildered, and Bormann smiled. 'Typical English schoolboy humour. This is apparently the British Special Operations Executive term for a radio operator.'

'Oh, I see.' Rattenhuber returned to the file. 'Through marriage, she is related to most of the great French families.'

'Which is why she is at Arlberg. So – who's next?'

'Madame Claudine Chevalier.'

'The concert pianist?'

'That's right, Reichsleiter.'

'She must be seventy at least.'

'Seventy-five.'

'A national institution. In 1940 she made a trip to Berlin to give a concert at the Führer's special request. It made her very unpopular in Paris at the time.'

'A very clever front to mask her real activities, Reichsleiter. She was one of a group of influential people who organized an escape line which succeeded in spiriting several well-known Jews from Paris to Vichy.'

'So – an astute old lady with nerve and courage. Does that dispose of the French?'

'No, Reichsleiter. There is Paul Gaillard to consider.'

'Ah, the one-time cabinet minister.'

'That is so, Reichsleiter. Aged sixty. At one time a physician and surgeon. He has, of course, an international reputation as an author. Dabbled in politics a little before the war. Minister for Internal Affairs in the Vichy government who turned out to be signing releases of known political offenders. He was also suspected of being in touch with de Gaulle. Member of the French Academy.'

'Anything else?'

'Something of a romantic, according to the security report. Joined the French Army as a private soldier in 1915 as some sort of public gesture against the government of the day. It seems he thought they were making a botch of the war. Flirted with Communism in the twenties, but a visit to Russia in 1927 cured him of that disease.'

'What about his weaknesses?'

'Weaknesses, Reichsleiter?'

'Come now, Willi, we all have them. Some men like women, others play cards all night or drink, perhaps. What about Gaillard?'

'None, Reichsleiter, and the State Security report is really most thorough. There is one extraordinary thing about him, however.'

'What's that?'

'He's had a great love of ski-ing all his life. In 1924 when they held the first Winter Olympics at Chamonix, he took a gold medal. A remarkable achievement. You see, he was thirty-nine years of age, Reichsleiter.'

'Interesting,' Bormann said softly. 'Now that really does say something about his character. What about the Englishman?'

'I'm not too certain that's an accurate description, Reichsleiter. Justin Fitzgerald Birr, 15th Earl of Dundrum: an Irish title, and Ireland is the place of his birth. He is also 10th Baron Felversham. The title is, of course, English and an estate goes with it in Yorkshire.'

'The English and the Irish really can't make up their minds about each other, can they, Willi? As soon as there's a war, thousands of Irishmen seem to join the British Army with alacrity. Very confusing.'

'Exactly, Reichsleiter. Lord Dundrum, which is how people address him, had an uncle who was a major of infantry in the first war. An excellent record, decorated and so on, then in 1919 he went home, joined the IRA and became commander of a flying column during their fight for independence. It apparently caused a considerable scandal.'

'And the earl? What of his war record?'

'Age thirty. DSO and Military Cross. At the beginning of the war he was a lieutenant in the Irish Guards. Two years later a lieutenant-colonel in the Special Air Service. In its brief existence his unit destroyed 113 aircraft on the ground behind Rommel's lines. He was captured in Sicily. Made five attempts to escape, including two from Colditz. It was then they decided that his special circumstances merited his transfer to Arlberg as a prominenti.'

'Which explains the last and most important point concerning the good Earl of Dundrum.'

'Exactly, Reichsleiter. It would seem the gentleman is, through his mother, second cousin to King George.'

'Which certainly makes him prominent, Willi. Very prominent indeed. And now – the best saved till last. What about our American friend?'

'Brigadier General Hamilton Canning, age forty-five.'

'The same as me,' Bormann said.

'Almost exactly. You, Reichsleiter, I believe, were born on the 17th of June. General Canning on the 27th of July. He would seem typical of a certain kind of American – a man in a perpetual hurry to get somewhere.'

'I know his record,' Bormann said. 'But go through it again for me.'

'Very well, Reichsleiter. In 1917 he joined the French

Foreign Legion as a private soldier. Transferred to the American Army the following year with the rank of second-lieutenant. Between the wars he didn't fit in too well. A trouble-maker who was much disliked at the Pentagon.'

'In other words he was too clever for them, read too many books, spoke too many languages,' Bormann said. 'Just like the High Command we know and love, Willi. But carry on.'

'He was a military attaché in Berlin for three years. Nineteen thirty-four to thirty-seven. Apparently became very friendly with Rommel.'

'That damn traitor.' Bormann's usually equable poise deserted him. 'He would.'

'He saw action on a limited scale in Shanghai against the Japanese in 1939, but he was still only a major by 1940. He was then commanding a small force in the Philippines. Fought a brilliant defensive action against the Japanese in Mindanao. He was given up for dead, but turned up in a Moro junk at Darwin in Australia. The magazines made something of a hero of him, so they had to promote him then. He spent almost a year in hospital. Then they sent him to England. Some sort of headquarters job, but he managed to get into combined operations.'

'And then?'

'Dropped into the Dordogne just after D-Day with British SAS units and Rangers to work with French partisans. Surrounded on a plateau in the Auvergne Mountains by SS paratroopers in July last year. Jumped from a train taking him to Germany and broke a leg. Tried to escape from hospital. They tried him at Colditz for awhile but that didn't work.'

'And then Arlberg.'

'It was decided, I believe, by Reichsführer himself, that he was an obvious candidate to be a prominenti.'

'And who do we have in charge of things at Schloss Arlberg, Willi?'

'Oberstleutnant Max Hesser, of the Panzer Grenadiers. Gained his Knight's Cross at Leningrad where he lost his left arm. A professional soldier of the old school.'

'I know, Willi, don't tell me. Held together by guts and piano wire. And who does he have with him now?'

'Only twenty men, Reichsleiter. Anyone capable of front-line action has been taken from him in the past few weeks. Oberleutnant Schenck, now his second-in-command, is fifty-five, a reservist. Sergeant-Major Schneider is a good man. Iron Cross Second and First Class, but he has a silver plate in his head. The rest are reservists, mostly in their fifties or cripples.'

He closed the last file. Bormann leaned back in his chair, fingertips together. It was quiet now except for the faintest rumblings far above them as the Russian artillery continued to pound Berlin.

'Listen to that,' Bormann said. 'Closer by the hour. Do you ever wonder what comes after?'

'Reichsleiter?' Rattenhuber looked faintly alarmed.

'One has plans, of course, but sometimes things go wrong, Willi. Some unexpected snag that turns the whole thing on its head. In such an eventuality, one needs what I believe the Americans term an "ace-in-the-hole".'

'The prominenti, Reichsleiter? But are they important enough?'

'Who knows, Willi? Excellent bargaining counters in an emergency, no more than that. Madame Chevalier and Gaillard are almost national institutions and Madame de Beauville's connections embrace some of the most influential families in France. The English love a lord at the best of times, doubly so when he's related to the King himself.'

'And Canning?'

'The Americans are notoriously sentimental about their heroes.'

420

He sat there, staring into space for a moment.

'So what do we do with them?' Rattenhuber said. 'What does the Reichsleiter have in mind?'

'Oh, I'll think of something, Willi,' Bormann smiled. 'I think you may depend on it.'

4

And at Schloss Arlberg on the River Inn, 450 miles south from Berlin and fifty-five miles north-west of Innsbruck, Lieutenant-Colonel Justin Birr, 15th Earl of Dundrum, leaned from the narrow window at the top of the north tower and peered down into the darkness of the garden, eighty feet below.

He could feel the plaited rope stir beneath his hands, and behind him in the gloom Paul Gaillard said, 'Is he there?'

'No, not yet.' A moment later the rope slackened, there was a sudden flash of light below, then darkness again. 'That's it,' Birr said. 'Now me, if I can get through this damned window. Hamilton certainly can pick them.'

He stood on a stool, turned to support himself on Gaillard's shoulders and eased his legs into space. He stayed there for a moment, hands on the rope. 'Sure you won't change your mind, Paul?'

'My dear Justin, I wouldn't get halfway down before my arms gave out.'

'All right,' Birr said. 'You know what to do. When I get down, or perhaps I should say *if* I do, we'll give you a flash. You haul the rope up, stick it in that cubbyhole under the floorboards then get to hell out of it.'

'You may rely on me.'

'I know. Give my regards to the ladies.'

'*Bon chance*, my friend.'

Birr let himself slide and was suddenly alone in the darkness, swaying slightly in the wind, his hands slipping from knot to knot. *Home-made rope and eighty feet to the garden. I must be mad.*

It was raining slightly, not a single star to be seen anywhere and already his arms were beginning to ache. He let himself slide faster, his feet banging against the wall, scratching his knuckles, at one point twirling round madly in circles. Quite suddenly, the rope parted.

My God, that's it! he thought, clamping his jaws together in the moment of death to stop himself from crying out, then hit the ground after falling no more than ten feet and rolled over in wet grass, winded.

There was a hand at his elbow, helping him to his feet. 'You all right?' Canning said.

'I think so.' Birr flexed his arms. 'A damn close thing, Hamilton, but then it usually is when you're around.'

'We aim to please.' Canning flashed his torch upwards briefly. 'Okay, let's get moving. The entrance to the sewer I told you about is in the lily pond on the lower terrace.'

They moved down through the darkness cautiously, negotiated a flight of steps and skirted the fountain at the bottom. The ornamental lily pond was on the other side of a short stretch of lawn. There was a wall at the rear of it, water gushing from the mouth of a bronze lion's head, rattling into the pool below. Birr had seen it often enough on exercise. 'Okay, here we go.'

Canning sat down and lowered himself into the water, knee-deep. He waded forward, Birr followed him and found the American crouched beside the lion's head in the darkness.

'You can feel the grille here, half under the water,' Canning whispered. 'If we can get that off we're straight into the main drainage system. One tunnel after the other all the way down to the river.'

'And if not?' Birr inquired.

'Short rations again and a stone cell, but that, as they say, is problematical. Right now we've got about ten minutes before Schneider and that damned Alsatian of his come by on garden patrol.'

He produced a short length of steel bar from his pocket, inserted it in one side of the bronze grille and levered. There was an audible crack, the metal, corroded by the years, snapping instantly. He pulled hard and the entire grille came away in his hands.

'You see how it is, Justin, All you have to do is live right. After you.'

Birr crouched down on his hands and knees in the water, and switching on his torch crawled through into a narrow brick tunnel. Canning moved in behind him, pulling the grille back into place.

'Don't you think you're getting a little old for Boy Scouts, Hamilton?' Birr whispered over his shoulder.

'Shut up and get moving,' Canning told him. 'If we can reach the river and find a boat by midnight, we'll have six or seven hours to play with before they find we're gone.'

Birr moved on, crawling on hands and knees through a couple of feet of water, the torch in his teeth. He emerged after a few yards into a tunnel that was a good five feet in diameter so that he could actually walk if he crouched a little.

The water was only about a foot deep here, for the tunnel sloped downwards steeply and the smell was not unpleasant, like old leaves and autumn on the river in a punt.

'Keep going,' Canning said. 'From what I found out from that gardener, we emerge into the main sewer pretty quickly. From there, it's a straight run down to the Inn.'

'I can smell it already,' Birr told him.

A few minutes later the tunnel did indeed empty into the main sewer in a miniature waterfall. Birr flashed his torch at the brown foam-flecked waters which rushed by several feet below.

'My God, just smell it, Hamilton. This really is beyond a joke.'

'Oh, get in there, for Christ's sake.' Canning gave him a shove and Birr dropped down, losing his balance and disappeared beneath the surface. He was on his feet in an instant and stood there cursing, still clutching his torch. 'It's liquid shit, Hamilton. Liquid shit.'

'You can have a wash when we get to the river,' Canning said as he lowered himself down to join him. 'Now let's make time.'

He started down the tunnel, torch extended before him, and Birr followed for perhaps sixty or seventy yards and then the tunnel petered out in a blank wall.

'That's it then,' Birr said. 'And a bloody good job too as far as I'm concerned. We'll have to go back.'

'Not on your sweet life. The water's got to go some-where.' Canning slipped his torch into his pocket, took a deep breath and crouched. He surfaced at once. 'As I thought. The tunnel continues on a lower level. I'm going through.'

Birr said, 'And what if it's twenty or thirty yards long, you idiot – or longer? You'll not have time to turn and come back. You'll drown.'

'So I'll take that chance, Justin.' Canning was tying one end of the rope about his waist now. 'I want out – you understand? I've no intention of sitting on my ass up there in the castle waiting for the Reichsführer's hired assassins to come and finish me off.' He held out the other end of the rope. 'Fasten that round your waist if you want to come too. If I get through, I'll give it a pull.'

'And if not?'

'Winter roses on my grave. Scarlet ones like those Claire cultivated in the conservatory.' He grinned once, took a deep breath and disappeared beneath the surface of the water.

Justin Birr waited. The electric torch gave only a minimal light, barely sufficient to pick out the slime on the ancient stone walls or the occasional rat that swam past in the dark water. The stench was frightful – really most unpleasant – and by now the cold had cut through to his very bones, or so it seemed.

He was aware of a sudden tug and hesitated, wondering for the moment whether it was simply imagination. There was another tug, more insistent this time. 'All right, damn you,' he said and extinguished the torch and put it in his breast pocket. His hands felt under the water for the edge of the arched roof. He took a deep breath and went down.

His feet banged against the stonework, but he kicked desperately, aware of the rope tugging at his waist, and then, just when he was convinced he couldn't keep going any longer, he saw a faint light ahead and surfaced, gasping for breath.

Canning, crouching out of the water on the side of a larger tunnel, reached down to pull him up. 'Easy does it.'

'Really, Hamilton, this particular small jaunt of yours is getting out of hand. I smell like a lavatory gone wrong and I'm frozen into the bargain.'

Canning ignored him. 'Listen – I can hear the river. Can't be far now.'

He set off at a fast pace, slipping and sliding on the slope of the tunnel, and Birr got to his feet wearily and went after him. And then Canning was laughing excitedly and running, splashing knee-deep in the brown water.

'I can see it. We're there.'

'Indeed you are, gentlemen. Indeed you are.'

A brilliant spot was turned on, flooding the tunnel with light. Birr hesitated, then went forward and dropped on his hands and knees beside Canning who crouched at the large circular grille which blocked the end of the tunnel. Schneider knelt on one knee at the other side, several armed men behind him.

'We've been waiting for you, gentlemen. Magda was growing impatient.'

His Alsatian bitch whined eagerly, pushing her muzzle

between the bars. Canning tugged at her ears. 'You wouldn't hurt me, you silly old bitch, would you?'

'All right, Sergeant-Major,' Justin Birr said. 'We'll come quietly.'

Oberstleutnant Max Hesser leaned back in his chair, got out his cigarette case and opened it one-handed with a skill born of long practice. Oberleutnant Schenck waited at the other side of the desk. He was dressed for duty, a pistol at his belt.

'Extraordinary,' the colonel said. 'What on earth will Canning get up to next?'

'God knows, Herr Oberst.'

'And the note you received telling you that the escape attempt was to take place. You say it was unsigned?'

'As you may see for yourself, Herr Oberst.'

He passed a slip of paper across and Hesser examined it. ' "Canning and Birr escaping through the main sewer tonight." Crudely done in pencil and block capitals but perfect German.' He sighed. 'So there is a traitor in the camp. One of their friends betrays them.'

'Not necessarily, Herr Oberst, if I might make a suggestion.'

'But of course, man. Carry on.'

'The general's knowledge of the sewer and drainage system must have been gained from somewhere. One of the soldiers or a servant, perhaps.'

'Ah, I see your point,' Hesser said. 'Who took a bribe, then slipped you that anonymous note to make sure the escape attempt would prove abortive.' He shook his head. 'I don't like it, Schenck. It leaves a bad taste.' He sighed. 'Anyway, I suppose I'd better have them in.'

Schenck withdrew and Hesser stood up and moved to the drinks cabinet. He was a handsome man in spite of the deep scar which bisected his forehead, curving into the right eye which was now glass; the uniform was trim and well-fitting, the empty left sleeve tucked into the belt.

He was pouring himself a brandy when the door opened behind him. He turned as Schenck ushered Canning and Birr into the room, Schneider behind them.

'Good God in heaven,' Hesser said.

They indeed presented a sorry sight, barefoot, covered in filth, water dripping on to the carpet. Hesser hurriedly filled another two glasses.

'From the looks of you, I'd say you needed it.'

Canning and Birr slopped forward. 'Very civil of you,' Birr said.

Canning grinned and raised his glass. 'Prosit.'

'And now to business.' Hesser went back to his desk and sat down. 'This is a nonsense, gentlemen. It must stop.'

'The duty of an officer to make every attempt to achieve his liberty and rejoin his unit,' Canning said. 'You know that.'

'Yes, under other circumstances I would agree with you, but not now. Not on the 26th of April, 1945. Gentlemen, after five and a half years, the war draws to a close. It's almost over – any day now. All we have to do is wait.'

'What for – an SS execution squad?' Canning said. 'We know what the Führer told Berger when he asked about the prominenti. He said shoot them. Shoot all of them. Last I heard, Himmler agreed with him.'

'You are in my charge, gentlemen. I have tried to make this plain many times before.'

'Great,' Canning said. 'And what happens if they drive up to the front door with a directive from the Führer. Will you pull up the drawbridge or order us to be shot? You took the soldier's oath, didn't you, just like everyone else in the German armed forces?'

Hesser stared up at him, very white, the great scar glowing angrily. Birr said gently, 'He does have a point, Colonel.'

Hesser said, 'I could put you gentlemen on short rations and confine you to your cells, but I won't. Under the circumstances and considering the point in time at which we all stand, I shall have you returned to prisoner's section and your friends. I hope you will respond in kind to this gesture.'

Schenck placed a hand on Canning's arm and the general pulled himself free. 'For God's sake, Max.' He leaned across the desk, voice urgent. 'There's only one way out for you. Send Schenck here in search of an Allied unit while there's still time. Someone you can surrender to legally, saving your own honour and our skins.'

Hesser stared at him for a long moment, then said, 'Have the general and Lord Dundrum returned to their quarters now, Schenck.'

'Herr Oberst.' Schenck clicked his heels and turned to the two men. 'General?'

'Oh, go to hell,' Canning told him, turned and walked out.

Birr paused. For a moment it was as if he intended to say something. Instead, he shrugged and followed. Schenck and Schneider went after them. Hesser went back to the cabinet and poured himself another drink. As he was replacing the bottle, there was a knock on the door and Schenck came back in.

'Would you care for one?' Hesser asked.

'No thank you, Herr Oberst. My stomach takes kindly only to beer these days.'

He waited patiently. Hesser walked across to the fire. 'You think he's right, don't you?' Schenck hesitated and Hesser said, 'Come on, man. Speak your mind.'

'Very well, Herr Oberst. Yes, I must say I do. Let's get it over and done with, that's my attitude. If we don't then I greatly fear that something terrible may take place here, the results of which may drag us all down.'

'You know something?' Hesser kicked a log that rolled forward back into place in a shower of sparks. 'I'm inclined to agree with you.'

Canning and Birr, followed by Schneider, two soldiers with Schmeissers and Magda, crossed the main hall and mounted the staircase, so wide that a company of soldiers could have marched up line abreast.

'I was once shown over MGM studios by Clark Gable,' Birr said. 'This place often reminds me of Stage Six. Did I ever tell you that?'

'Frequently,' Canning told him.

They crossed the smaller, upper landing and paused at an oaken, iron-bound door outside of which stood an armed sentry. Schneider produced a key about a foot long, inserted it in the massive lock and turned. He pushed open the door and stood back.

'Gentlemen.' As they moved in he added, 'Oh, by the way, the upper section of north tower is out of bounds and, in future, there will be two guards in the water garden at all times.'

'That's really very considerate of you,' Birr said. 'Don't you agree, General?'

'You can play that vaudeville act all night, but I've had it,' Canning said and started up the dark stone stairway.

Birr followed him and the door clanged shut behind them. They were now in north tower, the central keep of the castle, that portion to which in the old days the defenders had always retreated in the last resort. It was completely isolated from the rest of Schloss Arlberg, the lowest window fifty feet from the ground and heavily barred. It made, a relatively secure prisoner's section under most circumstances and meant that Hesser was able to allow the inmates a certain freedom, at least within the confines of the walls.

Madame Chevalier was playing the piano, they could hear her clearly – a Bach prelude, crisp and ice-cold, all technique, no heart. The kind of thing she liked to play to combat the arthritis in her fingers. Canning opened the door of the dining hall.

It was a magnificent room, a high arched ceiling festooned with battle standards from other times, a magnificent selection of fifteenth- and sixteenth-century armour on the walls. The fireplace was of baronial proportions. Gaillard and Claire de Beauville sat beside the log fire, smoking and talking quietly. Madame Chevalier was at the Bechstein.

At the sight of Canning and Birr, she stopped playing, gave a howl of laughter and started into the 'Dead March' from *Saul*.

'Very, very humorous,' Canning told her. 'I'm splitting my sides laughing.'

Claire and Paul Gaillard stood up. 'But what happened?' Gaillard said. 'The first I knew that there was anything amiss was when men arrived to lock the upper tower door. I'd just come down after securing the rope.'

'They were waiting for us, that's what happened,' Birr said. 'Dear old Schneider and Magda panting eagerly over Hamilton as usual. He's become the great love of her life.'

'But how could they have known?' Claire demanded.

'That's what I'd like to know,' Canning said.

'I should have thought it obvious.' Birr crossed to the sideboard and helped himself to a brandy. 'That gardener, Schmidt. The one you got the information about the drainage system from. Maybe a hundred cigarettes wasn't enough.'

'The bastard,' Canning said. 'I'll kill him.'

'But after you've had a bath, Hamilton – please.' Claire waved a hand delicately in front of her nose. 'You really do smell a little high.'

'Camembert – out of season,' said Gaillard.

There was general laughter. Canning said grimly, 'The crackling of thorns under a pot, isn't that what the good book says? I hope you're still laughing, all of you, when the Reichsführer's thugs march you out to the nearest wall.' He walked out angrily during the silence that followed. Birr emptied his glass. 'Strange, but I can't think of a single funny thing to say, so, if you'll excuse me . . .'

After he'd gone, Gaillard said, 'He's right, of course. It isn't good. Now if Hamilton or Lord Dundrum had got away and reached American or British troops, they could have brought help.'

'Nonsense, this whole business.' Claire sat down again. 'Hesser would never stand by and see us treated like that. It isn't in his nature.'

'I'm afraid Colonel Hesser would have very little to do with it,' Gaillard said. 'He's a soldier and soldiers have a terrible habit of doing what they're told, my dear.'

There was a knock at the door, it opened and Hesser came in. He smiled, his slight half-bow extending to the three of them, then turned to Madame Chevalier.

'Chess?'

'Why not?' She was playing a Schubert nocturne now, full of passion and meaning. 'But first settle an argument for us, Max. Paul here believes that if the SS come to shoot us you'll let them. Claire doesn't believe you could stand by and do nothing. What do you think?'

'I have the strangest of feelings that I will beat you in seven moves tonight.'

'A soldier's answer, I see. Ah, well.'

She stood up, came round the piano and moved to the chess table. Hesser sat opposite her. She made the first move. Claire picked up a book and started to read. Gaillard sat staring into the fire, smoking his pipe. It was very quiet.

After a while the door opened and Canning came in, wearing a brown battledress blouse and cream slacks.

Claire de Beauvoir said, 'That's better, Hamilton. Actually you really look rather handsome tonight. Crawling through sewers must be good for you.'

Hesser said, without looking up, 'Ah, General, I was hoping you'd put in an appearance.'

'I'd have thought we'd seen enough of each other for one night,' Canning told him.

'Perhaps, but the point you were making earlier. I think your argument may have some merit. Perhaps we could discuss it in the morning. Let's say directly after breakfast?'

'Now you're damn well talking,' Canning said.

Hesser ignored him, leaned forward, moved a bishop. 'Checkmate, I think.'

Madame Chevalier examined the board and sighed. 'Seven moves you told me. You've done it in five.'

Max Hesser smiled. 'My dear Madame, one must always try to be ahead of the game. The first rule of good soldiering.'

And in Berlin, just after midnight, Bormann still sat in his office, for the Führer himself worked through the night these days, seldom going to bed before 7 a.m., and Bormann liked to remain close. Close enough to keep others away.

There was a knock at the door and Rattenhuber entered, a sealed envelope in his hand. 'For you, Reichsleiter.'

'Who from, Willi?'

'I don't know, Reichsleiter. I found it on my desk marked Priority Seven.'

Which was a code reference for communications of the most secret sort, intended for Bormann's eyes alone.

Bormann opened the envelope, then looked up, no expression in his eyes. 'Willi, the Fieseler Storch in which Feldmarschall Greim and Hannah Reitsch flew in to Berlin has been destroyed. Get on to Gatow at once. Tell them they must send another plane by morning, one capable of flying directly out of the city.'

'Very well, Reichsleiter.'

Bormann held up the envelope. 'Know what's in here, Willi? Some very interesting news. It would appear that our beloved Reichsführer, dear Uncle Heini, has offered to surrender to the British and Americans.'

'My God,' Rattenhuber exclaimed.

'But what will the Führer say, Willi, that's the most interesting thing.' Bormann pushed back his chair and stood up. 'Let's go and find out, shall we?'

5

From his window, Hesser could see out across the court-yard and outer walls to the road winding steeply down the valley to the river below. Beyond the trees was the tiny village of Arlberg, looking rather like something out of a fairy tale by the Brothers Grimm, the pine trees on the lower slopes of the mountain behind it green against the snow. In fact it was snowing again now, only slightly, but for a moment, it seemed to make the world a cleaner, more shining place. Some throwback to childhood probably.

The door opened behind him and Schenck entered. Hesser said, 'Snowing again. It's hanging on this year.'

'True, Herr Oberst,' Schenck said. 'When I passed through the village early this morning I noticed the woodcutters' children from the outlying districts ski-ing to school.'

Hesser moved to the drinks cabinet and poured himself a brandy. Schenck tried to stay suitably impassive and Hesser said, 'I know, the road to ruin, but it's bad this morning. Worse than usual and this helps a damn sight more than those pills.'

He could feel his left arm in every detail within the empty sleeve, every wire inside his broken body, and the glass eye was sheer torture.

'What does it matter anyway? The same roads all lead to hell in the end. But never mind that now. Did you try Berlin again this morning?'

'Yes, Herr Oberst, but we're just not succeeding in getting through.'

'And the radio?'

'*Kaput*, Herr Oberst. Stern found a couple of valves gone.'

'Can't he replace them?'

'When he opened the box of spares they had all suffered damage in transit from the look of things.'

'Are you trying to tell me we've no kind of communication at all with anyone?'

'For the moment I am afraid that is true, Herr Oberst, but with luck we should still get through to Berlin if we keep trying and Stern is out in a field car now, touring the district to see if he can find the spares he needs.'

'Very well. Is there anything else?'

'General Canning and Colonel Birr are here.'

'All right, show them in. And Schenck,' he added as the old lieutenant moved to the door.

'Herr Oberst.'

'You stay, too.'

Canning wore a sidecap and olive drab officer's trenchcoat. Birr was in a reversible camouflage and white winter uniform smock with a hood, of a type issued generally in the German Army on the Eastern Front.

Hesser said, 'Ready for exercise, I see, gentlemen.'

'Never mind that,' Canning said brusquely. 'What have you decided?'

Hesser raised a hand defensively. 'You go too fast, General. There is a great deal to consider here.'

'For Christ's sake,' Canning said. 'Here we go again. Are you going to do something positive or aren't you?'

'We've been trying to get through to Prisoner of War Administration Headquarters in Berlin since last night without success.'

'Berlin?' Canning said. 'You must be joking. The Russians are walking all over it.'

'Not quite,' Hesser said evenly. 'The Führer, you may be dismayed to know, still lives and there are considerable German forces in the capital.'

'Four hundred and fifty miles away,' Canning said

urgently. 'This is here, Max. What are *you* going to do *here*, that's what I want to know.'

'Or to put it another way,' Birr said, 'have you thought any more about sending Lieutenant Schenck to look for a British or American unit, perhaps in company with one of us.'

'No.' Hesser slammed his good hand against the desk. 'That I will not permit. That would be going too far. I am a German officer, gentlemen, you must not forget that. I serve my country the best way I can.'

'So what in the hell is that supposed to mean?' Canning demanded.

Hesser frowned, thinking for a moment, then nodded. 'For today I will still keep trying to reach Berlin. I must know what their definite orders are in this matter.' Canning started to protest, but Hesser cut him short. 'No, this is the way I intend to handle things. You must make up your mind to it. First, to use a phrase you are fond of, we try channels.'

'And then?' Birr asked.

'If we are no further forward by this time tomorrow, I shall consider sending Oberleutnant Schenck out into the wide world to see what he can find. Always supposing he is willing to take his chances.' He turned to Schenck. 'I will not make this an order, you understand?'

Schenck smiled bleakly. 'I shall be happy to do as the Herr Oberst sees fit.'

'Why waste another day?' Canning began, but Hesser simply stood up.

'That is all I have to say, gentlemen. Good morning.' He nodded to Schenck. 'You will take the general and Colonel Birr to exercise now.'

It was cold in the water garden, snow flying every which way in the wind. The guards on each gate wore parkas and Schneider trailed along at the rear of Canning and

Birr with Magda. Canning turned at one point and snapped his fingers. The Alsatian strained at her lead and whined.

'Oh, let her go, man,' he snapped at Schneider in German.

Schneider slipped her chain reluctantly and the bitch ran to Canning and licked his hand. He knelt and fondled her ears and said, 'Well, what do you think?'

'More than I'd hoped for. Hesser's a Prussian, remember. A professional soldier of the old school, God and the Fatherland branded on his backbone. You're asking him to throw in his hand. Not only to string up the white flag, but to go running around trying to attract somebody's attention with it. That's expecting a hell of a lot. I'd settle for what you've got if I were you.'

'Yes, maybe you're right.' Canning stood up as Paul Gaillard and Madame Chevalier appeared from the lower water garden, walking briskly. She wore a German military greatcoat and a headscarf and Gaillard had on a black beret and overcoat.

'How did you get on?' the Frenchman demanded as they approached.

'Oh, you tell them, Justin,' Canning said. 'I've had enough for one day.'

He moved away, Magda at his knee, went down the steps past the lily pond and entered the conservatory. Schneider followed, but stayed in the porch.

It was warm and humid in there, plants everywhere, palms and vines, heavy with grapes. He followed the black and white mosaic of the path and came to the centre fountain where he found Claire de Beauville tending the scarlet winter roses that were her special pride.

Canning paused for a moment, watching her. She was really beautiful, the dark hair pulled back to the nape of the neck, exposing the oval triangle of the face. The high cheekbones, the wide, quiet eyes, the generous mouth.

He was conscious of the old, familiar stirring and the slight feeling of anger that went with it.

Orphaned at an early age and supported by an uncle in the shipping business in Shanghai, whom he never saw, he had spent most of his youth at boarding schools of one kind or another before he finally entered West Point. From that moment, he had given his all to the army; sacrificed everything to the demands of military life with single-minded devotion. He had never felt the need for wife or family. There had been women, of course, but only in the most basic way. Now, everything had changed. For the first time in his life, another human being could touch him and that was not a concept that fitted comfortably into his scheme of things.

Claire turned, gardening fork in one hand, and smiled. 'There you are. What happened?'

'Oh, we have to wait another twenty-four hours. Max wants to make one last attempt to get in touch with Prisoner of War Administration Headquarters in Berlin. The correct Junker officer, right to the bitter end.'

'And you, Hamilton, what do you want?'

'To be free now,' he said, his voice suddenly urgent. 'It's been too long, Claire, don't you see?'

'And you've missed too much, isn't that it?' He frowned and she carried on. 'The war, Hamilton. Your precious war. Bugles faintly on the wind, the smoke of battle. Meat and drink to you; what your soul craves. And who knows, if you were free now, there might still be the chance to get involved. Have one last glorious fling.'

'That's a hell of a thing to say.'

'But true. And what can I offer as a substitute? Only winter roses.'

She smiled slightly. He caught her then, pulling her into his arms, his mouth fastening hungrily on hers.

Ritter, seated at the piano in the canteen, was playing a Chopin étude, a particular favourite of his. It was a piece which comforted him, in spite of the fact that this present instrument was distinctly out of tune. It reminded him of other days. Of his father and mother and the small country estate in Prussia where he had been raised.

The Russians were shelling constantly now, the sound of the explosions audible even at that depth, the concrete walls trembling. There was that all-pervading smell of sulphur, dust everywhere.

A drunken SS lieutenant lurched against the piano, slopping beer over the keys. 'We've had enough of that rubbish. What about something rousing? Something to lift the heart. A chorus of "Horst Wessel", perhaps?'

Ritter stopped playing and looked up at him. 'You're speaking to me, I presume?' His voice was very quiet, yet infinitely dangerous, the white face burning, the eyes dark.

The lieutenant took in the Knight's Cross, the Oak Leaves, the Swords, the rank insignia and tried to draw himself together. 'I'm sorry, Sturmbannführer. My mistake.'

'So it would appear. Go away.'

The lieutenant moved off to join a noisy jostling throng as drunk as himself. A young nurse in service uniform was passing by. One of them pulled her across his knee. Another slipped a hand up her skirt. She laughed and reached up to kiss a third hungrily.

Ritter, totally disgusted, helped himself to a bottle of Steinhager at the bar, filled a glass and sat at an empty table. After a while, Hoffer entered. He looked around the canteen, then came across quickly, his face pale with excitement.

'I saw a hell of a thing a little while ago, Major.'

'And what would that be?'

'General Fegelein being marched along the corridor by two of the escort guard, minus his epaulettes and shoulder flashes. He looked frightened to death.'

'The fortunes of war, Erich. Get yourself a glass.'

'Good God, Major, a general of the SS. A Knight's Cross holder.'

'And like all of us in the end, clay of the most common variety, my friend – or at least his feet were.'

'We shouldn't have come here to this place.' Hoffer glanced about him, his face working. 'We're never going to get out. We're going to die here like rats and in bad company.'

'I don't think so.'

There was an immediate expression of hope on Hoffer's face. 'You've heard something?'

'No, but all my instincts tell me that I shall. Now get yourself a glass and bring that chessboard over here.'

Bormann and Rattenhuber, watching from a doorway at the rear of the room, had observed the entire scene. Rattenhuber said, 'His mother was a really big aristocrat. One of those families that goes all the way back to Frederick.'

'Look at him,' Bormann said. 'Did you see the way he handled that drunken swine? And I'll tell you something, Willi. A hundred marks says he hasn't raised his arm and said Heil Hitler for at least two years. I know his kind. They salute like a British Guards officer – a finger to the peak of the cap. And the men, Willi. Shall I tell you what they think, even the men of the SS? Would you imagine they'd still follow old peasants like you and me?'

'They follow.' Rattenhuber hesitated. 'They follow their officers, Reichsleiter. They have discipline, the Waffen-SS. The finest in the world.'

'But Ritter, Willi. A man like him, they'll follow into the jaws of hell, and you know why? Because men like him don't give a damn. They're what they are. Themselves alone.'

'And what would that be, Reichsleiter?'

'In his case, a very gentle perfect knight. You see, Willi? All that reading I do – even English literature. They think me Bormann the boor, Goebbels and company, but I know more than they do – about everything. Don't you agree?'

'But of course, Reichsleiter.'

'And Ritter – fine Aryan stock, like one of those idealized paintings the Führer loves so much. A standard impossible for the rest of us to attain. Forget the nasty things, Willi. The rapes, the burnings, the camps, the executions. Just think of the ideal. The finest soldier you've ever known. Decent, honourable, chivalrous and totally without fear. What every soldier in the Waffen-SS would like to imagine himself to be, that's what Ritter *is*.'

'And you think these Finnish barbarians we discussed earlier would concur?'

'The Knight's Cross, Willi, with Oak Leaves *and* Swords? What do you think?'

Rattenhuber nodded. 'I think that perhaps the Reichsleiter would like me to bring him to the office now.'

'Later, Willi. Now I must go to the Führer. The news of Himmler's defection and Fegelein's cowardice have considerably angered him. He needs me. You speak to Ritter, Willi, when he's had a drink or two. Judge if it's changed him. I'll see him later. After midnight.'

The shelling increased in intensity, the thunder overhead continuous now, so that the walls shook constantly and in the canteen behaviour deteriorated considerably. The place was crowded with a noisy, jostling throng, here and there a drunk lying under the table.

When Rattenhuber returned a couple of hours later, Ritter and Hoffer were still at the table at the rear of the room, playing chess.

Rattenhuber said, 'May I join you?'

Ritter glanced up. 'Why not.'

Rattenhuber winced as a particularly thunderous explosion shook the entire room. 'I didn't like the sound of that. Do you think we're safe here, Major?'

Ritter looked at Hoffer. 'Erich?'

Hoffer shrugged. 'Seventeen point five calibre is the heaviest they've got. Nothing that could get down this far.'

'A comforting thought.' Rattenhuber offered them both cigarettes.

Ritter said, 'Hoffer saw a strange sight some hours ago. General Fegelein being led along the corridor under escort, minus epaulettes and insignia.'

'Yes, very sad. A disgrace to all of us,' Rattenhuber said. 'He cleared off yesterday. When the Führer found he was missing, he sent a detachment out looking for him. The fool was actually at his own house in Charlottenburg in civilian clothes and with a woman. They took him outside and shot him half an hour ago.'

Ritter showed no emotion whatsoever. 'If what you say is so, then there could be no other penalty.'

'No, we can't just leave the war by taking off our uniform and putting on a raincoat, not at this stage,' Rattenhuber said. 'Not any of us.' He lit another cigarette. 'By the way, Major, the Reichsleiter would like to see you a little later on. I'd be obliged if you'd hold yourself in readiness.'

'Naturally,' Ritter said. 'I'm at the Reichsleiter's orders.' The slight, sardonic smile that touched his mouth had an edge of contempt to it. 'Was there anything else?'

Rattenhuber felt in some curious way as if he was being dismissed. 'No,' he said hurriedly. 'I'll look for you here.'

An SS orderly entered the room, gazed around quickly, then bore down on them. He clicked his heels and offered a signal to Rattenhuber. Rattenhuber read it, his face broke into a delighted smile and he waved the orderly away.

'Excellent news. The Fieseler Storch in which Feld-marschall von Greim and Hannah Reitsch flew into Berlin on the 26th was destroyed this morning by artillery fire.'

'So, the Feldmarschall is also a permanent guest here?' Ritter said. 'Bad luck.'

'No, he got away this evening in a replacement plane, an Arado trainer piloted by Hannah Reitsch after she'd made two unsuccessful attempts. They took off near the Brandenburger Tor.' He stood up. 'You must excuse me. The Reichsleiter has been waiting for such news and the Führer also.' He went out.

Hoffer said, 'But what does he want you for?'

'I expect I'll find that out when he sees me,' Ritter said. He nodded at the chessboard. 'And now, if you don't mind, it's your move.'

Just before midnight, Walter Wagner, a city councillor and minor official of the Propaganda Ministry, was hustled into the bunker under armed guard. Totally bewildered and still not quite believing what was happening to him, at approximately one o'clock in the morning he married Adolf Hitler and Eva Braun. The only other two people present were the witnesses, Martin Bormann and Josef Goebbels, Reich Minister for Propaganda.

A wedding breakfast was served immediately afterwards at which champagne was available in copious quantities. At approximately two o'clock, the Führer went into an adjoining room to dictate his will and final political testament to one of his two secretaries, Frau Junge. Bormann, who had been waiting for an appropriate moment, seized his chance and left also.

Rattenhuber was waiting for him in the corridor. 'And now we've got that out of the way, I'll see Ritter,' the Reichsleiter said. 'Bring him to me, Willi.'

When Rattenhuber ushered Ritter into the office, there was a particularly intensive bombardment taking place. The Reichsleiter looked up as smoke and dust drifted from the ventilator. 'If that hadn't been happening for some days now, I'd be alarmed.'

'Not pleasant,' Ritter said.

'No place to be at the moment – Berlin – if it can be avoided.'

Rattenhuber took up his position beside the door. There was a long silence during which Bormann gazed up at the young SS officer calmly. Finally he said, 'You would like to leave Berlin, Sturmbannführer?'

Ritter actually smiled. 'I think you may say that I would dearly love to, Reichsleiter, but I would not have thought it a possibility now.'

'Oh, all things are possible to men who are willing to dare anything. I had formed the opinion that you were of that breed. Am I right?'

'If you say so.'

'Good, we must see if we can accommodate you then. This man of yours – Hoffer. He is to be trusted?'

'With my life – yes,' Ritter said. 'I would not depend too much on his loyalty to any political idea, however – not at this stage.'

'In other words, a man of sound sense and judgement. I like that.' Bormann turned the map which lay before him. 'You know this area here, north-west of Innsbruck on the Inn River?'

'I know where it is,' Ritter said. 'Let's put it that way. My unit was in that general area when I left. Perhaps fifty miles away.'

'Not now,' Bormann said. 'What was left of them was wiped out by tanks of the American 6th Army Group a hundred miles or more from there yesterday morning.'

For a moment his voice seemed to fade for Ritter as he thought of the regiment, old comrades, Colonel Jäger.

He came back to reality to hear Bormann saying, 'I'm sorry – a bad shock for you.'

'No matter,' Ritter said. 'An old and tired story, repeated many times. Please continue.'

'Very well. This entire area, the triangle between Innsbruck, Salzburg and Klagenfurt, is still in our hands, but the situation is very fluid. The enemy are probing in with great care because they believe the stories they've heard of an Alpine fortress where we can hold out for years. Once they appreciate the truth of the situation, they'll be through to Berchtesgaden like a hot knife into butter.'

'And this could happen at any time?'

'Undoubtedly. So, to accomplish what I seek we must move fast.'

'And what would that be, Reichsleiter?'

Bormann picked up a pencil and drew a circle around Arlberg. 'Here at Schloss Arlberg on the Inn, you will find five important prisoners. What we call prominenti. One of them is the American general, Canning. Who the others are needn't concern you at the moment. It's enough to know that they are all people held in special regard by the individual nations. You can read the files later.'

'A moment,' Ritter said. 'You speak as if you expect me to go there in person. As if it is an accomplished fact. But this would first mean leaving Berlin.'

'Naturally.'

'But how can this be?'

'You may have heard that the Fieseler Storch in which Feldmarschall von Greim and Hannah Reitsch flew into Berlin was destroyed yesterday.'

'Yes, I know that. They flew out last night in a replacement, an Arado training plane.' And then, with a sudden flash of insight, Ritter saw it all. 'Ah, I see now. The Fieseler Storch –'

'– Is in a garage at the back of an automobile showroom just off the main avenue near Brandenburger Tor. I'll give you the address before you leave. You will fly out tonight, or probably just after midnight tomorrow, the best time to evade the Russian anti-aircraft. About ten miles from Arlberg, here at Arnheim, there's an airstrip. Used for mountain rescue operations before the war. No one there now. You should arrive by breakfast time.'

'Then what?'

'You'll find transport. It's all arranged. Even my enemies admit I'm an organizer.' Bormann smiled. 'You will proceed from there to Arlberg where you will take charge of the five prisoners I have mentioned and bring them back to Arnheim with you. They'll be picked up from there by transport plane later in the day. Any questions?'

'Several. The purpose of this operation?'

'The prisoners, you mean?' Bormann waved a hand. 'Put out of your mind any wild rumours you may have heard about the execution of prominent persons. I abhor waste, Major, believe me. These people will be useful bargaining counters when we reach the situation of having to sit down and discuss peace terms with our enemies.'

'Hostages might be a better word.'

'If you like.'

'All right,' Ritter said. 'But what about the situation at the castle? Who's in charge?'

'Soldiers of the Wehrmacht, but only just. A Colonel Hesser – a good man, but crippled – and nineteen or twenty old men. Reservists. Nothing to worry about.'

'And I'll have a piece of paper, I suppose, ordering him to hand them over?'

'Signed by the Führer himself.'

'What if he refuses – not that I'm trying to be difficult, you understand. It's just that after six years of service I've got accustomed to the fact that in war anything can happen, especially when one expects the opposite. I like to take care of all eventualities.'

'And so you shall.' Borman indicated the map again. tapping with his pencil. 'At this very moment no more than ten miles west of Arnheim you'll find an SS unit or what's left of it. Thirty or forty men according to my information.'

'These days, as the Reichsleiter knows, the term SS can cover a multitude of sins. Are they German?'

'No, but first-rate troops. Finns, who were with Wiking Division in Russia operating mainly as ski troops.'

'Mercenaries?' Ritter said.

'Soldiers of the Waffen-SS whose contract does not expire until 9 a.m. on the 1st May. You will hold them to their contract and bend them to your purpose until you have secured your prisoners. Do you understand me?'

'I believe so.'

'Good.' Bormann handed him a small folder. 'Everything you need is in there, including the address of the garage where you'll find the Stork. The pilot's name is Berger. He's SS too, so you see, it's all being kept in the family. Oh, and there's just one other rather important thing.'

'What's that, Reichsleiter?'

'Someone will be going along with you, as my personal representative, just to see that everything goes all right. A Herr Strasser. I hope I can rely on you to offer him every courtesy.'

Ritter stood looking down at the folder which he gripped tightly in both hands. 'Is there something worrying you, Major?' Martin Bormann asked gently.

'The prisoners,' Ritter said and looked up. 'I want your assurance, your personal word on your honour, that no harm will come to them. That the situation will be exactly as you have stated.'

'My dear Ritter.' Bormann came round the desk and put a hand on his shoulder. 'Anything else would simply be stupid and I'm not that, believe me.'

Ritter nodded slowly. 'As you say, Reichsleiter.'

'Good,' Bormann said. 'Excellent. I'd get some sleep now if I were you. Rattenhuber here will see that you and Hoffer get a pass that will get you out of here some time tomorrow afternoon. I may not see you again before you go, although I'll try. If not, good luck.'

He held out his hand. Ritter hesitated, then took it briefly. Rattenhuber held open the door for him. As he closed it, Bormann went round the desk. When he turned there was a strange expression on his face.

'My honour, Willi. He asked me to swear on my honour. Did you ever hear of such a thing with almost everyone else I know doubting its very existence for the past twenty years or more?'

Hoffer was waiting in the canteen and leaned over excitedly as Ritter sat down. 'What was it all about?'

'I'm not sure, Erich,' Ritter said. 'You see, there was what he told me and what he missed out. Still, for what it's worth . . .'

He leaned forward, his hands on the folder, and started to talk.

6

At Schloss Arlberg it was still snowing when Schenck knocked at the door and entered Hesser's office. The colonel was standing at the window, looking out across the valley. He turned and walked to the desk.

'So, the situation is still the same?'

'I'm afraid so, Herr Oberst. We are still unable to get through to Berlin.'

'And the radio?'

'Stern has visited every village in these parts without success. There are certain to be radios in the area, of course, that may well use the right type of valve, but as the Herr Oberst knows, their possession in this district has been declared illegal for more than a year now. Those individuals guilty of breaking the law are unlikely to admit to the fact at this stage.'

'Understandable in the circumstances.' Hesser sat down. 'The time for a definite decision has come.'

'So it would appear, Herr Oberst.'

Hesser sat for a moment, plucking at his empty sleeve. 'As I said yesterday, I will not make an order of this business. I would be failing in my duty if I didn't point out that it could be extremely hazardous. In the fluid state of the front line in this area, any enemy unit you run into may be inclined to shoot first and ask questions afterwards. You understand this?'

'Perfectly.'

'And you're still willing to take a chance?'

'Herr Oberst,' Schenck said, 'I'm an old man by military standards, perhaps too old for this sort of game.

I last saw action on the Western Front in 1918, but it would be quite out of the question for you to go, sir, and certainly improper to send one of the other ranks on such a mission. As I am the only other available officer, it would seem to me that we have little choice in the matter.'

'Who would you take with you?'

'Schmidt, I think. He's my own age, but an excellent driver. We'll take one of the field cars.'

'Very well,' Hesser said. 'It would seem, as you say, that there is no other choice. Please bring General Canning and Colonel Birr and I'll inform them of my decision.'

'They are outside now, Herr Oberst.'

Schenck moved to the door and Hesser said, 'Schenck?'

'Herr Oberst.'

'I appreciate this. You're a brave man.'

'No, Herr Oberst, anything but that. A very frightened man.' Schenck smiled. 'But I do have a wife and two daughters I'm more than anxious to see again. What I do now, I'm doing for them. The best thing for all of us, believe me.'

'Yes, perhaps you're right.'

Schenck went out and returned a few moments later with Canning and Birr. The general came forward eagerly. 'Well, have you come to a decision?'

Hesser nodded. 'Oberleutnant Schenck will be leaving.' Here, he glanced at his watch. 'At noon precisely. He'll take a field car and one driver with him and he will search for an Allied unit somewhere in the general direction of Innsbruck. You agree, Schenck?'

'Whatever you say, Herr Oberst.'

'Thank God you've come to your senses,' Canning said. 'Can we go now and tell the others?'

'I don't see why not.'

Canning and Birr turned to the door and Hesser stood up. 'One thing before you go.'

'What's that?' Canning turned impatiently.

'Oberleutnant Schenck and Corporal Schmidt will be running a considerable personal risk in this business. I hope you appreciate that.'

Canning frowned and it was Birr who held out his hand to Schenck. 'We certainly do and I, for one, would like to thank you now on behalf of all of us.'

'I will do my best, Herr Oberst,' Schenck smiled briefly, 'to stay alive for all our sakes.'

Paul Gaillard and Claire were sitting at the window in the dining hall when Canning and Birr entered, Madame Chevalier at her daily practice at the piano. She stopped playing at once.

Gaillard stood up. 'What happened?'

'We go,' Canning said excitedly. 'Or at least, Schenck does. He leaves at noon.' He stood in front of the fire, hands behind his back. 'Do you folks realize that with any kind of luck he could be back here in a matter of hours? That by this evening we could be free.'

Birr lit a cigarette. 'On the other hand, if he runs into the wrong sort of trigger-happy bunch, he could also be dead by then. Have you considered that?'

'Nonsense,' Canning said. 'Schenck spent four years on the Western Front in the First World War. Wounded three times. He's too old a bird to get knocked off now.'

'But if he does, Hamilton' – Claire walked to the fire and sat down – 'what do we do?'

'Then it may be necessary for us to take more positive action ourselves.' Canning crossed to the door and opened it. He turned. 'I know one thing. If anybody tries to take me out of here, SS or whoever, they're going to have to do it the hard way.'

He went out, closing the door behind him.

When Rattenhuber went into Bormann's office the Reichsleiter was writing away at his desk. 'I'll only be a moment, Willi. I missed my diary entry last night. I was with the Führer for hours.' After a while he put down his pen and closed the book. 'So, Willi, and how are things going out there? How's morale?'

Rattenhuber looked uncomfortable. 'Morale, Reichsleiter?'

'Come on, man. No need to beat about the bush at this stage of the game.'

'Very well, Reichsleiter. If you must know, it's a total disgrace. I've never seen so many drunks in uniform in all my life. The canteen is full of them. And the women aren't behaving any better. Everything seems to be going to pieces.'

'What do you expect, Willi? You know why the Russian artillery has stopped? Because they were killing their own people as their tanks and infantry pushed towards Wilhelmplatz. According to the latest reports they've come to a halt no more than 500 metres from the Chancellery. There's heavy fighting in Belle-Allianceplatz and in the Potsdamerstrasse, though I understand our troops are holding their own near Bismarckstrasse.'

'But what about Wenck's Army?'

'Still maintaining its links with Reimann's Corps, but that's no use to us, Willi. We're finished.'

Rattenhuber looked shocked. 'Finished, Reichsleiter?'

'Oh, for quite some time now, didn't you know? When Steiner's counter-attack failed to materialize on the 22nd, the Führer announced then that the war was lost. That he intended to die in Berlin. Did you know that at his wedding breakfast he actually talked of suicide?'

'My God!' Rattenhuber said in horror.

'Perhaps the greatest service he could render the German people.'

He seemed to be waiting for some kind of comment. Rattenhuber licked dry lips nervously. 'Reichsleiter?'

'An interesting thought. To die for the cause, if you are the right person, can sometimes be more important than to live.' He smiled gently, contriving to look even more sinister than usual. 'But for lesser mortals, such excesses are not always necessary. You, for instance, Willi.'

'Me, Reichsleiter? I don't understand.'

'Your destiny is to live, Willi. To put it simply, you are to leave this evening.'

Rattenhuber stared at him in astonishment. 'Leave Berlin, you mean?'

'Together with the Führer's army adjutant, Johannmeier, Lorenz from the Propaganda Ministry, and Zander. His task is to take a copy of the Führer's political testament and will to Admiral Dönitz. I suggested sending you as well and the Führer agreed.'

'I – I am honoured,' Rattenhuber stammered.

'I'm sure you are, Willi,' Bormann said dryly. 'But whether you reach Dönitz or not is problematical and of no particular consequence. There are other tasks for you now of more importance.'

Rattenhuber's face was pale. 'The Kamaradenwerk? It begins?'

'Of course, Willi. Did I not always say it would? In my end is my beginning. I read that once somewhere. Highly appropriate.'

There was a tremendous explosion somewhere close by, the walls of the bunker shook, a cloud of dust filtered in through the ventilator.

Bormann glanced up, showing absolutely no sign of fear. 'There goes the Ivan artillery again. You know, in some ways it reminds me of the *Twilight of the Gods*. All the forces of evil are in league against them and then suddenly a new citadel arises, more beautiful than ever, and Baldur lives again.' He turned, his face grave. 'It will be so for us, Willi, for Germany. This I promise you.'

And Rattenhuber, in spite of the noise of the shells landing without cease thirty metres above his head, the sulphurous stench, the dust which threatened to choke him, straightened his shoulders.

'I, too, believe, Reichsleiter. Have never ceased to believe in the destiny of the German people.'

'Good, Willi. Excellent.' Bormann took a letter from his desk and shook the dust from it. 'This is the reason it is so important you get out of Berlin and that clown Dönitz has nothing to do with it.'

At Schloss Arlberg in the main courtyard Schenck was preparing to leave. He stood beside the field car, the collar of his greatcoat turned up against the snow, and waited as Corporal Schmidt made a final check on the engine.

'Everything all right?' Schenck asked.

'As far as I can see, Herr Leutnant.'

'Good man.'

As he turned, Hesser, Canning and Birr came down the steps of the main entrance and moved across the courtyard.

'All set, Schenck?' Hesser demanded.

'Yes, Herr Oberst.'

'Good. General Canning has something for you.'

Canning held out an envelope. 'This is a letter I've written, explaining the situation here. Hand it to the first British or American officer you come to. I think it should do the trick.'

'My thanks, General.' Schenck put the envelope in his pocket, then unfastened the service belt that carried the holstered Walther automatic pistol at his waist. He held it out to Hesser. 'Under the circumstances, I shan't be needing this.' He reached inside the field car and picked up Corporal Schmidt's Schmeisser from the rear seat. 'Or this.'

Hesser hesitated, then took them. 'Perhaps the wiser course.'

'I think so, sir.' Schenck nodded to Schmidt, who started the engine. The Oberleutnant drew himself together and delivered a punctilious military salute. 'Herr Oberst – gentlemen.'

They all saluted in return, he climbed into the passenger seat and nodded. Schmidt drove away, out of the main entrance across the drawbridge and they disappeared into the first bend of the road.

As the sound of the engine faded, Birr said, 'You know, I've just thought of something?'

'What's that?' Canning asked.

'That if Schenck runs into a German unit and they find that letter on him, it isn't going to do him a great deal of good.'

'I know,' Canning said harshly. 'I thought of that when I was writing the damn thing, but at this stage of the game, he must just take his chance – like the rest of us,' he added and turned and walked back across the courtyard.

At approximately four o'clock in the afternoon, Rattenhuber conducted Ritter and Hoffer to the bunker exit leading on to Hermann-Goringstrasse. They each had a small field pack loaded with provisions for the journey and wore camouflaged ponchos and steel helmets. They were armed with Schmeisser machine pistols and in true SS fashion carried two stick grenades in the top of each boot.

The artillery barrage was still as relentless as ever and there was the sound of heavy fighting up near Potsdamerplatz.

Rattenhuber put a hand on Ritter's shoulder. 'What can I say, except good luck and God go with you?'

God? Ritter thought. *Is he on my side, too?* He smiled ironically, tapped Hoffer on the shoulder and moved out. As there was a burst of machine-gun fire, Rattenhuber watched them flatten themselves into the ground. A moment later they were up and running safely into the ruined buildings opposite.

Bormann moved out of the shadows behind him. 'So, they are on their way, Willi.'

'Yes, Reichsleiter.'

Bormann glanced at his watch. 'I can afford to be away from the bunker for perhaps three hours at the most. In any case, you, too, must be back by then to make your own departure on schedule. We must move fast.'

'Yes, Reichsleiter.'

Rattenhuber hurried away into the darkness of the vehicle ramp. A moment later, there was the sound of an engine starting and he drove out of the shadows at the wheel of a field car. There was an MG34 machine gun in the back and Bormann mounted it on the windshield swivel and got in. Rattenhuber put on a steel helmet and offered the Reichsleiter another.

Bormann shook his head. 'If there's a bullet for me that won't save me. I haven't worn one since my field artillery days in 1918. Now, let's get moving. We haven't got time to waste.'

Rattenhuber accelerated away, driving very fast and, they turned out of Hermann-Göringstrasse and moved in the general direction of Potsdamerplatz.

Once past Tiergarten, Ritter and Hoffer moved fast through the blocks of apartment houses. A continuous mortar barrage fell around them, and after a while a squadron of Russian fighter bombers came in low over the rooftops, spraying everything in sight with cannon fire.

They dodged into a doorway beside a sandbagged gun emplacement from which Hitler Youth fired light machine guns ineffectually into the sky.

'My God,' Hoffer said in disgust. 'Children playing soldiers, and for all the good they're doing they might as well be firing Christmas toys.'

'But willing to die, Erich,' Ritter said. 'They still believe.'

He was examining the rough map which Rattenhuber had given him. Hoffer tugged at his sleeve. 'And us, Major. What about us? What in the hell are we doing here? What's the point?'

'Survival, Erich,' Ritter said. 'A game we've been playing for quite some time now, you and I. We might as well see it through. Who knows? It could prove interesting.'

'That's all it's ever been to you, isn't it?' Hoffer said. 'Some kind of black joke. That's why you can only smile with that curl to your lips.'

'And still there when you fold my hands on my chest, Erich,' Ritter told him. 'I promise you. Now let's get moving. We've about a quarter of a mile to go.'

They moved from street to street, from one mortar crater to the next, through the charnel house that was Berlin, passing on the way groups of terrified civilians, mostly women and children and the soldiers of the Volkssturm, mainly tired old men, most of them already walking corpses.

Finally, they reached the East-West Avenue, saw the Victory Column in the distance. There were few people here now and for some reason the bombardment seemed to have faded and the avenue was strangely quiet and deserted.

'Over here,' Ritter said, and darted towards the side-street opposite. The showrooms on the corner were shattered, plate glass windows gaping. The sign above the main entrance said 'Burgdorf Autos'.

Ritter led the way along the pavement and paused outside the garage doors at the rear. They were closed. 'This is it,' he said. There was a judas gate to one side. He turned to Hoffer and grinned lightly. 'I'll lead, you cover.'

Hoffer cocked the Schmeisser and flattened himself

against the wall. Ritter tried the handle of the gate gingerly. It opened to his touch. He paused, then shoved the door open and went in fast, going down hard. There was a burst of machine-gun fire, a pause, then Hoffer fired an answering burst round the door.

In the silence as the echoes died Ritter called, 'Friends. We're looking for Obersturmführer Heini Berger.'

It was very quiet, the garage a place of shadows in the evening light. A voice called softly, 'Identify yourselves.'

'Valhalla Exchange,' Ritter called.

He could see the Fieseler Storch now, over to one side, and then a boot scraped and a young, dark-haired SS officer in camouflage uniform moved out of the shadows. His old-style, field-service cap was tilted at a rakish angle and he carried an American Thompson sub-machine gun in one hand.

'Nice to see you,' he said. 'For a moment there, I thought you might be a bunch of Ivans smelling out foxes.'

Ritter nodded towards the Thompson which carried a round 100-drum magazine. 'They'd have been in for a nasty surprise.'

Berger grinned lazily. 'Yes, a little item I picked up in the Ardennes. I always did like to overdo things.' He put a cigarette in his mouth and flicked a lighter made from a Russian rifle bullet.

'What about Herr Strasser?' Ritter said, looking around.

'Oh, he isn't due for a while yet.' Berger sat down on a packing case, putting the Thompson on the floor. 'No rush – we're not due out of here until midnight.'

'I see.' Ritter sat down beside him and Hoffer wandered over to the Storch. 'This man Strasser – you know him?'

Berger hesitated perceptibly. 'Don't you?'

'Never met him in my life before.'

'Neither have I. I'm just the bloody bus driver on this show.'

Ritter nodded towards the Stork. 'We're not going to make the Bavarian Alps in one hop in that.'

'No, we're scheduled to put down halfway at an airstrip in the Thuringian Forest, west of Plauen. Always supposing it's still in our hands.'

'And if it isn't?'

'An interesting thought.'

'You think we'll make it? Out of Berlin, I mean?'

'I don't see why not. Hannah Reitsch made it with Greim, didn't she?'

'Not in total darkness, which it will be when we take off.'

'Yes, I was aware of that fact,' Berger said 'On the other hand, it does mean that the Russians won't be expecting us They aren't likely to have any fighters up. No need now they've taken Templehof and Gatow. With any kind of luck, we could be away before they know what's happening.'

'But you would still have to take off along the avenue in the dark,' Ritter said. 'And the Victory Column . . .'

'I know. Very large and very solid. Still, I expect I'll manage to think of something.' There were a couple of old sacks on the floor and he lay down on them, cradling the Thompson in his arms. 'I think I'll get a little shut-eye. Something tells me I'm going to need it. If you wouldn't mind watching the front door and give me a push when Strasser comes.'

He pulled the peak of his service cap over his eyes. Ritter smiled slightly and turned to Hoffer, who looked bewildered. 'What's going on, Major? What's he playing at?'

'He's sleeping, Erich. Very sensible under the circumstances. Now, do you want to take the first watch or shall I?'

It was towards evening when Oberleutnant Schenck and Schmidt drove into the village of Graz on the road to Innsbruck. It was completely deserted, not a soul in sight. They had travelled a distance of approximately forty miles since leaving Arlberg, had lost nearly three hours on the way due to a fault in the field car's fuel system. It had taken Schmidt that length of time to diagnose what was wrong and put it right.

They hadn't seen a single soldier, of either side, and there had also been a total absence of refugees on the road. But that made sense. Typical peasants, these mountain people. They would stick with their land, whatever happened. No running away for them. Nowhere to go.

A curtain moved at a ground-floor window of a house opposite. Schenck got out of the field car, crossed the street and knocked at the door. There was no response so he kicked impatiently. 'Come on, for God's sake!' he called. 'I'm Austrian like you. I'm not here to cause trouble.'

After a while, the bolts were drawn and the door opened. An old, white-haired man with a bristling white moustache stood there, a young woman cowering behind him holding a baby.

'Herr Leutnant,' he said civilly enough.

'Where is everybody?'

'They stay inside.'

'Waiting for the Americans to come?'

'Or the British or the French.' He managed a smile. 'As long as it isn't the Russians.'

'Are there any German units left in this area?'

'No – there were some Panzers but they pulled out two days ago.'

'And the other side? Have you seen anything of them?' The old man hesitated and Schenck said, 'Come on. It's important.'

'This morning I visited my son's farm just to see if everything was all right. He's away in the army and his wife here is staying with me. It's three miles down the road from here. There were English troops camped in the meadow and using the farm buildings, so I came away.'

'What kind of troops? Tanks – infantry?'

461

The old man shook his head. 'They'd put up a great many tents, large tents, and there were ambulances coming in and out all the time. All their vehicles carried the red cross.'

'Good.' Schenck felt a surge of excitement. 'I won't bother you any more.'

He hurried back to the field car and climbed in. 'Three miles down the road, Schmidt. A British Army field hospital from the sound of it.'

It's going to work, he thought. It's going to be all right. It couldn't be better. Schmidt accelerated out of the square, bouncing over the cobbles, between the old medieval houses that leaned out, almost touching each other so that there was only room for one vehicle along the narrow street.

They came round a corner and entered another smaller square and found a British Army field ambulance bearing down on them. Schmidt spun the wheel desperately, skidded on the light powdering of snow. For a single frozen moment in time, Schenck was aware of the sergeant in the leather jerkin, the young private in tin hat sitting beside him and then they collided with the ambulance's front offside wheel and bounced to one side, mounting the low parapet of the fountain in the centre of the square and turning over.

Schmidt had been thrown clear and started to get up. Schenck, who was still inside the field car, saw the young private in the tin hat jump out of the ambulance, a Sten gun in his hand. He fired a short burst that drove Schmidt back across the parapet into the fountain.

Schenck managed to get to his feet and waved his arms. 'No!' he shouted. 'No!'

The boy fired again, the bullets ricocheting from the cobbles. Schenck felt a violent blow in his right shoulder and arm and was thrown back against the field car.

He was aware of voices – raised voices. The sergeant was swinging the boy round and wrenching the Sten gun away from him. A moment later, he was kneeling over Schenck.

Schenck's mouth worked desperately as he felt himself slipping away. He managed to get the letter from his pocket, held it up in one bloodstained hand. 'Your commanding officer – take me to him,' he said hoarsely in English. 'A matter of life and death,' and then he fainted.

Major Roger Mulholland of 173rd Field Hospital had been operating since eight o'clock that morning. A long day by any standards and a succession of cases any one of which would have been a candidate for major surgery under the finest hospital conditions. All he had were tents and field equipment. He did his best, as did the men under his command, as he'd been doing his best for weeks now, but it wasn't enough.

He turned from his last case, which had necessitated the amputation of a young field gunner's legs below the knees, and found Schenck laid out on the next operating table, still in his army greatcoat.

'Who the hell is this?'

His sergeant-major, a burly Glaswegian named Grant, said, 'Some Jerry officer driving through Graz in a field car. They collided with one of the ambulances. There was a shoot-out, sir.'

'How bad is he?'

'Two rounds in the shoulder. Another in the upper arm. He asked to be taken to the CO. Kept brandishing this in his hand.'

He held up the bloodstained letter. Mulholland said, 'All right, get him ready. Come one, come all.'

He opened the envelope, took out the letter and started to read. A moment later he said, 'Dear God Almighty, as if I didn't have enough to take care of.'

7

At a stage in the war when it had become apparent to him that Germany was almost certain to lose, Karl Adolf Eichmann, head of the Jewish Office of the Gestapo, ordered a shelter to be constructed according to the most stringent specifications, under his headquarters at 116 Kurfürstenstrasse. It had its own generating plant and ventilating system and was self-sufficient in every respect.

The entire project was carried out under conditions of total secrecy, but in the Third Reich nothing was secret from Martin Bormann for long. On making the happy discovery and needing a discreet establishment for purposes of his own, he had announced his intention of moving in, and Eichmann, too terrified to argue, agreed, putting up with the inconvenience of the arrangement until March when he'd decided to make a run for it.

When Bormann and Rattenhuber arrived the place seemed deserted. The front door hung crazily on its hinges, the windows gaped and the roof had been extensively damaged by shelling. Rattenhuber drove along the alley at one side, wheels crunching over broken glass, and pulled into the courtyard at the rear of the building.

For the moment the artillery bombardment had faded and most of the shooting that was taking place was some little way off. Bormann got out and walked down a sloping concrete ramp to a couple of grey-painted, steel doors. He hammered with the toe of his boot. A grille was opened. The man who peered through had SS decals on his steel helmet. Bormann didn't say a word. The grille slammed shut and a moment later the doors opened electronically.

Rattenhuber drove down the ramp, pausing for Bormann to get back in, and they entered a dark tunnel, passing two SS guards, and finally came to a halt in a brightly lit concrete garage.

There were two more SS guards and a young, hard-faced Hauptsturmführer. Like his men, he wore a sleeve-band on his left arm that carried the legend 'RFSS'. Reichsführer der SS. The cuff-title of Himmler's personal staff, a device of Bormann's to deter the curious.

'So, Schultz, how goes it?' Bormann asked.

'No problems, Reichsleiter.' Schultz delivered a perfect party salute. 'Are you going up?'

'Yes, I think so.'

Schultz led the way towards a steel elevator and pressed the button. He stood back. 'At your orders, Reichsleiter.'

Bormann and Rattenhuber moved inside, the colonel pressed the button to ascend and the doors closed. He carried his Schmeisser and there was a stick grenade tucked into his belt.

'Not long now, Willi,' Bormann said. 'The culmination of many months of hard work. You were surprised, I think, when I brought you into this affair?'

'No – an honour, Reichsleiter, I assure,' Rattenhuber said. 'A great honour to be asked to assist with such a task.'

'No more than you deserve, Willi. Zander was not to be trusted. I needed someone of intelligence and discretion. Someone I could trust. This business is of primary importance, Willi, I think you know that. Essential if the Kamaradenwerk is to succeed.'

'You may rely on me, Reichsleiter,' Rattenhuber said emotionally. 'To the death.'

Bormann placed an arm about his shoulders. 'I know I can, Willi. I know I can.' The lift stopped, the door opened. A young man in thickly lensed glasses and a white doctor's coat stood waiting. 'Good evening, Reichsleiter,' he said politely.

'Ah, Scheel, Professor Wiedler is expecting me. I trust.'

'Of course, Reichsleiter. This way.'

The only sound was the hum of the generators as they walked along the carpeted corridor. He opened the door at the end and ushered them through into a working laboratory, furnished mainly with electronic equipment. The man who sat in front of a massive recording machine in headphones was attired, like Scheel, in a white coat. He had an intelligent, anxious face and wore gold-rimmed, half-moon reading spectacles. He glanced round, took off the reading spectacles and got up hastily.

'My dear professor.' Bormann shook hands affably. 'How goes it?'

'Excellent, Reichsleiter. I think I may say, it couldn't have gone any better.'

Fritz Wiedler was a doctor of medicine of the Universities of Heidelberg and Cambridge. A fervent supporter of National Socialism from its earliest days, a Nobel prizewinner for his researches in cell structure and one of the youngest professors the University of Berlin had ever known, with a reputation as one of the greatest plastic surgeons in Europe.

He was a supreme example of a certain kind of scientist, a man totally dedicated to the pursuit of his profession with a fervour that could only be described as criminal. For Wiedler, the end totally justified the means, and when his Nazi masters had come to power he prospered mightily.

He had worked with Rascher on low-pressure research for the Luftwaffe using live prisoners as guinea pigs. Then he had tried spare-part surgery, using the limbs of prisoners where necessary at Geghardt's sanatorium near Ravensbrück where Himmler often went in search of cures for his chronic stomach complaint.

But it was as a member of the SS Institute for Research and Study of Heredity that he really came into his own, working with Mengele at Auschwitz on the study of twins,

466

first alive and later dead, all to the greater glory of science and the Third Reich.

And then Bormann had recruited him. Had offered him the chance of the ultimate experiment. In a sense, to create life itself. A challenge that no scientist worth his salt could possibly have turned down.

'Where are the rest of the staff?' Bormann asked.

'In the rest room, having their evening meal.'

'Five nurses. Three females, two male, am I right?'

'That is correct, Reichsleiter. Is there anything wrong?'

'Not at all,' Bormann said tranquilly. 'It's just that in these difficult times people tend to panic and make a run for it. I just wanted to make sure none of your people had.'

Wiedler looked shocked. 'None of them would think of such a thing, Reichsleiter, and besides they'd never get past the guards.'

'True,' Bormann said. 'So – it goes well, you say. Are we ready yet?'

'I think so, Reichsleiter. You must judge for yourself.'

'Let's get on with it then.'

Wiedler took a bunch of keys from his pocket, selected one and moved to a door at the other end of the laboratory. Bormann, Rattenhuber and Scheel followed. Wiedler inserted the key in the lock, the door swung open.

Music was playing, Schubert's Seventh Symphony, slow, majestic, the sound of it filling the room. Wiedler led the way in. They followed.

A man in flannel slacks and brown shirt was sitting at a table under a hard, white light, reading a book, his back towards them.

Wiedler said, 'Good evening, Herr Strasser.'

The man called Strasser pushed back his chair, got to his feet and turned and Martin Bormann gazed upon the mirror image of himself.

Rattenhuber's startled gasp had something of horror in it. 'My God!' he whispered.

'Yes, Willi, now you know,' Bormann said and held out his hand. 'Strasser, how are you?'

'Never better, Reichsleiter.'

The voice was identical and Bormann shook his head slowly. 'Not that I can tell with certainty. I mean who knows exactly how he speaks, but it seems all right to me.'

'All right?' Scheel said indignantly. 'Reichsleiter, it's perfect, I assure you. Three months we've worked, day and night, using the very latest in recording devices, using tape instead of wire. Here, we'll demonstrate. When I switch on the microphone, say something, Reichsleiter. Anything you like.'

Bormann hesitated then said, 'My name is Martin Bormann. I was born on June the 17th, in Halberstadt in Lower Saxony.'

Scheel ran the tape back, then played it. The reproduction was excellent. Then he nodded to Strasser. 'Now you.'

'My name is Martin Bormann,' Strasser said. 'I was born on June the 17th, in Halberstadt in Lower Saxony.'

'There, you see?' Scheel said triumphantly.

'Yes, I must agree.' Bormann tilted Strasser's chin. 'I might as well be looking into the mirror.'

'Not quite, Reichsleiter,' Wiedler said. 'If you stand side by side, a close examination does indicate certain features as not being quite the same, but that doesn't matter. The important thing is that no one will be able to tell you apart. And there are scars, not many, it's true, but I've arranged it so they appear as creases in the skin, the natural product of age.'

'I can't see them,' Bormann said.

'Yes, I don't think I've ever worked better with a knife, though I do say it myself.'

Bormann nodded. 'Excellent. And now I would have a word with Herr Strasser alone.'

'Certainly, Reichsleiter,' Wiedler said.

He and Scheel moved out and Bormann pulled Rattenhuber back. 'The question of the staff, Willi. You know what to do.'

'Of course, Reichsleiter.'

He went out and Bormann closed the door and turned to face himself. 'So, Strasser, the day is finally here.'

'So it would appear, Reichsleiter. The Kamaradenwerk? It begins?'

'It begins, my friend,' said Martin Bormann, and he started to unbutton his tunic.

Wiedler and the other waited patiently in the laboratory. It was perhaps twenty minutes later that the door opened and Bormann and Strasser appeared. The Reichsleiter was in uniform. Strasser wore a slouch hat and a black leather coat.

'And now, Reichsleiter –' Professor Wiedler began.

'It only remains to say goodbye,' Martin Bormann said.

He nodded to Rattenhuber who was standing by the door. The colonel's Schmeisser bucked in his hands, a stream of bullets knocking Wiedler and Scheel back against the wall. Rattenhuber emptied the magazine and replaced it with a fresh one.

He turned to Bormann, face pale.

'The staff?' Bormann inquired.

'I locked them in.'

Bormann nodded approvingly. 'Good – finish it.'

Rattenhuber went outside. A moment later there was the rattle of the Schmeisser sounding continuously above a chorus of screams. The Russian artillery had started again, the building shook violently far above their heads.

Rattenhuber came back in, walking slowly. 'It is done, Reichsleiter.'

Bormann nodded. 'Good – finish off here now and we'll go downstairs.'

He walked out into the corridor, followed by Strasser. Rattenhuber took the stick grenade from his belt and tossed it in through the door of the laboratory. As the reverberations died away, there was the angry crackling of flames as chemicals ignited.

Smoke drifted out into the corridor as Bormann and Strasser reached the elevator and Rattenhuber ran towards them. 'No need to panic,' Bormann said. 'Plenty of time.'

The elevator doors opened. They stepped inside and started down.

When the doors opened at the bottom, Schultz was waiting, A Walther in his hand, his two SS guards behind him, Schmeissers ready.

'No need to worry,' Bormann said. 'Everything's under control.'

'As you say, Reichsleiter,' Schultz said, and then he looked at Strasser and his mouth opened in amazement.

'We are leaving now, Schultz, all of us,' Bormann said gently. 'Bring in the rest of your men.'

Schultz turned, walked a few paces and whistled, fingers in teeth. A moment later the two guards from the garage door ran down the ramp.

'If you'd line them up, I'd just like a word about the situation we're going to find outside,' Bormann said.

'Reichsleiter.' Schultz barked orders at his men, they lined up and he stood in front of them.

'You have done good work. Excellent work ' Behind Bormann, Rattenhuber was climbing into the field car behind the MG34. 'But now, my friends, the time has come to part.'

In the final moment, Schultz realized what was

happening. His mouth opened in a soundless cry, but by then Rattenhuber was working the machine gun, driving Schultz and his men back in a mad dance of death across the concrete.

When he finally stopped, a couple of them were still twitching. 'Finish it,' Bormann ordered.

Rattenhuber picked up his Schmeisser, walked across to the guard and fired a short burst into the skull of one who still moved. He moved back hastily as blood and brains sprayed his boots and in the same moment became aware of the harsh metallic click as the MG34 was cocked again.

He swung round to find Strasser standing in the field car behind the machine gun. 'To the death, Willi, isn't that what you said?'

His fingers squeezed, the face beneath the brim of the slouch hat totally lacking in any kind of emotion. It was the last thing Willi Rattenhuber saw before he died.

Strasser stopped firing and jumped down. 'It's time I was away. I'll take Schultz's Mercedes.'

'And me?'

'I suggest you wait here till eleven o'clock. Start back to the bunker then. You should arrive around midnight, allowing for the state of the streets.'

'Dangerous times,' Bormann said. 'An artillery shell, a piece of shrapnel, a stray bullet, not to mention the possibility of running into a Russian patrol.'

'Like the Führer, I walk with the certainty of a sleep-walker,' Strasser said. 'I wear invisible armour, believing completely that nothing will happen to me – to either of us. A great deal depends on us, my friend. The future of many people.'

'I know.'

Strasser smiled. 'I must go now.'

He crossed to the open Mercedes tourer and climbed behind the wheel. As he started the engine, Bormann picked up a Schmeisser and hurried across to him. 'Take this.'

'No thanks, I won't need it,' Strasser said, and he drove away up into the darkness of the ramp.

Ritter was squatting on the ground, his back against the wall, Schmeisser across his knees. His eyes were closed, but he wasn't really asleep and heard the sound of the approaching vehicle as soon as Hoffer, who was on guard.

'Major!' Hoffer called.

'I know,' Ritter said.

He stood beside the sergeant-major listening, and Berger joined them. 'It isn't a tank anyway.'

'No, some sort of car,' Ritter said.

It braked to a half outside, and steps approached. The three men waited quietly in the darkness, there was a pause, a slight, eerie creaking and then the judas gate opened. Ritter and Berger flashed their torches at the same moment and picked Strasser out of the darkness.

'Herr Strasser,' Berger said cheerfully. 'We were just getting ready to go into blazing action. Why can't you whistle a few bars of "Deutschland Über Alles" or something?'

'If you could get the doors open I have a Mercedes outside that would probably be better under cover. We don't want to attract any unwelcome attention.'

Hoffer said, 'My God, it's the –'

Strasser turned towards them. He looked directly at Ritter and said calmly, 'Strasser – the name is Heinrich Strasser. I'm here to act on behalf of the Head of the Party Chancellery in the matter you already know of. You were expecting me, Major?'

'Oh, yes,' Ritter said. 'You were expected.' He turned to Hoffer as Berger opened the garage doors. 'Bring in Herr Strasser's car for him, Erich.'

Strasser put an arm around Berger's shoulders. 'Have we got any chance of getting away with this thing?'

'I don't see why not,' Berger told him. 'To try such a thing at all at this stage is something they won't even be considering. At least, that's what I'm counting on.'

They moved towards the Stork, talking in low tones. Hoffer drove the Mercedes into the garage and Ritter closed the doors again.

The sergeant-major whispered, 'But that man isn't Herr Strasser. It's the Reichsleiter himself. What's going on here?'

'I know, Erich, and Berger said they hadn't met, when it's obvious they know each other very well indeed.'

'So Berger knows who he really is?'

'And who would that be, Erich?' Ritter put a cigarette in his mouth. 'Martin Bormann or Heinrich Strasser – what's in a name, and if he prefers one to the other, who are we to argue?'

'Major Ritter,' Strasser called. 'One moment, if you don't mind.' They crossed to the plane and Strasser looked at his watch. 'Nine o'clock now. Captain Berger thinks we should leave around midnight.'

'So I understand,' Ritter said. 'What about take-off? I mean, it will be pitch dark, unless they send bombers over and start a few more fires, that is.'

'When we go, we go very fast,' Berger said. 'I've got a case of parachute flares in the Stork. I'll start the engine, and the moment I'm ready to go, I'd like you to fire the first one. After the first hundred yards, another. We might even need a third, I'm not sure. You'll be able to fire the pistol quite easily through the side-window.'

'During the actual take-off period then we will be considerably exposed,' Strasser said.

'For two or three minutes only. Of course, once we're airborne, the darker the better, but unless you want to end up on top of the Victory Column . . .' He shrugged.

'Anything but that, Captain,' Strasser said. 'It should, however, prove an exhilarating few minutes.'

Ritter went and sat on a packing case near the door. He put a cigarette in his mouth and felt for a match. Strasser walked across and produced a lighter.

'Thank you,' Ritter said.

'Is there anything you would like me to explain?'

'I don't think so,' Ritter said. 'The Reichsleiter's orders were quite explicit.'

'Good, then I think I'll get a little rest. Something tells me I'm going to need my strength before the night is out.'

He moved away, and Hoffer, who had been hovering nearby, came and squatted beside Ritter, his back against the wall. 'Well, what did he have to say?'

'What did you expect?' Ritter asked.

'Didn't he offer you some sort of explanation?'

'He asked me if there was anything I'd like him to explain, I said there wasn't. Is that what you meant?'

'Yes, Major.' Hoffer's voice sounded totally resigned now. 'That was exactly what I meant.'

At 11.30 the Russian bombardment started again. spasmodically at first, but within fifteen minutes it was in full throat.

Berger stood by the doors, checking his watch in the light of his torch. At five minutes to midnight precisely he said, 'All right, let's have those doors open and take her out.'

The night sky was very dark, occasionally illuminated by brilliant flashes as shells exploded, although they seemed to be concentrating on the area further to the east. The four men took the Stork out between them, two on each wing, and turned her round in the side-street. There was just enough room, the wall on either side only inches away from the wing-tips.

The sounds of battle increased in the middle distance and Berger, who pushed beside Ritter, said, 'Just think, hundreds of thousands of people trapped in this holocaust tonight face certain death and yet if the engine starts and the propeller turns, we by some special dispensation will live.'

'Perhaps – perhaps not.'

'You've no faith, my friend.'

'Ask me again when we're passing over the Victory Column.'

They turned the Stork into the East-West Avenue, the wheels crunching over broken glass.

'What about your wind direction, Berger?' Strasser asked. 'These things should always be pointing the right way, am I right?'

'As far as I can judge, there's a cross-wind,' Berger said 'North to south, not that it makes much difference. We don't after all, have a great deal of choice.'

The avenue was very dark and quiet, the Russian artillery devoting itself exclusively to the district around Potsdamerplatz. Berger said, 'Right, everybody in except Major Ritter.'

Ritter said, 'What do you want me to do?'

Berger handed him a flare gun and cartridge. 'Walk up the avenue about fifty yards and wait. The moment you hear the engine start, fire the pistol, then turn and run back as fast as you like.'

'All right,' Ritter said. 'I think I can handle that.'

Hoffer pulled at his sleeve. 'Let me, Major.'

'Don't be stupid,' Ritter said coldly.

He walked away into the darkness, suddenly angry, with himself as well as Hoffer. The sergeant-major meant well, he knew that, but there were times . . . Perhaps they'd been together for too long.

He was counting out the paces under his breath as he walked, and now he paused and rammed the cartridge home. It was quiet except for the dull rumble of the guns, and when the engine of the Fieseler Storch roared into life, the noise was shattering.

Ritter raised the pistol and fired a couple of seconds later, the flare started to descend on its parachute, bathing the avenue in a cold, white glare for a few moments only.

There were two Russian tanks and half a company of infantry sixty or seventy yards up the street. Ritter saw the white faces, heard the voices raised excitedly, and turned and ran like hell towards the Stork.

They picked him up on the move, Strasser holding the door open while Hoffer reached out to grab him by the scruff of the neck, and already the Russians were firing.

Ritter fell into the cabin on hands and knees and Berger yelled excitedly, 'More light! I'm going to need more light!'

Ritter fumbled in the box for another flare. The Stork was roaring down the avenue now, its tail lifting, but already one of the tanks had started to move. Berger had to swerve violently at the last moment, his starboard wing-tip just missing the tank's turret, and for a moment seemed to lose control.

But a second later and he was back on course again. Ritter put his hand out of the window and discharged the flare. In its sudden glare, the Victory Column seemed terrifyingly close, but Berger held on grimly. She yawed to starboard in the cross-wind and he applied a little rudder correction.

And then, quite suddenly, they were airborne, lifting off the avenue in a hail of rifle bullets, the Victory Column rushing to meet them.

'We'll hit! We'll hit!' Hoffer cried, but Berger held on grimly, refusing to sacrifice power for height, and only at the very last moment did he pull the column back into his stomach, taking the Stork clear of the top of the Victory Column by fifteen or twenty feet.

'Dear God, we made it. How truly amazing,' Strasser said.

'Surely you never doubted me, Reichsleiter?' Heini Berger laughed, unaware in the excitement of the moment of his slip of the tongue, stamped on the right rudder and turned away across what was left of the rooftops of Berlin.

It was at roughly the same moment that the SS guard on duty at the exit of the bunker leading on to Hermann-Göringstrasse heard a vehicle approach. A field car turned into the entrance of the ramp and braked to a halt. The driver, a shadowy figure in the gloom, got out and came forward.

'Identify yourself!' the sentry demanded.

Martin Bormann moved into the circle of lamplight. The sentry drew himself together. 'I'm sorry, Reichsleiter. I didn't realize it was you.'

'A bad night out there.'

'Yes, Reichsleiter.'

'But it will get better, my friend, very soon now, for all of us. You must believe that.'

Bormann patted him on the shoulder and moved down the ramp into the darkness.

8

There was no immediate easing of tension in the Stork for, as they flew across Berlin, the Russian artillery bombardment seemed to chase them all the way. There were numerous fires in many parts of the city and the darkness crackled with electricity on the edge of things as one shell after another found its target.

'Something to remember, eh, Major?' Strasser said. looking down at the holocaust. 'The *Twilight of the Gods.*'

'All we need is a score by Wagner,' Ritter said, 'to enjoy ourselves thoroughly. We have been well trained, we Germans, to appreciate the finer things.'

'Oh, it could be worse,' Strasser pointed out. 'We could be down there.'

The Stork rocked violently and something rattled against the fuselage. 'Anti-aircraft fire,' Berger cried. 'I'm going down.'

He threw the Stork into a sudden, violent corkscrew that seemed to last for ever, the whine of the engine rising to fever-pitch; and finally and only when the fires below seemed very close indeed, he pulled back the column and levelled out.

Hoffer turned his head away and was violently sick. Strasser said, with a slight edge of contempt to his voice, 'He has no stomach for it, I think, your sergeant-major.'

'So what?' Ritter said. 'They tell me Grand Admiral Dönitz is sick every time he puts to sea, but he's still Germany's greatest sailor.'

Gradually, the flames, the darting points of light on the ground, faded into the night. Berger shouted above the roar of the engine, 'I'll tell you something now we're out of it. I never thought we'd make it. Not for a moment.'

'You did well,' Strasser said. 'A brilliant piece of flying.'

It was Ritter, suddenly irritated, who said, 'Not out of the woods yet.'

'Nonsense,' Berger shouted. 'A milk run from now on.'

And he was right, for conditions generally could not have been more in their favour. They flew on through the night at 500 feet in darkness and heavy rain, Berger sitting there at the controls, a slight, fixed smile on his mouth, obviously thoroughly enjoying himself.

Hoffer fell asleep; Strasser, who was sitting next to Berger, made notes in his diary in the light from the control panel. Ritter smoked a cigarette and watched him, wondering what was going on behind the eyes in that calm, expressionless face, but that was a pointless exercise. Just as much a waste of time as asking himself what in the hell he was doing here.

It was like a chess game. You made a move in answer to one. A totally open-ended situation. No means of knowing what the end would be until it was reached. And in the final analysis, did it really matter? He leaned back in his seat and closed his eyes.

He came awake instantly in response to a hand on his shoulder. Strasser said, 'We're close to Plauen now. Berger's trying to raise the airstrip.'

Ritter glanced at his watch and saw, with a slight shock of surprise, that it was three o'clock. He turned to Hoffer. 'How are you?'

'Better, Major, much better, now that there's nothing left to come. I never could stand flying – any kind of flying. Remember that transport plane which brought us out of Stalingrad?'

Berger was talking away, using his throat mike. 'Red Fox, this is Valhalla. Do you read me?' There was only the confused crackling of the static. He tried again, adjusting one of the dials. 'Red Fox, this is Valhalla.' A moment later a voice broke through the static. 'Valhalla, this is Red Fox. I read you strength five.'

'I am coming in now for refuelling as arranged.' Berger said. 'What is your situation?'

'Heavy rain, slight ground mist, visibility about 150 yards. We'll put the landing lights on for you.'

'All the comforts of home,' Berger said. 'My thanks.' A moment later, two parallel lines of light flared in the darkness to starboard. 'I can see you now,' he called. 'I'm coming in.'

He turned into the wind and started his descent. Ritter said, 'Do we stay here for any length of time?'

'For as long as it takes to fill the tanks,' Strasser said. 'We've still got a long way to go.'

They drifted down through the rain and mist into the light, there was the sudden squeal of the tyres biting as Berger applied the brakes, they slowed, the tail going down.

And then Berger gave a cry of dismay for the trucks that raced out of the darkness on either side, converging on them, had red stars emblazoned on their sides.

'Get out of it!' Strasser cried.

Berger increased engine revs. The soldiers in the trucks were already firing. A bullet shattered one of the side-windows. Ritter shoved the barrel of a Schmeisser through and loosed off a long burst. And then they were really moving again, racing towards the end of the runway, the trucks trying to keep up with them and losing. Berger pulled back the column, they climbed up into the darkness.

He levelled off at 3,000 feet. Strasser said, 'Now what?'

For the first time his composure seemed to have deserted him and he actually looked worried. For some reason Ritter found the spectacle strangely comforting.

'The only thing I'm certain of at the moment is that I've got fuel for forty minutes, and that includes the reserve tank,' Berger said. And in the crisis it was Ritter he turned to. 'Have a look at the Luftwaffe area map, the one on top. See what there is close to our line fifty miles south of here.'

Ritter spread the map across his knees and switched on his torch. 'There's a place called Plodin marked with a red ring. Perhaps forty miles. According to the key that means reserve feeder station. What's that?'

'Part of the back-up system for night-fighters. The sort of place they can put down if they run into trouble. A hangar and a single runway, usually grass. Probably a private air club before the war. I'll see if I can raise them.'

'You raised somebody last time,' Strasser said. 'They answered in excellent German and look what happened.'

'All right, what do you want me to do?' Berger demanded. 'I can't see what we're getting in to unless I go down because you won't get even a touch of grey in the sky before four o'clock. I'll be out of fuel twenty minutes before then by my reckoning. You may have read that in such situations people often jump for it. Unfortunately, we only have one parachute and I'm sitting on it.'

'All right, I take the point,' Strasser said. 'Do as you think fit.'

He sat there, his jaw working, fists tightly clenched. He's thrown, Ritter thought, and badly because, for once, he isn't in charge. He has no control. He isn't playing the game – game's playing him.

Berger was using plain language. 'This is Fieseler Storch AK40, calling Plodin. I am dangerously short of fuel and urgently require assistance. Come in, please.'

There was an immediate response. A voice said urgently, 'Suggest you try elsewhere. We've been completely cut off by Russian troops since seven o'clock last night.'

'I'm afraid I have no choice in the matter,' Ritter told him. 'My estimated time of arrival is o-three-forty. Five minutes after that, and if I'm still airborne, I'll be gliding.'

There was silence, only the static, and then the voice said, 'Very well, we'll do what we can.'

'Right, gentlemen, here we go again,' Berger said, and he started to descend.

Two aircraft were burning at the side of the runway as they went in. 'Expensive landing lights,' Berger said, 'but I'm grateful, nevertheless.'

There were a couple of hangars, a small control tower, a complex of huts a hundred yards or so away, some trucks parked beside them. There was no sound of conflict, no shooting, only the two planes burning at the side of the runway as they touched down, an old Dornier 17 and a Ju 88 nightfighter.

As Berger taxied towards the control tower, half a dozen ground crew ran forward, two of them carrying wheel blocks, and the door opened and an officer stood there framed in the light.

He was an Oberleutnant, his Luftwaffe *fliegerblüse* open at the neck. He was twenty-three or four, badly in need of a shave and looked tired.

Berger held out his hand. 'Heini Berger. Not too worried about blackout, I see?'

'What would be the point?' the Oberleutnant said. 'With those two blazing like the candles on a Christmas tree. Our water main was fractured in the initial bombardment so we've no fire-fighting facilities. My name's Fränkel, by the way.'

'You are in command here?' Strasser asked.

'Yes, the commanding officer, Captain Hagen, was killed last night. Russian tanks shelled us at eleven o'clock and raked the buildings with machine-gun fire.'

'No infantry attack?' Ritter asked.

Fränkel took in the uniform, the Knight's Cross with Oak Leaves and Swords, and straightened his shoulders.

'No, they stayed out there in the dark, Sturmbannführer. Shelled us again approximately an hour ago. That's when the planes got it.'

Ritter walked forward into the shadows. There were bodies here and there and on the far side of the runway, another Junkers tilted forward on its nose, tail up, an enormous ragged furrow in the ground indicating where it had belly-landed.

He turned and came back to the others. 'How many men have you left?'

'Half a dozen,' Fränkel said. 'The aircrews of those planes all got away before we were hit. And then there are some of your people. Arrived last night just before the Russians. They're down at the huts now. You can just see their trucks – four of them.'

'My people?' Ritter said. 'You mean by this SS, I presume. Which unit?'

'Einsatzgruppen, Sturmbannführer.'

Ritter's face was very pale. He reached out and grabbed Fränkel by the front of his *fliegerblüse*. 'You will not mention scum like that in the same breath as Waffen-SS, you hear me?'

Einsatzgruppen, action groups or special commandos, had been formed by Himmler prior to the invasion of Russia. They were, in effect, extermination squads, recruited from the gaols of Germany, officered by SD and Gestapo officers. Occasionally soldiers of the Waffen-SS convicted of some criminal offence were transferred to them as a punishment. The phrase scum of the earth summed them up perfectly.

It was Strasser who moved forward to pull Ritter away. 'Easy, Major. Easy does it. What are they doing now, down there?'

'Drinking,' Fränkel said. 'And they have some women with them.'

'Women?'

'Girls – from the camps. Jewish, I think.'

483

There was a nasty silence. Berger said, nodding towards the blazing wrecks, 'Why didn't they fly those out of it while the going was good?'

'They landed here because they were low on fuel in the first place and we didn't have any. Used our last a fortnight ago.'

'No fuel,' Strasser cut in. 'But you must have something surely, and the Stork doesn't need much. Isn't that right, Berger?'

'If it was only ten gallons you wanted, I still couldn't oblige,' Fränkel said.

Berger looked towards the Junkers on the far side of the hangar, the one which had crash-landed. 'What about that? Nothing in the tanks?'

'We syphoned the fuel out of her a couple of weeks ago.' Fränkel hesitated. 'There could be a few gallons left, but not enough to get you anywhere.'

There was a sudden burst of laughter and singing from the huts. Ritter said to Berger, 'Am I right in assuming that a workhorse like the Fieseler Storch doesn't necessarily need high-octane aviation spirit to be able to fly?'

'No. She'll function on stuff a lot more crude than that. Reduced performance, of course.'

Ritter nodded towards the huts. 'Four trucks down there. I should think their tanks between them would hold forty or fifty gallons. Would it do?'

'I don't see why not,' Berger said. 'Especially if we can syphon a few gallons out of the Junkers to mix with it.'

Ritter said to Fränkel, 'All right?'

The Oberleutnant nodded. 'As far as I'm concerned. But the gentlemen of the Einsatzgruppen may have other ideas.'

Strasser said, 'We are on a special mission of vital importance to the Reich. My orders are signed by the Führer himself.'

'Sorry, Mein Herr,' Fränkel said, 'but strange things are happening in Germany today. There are actually

484

people around for whom that kind of talk doesn't cut much ice. I suspect that's particularly true of these characters.'

'Then we must change their minds for them,' Ritter said. 'How many are there?'

'Thirty or so.'

'Good. Put a couple of your men to the task of syphoning the JU. Send the rest to the trucks. I'll deal with these –' here he hesitated. 'These gentlemen of the Einsatzgruppen.' He turned to Strasser. 'You agree?'

Strasser smiled slightly. 'My dear Ritter, I wouldn't miss it for anything.'

There was no one at the trucks, no guard at the steps leading up to the door of the mess hall as Ritter marched briskly across the compound, Strasser a pace behind his left shoulder.

'I must be mad,' Strasser said.

'Oh, I don't know. Like we used to say about those chairborne bastards at HQ, it does a man good to get up off his backside occasionally and go up front to see what it's like for the ordinary troops. A little action and passion for you, Reichsleiter.'

He paused at the bottom of the steps to adjust his gloves. Strasser said, 'Why do you call me that, Major?'

'You mean I'm mistaken?'

'To the best of my knowledge, Reichsleiter Martin Bormann is at present in his office in the Führerbunker in Berlin. Even in this day and age, it would take a rather large miracle for a man to be in two places at once.'

'Simple enough if there were two of him.'

'Which would raise the problem of who is real and who is only the image in the mirror,' Strasser said. 'A neat point, but relevant, I think you'll agree.'

'True,' Ritter said. 'And perhaps in the final analysis, an academic point only.' He smiled ironically. 'Shall we go in now?'

He opened the door and stepped into the light. At first he and Strasser went completely unnoticed, which was hardly surprising for the men who crowded the tables before them were mostly drunk. There were perhaps a dozen girls huddled into a corner at the far end of the room – hair unkempt, tattered clothes, faces grimy with dirt. In fact, the faces were the most interesting feature about them, the eyes dull, totally without hope, the look of trapped animals waiting for the butcher's knife.

There was a burly Hauptsturmführer seated at one end of the longest table. He was a brute of a man with slanting eyes and high Slav cheekbones. He had a small, dark-haired girl on his knee, an arm around her neck, holding her tight, while his other hand was busy under her skirt. She couldn't have been more than sixteen.

And she saw Ritter first, her eyes widening in amazement, and the Hauptsturmführer, becoming aware of her stillness, turned to see what she was looking at.

Ritter stood, hands on hips, legs slightly apart, and it was as if a chill wind had swept into the room, Death himself come to join them. The Hauptsturmführer took in that magnificent black uniform, the decorations, the dark eyes under the peak of the service cap, the silver death's-head gleaming.

'You are in charge here, I presume?' Ritter inquired softly.

The captain shoved the girl off his knee and stood up. The room had gone absolutely quiet. 'That's right,' he said. 'Grushetsky.'

'Ukrainian?' Ritter said, his distaste plain. 'I thought so.'

Grushetsky turned red with anger. 'And who in the hell might you be?'

'Your superior officer,' Ritter told him calmly. 'You're aware that there are Russians out there in the dark who might have a more than passing interest in getting their hands on you, and yet you don't even post a guard.'

'No need,' Grushetsky said. 'They won't come in before dawn, I know how they work. We'll be driving out of here long before then. In the meantime . . .' He put an arm around the girl and pulled her close.

'Sorry,' Ritter said. 'But you won't be driving anywhere, I'm afraid. We need your petrol for our aircraft.'

'You what?' Grushetsky cried.

'Show him your orders,' Ritter said casually to Strasser. He glanced at the girl again, ignoring Grushetsky, then walked to the end of the room and looked at the others.

Strasser said, 'I'll read it to you. From the Leader and Chancellor of the State. Most secret. You recognize the name at the bottom of the page, I trust. Adolf Hitler.'

'Yes, well, he's in Berlin and this is here,' Grushetsky said. 'And you take that petrol from those tanks over my dead body.'

'That can be arranged.' Ritter raised his right arm casually and clicked his fingers. A window was smashed as a Schmeisser poked through, Berger's smiling face behind it. The door crashed open and Hoffer came in holding another Schmeisser.

'You see,' Ritter said to the girl whom Grushetsky had released now. 'It is still possible for the best to happen in this worst of all possible worlds. What's your name?'

'Bernstein,' she said. 'Clara Bernstein.'

He recognized her accent instantly. 'French?'

'That's what it says on my birth certificate, but to you bastards, I'm just another dirty Jew.'

In a strange way it was as if they were alone. 'What do you want me to do – say I'm sorry?' Ritter asked her in French. 'Would that help?'

'Not in the slightest.'

'Positive action then, Clara Bernstein. You and your friends go now. Out there in the darkness beyond the perimeter wire there are Russian soldiers. I suggest you turn towards them, hands high in the air, yelling like hell. I think you will find they will take you in.'

'Here, what in the hell is going on here?' Grushetsky demanded in his bad German.

Ritter rounded on him. 'Shut your mouth, damn you. Feet together when you speak to me, you understand? Attention, all of you.'

And they responded, all of them, even those far gone in drink trying to draw themselves together. The girl called to the others in German. They hesitated. She cried, 'All right, stay and die here if you want, but I'm getting out of it.'

She ran outside and the rest of the girls broke instantly and went after her. Their voices could be heard clearly as they ran across the runway to the perimeter wire.

Ritter paced up and down between the tables. 'You believe yourselves to be soldiers of the German Reich, a natural assumption in view of the uniforms you wear, but you are mistaken. Now, let me tell you what you are, in simple terms, so that you can understand.'

Grushetsky gave a roar of rage and pulled out his Luger, and Strasser, who'd been waiting for something like this to happen for the past few minutes, fired twice through the pocket of his leather coat, shattering the Ukrainian's spine, killing him instantly, driving him across one of the tables.

Several men cried out and reached for weapons and Berger and Hoffer both fired at the same moment, dropping four men between them.

Ritter said to Hoffer, 'All right – collect their weapons and hold them here until we're ready to go.'

One of the Einsatzgruppen took an involuntary step forward. 'But Sturmbannführer. Without weapons we shall be totally unable to defend ourselves, and the Russians –'

'Can have you,' Ritter said, and he walked outside, followed by Strasser.

Fränkel walked to meet them. 'It's worked quite well. We've managed to get about fifteen gallons of aviation fuel out of the Junkers. Mixed with petrol from the trucks, it means we can give you full tanks.'

'How long?' Strasser asked. 'Before we're ready to go?'

'Five or ten minutes.'

Ritter offered the young Luftwaffe lieutenant a cigarette. 'I'm sorry we can't take you with us, you and your men. We leave you in a bad situation.'

'The moment you've gone, I'm going to go out there and ask for terms,' Fränkel said. 'I can't see much point in any other course of action, not at this stage.'

'Perhaps you're right,' Ritter said. 'And I'd keep those bastards back there in the mess hall under lock and key until the Russians get here, if I were you. It might help.'

A sergeant hurried towards them and saluted. 'The Stork's all ready to go now, Herr Leutnant.'

There was some movement out there in the darkness beyond the perimeter, the sound of an engine starting up. Ritter turned and shouted, 'Berger – Erich! Let's get out of here. It looks as if the Russians are starting to move in.'

He ran back towards the hangar, followed by Strasser. As they scrambled up into the cabin of the Stork, Hoffer and Berger arrived. Berger didn't even bother to strap himself in. He got the door closed and started the engines instantly so that the Stork was moving down the runway and turning into the wind in a matter of seconds.

The flames from the burning planes had died down and the field was almost totally dark now. 'If you believe in prayer, then now's the time.' Berger cried and he pushed up the engine revs and took the Stork forward.

They plunged headlong into darkness and Ritter leaned back in the seat and closed his eyes, totally unafraid, consumed only by curiosity to know what it would be like. Was this it? he asked himself. Could this possibly be the final moment after all these years? And then the Stork lifted as Berger pulled back the stick and they climbed up into the darkness.

Ritter turned to find Strasser examining the bullet holes in his coat. 'My thanks, but I hardly expected to see the day when you would lay yourself on the line to defend the rights of Jews.'

'What happens to those girls back there is a matter of complete indifference to me,' Strasser told him. 'You, on the other hand, are an essential part of this operation which could well fail without you. That was the only reason I shot that Slavic ape back there.'

'I should be thankful for small mercies, it would seem.'

'No more empty gestures, my dear Ritter, I beg you.'

'Empty?'

'A fair description. I should imagine the Russians will rape those girls with an enthusiasm at least equal to that of Grushetsky and his motley crew, or had you really imagined it would be different?'

Dawn was a gradual affair from about 4.30 as they flew onwards through heavy cloud – at first merely an impression of light, no more than that. Strasser and Hoffer both slept, but Berger seemed as cheerful and relaxed as ever, whistling softly between his teeth.

'You love it,' Ritter said. 'Flying, I mean?'

'More than any woman.' Berger grinned. 'Which is saying a lot. For a long time I worried about what I would do when it was all over – the war, I mean. No more flying, not for the defeated.'

'But now you don't?'

It was a statement as much as a question and caught Berger off-guard. 'Plenty of places to go, when you think about it. Places where there's always work for a good pilot. South America, for instance. The Reichs . . .' He pulled himself up quickly. 'Herr Strasser already has a pipeline organized that should ensure that some of us live to fight another day.'

'A charming prospect,' Ritter said. 'I congratulate you.'

When he leaned back, he realized that Strasser was awake and watching through half-opened eyes. He smiled and leaned forward, a hand on Berger's shoulder.

'He likes to talk, my young friend here. A conversationalist by nature. A good thing he's such a brilliant pilot.'

Strasser was smiling genially, but his fingers were hooked into the shoulder so tightly that Berger winced with pain. 'I'll take her up now,' he shouted. 'Try and get above this shit and see what's what. We should be nearly there.'

He pulled back the stick and started to climb, but the heavy cloud showed no signs of diminishing. Finally, he levelled out. 'No good. I'll have to try it the other way. Nothing else for it. Hang on and we'll see what the state of things is downstairs.'

He pushed the column forward, taking the Stork into a shallow dive. The cloud became darker, more menacing, boiling around them, hail rattling against the fuselage, and Berger had to hang on to the column with all his strength. They were at 4,000 feet and still descending, Berger hanging on grimly, and Hoffer gave an involuntary cry of fear. And then at 3,000 feet they emerged into the light of day and found themselves, as Berger levelled out, drifting along the course of a wide valley, pine trees very green against the snow, the peaks of the Bavarian Alps rising on either side of them.

'Somebody on board must live right,' Berger said. 'Now have a look on the Luftwaffe area map and see if you can find Arnheim, Major.'

It was no more than a feeder station, had never been more than that. There was a single runway, two hangars. No control tower – simply a couple of single-storeyed concrete huts with tin roofs.

Snow was falling gently, but there was no wind to speak of and the Fieseler Storch came in from the north like a grey ghost, her engine barely a murmur. Her wheels touched and there were two puffs of white smoke as snow spurted beneath them.

Strasser said, 'Straight up to the hangars. I want her under cover.'

'All right.' Berger nodded.

When they were close enough, Strasser, Ritter and Hoffer all got out and opened the hangar doors between them. Berger taxied inside and cut the engine. He laughed out loud as he jumped to the ground.

'So we made it. The Victory Column to Arnheim in five and a half hours.' He helped Ritter pull the door across. 'Smell that mountain air.'

Hoffer had gone through the connecting door into the next hangar, and now he returned. 'There's a field car in there, Major,' he told Ritter. 'A basket in the back.'

'Good,' Strasser said. 'I've been expecting that.'

He led the way in and the others followed. The basket was of the picnic type. There was also a small leather suitcase with it. Strasser placed it on the bonnet of the car and opened it. Inside there was a radio transmitter and receiver of a kind Ritter had never seen before.

'Excellent,' Strasser said. 'The best in the world at the present time. Came to us by courtesy of an agent of the British Special Operations Executive.' He checked his watch. 'Five-thirty – am I right?'

'So it would appear,' Ritter said.

'Good.' Strasser rubbed his hands briskly. 'There's a nip in this mountain air. We'll have something to eat, a hot drink and then . . .'

'Something to eat?' Berger said.

'But of course. What do you think is in the basket?'

Berger unstrapped it and raised the lid. Inside there were three loaves of black bread, sausages, butter, boiled eggs, two large vacuum flasks and a bottle of schnapps.

Berger unscrewed the cap of one of the flasks and removed the cork. He inhaled deeply, an expression of delight appearing on his face.

'Coffee – hot coffee.' He poured a little into the cup and tasted it. 'And it's real,' he announced. 'A miracle.'

'See how good I am to you,' Strasser said.

'You certainly have a flair for organization,' Ritter told him.

'It's been said before.' Strasser glanced at his watch.

'And then?' Ritter said. 'After we've eaten? You were saying?'

Strasser smiled. 'I'm expecting another aircraft at seven o'clock. A very reliable man, so he should get here right on time.' Ritter opened the small judas gate, set in the main gate, and stepped outside, turning his face up to the snow. 'What air. It makes things feel clean again.'

Hoffer passed Ritter a cup of coffee and a piece of black bread. 'But I don't understand, Major. This other plane he's expecting. Who is it? Why won't he tell us?'

'Probably the Führer himself, Erich.' Ritter smiled. 'After the events of the past couple of days, nothing would surprise me.'

It was at precisely five minutes to seven when Heini Berger, lounging against the bonnet of the field car, smoking a cigarette, straightened. 'There's a plane coming now, I hear it.'

Ritter opened the judas and stepped outside. Snow was still falling softly, the flakes brushing against his face when he looked up. The sound was still some distance away, but real enough.

He went back inside. 'He's right.'

Strasser had the suitcase open, the microphone in his hand. He adjusted the dials and said, in English, to everyone's surprise, 'Valhalla Exchange. Valhalla Exchange. Plain language. Do you receive me.'

An American voice answered with startling clarity. 'Valhalla Exchange. Odin here. Am I cleared for landing?'

'All clear. Closing down now.'

He stowed the microphone and closed the case. Ritter said, 'Are we permitted to know what that was all about?'

'Later,' Strasser said impatiently. 'For the moment, let's get these doors open. I want him under cover and out of sight the moment he's landed.'

Ritter shrugged and nodded to Hoffer, and with Berger's assistance they got the doors open. The sound of the plane, whatever it was, was very close now and they all moved outside and waited.

And then, suddenly, she was there, coming in out of the greyness at the north end of the runway, twin-engined, camouflaged and entirely familiar to at least one man there, Berger, who cried 'God in heaven, that's an American Dakota.'

'So it would appear,' Strasser said.

'Is nothing impossible to you then?' Ritter asked.

'My dear Ritter, if I'd needed it, I could have had a Flying Fortress or an RAF Lancaster.'

The Dakota landed, snow rising in a cloud around her as she rolled forward, turning in towards them as Strasser waved his arms, and then she was close enough for them to see the pilot in the cockpit, the American Air Force insignia plain against the green and brown camouflage.

The plane taxied into the hangar; for a moment, the din was colossal, and then suddenly the engines cut. 'Right, get these doors closed,' Strasser ordered.

As they turned from the task, the hatch was opened and the pilot appeared. He had a dark saturnine face and appeared to be in his early thirties. He was wearing a side-cap with an SS death's-head badge and a flying jacket. He removed the jacket and caused something of a sensation.

He wore a beautifully tailored uniform of field-grey.

Under the eagle on his left sleeve was a Stars and Stripes shield and the cuff-title on his left wrist carried the legend 'George Washington Legion' in Gothic lettering. His decorations included the Iron Cross, Second and First Class, and he wore the Winter War Ribbon. When he spoke, his German was excellent, but with a definite American accent.

'So, you made it?' he said to Strasser. 'Amazing, but then, I should have learned to believe you by now.'

'Good to see you.' Strasser shook hands, then turned to the others. 'Gentlemen – allow me to introduce Hauptsturmführer Earl Jackson. This is Heini Berger who got us out of Berlin in the Stork.'

'Captain.' Berger shook hands. 'It gave me something of a shock when I saw you dropping down out of the sky, I can tell you.'

'And Sturmbannführer Karl Ritter.'

Jackson held out his hand, but Ritter ignored him and turned to Strasser. 'And *now* we talk, I think.'

'My dear Ritter,' Strasser began.

'Now!' Ritter said sharply and he opened the connecting door and went into the next hangar.

'All right,' Strasser said. 'What is it now?'

'This American, Jackson – who is he? I want to know.'

'Come now, Ritter, the Waffen-SS has recruited men from almost every nation possible, you know that. Everything from Frenchmen to Turks. There's even an English contingent, the Britisches Freikorps. There have been, admittedly, only a handful of Americans in the George Washington Legion. Ex-prisoners of war, recruited by prospects of unlimited liquor and women. Jackson is a different specimen, believe me. He flew for the Finns against the Russians in their first war, stayed on in their air force and got caught up in their second bout with the Russians when they joined our side. When the Finns sued for peace last year, he transferred to us.'

'A traitor is a traitor, however you wrap it up.'

'A point of view, but not objective enough, my friend. All I see is a superb pilot; a brave and resourceful man with a highly specialized background which makes him peculiarly suitable for my purposes. May I also add, that as his own people would most certainly hang him if ever they succeed in getting their hands on him, he has no other choice but to serve my cause. It is his only chance of life. Now, have you anything else to say?'

'I think you've made your point,' Ritter said.

Strasser opened the door and led the way back into the other hangar. He made no reference to what had happened, simply took a map from his pocket and unfolded it across the bonnet of the field car. They all crowded round.

'Here is Arnheim. Arlberg eight or nine miles south of here. Ten miles to the west, there's a farm marked on the edge of the forest. That's where the Finns are.'

'Do we all go?' Ritter asked.

'No, Hauptsturmführer Berger can stay with the planes.'

'And me?' Jackson said.

'No, you might well be useful in other ways. You come with us.' The American didn't look too pleased, but there was obviously nothing he could do about it. Strasser added, 'And from now on, as what might be termed the military part of the operation starts, Sturmbannführer Ritter will be in sole command.'

'You mean I have a totally free hand?' Ritter said.

'Well, a little advice now and then never hurt anyone, did it?' Strasser smiled. 'Still, no point in crossing over bridges until we come to them, Major. Let's get these Finnish barbarians sorted out first.'

9

At the field hospital, Mullholland had had a hard night. Eleven wounded from a skirmish near Innsbruck had been brought in at ten o'clock. He and his team had worked steadily through the night on cases of varying seriousness.

His final patient, a young lieutenant, had two machine-gun bullets in the left lung. Mullholland had used every trick in his now considerable repertoire for more than two hours. The boy had died at 7 a.m. after suffering a massive haemorrhage.

When Mullholland went outside it was snowing gently. He lit a cigarette and stood there, breathing deeply on the clean air, and Sergeant-Major Grant approached with a cup of tea.

'A rotten night, sir.'

'I could have done without it. The bloody war is as good as over, or so they tell us, and here we are, still up to our armpits in blood and destruction. If I sound depressed it's because I've just lost a patient. A bad way to start the day.' He sipped some of the tea. 'How's our German friend?'

'Not too bad, sir. He's been asking for you.'

'All right, Sergeant-Major,' Mullholland said wearily. 'Let's see what he wants.'

Grant led the way down the line of hospital tents and turned into No. 3. Schenck was in the end bed. He lay there, his heavily bandaged arm on top of the blankets. Mullholland unhooked the board from the end of the bed to check on his condition and Schenck's eyes fluttered open.

'Good morning, Herr Major.'

'And how are you today?'

'Alive, it would seem, for which I am grateful. I thought that perhaps the arm . . .'

'No, it's fine, or it will be. You speak excellent English.'

'I worked for ten years in the City of London, not far from St Paul's – for an export agency.'

'I see.'

There was a pause, then Schenck said, 'Have you had a chance to consider General Canning's letter?'

Mullholland sat on the edge of the bed, suddenly very tired. 'I'm in something of a difficulty here. This isn't a combat unit. We're medical people. I've been thinking that perhaps the best thing I can do is get on to brigade headquarters and see if they can manage anything.'

'Are they nearby?'

'Last I heard, about twenty miles west of here, but the situation, of course, is very fluid.'

Schenck tried to push himself up. 'Forgive me, Herr Oberst, but time is of the essence in this matter. I must stress that to our certain knowledge, orders from Berlin have gone out authorizing the execution of all prominenti. If the SS reach Arlberg first, then General Canning, your own Colonel Birr and the rest, are certain to die. Colonel Hasser wishes to avoid this situation at all costs and is willing formally to surrender his command immediately.'

'But the area between here and Arlberg is in a very confused state, no one knows that better than you yourself. It would require a fighting unit to get through. They could run into trouble.'

'A small patrol, that's all I ask. A couple of jeeps, perhaps. An officer and a few men. If I go with them to show the best route, we could be there in four hours with any kind of luck at all. They could return at once with the prisoners. General Canning and the others could be here by this evening.'

'And just as much chance that they might run into

498

units of your forces on the way back. They could be taking a hell of a chance, especially the ladies.'

'So, what do you suggest, Herr Major? That they wait for the SS?'

Mullholland sighed wearily. 'No, you're right, of course. Give me half an hour. I'll see what I can work out.'

He went straight to his command tent and sat behind the desk. 'It's a mess, isn't it, but he's right. We've got to do something.'

'I've been thinking, sir,' Grant said. 'What about the three Americans? Captain Howard, the Ranger officer and his men?'

Mullholland paused in the act of taking a bottle of Scotch from his drawer. 'The survivors of that mess on the Salzburg road last week? By God, you might have something there. What shape is Howard in?'

'It took about fifty stitches to sew him up, sir, if you remember. Shrapnel wounds, but he was on his feet when I last saw him yesterday and his sergeant and the other bloke weren't wounded.'

'See if you can dig him up and bring him to me.'

Grant went out. Mullholland looked at the whisky bottle for a long moment, then he sighed, replaced the cork and put the bottle back into the drawer, closing it firmly. He lit a cigarette and started on some paperwork. A few moments later, Grant entered.

'Captain Howard, sir.'

Mullholland looked up. 'Fine, Sergeant-Major. Show him in and see if you can rustle up some tea.'

Grant went out and Howard ducked under the flap a moment later. He wasn't wearing a helmet and a red, angry-looking scar bisected his forehead, stopping short of the left eye, the stitches still clearly visible. His left hand was heavily bandaged. He was very pale, the eyes sunken, an expression of ineffable weariness on his face.

My God, Mullholland thought, *this boy's had about all he can take and no mistake*. He smiled. 'Come in, Captain, sit down. With any luck we might get some tea in a few minutes. Cigarette?'

'Thank you, sir.'

Mullholland gave him a light. 'How are you feeling?'

'Fine.'

Which was as fair a lie as Mullholland had heard in many a day, but he carried on. 'I've got a problem I thought you might be able to help me with.'

Howard showed no emotion at all. 'I see, sir.'

'We carted a German officer in here yesterday with a couple of bullets in him. The unfortunate thing was that he'd been looking for an Allied unit anyway. Had a letter on him from an American general called Canning. Have you heard of him?'

'Hamilton Canning?'

'That's him. He's being held prisoner along with four other prominentis, as the Germans call them.' He pushed the bloodstained letter across the table. 'But you'll find all the details there.'

Howard picked up the letter, read it with lacklustre eyes. Grant came in with two mugs of tea and placed them on the desk. Mullholland motioned him to stay.

After a while, the American looked up. 'They seem to be in a mess, these people. What do you want me to do about it?'

'I'd like you to go and get them. Accept this Colonel Hesser's surrender formally, then return with the prisoners as soon as possible. The German officer who brought this letter, Lieutenant Schenck, is willing to return with you to show you the way. He was quite badly wounded, but I think we can fix him up well enough to stand the trip.'

'You want me to go?' Howard said.

'And those two men of yours. I've been thinking about it. We could give you an ambulance. Plenty of room then for the others for the return trip.'

'Have you any idea what it's like out there, sir, between here and Arlberg?'

500

'I can guess,' Mullholland said evenly.

'And you want me to go with two men and a crippled German?' Howard's voice was flat, unemotional. 'Is this an order?'

'No, I've no authority to order you to do anything, Captain, as I think you know. The blunt truth is that I just haven't got anyone else available. This is a medical unit, and as you've seen for yourself, we're up to our eyes in it.'

Howard stared down at the letter for a long moment, then he nodded slowly. 'I'll put it to my sergeant, Hoover, and Private Finebaum, if that's all right with you, sir. I I think, under the circumstances, they should have some choice in the matter.'

'Fine,' Mullholland said. 'But don't take too long about making your decision, please,' and he used the phrase Schenck had used to him. 'Time really is of the essence in this one.'

Howard went out and Mullholland looked up at Grant. 'What do you think?'

'I don't know, sir. He looks as if he's had it to me.'

'Haven't we all, Sergeant-Major?' Mullholland said wearily.

Finebaum and Hoover shared a pup tent at the end of the rows on the other side of the vehicle park. Hoover was busily writing a letter while Finebaum crouched in the entrance, heating beans in a mess tin on a portable stove.

'Beans and yet more beans. Don't these limeys eat anything else?'

'Maybe you'd prefer K-ration,' Hoover said.

'Oh, I've got plans for that stuff, Harry,' Finebaum said. 'After the war, I'm going to buy a whole load of that crap – war surplus, you understand? Then I'm going to take it round to my old grannie who runs a strictly Kosher house. So Kosher that even the cat's got religion.'

'You mean you're going to feed K-ration to the cat?'
'That's it.'

'And break that old woman's heart? I mean, what did she ever do to you?'

'I'll tell you what she did. The day the Japs bombed Pearl Harbour she called me in and said, Mannie, you know what you've got to do, then she opened the front door, pointed me in the general direction of the recruiting office and shoved.'

He spooned beans on to a tin plate and handed it to Hoover. The sergeant said, 'You talk too much, but I know how you feel. I'm bored to hell with this place too.'

'When are we going to get out of here?' Finebaum demanded. 'I mean, I respect and love our noble captain, nobody more so, but how much longer do we stand around and wait for him to find his goddamned soul.'

'You cut that out,' Hoover said. 'He's had about all he can take.'

'In this game there's only two ways to be – alive or dead. Now I've seen a lot of good men go under in the year I've served with you and him. But they're dead and I'm not. I don't rejoice in it, but it's a fact of life and I ain't going to sit and cry over them either.'

Hoover put down his plate. 'Why, you son of a bitch, I've just made a discovery. You're not doing it because you're here or a patriot or something. You're doing it because you like it. Because it gives you kicks like you've never had before.'

'Screw you!'

'What are you after – another battle star? You want to be right up there in the line with those other heroes?'

'What do you want me to do, go back to sewing on fly-buttons in an Eastside cellar for thirty bucks a week when I can't get work blowing clarinet? No thank you. Before I got back to that, I'd rather pull the pin on one of my own grenades. I'll tell you something, Harry.' His voice

502

was low, urgent. 'I live more in a single day, than I did in a year before the war. When my time comes, I hope I take it right between the eyes about one minute before they sign the peace treaty, and if you and the noble captain don't like it, baby, then you can do the other thing.'

He got up and, turning, found Howard listening. They stood there, neither Hoover nor Finebaum knowing what the hell to say. It was Howard who spoke first. 'Tell me, Finebaum – Garland, Anderson, O'Grady – all those other guys in the outfit, all the way across Europe since D-Day? Don't you ever think of them at all? Doesn't the fact of their deaths have any meaning for you?'

'Those guys are dead – so they're dead. Right, Captain? I mean, maybe some part of my brain is missing or something, but I don't see it any other way.'

'And you don't think they accomplished anything?'

'You mean the nobility of war, sir? The strength of our purpose and all that crap? I'm afraid I don't buy that either. The way I figure it, every day for the past 10,000 years, someone, somewhere in the world has been beating hell out of someone else. I think it's in the nature of the species.'

'You know something, Finebaum. I'm beginning to think you might have read a book or two.'

'Could be, Captain. That just could be.'

'All right,' Howard said. 'You want a little action – I've got a pretty large helping for you. Ever heard of General Hamilton Canning?'

He quickly outlined the situation. When he was finished, Finebaum said, 'That's the craziest thing I ever heard of. That's Indian territory out there.'

'Forty or fifty miles of it between here and Arlberg.'

'And they want *us* to go? Three guys in an ambulance with some kraut stretcher case.' He started to laugh. 'You know I like it, Captain. Yes, I definitely like it.'

'Okay, so you go and tell Sergeant-Major Grant we're

going. Tell him I'll go along in five minutes to speak to this German lieutenant, Schenck and move it. If we're going we've got to go now.'

Finebaum went off on the double and Howard squatted down and helped himself to coffee from the stove. Hoover said, 'You sure you're doing the right thing? You don't look too good.'

'You want to know something, Harry?' Howard said. 'I'm tired right through to my backbone. More tired than I've ever been in my life, and yet I can't sleep. I can't feel, I don't seem to be able to react.' He shrugged. 'Maybe I need to smell a little gunpowder. Maybe I've got like Finebaum and need it.' He stuck a cigarette between his lips. 'I know one thing. Right now, I'd rather be out there taking my chances than squatting on my backside here waiting for the war to finish.'

The Finns were encamped at a farm just off the main road about ten miles west of Arnheim. There were thirty-eight of them under the command of a Hauptsturmführer named Erik Sorsa.

The 5th SS Panzer Division Wiking was the first, and without a doubt the best, foreign division of the Waffen-SS composed mainly of Dutch, Flemings, Danes and Norwegians. The Finns had joined in 1941, providing ski-troop expertise so essential in the Russian campaign.

The losses on the Eastern Front by January 1945 had been so colossal that it was decided to raise a new regiment, a joint Germanic–Finnish affair. The project had foundered when the few dozen Finnish survivors, with Sorsa as their senior officer, had made it clear that they would not renew their contracts with the German government after 1 May. So, from Divisional Headquarters in Klagenfurt, had come the order which had sent them to the farm at Oberfeld to await further instructions, which was what they had been doing for precisely three weeks now.

Sorsa was a handsome, fair-haired young man of twenty-seven. His mountain cap was identical to that of the army in cut, the edelweiss on the left-hand side, the usual SS death's head at the front. His cuff title read 'Finnisches Freiwilligen Bataillon der Waffen-SS' in two lines, and his armshield was black with a white lion. He wore two Iron Crosses, the wound badge in silver and the Winter War ribbon.

He stood at the door of the farm, smoking a cigarette, watching half a dozen of his men ski-ing down through the trees on the hillside above, led by the unit's senior sergeant-major, Matti Gestrin. Gestrin soared over the wall by the barn, jumping superbly, and they followed him one by one with rhythmic precision, tough, competent-looking men in reversible winter war uniforms, white on one side, autumn-pattern camouflage on the other.

'Did you see anything?' Sorsa inquired.

'Were we supposed to?' Gestrin grinned. 'I thought we were just out for the exercise. Still no word from headquarters?'

'No, I think they've forgotten about us.'

Gestrin, in the act of lighting a cigarette, stopped smiling, looking beyond Sorsa's shoulder. 'From the looks of things, I'd say they've just found us again.'

The field car came down the track through the snow, Hoffer at the wheel, Ritter beside him wearing a camouflaged parka with the hood up over his cap. Strasser and Earl Jackson were in the back seat. Hoffer drove into the farmyard and braked to a halt. Sorsa and Gestrin stayed where they were by the front door, but the rest of the Finns moved forward perceptibly, one or two unslinging their Mauser infantry rifles. Sorsa said something quietly to them in Finnish.

'What did he say?' Strasser asked Jackson.

'He said, easy, children. Nothing I can't handle.'

Another dozen or fifteen Finns came out of the barn, mostly in shirt-sleeves and all carrying weapons of one sort or another. There was total silence as everyone waited, just the snow falling perfectly straight, and then, with a sudden whispering rush, another white-clad skier lifted over the wall to land perfectly, skidding to a halt a yard or two away from Sorsa. Another, and yet another followed.

It was poetry in motion, total perfection, and there was a slight fixed smile on Sorsa's face that seemed to say: 'That's what we are. What about you?'

Jackson murmured, 'The greatest skiers in the world, these boys. They knocked hell out of the Russians in the first winter war. And they're great throat-cutters, maybe I should have warned you.'

'Wait here,' Ritter said tonelessly. 'All of you.'

He got out of the field car and walked across the yard to Sorsa. For a moment he confronted the tall Finn, who could see only the death's-head in his cap, then said, 'Not bad – not bad at all.'

'You think so?' Sorsa said.

'A fair jump, certainly.'

'You could do better?'

'Perhaps.'

There were several pairs of skis leaning against the wall. Ritter helped himself, kneeling to adjust the bindings to fit his heavy Panzer boots.

Hoffer appeared at his side and knelt down. 'Allow me, Sturmbannführer.'

Sorsa took in the sergeant-major's black Panzer uniform, the Knight's Cross. There was a sudden change of expression in his eyes and he turned and glanced at Gestrin briefly.

Ritter stamped his feet and took the sticks Hoffer offered him. He smiled. 'A long time, Erich, eh?'

He pushed forward, past the field car, out of the gate, and started up the steep slope through the pine trees.

Nobody said a word. Everyone waited. He felt curiously calm and peaceful as he followed the zig-zag of the farm track, totally absorbed, thoroughly enjoying the whole thing.

When he turned, he was perhaps a hundred feet above the yard, the track the Finns had made clear before him. Every face was turned, looking up, and he suddenly felt immensely happy, laughter bubbling up inside him.

He threw back his head and howled like a wolf, the old Harz woodcutters' signal, and launched himself forward, away from the track of the Finns, taking the steepest slope, down, zig-zagging through the pine trees in a series of stem turns that were breathtaking in their audacity. And then he lifted, soaring effortlessly over the wall, the field car, drifting broadside for a second only, then turning on his left stick, landing in a spray of snow at a dead halt in a perfectly executed Stem Christiana, no more than a yard from Sorsa.

There was a shout of approval from the Finns. Ritter stood there, Hoffer kneeling to unfasten his bindings for him, then he threw back his hood, unbuttoned the parka and took it off.

'He should have been on the stage, that one,' Strasser whispered to Jackson.

Ritter tightened his gloves and spoke without looking at Sorsa. 'My name is Ritter, Sturmbannführer, 502nd SS Heavy Tank Battalion, and I am here to assume command of this unit under special orders from the Führer himself in Berlin.'

Sorsa looked him over, the Winter War Ribbon, the Iron Cross, First and Second Class, the silver badge which meant at least three wounds, the Knight's Cross with Oak Leaves and Swords, the dark eyes, the pale devil's face on him.

'Death himself come among us,' Matti Gestrin said.

'You will speak German, please, in my presence,' Ritter said calmly. 'I take it your men are capable of as much,

Hauptsturmführer, considering that they have been in the service of the Reich for some four years now?'

Sorsa said, 'Most of them, but never mind that now. What's this nonsense about orders from Berlin? I know nothing of this.'

'Herr Strasser?' Ritter called. 'You will please show this gentleman our orders.'

'With pleasure, Major.'

Strasser came forward, taking them from his pocket, and Ritter walked a few paces away, ignoring the Finns' stares, took out a silver case and selected a cigarette with care. Hoffer jumped to his side to offer him a light.

'Thank you, Sturmscharführer.'

It was a nicely calculated piece of theatre, a scene they had played many times before, usually with maximum effect.

Sorsa was examining the order Strasser had passed to him. From the Leader and Chancellor of the State. Most Secret. And he was there himself, mentioned by name, everything exactly as Ritter had said. Most explicit. And most amazing thing of all, the signature at the foot of the paper. *Adolf Hitler*.

He handed the paper back and Strasser replaced it in his wallet. 'Well?' Ritter said, without looking round. 'You are satisfied?'

'There is a situation here,' Sorsa said awkwardly. 'My comrades and I are contract soldiers.'

'Mercenaries,' Ritter said. 'I'm well aware of the fact. So?'

'My men have voted to go home to Helsinki. We have not renewed our contract.'

'Why should you?' Ritter said loud enough for all to hear. 'When your original one is still in force until nine o'clock tomorrow morning – or would you deny that fact?'

'No – what you say is true.'

'Then it would appear that you and your men are still soldiers of the Waffen-SS, and under the Führer-directive just shown to you by Herr Strasser here, I now assume command of this unit.'

There was a long, long moment while everyone waited for Sorsa's answer. 'Yes, Sturmbannführer.' There was a further pause and he raised his voice a little. 'Until nine o'clock tomorrow morning, we are still soldiers of the Waffen-SS. We have taken the blood money, sworn the oath and we Finns do not go back on our word.'

'Good.' Ritter turned to Gestrin. 'You will please bring the company to attention, Sergeant-Major. I wish to address them.'

There was a flurry of movement as Gestrin barked orders and finally the Finns were drawn up in two lines. Thirty-five of them, Ritter noted that. They stood there waiting in the falling snow as he paced up and down. Finally, he stopped and faced them, hands on his hips.

'I know you men. You were at Leningrad, Kurland, Stalingrad – so was I. You fought in the Ardennes – so did I. We've a lot in common, so I'll speak plainly. Captain Sorsa here says that you're Waffen-SS only until tomorrow morning. That you want to go home to Helsinki. Well, I've news for you. The Russians are into Berlin, they're with the American Army on the Elbe, cutting Germany in half. You're not going anywhere because there's nowhere to go and if the Ivans get their hands on you all you'll get is a bullet – and that's if you're lucky.'

The wind increased in force, driving snow down through the trees in a miniature blizzard.

'And I'm in the same boat because the Russians over-ran my parents' place a month ago. So, all we've got is each other and the regiment, but even if it's only till nine o'clock tomorrow morning, you're still soldiers of the Waffen-SS, the toughest, most efficient fighting men the world has ever seen, and from now on, you'll start acting that way again. If I ask you a question, you answer; *Jawohl, Sturmbannführer*. If I give you an order, you get those heels together and shout: *Zu befehl, Sturmbannführer.*

509

Do you understand me?' There was silence. He raised his voice. 'Do you understand me?'

'*Jawohl, Sturmbannführer,*' they chorused.

'Good.' He turned to Sorsa. 'Let's go inside and I'll explain the situation to you.'

The door opened directly into a large, stone-flagged kitchen. There was a wooden table, a few chairs, a wood fire burning on the hearth and a profusion of military equipment of various kinds, including several Panzerfausts, the one-man anti-tank weapons which had been produced in such quantities during the last few months of the war.

They all gathered round the table, Sorsa, Strasser, Earl Jackson, Hoffer. Ritter unfolded a map of the area. 'How many vehicles do you have?'

'One field car, three troop-carrying half-tracks.'

'And weapons?'

'A heavy machine gun in each half-track, otherwise only light infantry weapons and grenades. Oh, and a few Panzerfausts, as you can see.'

Strasser said, 'Aren't you overreacting just a little, Major? After all, if things go as smoothly as they should, this could simply be a matter of driving into the Schloss and driving out again half an hour later.'

'I stopped believing in miracles some considerable time ago.' Ritter tapped his finger on the map and said to Sorsa, 'Schloss Arlberg. That's our objective. Herr Strasser here will now tell you what it's all about and you can then brief the men. We leave in half an hour.'

IO

It was just after ten o'clock and Colonel Hesser was working away at his desk when there was a knock at the door and Schneider entered.

Hesser glanced up eagerly. 'Any news of Schenck?'

'I'm afraid not, sir.'

Hesser threw down his pen. 'He should have been back by now. It doesn't look good.'

'I know, sir.'

'Anyway, what did you want?'

'Herr Meyer is here, sir, from the village. There's been some sort of accident. His son, I believe. He wants to know if Herr Gaillard can go down to the village with him. He's the only doctor for miles around at the moment.'

'Show him in.'

Johann Meyer was Mayor of Arlberg and owner of the village inn, the Golden Eagle. He was a tall robust-looking man with iron-grey hair and beard, a well-known guide in the Bavarian Alps. Just now he was considerably agitated.

'What's the trouble, Meyer?' Colonel Hesser asked.

'It's my boy, Arnie, Herr Oberst,' Meyer said. 'Trying the quick way down the mountain again, tried jumping a tree and ended up taking a bad fall. I think he may have broken his left leg. I was wondering whether Herr Gaillard . . .'

'Yes, of course.' Hesser nodded to Schneider. 'Find Gaillard as fast as you can, and take him and Herr Mayer back to the village in a field car.'

'Shall I stay with him, Herr Oberst?'

'No, I need you here. Take one of the men with you and leave him there. Anyone will do. Oh, and tell Gaillard that I naturally assume that under the circumstances he offers his parole.'

Gaillard was in fact at that very moment engaged in an animated discussion about their situation with Canning and Birr.

'We can't go on like this, it's crazy,' Canning said. 'Schenck should have been back last night. Something's gone wrong.'

'Probably lying dead in a ditch somewhere,' Birr said. 'I did tell you, remember?'

'Okay, so what do we do?'

'Well,' Gaillard said. 'The garrison of this establishment is composed mainly of old men or cripples, as no one knows better than I do. I've been treating them all for months now. On the other hand they still outnumber the three of us by about seven to one and they are armed to the teeth.'

'But we can't just sit here and wait for it to happen,' Canning said.

Claire, sitting by the fire with Madame Chevalier, said, 'Has it ever occurred to you, Hamilton, that you just might be making a mountain out of a molehill here? An American or British unit could roll up to that gate at any time and all our troubles would be over.'

'And pigs might also fly.'

'You know what your trouble is?' she told him. 'You want it this way. Drama, intrigue, up to your ears in the most dangerous game of all again.'

'Now you listen to me,' he began, thoroughly angry, and then the door opened and Schneider entered.

He clicked his heels. 'Excuse me, Herr General, but Dr Gaillard is wanted urgently in the village. Herr Meyer's son has had a ski-ing accident.'

'I'll come at once,' Gaillard said. 'Just give me a moment to get my bag.'

He hurried out, followed by Schneider. Birr said, 'Always work for the healers, eh? Nice to think there are people like Gaillard around to put us together again when we fall down.'

'Philosophy now?' Canning said. 'May God preserve me.'

'Oh, he will, Hamilton. He will,' Birr said. 'I've got a feeling the Almighty has something very special lined up for you.'

As Claire and Madame Chevalier started to laugh, Canning said, 'I wonder whether you'll still be smiling when the SS drive into that courtyard down there?' and he stalked angrily from the room.

Arnie Meyer was only twelve years old and small for his age. His face was twisted in agony, the sweat springing to his forehead, trickling down from the fair hair. He had no mother and his father stood anxiously at one side of the bed and watched as Gaillard cut the trouser leg open with a pair of scissors.

He ran his fingers around the angry swelling below the right knee and, in spite of his gentleness, the boy cried out sharply.

'Is it broken, Herr Doctor?' Meyer asked.

'Without a doubt. You have splints, of course, with your mountain rescue equipment?'

'Yes, I'll get them.'

'In the meantime I'll give him a morphine injection. I'll have to set the leg and that would be too painful for him to bear. Oh, and that private Schneider left, Voss I think his name is. Send him in here. He can assist me.'

The mayor went out and Gaillard broke open a morphine ampoule. 'Were you coming down the north track again?'

'Yes, Herr Doctor.'

'How many times have I warned you. Out of sun among the trees, when it's below freezing, conditions are too fast for you. Your father says you tried to jump a tree, but that isn't true, is it?' Here, he gave the boy the injection.

Arnie winced. 'No, Herr Doctor,' he said faintly. 'I came out of the track on to the slope and tried to do a Stem Christiana like I've seen you do, only everything went wrong.'

'As well it might, you idiot,' Gaillard told him. 'Frozen ground – hardly any snow. What were you trying to do? Commit suicide!'

There was a knock at the door and Private Voss came in, a small middle-aged man with steel spectacles. He was a clerk from Hamburg whose bad eyes had kept him out of the war until the previous July.

'You wanted me, Herr Doctor?'

'I'll need your assistance in a short while to set the boy's leg. Have you ever done anything like this before?'

'No.' Voss looked faintly alarmed.

'Don't worry. You'll soon learn.'

Meyer came back a moment later with mountain-rescue splints and several rolls of bandage.

'If I had hospital facilities, I'd put this leg in a pot,' Gaillard said. 'It is absolutely essential that once it's set, it remains immobile, especially so in the case of a boy of this age. It will be your responsibility to see that he behaves himself.'

'He will, I promise you, Herr Doctor.'

'Good, now let's see how brave you can be, Arnie?'

But Arnie, in spite of the morphine, fainted dead away at the first touch. Which was all to the good, of course, for Gaillard was really able to get to work then, setting the bone with an audible crack that turned Voss's face pale. The little private hauled on the foot as instructed and held a splint on the other side from Meyer as Gaillard skilfully wound the bandages.

When he was finished, the Frenchman stepped back and smiled at Meyer. 'And now, my friend, you can serve me a very large brandy from your most expensive bottle. Nothing less than Armagnac will be accepted.'

'Do we return to the castle now, Herr Doctor?' Voss asked.

'No, my friend. We adjourn to the bar with the mayor here, who will no doubt consider your efforts no less worthy of his hospitality. We will wait there until my patient recovers consciousness, however long it takes. Possibly all day, so be prepared.'

They started downstairs and at the same moment heard a motor vehicle draw up outside. Meyer went to the window on the landing halfway down, then turned. 'There's a military ambulance outside, Herr Doctor, and it isn't German from the looks of it.'

Gaillard joined him at the window in time to see Jack Howard jump down from the passenger seat and stand looking up at the Golden Eagle, a Thompson gun under one arm.

Gaillard got the window open. 'In here,' he called in English. 'A pleasure to see you.' Howard looked up, hesitated then advanced to the door. Gaillard turned to Voss. 'A great day, my friend, perhaps the most important in your life because from this moment, for you, the war is over.'

The journey in the ambulance from the field hospital had been a total anti-climax. They had driven through countryside covered in snow, from which the population seemed to have vanished, a strange, lost land of deserted villages and shuttered farms. Most important of all, except for a few abandoned vehicles at various places, they had seen no sign of the enemy.

'But where in the hell is everybody?' Hoover demanded at one point.

'With their heads under the bed, waiting for the axe to fall,' Finebaum told him.

'Alpine Fortress,' Hoover said. 'What a load of crap. One good armoured column could go from one end of this country to the other in a day as far as I can see and nobody to stop them.' He turned to Howard. 'What do you think, sir?'

'I think it's all very mysterious,' Howard said. 'And that's good because if my map reading is correct, we're coming down into Arlberg now.'

They came round the corner, saw the village at the bottom of the hill, the spires of the castle peeping above the wooded crest on the other side of the valley.

'And there she is,' Finebaum said. 'Schloss Arlberg. Sounds like a tailor I used to know in East Manhattan.'

They drove down through the deserted street, turned into the cobbled square and halted in front of the Golden Eagle.

'Even here,' Hoover said, 'not a soul in sight. It gives me the creeps.'

Howard reached for his Thompson gun and got out of the cab. He stood there looking up at the building and then a window was thrown open and a voice called excitedly in English with a French accent, 'In here!'

Gaillard embraced the American enthusiastically. 'My friend, I don't think I've ever been more pleased to see anyone in my life. My name is Paul Gaillard. I am a prisoner with several others here at Schloss Arlberg.'

'I know,' Howard said. 'That's why we're here. Jack Howard, by the way.'

'Ah, then Schenck got through?'

'Yes, but he stopped a couple of bullets on the way. He's outside now in the ambulance.'

'Then I'd better take a look at him. I was once a doctor by profession. It has come in useful of late.'

Just then Voss appeared hesitantly at the bottom of the stairs. Finebaum called a warning from the doorway.

'Watch it, Captain.'

As he raised his M1, Gaillard hastily got in the way. 'No need for that. Although poor Voss here is technically supposed to be guarding me he has, to my certain knowledge, never fired a shot in anger in his life.' Finebaum lowered his rifle and Gaillard said to Howard, 'There will be no need for shooting by anyone, believe me. Colonel Hesser has already said that he will surrender to the first Allied troops who appear. Didn't Schenck make this clear?'

'It's been a long, hard war, Doctor,' Finebaum said. 'We only got this far by never taking a kraut on trust.'

'Like perspective, I suppose, it's all a question of your point of view,' Gaillard said. 'It has been my experience that they are good, bad or indifferent as the rest of us. Still, I'd better have a look at Schenck now. Voss, please to bring my bag.'

At the door, he paused, looking at the ambulance, then glanced along the street. 'There are no others? No one else is coming?'

'You were lucky to get us,' Howard told him.

He opened the rear door of the ambulance and Gaillard climbed inside. Schenck lay there, the heavily bandaged arm outside the blankets, the eyes closed. He opened them slowly and on finding Gaillard, managed a smile.

'So, Doctor, here we are again.'

'You did well.' Gaillard felt his pulse. 'What about Schmidt?'

'Dead.'

'He was a good man, I'm sorry. You have a slight fever. Is there much pain?'

'For the past hour it has been hell.'

'I'll give you something for that, then you can sleep.'

He opened the bag which Voss had brought, found a

morphine ampoule and gave Schenck an injection, then he climbed out of the ambulance again.

'Will he be okay?' Howard asked.

'I think so.'

They went back into the inn and found Hoover and Finebaum at one end of the bar, Voss at the other looking worried. Meyer had the Armagnac out and several glasses.

'Excellent,' Gaillard said. 'Herr Meyer, here, who is Mayor of Arlberg as well as a most excellent inn-keeper, was about to treat me to a shot, as I believe you Americans call it, of his best brandy. Perhaps you gentlemen will join me.'

Meyer filled the glasses hurriedly. Finebaum grabbed for his and Hoover said, 'Not yet, you dummy. This is a special occasion. It calls for a toast.'

Howard turned to Gaillard. 'I'd say it was your prerogative, Doctor.'

'Very well,' Gaillard said. 'I could drink to you, my friends, but I think the circumstances demand something more appropriate. Something for all of us. For you and me, but also for Schenck and Voss and Meyer here, all those who have suffered the disabilities of this terrible war. I give you love and life and happiness, commodities which have been in short supply for some considerable time now.'

'I'll drink to that,' Finebaum said, and emptied the glass at a swallow.

'We'd better get on up to the castle now,' Howard said.

'Where you will find them awaiting your arrival with a considerable degree of impatience, General Canning in particular,' Gaillard told him. 'I'll hang on here for the moment. I have a patient upstairs.'

'Okay, Doctor,' Howard said. 'But I'd better warn you. My orders are to pick you people up, turn straight round and get the hell out of it. I'd say you've got an hour – that's all.'

They moved outside. Finebaum said, 'What about the kraut? We take him along?'

'Voss stays with me,' Gaillard said firmly. 'I'll very probably need him.'

'Anything you say, Doctor.' Howard shoved Finebaum up into the cab of the ambulance. 'Finebaum's survived on the idea the only good one is a dead one for so long, it's become a way of life.'

'So what does that make me, some kind of animal? It means I'm alive, doesn't it?' Finebaum leaned down to Gaillard as Hoover started the engine. 'You look like a philosopher, Doc. Here's some philosophy for you. A funny thing about war. It gets easier as you go along.'

The ambulance drove away across the square. Meyer, who was standing in the porch, said in German, 'What did he say, the small one, Herr Doctor?'

'He said a terrible thing, my friend.' Gaillard smiled sadly. 'But true, unfortunately. And now, I think, we'll take another look at this boy of yours.'

Hesser was seated at his desk writing a letter to his wife when the door was flung open unceremoniously and Schneider rushed in. He had the Alsatian with him and his excitement had even infected the dog, which circled him, whining, so that the lead got tangled in his legs.

'What is it, man?' Hesser demanded. 'What's wrong with you?'

'They're coming, Herr Oberst. A British vehicle has just started up the hill.'

'Only one? You are certain?'

'They've just phoned through from the guardhouse, Herr Oberst. An ambulance, apparently.'

'Strange,' Hesser said. 'However, we must prepare to receive them with all speed. Turn out the garrison and notify General Canning and the others. I'll be down myself directly.'

Schneider went out and Hesser sat there, hand flat on the table, a slight frown on his face. Now that the

moment had come he felt curiously deflated, but then that
was only to be expected. The end of something, after all,
and what did he have to show for it? One arm, one eye.
But there was still Gerda – and the children – and it was
over now. Soon he could go home. When he got up and
reached for his cap and belt he was actually smiling.

As the ambulance came out of the last bend and Schloss
Arlberg loomed above them, Finebaum leaned out of the
cab and looked up at the pointed roofs of the towers in awe.

'Hey, I seen this place before. The moat, the drawbridge – everything. *The Prisoner of Zenda*. Ronald Cole-
man swam across and some dame helped him in through
the window.'

'That was Hollywood, this is for real, man,' Hoover
said. 'This place was built to stand a siege. Those walls
must be ten feet thick.'

'They're hospitable enough, that's for sure,' Howard
said. 'They've left the gate open for us. Straight in,
Harry, nice and slow, and let's see what we've got here.'

Hoover dropped into bottom gear and they trundled
across the drawbridge. The iron-bound gates stood open
and they moved on through the darkness of the entrance
tunnel and emerged into the great inner courtyard.

The garrison was drawn up in a single line, all eighteen
of them, Colonel Hesser at the front. General Canning,
Colonel Birr, Claire and Madame Chevalier stood together at the top of the steps leading up to the main
entrance.

The ambulance rolled to a halt and Howard got out.
Hesser called his men to attention and saluted politely.
'My name is Hesser – Oberstleutnant, 42nd Panzer
Grenadiers, at present in command of this establishment.
And you, sir?'

'Captain John H. Howard, 2nd Ranger Battalion,
United States Army.'

Hesser turned and called, 'General Canning – Colonel Birr. Will you join me, please?'

They came down the steps and crossed the yard. It was snowing quite hard now. Howard saluted and Canning held out his hand. 'We're certainly pleased to see you, son, believe me.'

'Our pleasure, General.'

Hesser said, 'Then, in the presence of these officers as witnesses, I formally surrender this establishment, Captain Howard.' He saluted, turned and said to Schneider, 'Have the men lay down their arms.'

There was a flurry of movement. Within a matter of seconds, the men were back in line, their rifles standing in three triangular stacks before them.

Hesser saluted again. 'Very well, Captain,' he said. 'What are your orders?'

Sorsa headed the German column in one of the armoured half-tracks, Ritter and Hoffer, Strasser and Earl Jackson next in line in their field car, the rest of the Finns trailing behind.

Just after noon they emerged from a side-road to join the road from Innsbruck to Arlberg, the road along which the ambulance had passed a short time before. As they reached the crest of the hill above the village, Sorsa signalled a halt. Ritter, Strasser and Jackson got out of the field car and went to join him.

'What is it?' Ritter demanded.

'Something's passed along this road very recently. Heavy vehicle. See the tyre marks. It stopped here before starting down to the village.'

There was fresh oil on the snow. Ritter looked down the hill. 'So this is Arlberg?'

'Quiet little place, isn't it?' Earl Jackson said. 'They're certainly staying out of the way down there.'

Ritter held out his hand for Sorsa's field-glasses and

521

trained them on the turrets of Schloss Arlberg peeping above the crest of the far ridge. He handed them back to Strasser. 'Nothing worth seeing. The vehicle which has preceded us could be anything, but under the circumstances, I think we should press on.'

'I agree,' Strasser said, and for the first time seemed less calm than usual, filled with a kind of nervous excitement. 'Let's get there as fast as possible and get things sewn up. We've come too far for anything to be allowed to go wrong now.'

They got back into the vehicles, Sorsa waved the column on and they started down the hill.

It was Meyer who saw them first when they were half-way down; sheer luck that he'd gone to the landing window to close it. He took one look, then hurried to the bedroom where Gaillard was checking on the boy, who was still unconscious.

'There's an SS column coming down the hill,' Meyer said. 'Three half-tracks, two field cars. About forty men in all.'

Voss's face turned deathly pale. Gaillard said, 'You're certain?'

Meyer opened a cupboard and took out an old brass telescope. 'See for yourself.'

They all went out on to the landing and Meyer levelled the telescope on the lead half-track. Immediately the divisional signs on the vehicle leapt into view, the SS runes, the death's head painted in white. He moved on to the field car, picking out Ritter, first, then Strasser.

He frowned and Meyer said, 'What is it, Herr Doctor?'

'Nothing,' Gaillard said. 'There's a civilian with them I thought I knew for a moment, but I must be wrong. They're mountain troops judging by their uniform and the skis they carry in the half-tracks.'

He closed the telescope and handed it to Meyer. Voss plucked at his sleeve. 'What are we going to do, Herr Doctor? Those devils are capable of anything.'

'No need to panic,' Gaillard said. 'Keep calm above all things.' He turned to Meyer. 'They'll be here within the next two or three minutes. Go out and meet them.'

'And what about the Americans? Look, the tracks of the ambulance are plain in the snow. What if they ask me who made them?'

'Play it by ear, that one. Whatever happens don't tell them Voss and I are here. We'll keep out of sight for the time being. We can always clear off the back way if we have to, but I want to see how the situation develops here first, and besides, Arnie is going to need me when he wakes up.'

'As you say.' Meyer took a deep breath and started downstairs as the first vehicle braked to a halt outside. Gaillard and Voss, peering round the edge of the curtain, saw Ritter, Strasser and Earl Jackson get out of the field car.

'Strange,' Gaillard said. 'One of the SS officers has a Stars and Stripes shield sewn on to his left sleeve below the eagle. What on earth does that mean?'

'I don't know, Herr Doctor,' Voss whispered. 'Where the SS are concerned, I've always kept well out of the way. Who's the one in the leather coat speaking to Meyer now? Gestapo, perhaps!'

'I don't know,' Gaillard said. 'I still have that irritating feeling we've met somewhere before.' He eased the window open in time to hear Sorsa shout an order to Matti Gestrin in the rear half-track. 'My God,' Gaillard whispered, 'they're Finns.'

He peered down at them, suddenly fearful. Hard tough, competent-looking men, armed to the teeth, and there was only one road up to the castle, one road down. He turned and grabbed Voss by the shirt-front.

'Right, my friend, your chance to be a hero for the first time in your miserable life. Out of the back door, through the trees and take the woodcutter's track up to the castle and run till your heart bursts. Tell Hesser the SS are coming. Now get moving!' And he shoved Voss violently along the landing towards the back stairs.

As he turned to the window again, Ritter was saying to Meyer, 'From these tracks a vehicle would seem to have passed this way during the past half-hour. A heavy vehicle. What was it?'

The direct question, and in the circumstances there was only one answer Meyer could give. 'It was an ambulance, Sturmbannführer.'

'A German ambulance?' Strasser asked.

'No, mein Herr. A British Army ambulance. There were three American soldiers in the cab. One was an officer – a captain, I think.'

'And they took that street there out of the square?' Ritter nodded. 'Which leads to?'

'Schloss Arlberg.'

'And is there any other way up or down?'

'Only on foot.'

'One more question. How many men in the garrison at Schloss Arlberg now?'

Meyer hesitated, but he was a simple man with his son to consider, and Ritter's pale face, the dark eyes under the silver death's-head, were too much.

'Eighteen, Sturmbannführer. Nineteen with the commandant.'

Ritter turned to the others. 'What you might call a damn close thing.'

'No problem, surely,' Strasser said.

'Let's go and see, shall we?' Ritter replied calmly, and he turned back to the field car.

Meyer waited on the step until the last half-track in the column had disappeared up the narrow street before going back inside. Gaillard was at the bottom of the stairs.

'Well?' the Frenchman demanded.

'What could I do, I had to tell them?' Meyer shivered. 'But now what, Herr Doctor? I mean, what can they do up there in the castle? Colonel Hasser has no option but to turn your friends over to the SS now.'

But before Gaillard could reply, Arnie called out feverishly from the bedroom and Gaillard turned and hurried upstairs.

In the courtyard, the prominenti were making ready to leave. Schenck had been left on board the ambulance and three German soldiers were loading the prisoners' personal belongings. Claire and Madame Chevalier waited in the porch while Hesser, Birr and Canning stood at the bottom of the steps, smoking cigarettes. Beyond the ambulance, the rest of the tiny garrison still stood in line before their stacked rifles.

It was Magda, Schneider's Alsatian, who first showed signs of agitation, whining and straining at her leash and then breaking into furious barking.

Canning frowned. 'What is it, old girl? What's wrong with you?'

There was the hollow booming of feet thundering across the drawbridge and Voss staggered out of the tunnel.

'Herr Oberst!' he called weakly, lurching from side to side like a drunken man. 'The SS are coming! The SS are coming!'

Hesser reached out his one good arm to steady Voss as he almost fell, chest heaving, sweat pouring down his face.

'What are you telling me, man?'

'SS, Herr Oberst. On their way up from the village. It's

true. Finnish mountain troops in the charge of a Sturmbannführer in Panzer uniform.'

Canning caught him by the arm and pulled him round.
'How many?'

'Forty or so all together. Three half-tracks and two
field cars.'

'What kind of armaments did they carry?'

'There was a heavy machine gun with each vehicle,
Herr General, I noticed that. The rest was just the usual
hand stuff. Schmeissers, rifles and so on.'

Finebaum said to Hoover, 'They keep telling me the
war's over, but here we are, the three of us, with nineteen
kraut prisoners on our hands and forty of those SS bastards
coming round the bend fast.'

Howard turned to Canning. 'It's an impossible situation,
sir, and even if we tried to make a run for it, we'd just
run slap into them. There's only one road in and out of
here.'

Canning turned to face Hesser, trying to think of the
right words, but strangely enough it was Madame
Chevalier who played a hand now.

'Well, Max,' she called. 'What's it to be? Checkmate
or have you still got enough juice left in you to act like
a man?' She moved forward, leaning on Claire's shoulder.
'Not for us, Max, not even for yourself. For Gerda, for
your children.'

Max Hesser stared up at her wildly for a moment, then
he turned to the garrison. 'Grab your rifles, quick as you
like. Schneider – take two men, get to the guardroom
on the double and shut the gates.'

There was a sudden flurry of activity. He turned to
Canning, drew himself up and saluted formally. 'General
Canning, as you are the senior Allied officer here, I place
myself and my men at your command. What are your
orders, sir?'

Canning's nostrils flared, his eyes sparkled, tension
erupting from deep inside him in a harsh laugh. 'By God,

that's more like it. All right, for the time being, deploy your men on the walls above the guardroom and let's see what these bastards want.' He clapped his hands together and shouted furiously, 'Come on, come on, come on! Let's get this show on the road.'

The column, Sorsa still leading the way in the front half-track, was no more than fifty yards from the castle entrance when the gates clanged shut. Sorsa immediately signalled a halt.

Ritter stood up in the field car and called, 'Line of assault. Quickly now.'

The Finns moved into action instantly. The other two half-tracks took up position on either side of Sorsa, the machine-gun crews made themselves ready for action, the rest of the men jumped to the ground and fanned out.

There was silence for a moment after the engines were cut. Ritter raised his field-glasses and looked to where there was movement on the wall.

'What is it? What's happening?' Strasser demanded.

'Interesting,' Ritter said softly. 'I see American helmets up there together with German ones. Perhaps the Third World War has started?'

On the wall, Canning, Birr, Hesser and Howard grouped together in the shelter of the west guardroom turret and peered out.

'Now what?' Birr said. He carried a Schmeisser in one hand, and Canning a Walther pistol.

'We'll stir things up a bit, just to show them we mean business.' Canning moved to where Schneider crouched beside the machine-gun crew who had positioned their weapons to point out through an embrasure beside one of the castle's eighteenth-century cannon. 'I want you to fire a long burst into the ground about ten yards in front of the lead half-track,' he said in German.

Schneider turned in alarm and looked to Hesser. 'Herr Oberst, what do I do?'

'As General Canning commands,' Hesser said. 'We are under his orders now.'

Schneider patted the lead gunner on the shoulder. He was another reservist, a man named Strang, who like most of them had never in his life fired a shot in anger. He hesitated, sweat on his face, and Finebaum slung his M1, pushed him out of the way and grabbed for the handles.

'Maybe you got qualms, Uncle, but not me.'

He squeezed off a long burst, swinging the barrel so that snow and gravel spurted in a darting line right across the front of the half-tracks.

Ritter turned, arms flung wide. 'No return fire. It's a warning only.'

Hoover whispered to Howard. 'Did you see that? Those guys didn't even move.'

Finebaum got up and turned. 'They're hot stuff, Harry, believe me. I tell you, this thing could get very interesting.'

Ritter jumped down from the field car and Sorsa moved to meet him. 'Do we go in?'

'No, first we talk. They'll want to talk, I think.' He turned to Strasser. 'You agree?'

'Yes, I think so. Hesser will already be beginning to have second thoughts. Let's give him a chance to change his mind.'

'Good,' Ritter said, and called to Hoffer, 'Over here, Erich. We'll go for a little walk, you and I.'

'*Zu befehl, Sturmbannführer*,' Hoffer replied crisply.

'I, too, could do with some exercise, I think,' Strasser said. 'If you've no objection, Major Ritter?'

'As you like.'

Strasser turned to Earl Jackson. 'You stay back out of the way. Borrow a parka and get the hood up. I don't want them to see you, you understand?'

Jackson frowned, but did as he was told, moving back to one of the half-tracks.

Sorsa said, 'What if they open fire?'

'Then you'll have to take command, won't you?' Ritter said and started forward.

Their feet crunched in the snow. Ritter took out his case, selected a cigarette and offered one to Strasser.

'No thank you. I never use them. You are surprised, I think, that I felt the need for exercise?'

'Perhaps. On the other hand I could say that it shows confidence in my judgement.'

'Or a belief in my own destiny, have you considered that?'

'A point of view, I suppose. If it's of any comfort, good luck to you.'

On the wall, Canning said, 'By God, he's a cool one, the devil in black out there. Obviously in need of conversation.'

'What do we do, General?' Hesser asked.

'Why, accommodate him, of course. You, me and Captain Howard here. Not you, Justin. You stay up here in command, just in case some trigger-happy jerk in one of the half-tracks decides to open up.' He smiled savagely, giving every appearance of thoroughly enjoying himself. 'All right, gentlemen. Let's see what they have to say.'

Ritter, Strasser and Erich Hoffer paused at their side of the drawbridge and waited. After a while, the small judas in the main gate opened and Canning stepped out, followed by Hesser and Howard. As they came forward, Ritter and his party moved also and they met in the middle of the drawbridge.

Ritter saluted and said in excellent English, 'Sturmbannführer Karl Ritter, 502nd SS Heavy Tank Battalion at present in command of this unit, and this is Herr Strasser.'

'Of the Prisoner of War Administration Department in Berlin,' Strasser put in.

'And I am Brigadier General Hamilton Canning of the Army of the United States, Captain Howard here Second Rangers. Oberstleutnant Hesser, you may know.'

It was all very polite, very formal, except for Jack Howard, whose face had turned deathly pale and who clutched the Thompson gun in his hands till the knuckles turned white. There was life in his eyes again for the first time in days, for he had recognized Ritter instantly.

'What can we do for you?' Canning said.

'Oberstleutnant Hesser.' Strasser produced the Hitler Directive and unfolded it. 'I have here an order from my department in Berlin signed, as you will see, by the Führer himself, ordering you to place the five prisoners remaining at Schloss Arlberg in my care.'

He held out the letter. Max Hessler waved it away. 'Too late, gentlemen. I surrendered my command to Captain Howard on his arrival not more than thirty minutes ago. General Canning is in command here now.'

There was silence for a while. The snow falling harder than ever, a sudden, small wind churning it into a miniature blizzard that danced around them.

Strasser said, 'This is a totally illegal act, Colonel Hesser. To my certain knowledge there has been no general surrender, no discussion of peace terms; cannot be while the Führer still lives to direct the struggle of the German people from his headquarters in Berlin.'

'There has been a surrender here,' Hesser said, 'according to the rules of war. I have done nothing dishonourable.'

'A surrender to three members of the American Army?' Strasser said. 'You tell me there is nothing dishonourable in this?'

'You will speak to me if you please,' Canning said. 'As this gentleman has made plain, I command here now as senior Allied officer present.'

'No, General, I think not,' Ritter said calmly. 'Our business is with the officer in command of Schloss Arlberg, and to us he must still be Oberstleutnant Max Hesser until relieved of that duty by the High Command of the German Army.' He turned to Hesser. 'You took an oath, Colonel Hesser, as did we all, I think. An oath as a German soldier to your Führer and the State.'

'To a madman,' Hesser said. 'Who has brought Germany to her knees.'

'But also to the State, to your country,' Ritter said. 'You and I are soldiers, Hesser, as General Canning here and Captain Howard. No difference. We play the game on our side, they on theirs. We can't hope to change the rules in the middle to suit our personal convenience. Not any of us. Is that not so, General?'

It was Howard who answered him. 'Is that how you see it? A game? Nothing more?

'Perhaps,' Ritter said. 'The greatest game of all where the stakes are a country and its people, and if a man can't stand by his own, he is less than nothing.'

He turned back to Hesser, waiting. Hesser said, 'It is my information that a direct order has gone to the SS from the Führer himself, authorizing the execution of all prominent prisoners. I consider this order monstrous. A direct violation of the Geneva Convention and a crime against humanity. I will not be a party to it and neither will the men of this garrison.'

Strasser said, 'This is, of course, total nonsense. A tissue of lies. As the representative for this area of the Prisoner of War Administration Department, I can give you my word on this absolutely.'

'Then why do you want us?' Canning asked. 'Tell me that?'

'All prominent prisoners are being brought together in one centre, for their own protection.'

'As hostages against the evil day?'

'A sensible precaution only, Herr General, I assure you.'

'Who for – you or us?'

There was another brief silence. The snow danced around them. Hesser said slowly, 'I stand by what I have done. General Canning is in command here now.'

'Which just about wraps it up,' Canning said. 'I can't see that we have anything further to discuss. If you'll take the advice of an old hand, Major, I'd say you and your men had better get the hell out of here while you still can. Let's go, gentlemen.'

He turned and walked back towards the gate briskly, Hesser at his side. Howard stayed there, holding the Thompson gun across his chest. Hoffer never took his eyes off him, his hand close to the butt of the holstered Walther at his belt. Ritter ignored him as he lit a cigarette calmly and examined the gate, the walls above.

'It would seem they mean business,' Strasser said.

Ritter nodded. 'So it would appear.'

He turned on his heel. Howard said, 'Major Karl Ritter, of the 502nd SS Heavy Tank Battalion, you said?'

Ritter turned slowly. 'That is correct.'

'We've met before.'

'Have we?'

'Last Wednesday morning. That little affair on the way to Innsbruck when you took out an entire British armoured column. I was one of the survivors, along with my two friends up there on the wall.'

'Congratulations,' Ritter said calmly. 'Your luck is good.'

'You can tell your man there to take his hand off the butt of that Walther. I'm not going to kill you – yet. I mean, that wouldn't be playing this game of yours according to the rules, now would it?'

'Your choice, my friend.'

'You'll be coming in?' Howard said. 'Or you'll try to?'

'Yes, I think so.'

'I'll be looking for you.'

Canning called from the gate, 'Captain Howard.' Howard turned and ran back through the snow.

'He means it, that one,' Strasser said. 'For the past five minutes I've had a finger on the trigger, imagining I might have to put another hole through the pocket of my coat. I wonder if he knew?'

'Oh, yes,' Ritter said. 'He knew'; and he turned and led the way back to the half-tracks.

'What in the hell kept you?' Canning demanded as Howard slipped inside and the gates closed. 'Go on – up on the wall and tell Colonel Birr I'll join you in a couple of minutes.'

Howard mounted the stone steps and Canning turned to Hesser. 'As I recall, you raised the drawbridge six or seven months back?'

'That's right, Herr General. To see if it was working.'

'Then let's see if the damn thing still does.'

Hesser nodded to Schneider, who immediately opened the door at the foot of the tower on the left-hand side of the gate and led the way in. He switched on the light, disclosing a massive steel drum, ten feet across, chains wrapped around it, lifting up into the gloom. There were great spoked wheels on either side.

'Let's get it done.' Canning moved to one of the wheels, Schneider ran to the other, and together they started to turn.

Howard crouched beside the cannon, peering out through the embrasure, watching Ritter and his two companions walk back towards the Finns. Hoover and Finebaum dropped down beside him.

'What was going on out there, Captain?' the sergeant asked. 'Between you and the kraut officer?'

'It was him,' Howard said. 'The guy who took the

column out Wednesday. His name's Ritter – Karl Ritter.'

'The guy in the Tiger who flattened the jeep?' Finebaum demanded. 'Are you saying that's him out there?' He raised the M1 and leaned across the cannon. 'Jesus, maybe I can still get him.'

Howard pulled him down. 'Not now,' he said. 'And anyway, he's mine.'

'Attack now!' Strasser said. 'The only way. Use the front half-track as a battering ram. Straight in while they're still wondering what our next move will be.'

'There are twenty armed men on that wall, armed to the teeth. At least one heavy machine gun mounted beside the old cannon between the turrets. I had a good look at that while I was lighting my cigarette. Rate of fire not far short of a thousand rounds a minute. You served in the first war, did you not, Herr Strasser? I should have thought you might have remembered what happens to those who attempt frontal attacks on heavy machine guns, skilfully positioned.'

'And in any case, the argument now becomes a wholly academic one.' Sorsa pointed and Strasser and Ritter turned in time to see the end of the drawbridge lift above the moat.

They watched as it continued its steady progress and finally came to a halt. Strasser said, 'So, a situation which can only be described as medieval. Impossible for us to get in . . .'

'And equally impossible for them to get out,' Ritter said. 'Which is, after all, the important thing. There is one thing which worries me, however.'

'What's that?' Strasser asked.

'The question of radio communication with the outside world. A distress call at random might well be picked up by some Allied unit or other in the vicinity.'

'No danger of that,' Strasser said. 'They've had

problems in the communication room at Schloss Arlberg for several days now. Believe me, Major, there is no way in which they can communicate with the outside world.'

'Another example of your flair for organization, I presume,' Ritter said. 'Anyway, that problem being solved, we will now leave, I think.'

'You mean that literally or do you have a plan?'

'The fact of our going may comfort the general and his friends, however temporarily. The question of planning must wait until I've handled the immediate situation.' He nodded to Sorsa. 'Move out and stop the column around the first bend out of sight of the castle.'

'*Zu befehl, Sturmbannführer.*'

From the walls, Canning and the others watched them go.

'What do you think, Hamilton?' Birr asked.

'I'm not sure,' Canning said. 'Strasser, the guy who said he was from the Prisoner of War Administration Department, intrigues me. I'm sure I've seen the bastard before somewhere.'

'And the other one – Ritter?'

'The kind who never lets go? Did you see his medals, for Christ's sake?'

'He has quite a reputation, this man,' Hesser said. 'Something of a legend. A great tank destroyer on the Eastern Front. They made much of him in the magazines last year.'

'And Strasser – you've never seen him before?'

'No – never.'

Canning nodded. 'Right, this is what we do. I want two lookouts in the top of the north tower linked to here by field telephone. From up there they should be able to see outside the walls for the entire circuit. Any kind of movement must be instantly reported. I want the rest of the garrison split into three fire parties of six or seven each, ready to rush to any point on the wall as directed by the lookouts.' He turned to Howard. 'You take charge of that operation with Hoover. Finebaum can accompany me as my runner.'

'I'm with you, General,' Finebaum said. 'We'll make a hell of a team, believe me.' He raised a hand deprecatingly. 'No disrespect intended, General.'

'Which remains to be seen.' Canning turned to Hesser. 'And now, I want to see the armoury. Everything you've got here.'

Beyond the first bend in the road, the column had halted. Ritter said to Sorsa, 'I'm returning to the village now. I'll take Sergeant-Major Gestrin and four men with me. They can use the other field car. You stay here with the half-tracks. I want fifteen or twenty men on skis circling those walls without pause. Keep to the woods, but make sure they can be seen. Field telephone communication at all times.'

'And then what?' Sorsa asked.

'I'll let you know,' Ritter said.

Paul Gaillard and Meyer were at the landing window as the two field cars drove into the square and pulled up outside the Golden Eagle. Gestrin and his men carried their skis in theirs and had a field radio.

Gaillard said, 'Better go down and find out what they want. I'll hide in the cupboard in the dressing room again if I hear anyone coming.'

Meyer went downstairs as the front door opened and Ritter led the way into the bar. Strasser and Jackson followed, then Hoffer, carrying Strasser's suitcase containing the radio.

Strasser said to Meyer, 'You have a room I can use personally?'

Meyer, with little option in the matter, said, 'Through here, mein Herr. My office.'

537

'Excellent.' Strasser turned to Earl Jackson. 'Tell me, the American pilot's uniform – they managed to procure one for you?'

'It's in the Dakota,' Jackson told him.

'Good. I want you to run up there now in one of the field cars and get it. Take a couple of Gestrin's men with you. And I want you back here as soon as possible.' Jackson hesitated, a look of puzzlement on his face, and Strasser said, 'No questions – just do it.'

Jackson turned and went out. Strasser picked up his case. 'And now,' he said to Ritter, 'if you will excuse me, I have a little communicating to do,' and he nodded to Meyer and followed him out.

Hoffer went behind the bar. 'A drink, Sturmbannführer?'

'Why not?' Ritter said. 'Brandy, I think,' and then he gave a slight exclamation and crossed the room quickly.

On the opposite wall hung a large framed eighteenth-century print of Schloss Arlberg, a perfect plan of the entire castle, every walk, every strongpoint, all clearly defined.

The armoury contained few surprises. Perhaps a dozen extra Schmeissers, twenty spare rifles, a couple of boxes of grenades, some plastic explosive. No heavy stuff at all.

'Plenty of ammunition, that's one good thing,' Canning said. He hefted a couple of Walther service pistols and said to the others, 'All right, let's go and see the ladies.'

They found Madame Chevalier warming herself in front of the log fire in the upper dining hall in north tower. Canning said, 'Where's Claire?'

'She went to her room. She was feeling the cold very badly. We stood outside too long.'

Canning held up the Walther. 'You know how to use one of those things?'

'I play a different instrument as you well know.'

538

'You'd better learn this one fast, believe me.' He turned to Finebaum. 'See if you can get the finer points. across to Madame Chevalier in a fast five minutes, soldier.'

'Anything you say, General.'

Madame Chevalier looked him over, horror on her face, and Finebaum tried his most ingratiating smile. 'They tell me you play piano, lady? You know "GI Jive"?'

Madame Chevalier closed her eyes momentarily, then opened them again. 'If you could show me how the pistol works now,' she said.

When Canning tried the handle on Claire's door it was locked. He knocked and called her name. It was two or three minutes before the bolt was drawn back and she peered out at him. Her eyes seemed very large, the face pale.

'I'm sorry, Hamilton. Come in,' she said.

He walked past her into the bedroom. 'You don't look too good.'

'As a matter of fact, I've just been thoroughly sick. I panicked down there when I heard that the SS had arrived.'

Canning remembered how her husband had died. 'It made you think of Étienne and what happened to him?'

When she looked up at him, her face was very pale. 'No, it made me think of myself, Hamilton. You see I'm a total physical coward and the very thought of those devils . . .'

He placed a finger on her lips and took the Walther from his pocket. 'I've brought you a life preserver. You know how to use it, I believe.'

She took it from him, holding it in both hands. 'On myself,' she said. 'Before I allow them to take me from this place.'

'Hush,' Canning kissed her gently. 'Nobody's taking

you anywhere, believe me. Now come down and join the others.'

Ritter had taken down the print from the wall and was examining it closely when Strasser entered.

'A useful find,' Ritter told him. 'A plan of Schloss Arlberg.'

'Never mind that now,' Strasser said. 'I've made an even more interesting discovery. Hoffer, bring friend Meyer in here.'

'What is it?' Ritter inquired.

'It appears that a certain Dr Paul Gaillard is actually on the premises. Meyer's boy broke a leg this morning.'

'You're sure of this?'

'Oh yes, my informant is completely reliable.'

Ritter frowned. 'You've been on the radio. Where to? The castle? You mean you've actually got an agent planted up there? I really must congratulate you, Reichsleiter. My apologies – Herr Strasser. That really is taking organization to the outer limits.'

'I do like efficiency you see, Major. A fatal flaw, if you like, all my life.'

The door opened and Hoffer ushered Meyer into the room. Strasser turned to him and smiled. 'So, Herr Mayer, it would appear you have not been strictly honest with us.'

A few moments later Paul Gaillard, bending over the still unconscious boy, heard footsteps on the stairs. They approached the door confidently. He hesitated, then withdrew into the dressing room and stepped into the cupboard.

There was a long period of silence, or so it seemed – a slight creaking and then, quite unexpectedly, the cupboard door opened and light flooded in.

Ritter was standing there. He didn't bother to draw

his pistol. Simply smiled and said, 'Dr Gaillard, I believe? Your patient seems to be reviving.'

Gaillard hesitated, then brushed past him and went into the other room where he found Strasser and Meyer bending over the boy, who was moaning feverishly.

Meyer turned in appeal to Ritter, his concern wholly for his son now. 'When you first arrived, Sturmbannführer, we didn't know what to think, the doctor and I. And there was the boy to consider.'

'Yes, I can see that,' Ritter said. 'How bad is he?'

'Not good,' Gaillard said. 'A badly broken leg – high fever. He needs constant attention, that's why I stayed. But I can't have you lot in here. You'll have to go.'

Ritter glanced at Strasser, who nodded slightly. Gaillard was ignoring them, sponging the boy's forehead. 'So, you didn't manage to get into the castle it would seem.'

'We will, Doctor, we will,' Ritter said. 'I'll have to put a sentry in here, of course, but we'll leave you to it for now.'

He nodded to Meyer, who went out. Gaillard said, 'All right, if you must, I suppose.' He glanced up, saw Strasser for the first time. His mouth opened wide, there was a look of astonishment on his face. 'Good God, I know you.'

'I don't think so,' Strasser said. 'My name is Strasser of the Prisoner of War Administration Department in Berlin, as the major here will confirm.'

Gaillard turned to Ritter, who smiled. 'We'll leave you to your patient, Doctor,' and he ushered Strasser outside and closed the door.

'Bormann,' Gaillard whispered. 'When was it we were introduced? Munich, 1935? Reichsleiter Martin Bormann. I'd stake my life on it.'

And at the same moment in the bunker in Berlin, Martin Bormann and General Wilhelm Burgdorf, Hitler's army adjutant, waited in the central passage outside the Führer's personal suite. As the man who had delivered the poison with which Field-Marshal Erwin Rommel had been obliged to kill himself after the July 20th plot, it might have been thought that Burgdorf would have been used to such situations, but just now he looked terrified and was sweating profusely.

At 3.30 there was a pistol shot. Martin Bormann rushed into the Führer's suite, followed by his valet, Heinz Linge and Colonel Otto Günsche, his SS adjutant. The room reeked of the cyanide which Eva Hitler had used to take her life. The Führer sprawled beside her, his face shattered.

Dr Stumpfegger, the Führer's personal doctor, and Linge, the valet, carried the body up to the Chancellery garden, wrapped in a grey blanket. Martin Bormann came next, carrying Eva Hitler.

A curious incident then took place, for the Führer's chauffeur, Erich Kempka, was reminded of the fact that in life Bormann had been Eva Hitler's greatest enemy. He stepped forward and took her body from the Reichsleiter for it did not seem right to him to leave her in his charge.

The bodies were placed in a shallow pit and fifty gallons of petrol poured over them and set on fire. As the flames cascaded into the sky, those present stood at attention, arms extended in a final party salute.

The Russians, at that point in time, were perhaps 150 yards away from the bunker.

12

Ritter sat at the desk in Meyer's office, going over the print of the ground-plan of Schloss Arlberg yet again. Hoffer stood by the door, waiting quietly. Ritter put down his pencil and sat back.

Hoffer said, 'Can it be done?'

'I don't see why not,' Ritter said. 'All it requires is good discipline and a little nerve and I think our Finns aren't noticeably lacking in either.'

The door opened and Strasser entered. 'Jackson is back.'

'Ah, yes,' Ritter said. 'You sent him to Arnheim. May one ask why?'

'First tell me of your plan of attack.'

'Very well.' Ritter looked down at the print of the castle again. 'I will wait until dark. In fact, well after. Say midnight when the defenders will already have been on the alert for a considerable period of time, which means they will be tired. No use moving in with the half-tracks because we alert them the instant we start the engines.'

'So?'

'A force of say twenty men will approach the edge of the moat under cover of darkness. Two of them will cross the moat, climb the drawbridge and set a couple of demolition charges. Very easy to make up from what we've got and it won't need a particularly powerful charge to blow those chains. Another charge against the gate timed to explode in the same instant.'

'I see,' Strasser said. 'The drawbridge falls, the gates

open and your shock-troops rush across to take possession?'

'Backed up by the half-tracks, which start moving the instant they hear the explosion. What do you think?'

'Very good,' Strasser said.

'Any weak points?'

'Only one. As it happens there's an outside floodlight at the entrance. They turned it on about fifteen minutes ago. I'm sure Sorsa will confirm that if you raise him on the field telephone.'

Ritter leaned back. 'You have an excellent and very immediate source of information.'

'So it would appear,' Strasser said, but made no effort to enlighten him. 'Of course, you could have a sniper shoot out this floodlight.'

'And immediately alert them to the fact that we were up to something.'

'An excellent plan, however, and it could still work.'

'How?'

'If we had someone able to do exactly the same thing from the inside.' Strasser walked to the door and opened it. 'All right?' he said.

Earl Jackson entered the room wearing a flying jacket with a sheepskin collar over the uniform of a captain in the United States Army Air Corps.

As Colonel Hesser and Schneider mounted the steps to the east wall, the wind dashed frozen sleet into their faces. It was bitterly cold and the sergeant-major adjusted his grip on Magda's lead.

'A bitch of a night,' Hesser said. 'Takes me back to forty-two and the Winter War. The kind of cold that eats into the brain.'

He shuddered, remembering, and Schneider said, 'I wouldn't think they'd bother us on a night like this.'

'Isn't that what we used to say about the Russians?' Hesser said. 'Until we learned better? And so, I presume, did Ritter. He's spent enough time on the Eastern Front, God knows.'

The sentries were spread woefully thin, not that he could do much about that. There was one at the east watchtower. Hesser had a word with him, then leaned out of an embrasure in the wall and looked back towards the pool of light at the gate.

'I wonder how long it will be before one of them can't resist shooting that out? I almost wish they would. An end to this damned uncertainty.'

'You think they'll come then, Herr Oberst?' Schneider asked.

'You saw Ritter for yourself, didn't you? Did he look like the kind of man to just run away? And what about those ski patrols, circling endlessly through the forest right up until dark. No, he's there all right. And when he's ready, you'll know about it. Anyway, let's check the water gate.'

They went down the watchtower steps. There was a small damp tunnel blocked by a heavy iron grille. A corporal called Wagner stood guard there, a veteran of the Eastern Front, his left arm partially wasted away from bad shrapnel wounds. He was leaning against the gate looking out, his Schmeisser ready in his right hand.

'Everything is in order here?' Hesser demanded.

'I'm not sure, Herr Oberst. I thought I heard something.'

They stood listening. Snow drifted through the grille and Hesser said, 'Only the wind.'

And then Magda whined, straining forward on the leash. 'No, Herr Oberst,' Schneider said. 'He's right. Something moves.'

He and Hesser drew their pistols. There was a distinct slithering sound on the other side of the moat, snow falling into the water, and then a hoarse whisper in English. 'Is there anyone there? Don't shoot. I'm an American officer.'

Someone entered the water. Hesser said to Schneider, 'Switch on your torch, a second only, then down on the ground.'

There was a pause, then Schneider's torch flashed, the beam picking Earl Jackson out of the darkness instantly. He was in the middle of the moat, swimming strongly, only his head and the sheepskin collar of his flying jacket showing above the water.

'*Kamerad!*' he called, gasping for breath. 'American officer. I'm looking for General Hamilton Canning.'

It was Finebaum, crouched in the shadow of the wall above the main gate, who spotted the momentary spot of light on his left. Below him, Howard and Hoover crouched against the wall, smoking cigarettes.

'Hey, Captain, there was a light down there below the east watchtower in the moat.'

They were on their feet instantly. 'You certain?' Howard leaned out of the embrasure. 'I can't see a thing.'

'There was a light. Just for a minute.'

'Okay, let's move it,' Howard said and started along the wall.

When they entered the water-gate tunnel, Jackson was on the other side from Hesser and his men, clutching the grille, knee-deep in water. 'Let me in, for Christ's sake. I've got to see General Canning.'

'What is it?' Howard demanded. 'What's going?'

Hesser switched on the torch without a word. Jackson blinked in the sudden light. He was soaked to the skin, water dripping from his uniform, teeth chattering. He tried to peer into the darkness at Howard.

'You American, buddy? For Christ's sakes, make these crazy bastards let me in. Another five minutes of this and I'll die of exposure.'

'Hey, he's right, Captain,' Finebaum said. 'He don't look too good.'

'Who are you?' Howard demanded.

'Harry Bannerman's the name. Crash-landed this morning about ten miles from here in a P47. Got picked up by an SS unit. They had me down in the village here until an hour ago. In an inn called the Golden Eagle.'

'How did you get away?'

'The landlord helped me – a guy called Meyer. There was another prisoner there. He put him up to it. A Frenchman named Gaillard. He told me to get up here fast and see General Canning. I've got information about when the krauts intend to hit this place.' He rattled the grille ineffectually, his voice breaking. 'Let me in, for Christ's sake – if you don't want to die, that is.'

'Okay,' Howard said to Hesser. 'Open the gate and drag him in – but fast. And you, Finebaum, I make personally responsible for blowing his backbone in half if he makes a wrong move.'

In the darkness among the trees on the far side of the moat, Strasser, Ritter and Hoffer listened to the clang of the grille shutting.

'So, he's in,' Ritter said. 'Let's hope they buy his story.'

'I don't see why not,' Strasser said. 'Jackson's strength, as I said before, lies in the fact that he's a genuine American, not the ersatz variety that let Skorzeny down so badly in the Ardennes.'

'So now we wait,' Ritter said.

'Until it's time for my part in this rather interesting drama.' Strasser smiled through the darkness. 'You know, I'm really rather looking forward to it.'

General Canning, Birr, Madame Chevalier and Claire were having a late supper of sandwiches and coffee when Hesser and Howard entered, followed by Jackson, an army blanket draped around his shoulders. Finebaum was right behind him, the muzzle of his M1 no more than an inch away from Jackson's backbone.

'What have we here?' Canning demanded, rising to his feet.

'Swam across the moat to the water gate, General,' Howard said. 'Claims to be an Army Air Corps officer. No papers – no identification on him whatsoever. Not even his dog tags.'

'They took them off me,' Jackson said. 'Those damned SS stripped me of everything. I mean, how many times do I have to tell you?'

'What outfit?' Canning demanded.

'Five hundred and tenth squadron, 405th group, sir. Operating out of what was a Luftwaffe base at Hellenbach until we took it four days ago.'

'What's your story?'

'My squadron was ordered to hit a Panzer column on the other side of Salzburg from here. This morning it was, General. We dropped our bombs dead on target, no problem, there being no Luftwaffe to speak of in this area any more. Then on the way back my battery went dead and I had to crash-land.'

'What was your aircraft?'

'P47 Thunderbolt, sir. I made it down in one piece in a clearing in the forest, then struck out for the main road. It's a pretty fluid situation in this area, General. There are plenty of our people around. It's just a question of knowing where.'

'And you say you were picked up by an SS unit?'

'That's right, sir. Mostly Finns, but there was a German officer in charge. A man called Ritter.'

'And they've been holding you all day?'

'That's right, sir, at an inn called the Golden Eagle in Arlberg.' There was a slight pause. He gazed around him wildly. 'Say, what goes on here? What do you people think I am – a kraut or something?'

'Well, I'll tell you, Captain,' Finebaum put in. 'Because it's really funny you should say that. When we were in the Ardennes in forty-four – and it was snowing then too, I might add – there was guys popping up all over the place, just like you, GI uniform – everything. Saying they'd lost their units, asking the way to Malmedy. Stuff like that. An interesting thing. They was all krautheads.'

'Any chance of you shutting this man up?' Canning inquired coldly.

Howard said, 'Button it, Finebaum.'

Canning said to Jackson, 'We're in a hell of a position in here, Bannerman. We can't afford to take anything on trust, you understand?'

'He says he's met Dr Gaillard, sir,' Howard put in.

Claire said excitedly, 'You've seen Paul?'

'Sure I've seen him.'

'How is he?'

'He's looking after a sick kid down there at the inn. Son of the landlord, a guy named Meyer.'

'And the SS have him?' Canning asked.

'Oh, yes. Major Ritter, the officer in command, lets him see to the kid regularly, but they had us locked up together for quite a while. Meyer brought our food and Gaillard saw him quite a lot each time he went to see to the kid. He's in a pretty bad way.'

'All right, how did you escape?'

'Well, it was mostly Meyer who made that possible. He overheard Ritter and some guy called Strasser – a civilian he has with him – discussing their plans for an attack just before dawn. They're going to put some guys across the moat with explosives to blow down your drawbridge. When Gaillard heard that, he told me I'd have to get away somehow and come and warn you people.'

'Which you seem to have managed without too much trouble,' Birr said.

'That was Meyer again. He tipped me off he'd leave

the back door near the kitchen unlocked. I asked to go to the lavatory, gave the Finn who was escorting me a shove at the right moment, got the door open and ran like hell.'

There was a long and heavy silence now in which everyone seemed to be looking at him. Jackson said, 'General, I'm Captain Harry Bannerman of the United States Army Air Corps and when that drawbridge of yours is blown to hell and gone just before dawn tomorrow, you'll know I was telling the truth. Just now, I'd settle for a cup of coffee, dry clothes and somewhere to lay my head.'

Canning smiled suddenly and held out his hand. 'I'll tell you something, son. All of a sudden I've decided to believe you.' He turned to Hesser. 'Can you find him some dry clothes?'

'Certainly,' Hesser said. 'If the Herr Captain doesn't mind German uniform. This way, if you please.'

Jackson started to follow him, paused and turned. 'Heh, there's just one thing, General. Something kind of funny. It doesn't mean a damn thing to me. Maybe it does to you.'

'What's that?' Canning asked him.

'This guy Strasser – the civilian I told you about?'

'Well?'

'It's just that he seems to swing a lot of weight. I mean a couple of times there he acted as if he was in charge and I heard Ritter call him Reichsleiter. That ring any bells with you?'

Hesser turned pale. 'Bormann?' he whispered.

'That's it.' Canning said excitedly. 'I knew I'd seen that ugly face somewhere before. Martin Bormann, Secretary to Hitler himself. I saw him just once on the stand at the Berlin Olympic Games in thirty-six.' He turned on Hesser. 'You didn't recognize him?'

'I've never laid eyes on Bormann in my life,' Hesser said. 'He's a man of the shadows, always has been.'

'Now we know why they wanted us so urgently,' Canning said. 'Hostages to bargain with in the hope he might save his rotten neck.' He rubbed his hands together excitedly. 'Good work, Bannerman. You've really earned your keep with that one. Take him away now, Max, and get some dry clothes on him.'

Hesser and Jackson went out. Madame Chevalier said, 'What does this mean, General? I've heard of this man, Bormann. A member of the inner circle, isn't that so?'

'Not a thing to worry about, I assure you,' Canning said. 'Now have some more coffee, sit down and take it easy and I'll be back in a moment.'

He went out with Howard and Finebaum, closed the door behind him and paused in the shadows at the head of the stairs.

'What do you think, sir?' Howard asked.

Canning looked down at Finebaum. 'Is he any good?'

'A sackful of medals He seems to have a talent for killing people, General.'

'Okay, soldier,' Canning said. 'You watch Bannerman like a hawk. Not too close, but be around just in case.'

'I'm your man, General.' Finebaum went down the stairs into the shadows.

'You don't believe Bannerman, sir?' Howard asked.

'I had a Scottish grandmother, Captain, from the Isle of Skye who used to say she had an instinct for things. No proof, because there was no need. She just knew. I sometimes think some of it rubbed off on me. Now get back to that gate. I'll join you there as soon as I can.'

He opened the door and went back into the dining hall.

When Howard climbed up to the ramparts above the gate it was snowing hard, large flakes drifting down through the yellow glare of the spotlight, spiralling in the slight wind. Hoover was up there with three Germans. Like them, the American was wearing a Wehrmacht winter-issue parka.

'Decided to change sides, I see,' Howard said. 'Kind of late in the war, isn't it?'

'The romantic in me,' Hoover said. 'My great-grandfather was in the Army of the Confederacy. We Hoovers just take to losing naturally, I guess. What about Bannerman?'

'He tells a convincing story. Says the opposition are going to hit us just before dawn. Slip a couple of guys across the moat with explosives and come running.'

He carried on to explain the rest of it, and when he was finished Hoover said. 'That last part doesn't make too much sense to me. I never even heard of this guy Bormann. Did you?'

'Somewhere or other,' Howard said. 'But I never thought he was particularly important. I mean, not like Ribbentropp or Goebbels or one of those guys. Sending someone like him sure lays it on the line how much they want to get their hands on these people as hostages.'

'Where's Finebaum?'

'Somewhere back there in north tower, keeping an eye out for Bannerman on General Canning's orders.'

One of the sentries said quickly in German, 'Something moves – out there.'

He grabbed Howard's arm and pointed. A moment later, Karl Ritter, Hoffer and Strasser moved out of the darkness into the circle of light.

'Hello, the wall,' Ritter called. 'Is General Canning there?'

Howard stayed back in the shadows. 'What do you want?'

'Herr Strasser would like a word with General Canning. He has a proposition to put to him.'

'Tell me,' Howard called.

Ritter shrugged. 'If that is your attitude, then I can see we are wasting your time. Thank you and good night.'

They turned to go and Hoover whispered, 'Sir, this could be important.'

'Okay, Harry, okay.' Howard leaned forward into the light. 'Hold it. I'll see what he says.'

A moment later he was speaking to Canning on the field telephone. 'It could be a trap, sir.'

'I don't think so,' Canning said. 'They must know they'd be cut down in half a second, those two, at the first sign of trouble, and I don't think they'd make that kind of sacrifice, not if Strasser is who Jackson says he is. No, drop the drawbridge and have them in. Send Strasser up here to me. Keep Ritter with you.'

A few moments later, the drawbridge started to descend with a rattle of chains. Ritter said softly, 'So, the fish bite. Are you always so correct in your prophecies?'

'Only where matters of importance are concerned,' Strasser said, and as the drawbridge thudded down into place, they walked across together, Hoffer following.

The judas opened and Howard peered through briefly. He stepped back and they moved inside. As he closed the gate and barred it, Howard said to Hoover, 'Take Herr Strasser up to north tower. General Canning is waiting. You, Major,' he continued to Ritter, 'will have to put up with my company until he gets back, I'm afraid.'

Strasser moved off, without a word, following Hoover. Hoffer stood, back to the gate, stony-faced. Ritter took out his case, selected a cigarette, then offered one to Howard.

'I must warn you. They're Russian, an acquired taste.'

Howard took one and leaned back against the wall, the butt of his Thompson braced against his hip. 'So, here we are again,' he said.

When Hoover knocked on the door and led the way into the upper dining hall, only Canning and Justin Birr stood by the fire. Strasser paused nonchalantly in the centre of the room, hands in the pockets of his leather coat, slouch hat slanted over one ear.

'Good evening, gentlemen.'

Canning nodded to Hoover. 'You can wait outside, Sergeant. I'll call you if I need you.'

The door closed. Strasser crossed to the fireplace and spread his hands to the blaze. 'Nothing like a log fire to take the chill off. It's cold out there tonight. The kind that eats into your bones like acid.'

Canning glanced at Birr and nodded. Birr crossed to the sideboard, poured a generous measure of brandy into a glass and returned.

'Just to show how humanitarian we are. Now what in the hell do you want, Bormann?'

Strasser paused in the act of drinking some of the brandy. 'Strasser, Herr General. The name is Strasser.'

'Strange,' Canning said. 'You look exactly like the man I saw in Berlin in 1936 standing on the rostrum behind Adolf Hitler at the Olympic Games. Reichsleiter Martin Bormann.'

'You flatter me, General. I am, I assure you, a relatively unimportant official of the Department of Prisoner of War Administration.'

'I have difficulty in imagining you as a relatively unimportant thing. But go on.'

'Let us consider your situation here. There are twenty-four of you in this garrison, twenty-six if we count the ladies. Most of your men are reservists who have never fought or cripples who can barely lift a rifle.'

'So?'

'We, on the other hand, have almost forty battle-hardened shock-troops to call upon. Men of the Waffen-SS, and whatever you may think, General, however much you disapprove, that means the best in the world.'

'Get on with it,' Justin Birr said. 'Just what are you trying to prove?'

'That if we decide to move against you, the consequences will be disastrous – for you.'

'A matter of opinion,' Canning said. 'But accepting

that what you say is true, what do you suggest we do about it. I mean, that is why you're here, isn't it? To offer us some kind of alternative solution. I mean before you try slipping a couple of men across the moat just before dawn to blow the drawbridge chains.'

'My goodness, somebody has been busy,' Strasser said. 'All right, General, it's simple. We have Dr Gaillard, whom we found at the Golden Eagle in Arlberg attending to the landlord's sick son. Sad, how good deeds can so often prove our undoing. However, if you and Colonel Birr will hand yourselves over, we'll be content with that and let the ladies go free.'

'Not a chance,' Canning said.

Strasser turned to Birr. 'You agree?'

'I'm afraid so, old stick. You see, we don't really trust you, that's the truth of it. Terribly sorry, but there it is.'

'And the ladies?' Strasser said. 'They have no say in this?'

Canning hesitated, then went and opened the door. He spoke briefly to Hoover, then returned. 'They'll be here directly.'

He and Birr lit cigarettes. Strasser turned to survey the room and immediately saw the great silver bowl of scarlet winter roses on the piano.

'Ah, my favourite flowers.' He was genuinely delighted and crossed the room to admire them. 'Winter roses. Like life in the midst of death – they fill the heart with gladness.'

The door opened and, as he turned, Claire de Beauville, Madame Chevalier and Earl Jackson entered the room. Strasser smiled at the American. 'We missed you for supper.'

'Sorry I couldn't stay.'

Strasser turned to Canning. 'An explanation of one or two things which was puzzling me. I was beginning to think you were a wonder-worker. It's nice to know you're just a man, like the rest of us.'

'Okay,' Canning said. 'I've had just about enough for one night. You wanted a word with the ladies – well, they're here, so make the most of it.'

'I can't imagine what you could possibly have to say to me that I would be interested in hearing, Monsieur,' Madame Chevalier said. 'Thankfully, I can use the time to some advantage.'

She sat down at the piano and started to play a Debussy nocturne. Strasser, not in the least put out, said, 'I have offered you ladies your freedom, guaranteed it, on condition that the General and Colonel Birr come quietly and with no fuss.'

Madame Chevalier ignored him and Claire simply walked across to the bowl of roses and buried her face in them.

Strasser said, 'I should have known. Above all flowers, they need delicate hands and infinite patience in their rearing. Your work, Madame?'

'Yes,' she said. 'So, as you can see, I am fully occupied and cannot leave at the present time.'

Canning moved in. 'You heard the lady.'

Strasser selected one of the blooms, snapped the stem and placed it in his buttonhole. 'Ah, well, it was worth the trip. You like winter roses, General?'

'Whatever it is, if Madame de Beauville cultivated it, I like.'

'Good,' Strasser said. 'I'll remember that at your funeral. One gets so bored with lilies. A single scarlet winter rose should look very well. And now, I think, I will bid you goodnight. There is obviously nothing more for me here.'

He walked to the door. Hoover glanced at Canning, who nodded. The sergeant led the way out.

There was a heavy silence and Madame Chevalier stopped playing. 'I must be getting old. Suddenly I feel cold – very, very cold.'

Strasser stepped through the judas, followed by Hoffer. As Ritter moved out Howard said softly, 'I'll be seeing you.'

'When?' Ritter said. 'Under the elms at dawn? Six paces each way, turn and fire? You take it all too seriously, Captain.'

He followed the others across. As they stepped on to the bank, the drawbridge lifted behind them.

'Are you satisfied?' Ritter asked Strasser softly.

'Oh, yes, I think so. Jackson should be well enough entrenched now. The rest is up to him.'

He started to whistle cheerfully.

It was just after midnight, and in Berlin at his office in the bunker Bormann worked steadily, the scratching of his pen the only sound, the noise of the Russian shelling muted far away. There was a light tap on the door. It opened and Goebbels entered. He looked pale and haggard, the skin drawn tightly over his face. A dead man walking.

Bormann put down his pen. 'How goes it?'

Goebbels passed a flimsy across the desk. 'That's the radiogram I've just dispatched to Plön.'

GRAND ADMIRAL DÖNITZ (*Personal and Secret*)
To be handled only by an officer.
Führer died yesterday, 1530 hours. In his will dated 29 April he appoints you as President of the Reich, Goebbels as Reich Chancellor, Bormann as party minister . . .

There was more, but Bormann didn't bother to read it. 'Paper, Josef. Just so much paper.'

'Perhaps,' Goebbels said. 'But we must preserve the formalities, even at this desperate stage.'

'Why?'

'For posterity, if nothing else. For those who will come after us.'

'Nobody comes after us. Not here – not in Germany

for many years to come. Our destiny lies elsewhere for the time being.'

'For you, perhaps, but not for me,' Goebbels said, his voice flat, toneless.

'I see,' Bormann said. 'You intend to emulate the Führer?'

'No shame in ending a life which will have no further value to me if I cannot stand at his side. I have no intention of spending the rest of my life running round the world like some eternal refugee. Preparations are already in hand. The children will be given cyanide capsules.'

'What, all six of them?' Bormann actually smiled. 'Thorough and painstaking to the end, I see. And you and Magda?'

'I have already detailed an SS orderly to shoot us when the moment comes.'

Bormann shrugged. 'Then I can only wish you better luck in the hereafter than you've had here.'

'And you?' Goebbels said.

'Oh, I'll try my luck in the outside world, I think. We should be all right here for the rest of today. I'll make a run for it tonight with Axmann, Sturmpfegger and one or two more. We intend to try the underground railway tunnel. That should get us to Friedrichstrasse Station all right. Mohnke is still holding out there with a battle-group of 3,000. SS, sailors, Volkssturm and a whole batch of Hitler Youth kids. They seem to be holding their own.'

'And then?'

'With their help we'll try to cross the Weidendammer Bridge over the Spree. Once on the other side, we should stand an excellent chance. Not many Russians in the north-western suburbs yet.'

'I can only wish you luck.' Suddenly Goebbels sounded very tired indeed. He turned to the door, started to open it and paused. 'What comes afterwards, if you get away?'

'Oh, I'll make out.'

'Come to think of it, you always did, didn't you?'

Goebbels went out, closing the door. Bormann sat there, thinking about what he had said. *I have no intention of spending my life running round the world like some eternal refugee.* He shrugged, picked up his pen and resumed his writing.

Jackson lay on the bed, waiting in the dark in the room they'd given him. He glanced at the luminous dial of his watch. It was twenty past midnight – ten minutes to go. He lit a cigarette and drew on it nervously. Not that he was afraid – simply keyed up. A brilliant suggestion of Strasser's to tell them he was the Reichsleiter. Coupled with Strasser's personal appearance, it had effectively clouded the entire issue. He was certain they'd accepted him completely now.

He checked his watch again. Time to go. He got up and padded to the door, and when he opened it, the passageway was deserted, a place of shadows partially illuminated by a single small bulb at the far end. He caught a brief glimpse of himself in a full-length gilt mirror. He was wearing Hesser's best uniform and it fitted rather well. He moved on, past one oil painting after another, blank eighteenth-century faces staring down at him. He turned the stairs at the end, paused by the white door on the small landing and knocked.

The door opened slightly and on the instant as if the occupant had been waiting. 'Valhalla Exchange,' Jackson whispered.

'Good – everything's ready for you,' Claire de Beauville said.

Jackson stepped into the room. On the washstand was plastic explosive, detonators and a Schmeisser. He put the explosive in one pocket, the detonators in the other and picked up the machine pistol.

'Anything else?' she said. Her face was pale, unnaturally calm.

'Yes. Some sort of hand-gun. Can you manage that?'
'I think so.'

She opened the drawer of the bedside locker and produced a Walther. Jackson checked that it was loaded, then pushed it down into his waistband at the small of his back under the tunic.

'I like an ace-in-the-hole, just in case things go wrong. Amazing how often even an expert search misses that particular spot. Have you spoken to him on the radio again since he was here?'

'Twenty minutes ago. Everything is arranged exactly as planned. They wait on you. You'll need a greatcoat and a cap to get you across the square unnoticed. There are men working out there. The small staircase at the end of the passage takes you to the main entrance hall, you'll find a cloakroom at the bottom, and the room that houses the drawbridge mechanism is first door on the left in the gate tunnel.'

'You've done well,' Jackson grinned. 'Well, mustn't stand here gossiping. Once more into the breach, dear friends . . .' and he picked up the Schmeisser and slipped out.

In the dining hall, Canning was standing alone in front of the fire when Hesser entered. 'Cold,' the German said. 'Too cold. Schneider said you wanted a word.'

'Yes. Let's say that drawbridge falls and the gates blow, what happens then?'

'They'll come in at full speed in those half-tracks, I should imagine.'

'Exactly. Armoured troop carriers and we don't even have anything capable of blowing off a track unless someone gets lucky and close enough with one of your stick grenades.'

'True, but you have some sort of solution, I think, or you would not be raising the matter.'

'We've been together too long, Max.' Canning smiled. 'Okay – that cannon in the centre of the square. Big Bertha.'

Hesser said. 'She hasn't been fired since the Franco–Prussian War.'

'I know, but she could still have one good belt left in her. Get Schneider on the job. You can soon make up some sort of charge. Prise open a few cartridges to make touch powder. Stoke the barrel up with old metal, chain, anything you can find, then have the men haul her down to the tunnel. Say twenty or thirty yards from the entrance. It could knock hell out of the first vehicle to come out of there.'

'Or simply explode in the face of whoever puts a light to the touch-hole.'

'Well, that's me,' Canning told him. 'I thought of it, so I'll stick with it.'

Hesser sighed. 'Very well, Herr General, you command here, not I,' and he went out.

13

Jackson went down the rear staircase quickly and paused at the bottom, staying well back in the shadows, but his caution was unnecessary for the hall was quite deserted. He opened the door on his left, slipped inside and switched on the light.

As Claire de Beauville had indicated, it was a cloakroom, and there was an assortment of coats and caps hanging on the pegs – even a couple of helmets. He hesitated, debating, then selected a field cap and heavy officer's greatcoat. He and Hesser were, after all, the same build, and it was a reasonable assumption that in the darkness he would be mistaken for the colonel by anyone who saw him.

When he opened the front door, snow filtered through. He moved out quickly and paused at the top of the steps to get his bearings. Most of the courtyard was in darkness, but in the centre a group of German soldiers, supervised by Howard and Sergeant Hoover, worked in the light of a storm lantern on Big Bertha.

Jackson went down the steps to the left and moved into the protecting dark, following the line of the wall towards the main gate. He paused at the end of the tunnel. It was very quiet except for an occasional murmur of voices from the men in the middle of the courtyard, and a sudden, small wind dashed snow in his face.

It was as if he was listening for something, waiting, he wasn't sure what for, and he felt a shiver of loneliness. Suddenly, in one of those instant flashes of recall, he was once again the fifteen-year-old minister's son, standing in a

Michigan snowstorm at one o'clock in the morning, despair in his heart. Home late and the door locked against him for the last time.

And from that to Arlberg – so much in between and yet in some ways so little. He smiled wryly, moved into the tunnel. First door on the left, Claire de Beauville had said. He held the Schmeisser ready and tried the handle of the iron-bound door. It opened gently, he pushed it wide and stepped inside.

The place was lit by a single bulb. Gunther Voss, Gaillard's erstwhile guard, sat in helmet and greatcoat on a stool by a small woodstove, back towards the door, reading a magazine.

'Is that you, Hans?' he demanded without turning round. 'About time.'

Jackson pushed the door shut with a very definite click. Voss glanced over his shoulder, his mouth gaped in astonishment.

'Just do as you're told,' Jackson said, 'and everything will be fine.'

He stepped lightly across the room, picked up Voss's Mauser rifle and tossed it on top of one of the bunks, out of the way.

'What are you going to do?' Voss asked hoarsely. He was absolutely terrified, sweat on his face.

'You've got it wrong, my friend. It's what you're going to do that counts.'

A cold breeze touched Jackson on the back of the neck, there was the faintest of creakings from the door. Finebaum said, 'That's it, hotshot – you're all through.'

Jackson turned in the same moment, the Schmeisser coming up, and Finebaum shot him through the right arm just above the elbow. Jackson was knocked back against the table, dropping the Schemisser. He forced himself up, clutching his arm, blood spurting between his fingers.

'What are you bucking for, a coffin?' Finebaum demanded, and he nodded to Voss. 'Search him.'

Voss went through Jackson's pockets of plastic explosive and the detonators. He held them up without a word and the door was flung open and Howard and Hoover rushed in.

'What goes on here?' Howard demanded.

Finebaum took one of the packets of plastic explosive from Voss and threw it across. 'Just like I said, Captain. The Ardennes all over again.'

Claire de Beauville, waiting in the darkness of her room, heard the shot. Her window looked out over the water garden, not the courtyard, so she couldn't see anything, yet the shot was trouble, whatever the cause. It meant that Jackson had failed. She lit a cigarette and sat on the bed in the dark, smoking nervously, but that wasn't any good. She had to know what had happened, there was no avoiding that fact. She opened the washstand door, took out another Walther automatic pistol, slipped it into her jacket pocket and went out.

When she went into the dining hall, Claudine Chevalier was already there with Canning, Birr and Hesser.

'What's happened?' Claire said. 'I heard a shot?'

'Nothing to be alarmed about.' Canning put an arm about her shoulders. 'Everything's under control. I've just had Howard on the field telephone from the gate. It seems friend Jackson wasn't all he pretended to be. They're bringing him up now.'

She turned away and moved to join Madame Chevalier by the fire. The door opened and Howard entered, followed by Jackson and Finebaum. Jackson was no longer wearing the greatcoat. A scarf was tied about his right arm, blood soaking through.

'Okay, what happened?' Canning demanded.

Howard held up the packets of plastic explosive. 'He was going to blow up the drawbridge winding gear with this. Lucky for all of us Finebaum was on the ball.'

Canning turned to Jackson. 'All right, Bannerman, or whatever your name is. Who are you? What are you?'

'Sorry, General,' Jackson said. 'I've been trying to work that one out for myself for the past thirty years with a total lack of success.'

Before Canning could reply, the door opened and Hoover looked in. 'General, sir?'

'What is it?'

'The German sentry who was on duty in the winding gear room, Private Voss, is out here asking to see you or Colonel Hesser. He says he has information about this man.'

'Let's have him in then.'

Hoover snapped his fingers and Voss stepped into the room. His army greatcoat and the helmet were too big for him and he looked faintly ridiculous.

'He doesn't speak English,' Hesser said. 'I'll deal with this. You've got something to say, Voss?' he carried on in German.

It poured out of Voss like a dam bursting, the words seeming to spill over themselves, and several times he gestured towards Jackson. He finally stopped and Hesser turned, a frown on his face.

'What is it?' Canning demanded. 'Good news or bad?'

Hesser looked at Jackson gravely. 'He says he's seen this man before, yesterday, at Arlberg sitting in a field car with Strasser and Ritter when they first drove into the square.'

'Is that so?'

'He was at that time wearing the uniform of a Hauptsturmführer in the SS.'

'Now that', Canning said, 'really is interesting. Where did you learn your American, Bannerman? I must congratulate you. They did a first-class job.'

'I think you'll find he was raised to it,' Hesser said. 'You see, Voss noticed that the armshield on this – this gentleman's uniform was a Stars and Stripes.'

There was a heavy silence. Canning glanced at Jackson,

then turned back to Hesser incredulously. 'Are you saying this man is a genuine American?'

'In the Waffen-SS, Herr General, there are what are known as the foreign legions. Units of volunteers raised from every country in Europe. There is even a Britisches Freikorps raised from English soldiers, recruited from prisoner-of-war camps.'

'And you're trying to tell me there are Americans who would sell out their country like that?'

'Not many,' Hesser said gently. 'A handful only. They are called the George Washington Legion.'

Canning turned, his arm swinging, and struck Jackson back-handed across the face. 'You dirty yellow bastard,' he shouted.

Jackson staggered back, cannoning into Madame Chevalier. In a second he had an arm around her throat and produced the Walther from the waistband at his back.

'Okay, just stand clear, all of you.'

Claire de Beauville remained where she was on his left, apparently frozen, hands thrust deep into the pockets of her jacket.

Jackson said, 'It's a funny old world, General. Not too long ago I was one of the gallant American boys flying for the Finns against the Russians. Remember that one? Then all of a sudden, the Finns are allies of the Nazis and back fighting the Russians again. Now that kind of thing can be just a little confusing.'

'You should have got out,' Canning said hoarsely.

'Maybe you're right. All I know is I was flying with the same guys against the same enemy. Hurricanes, by the way, with swastikas on them. Can you beat that?'

'Just let her go,' Canning said. 'She's an old woman.'

'I'm sorry, General. I can't do that. She's going to walk me right out of that front gate, aren't you, *liebling?*'

Claire stepped in close, her right hand came out of her pocket, clutching the Walther. She rammed the muzzle into his side and pulled the trigger.

The sound seemed very loud, sending shock-waves round the room. Jackson bucked, crying out in agony, and staggered back. She swung the Walther up, clutching it in both hands now, and pulled the trigger again and again until the gun was empty, driving him back against the wall beside the fireplace.

As his body slumped to the floor she threw the Walther away from her and turned to Canning, her face contorted. 'Hamilton?'

He opened his arms and she ran into them.

She lay on her bed in the dark, as Jackson had lain no more than an hour ago, waiting, afraid to move in case they came back. And then, finally, when all seemed quiet, she got up, went to the door and shot the bolt.

She lifted the washbasin out of its mahogany stand and took out the small compact radio which was secreted inside. An S-phone, they had told her. A British invention, far in advance of any German counterpart, obtained when an OSS agent in France had been picked up by the Gestapo.

She pressed the electronic buzzer that processed the call sign automatically and waited. Strasser's voice sounded in her ear almost instantly, clear and distinct.

'Valhalla here.'

'Exchange. It didn't work. He was caught in the act.'

'Dead?'

She hesitated, but only for a moment. 'Yes.'

'Very well. You'll have to do it yourself. You have sufficient materials left?'

'Yes.' She hesitated again. 'I'm not sure that I can.'

'No choice. You know the consequences if you fail. You should stand a good chance. The Jackson affair will have taken the edge off things. They won't be expecting a similar move from inside. Why should they?' He paused then said, 'I repeat; you know the consequences if you fail.'

'All right.' Her voice was barely a whisper, a dying fall. 'Good. Valhalla out.'

She sat there for a long, long moment, then got up slowly and took the S-phone back to the washstand. Then she got down on her knees, removed the bottom drawer and took out the two packets of plastic explosive and detonators that remained from what she had stolen from the armoury earlier.

Strasser, seated at the desk in Meyer's office, closed the lid of the case containing the radio and locked it. He sat there thinking for a moment, his face grave, then stood up and went out.

Ritter was seated by the fire in the bar enjoying a late supper. Cheese, black bread and beer. Hoffer lurked in the background as usual in case of need.

As Ritter looked up, Strasser said, 'Total failure, I'm afraid. He's dead.'

Ritter said calmly, 'What now?'

'The plan still stands. My agent will make another attempt.'

Ritter selected a cigarette from his case and lit it with a splinter from the fire. 'One thing puzzles me. Why didn't this contact of yours make the attempt in the first place? Why the elaborate charade with Jackson?'

'It's really very simple,' Strasser said. 'You see, she's a woman.'

Meyer went up the stairs from the kitchen carrying a tray containing sandwiches, a pot of coffee and a cup. The big Finn on the door regarded him impassively, one of the few who didn't speak a word of German as Meyer well knew. In fact, communication had proved impossible. He spoke fair English, but that had provoked no response, neither had the few phrases of French that he knew. He raised the tray and gestured inside. The Finn slung his Schmeisser, unlocked the door and stood back.

Gaillard was sitting beside the bed, wiping Arnie's damp forehead. The boy, obviously still in high fever, moaned, tossing and turning clutching at the blankets.

'Ah, there you are, Johann,' Gaillard said in German. 'I'm about ready for that.'

'How is he, Herr Doctor?'

'A little better, though you might not think it to look at him.'

Meyer put the tray on the bedside locker and started to pour the coffee. 'I was in the passageway that leads from the bar to the kitchen just now,' he said in a low voice. 'Don't worry about this one. He can't understand me.'

'So?'

'I heard Herr Strasser and Major Ritter talking. Something about the castle. Strasser said he had a contact in there. A woman.'

Gaillard looked up at him in astonishment. 'Impossible. There are only two women in the place. Madame Chevalier and Claire de Beauville. Frenchwomen to the core, both of them. What are you saying, man?'

'Only what I heard, Herr Doctor. I think they're waiting for something to happen.'

The Finn said something unintelligible, strode into the room and grabbed Meyer by the shoulder. He shoved him outside quickly and closed the door.

Gaillard sat there, staring into space. Impossible to believe. Meyer must have got it wrong. Must have. The boy cried out and Gaillard turned quickly, squeezed out his cloth in the bowl of water and wiped the forehead gently.

Claire de Beauville paused in the shadows at the bottom of the back stairs, listening. All was still. She opened the door on her left gently and stepped into the cloakroom. When she slipped out a few seconds later, she was wearing a military greatcoat and a steel helmet, both far too large for her, but that didn't matter. In the darkness, it was only the general impression that was important.

It was snowing lightly when she went outside and the entire courtyard was shrouded in darkness, no one working on Big Bertha this time. She took a deep breath to steady her nerves, went down the steps and started across to the gate.

There was a murmur of conversation up on the wall where the sentries talked in subdued voices. In the tunnel itself, silence. She hesitated at the door of the winding-gear room, then tried the handle gently. The door opened with a slight creak. It was dark in there. With a tremendous surge of relief, she stepped inside. Her groping hand found the switch and she turned on the light.

Canning was standing there with Hesser and Birr, Howard and Finebaum against the wall. She stood there, very pale, looking suddenly like some little girl in a macabre game of dressing-up that had gone wrong, lost in that ridiculous greatcoat and steel helmet.

'How did you know?' she said tonelessly.

'Well, I'll tell you, miss, you'll have to blame me for that.' Finebaum slung his M1, crossed to her side and searched her pockets, finding the explosive and detonators instantly. 'You see, the general here, being highly suspicious of our old pal Bannerman, put me on his tail. I was sitting it out up there in the passage by his room when he came out, and the plain fact is, miss, he called on you. The rest, as they say in the movies, you know. I didn't get a chance to tell the general about it right away because everything sort of happened on wheels after that.'

'That'll do, Finebaum,' Canning said.

'Anything you say, sir.'

Finebaum moved away. She stood there, defenceless. Canning glared at her, eyes burning, agony on his face.

It was Hesser who said, strangely gentle, 'Strasser is Bormann then?'

'I don't know. I've never met him. Remember the Gestapo security check on the castle two months ago when we were all interviewed personally? I received my instruction then from that SS colonel, Rattenhuber. He said he was acting for Bormann. A special radio was secreted in my room. I was given times when I could expect messages.'

'The damage to our own radio spares?' Hesser said. 'That was you?'

'Yes.'

'Why, for God's sake?' Canning cried harshly.

'It's really quite simple,' she said. 'Remember my husband, Étienne?'

'Of course. Shot dead while trying to escape from SD headquarters in Paris.'

'So I believed,' she said, 'until Rattenhuber was able to prove to me that wasn't true. Étienne is alive, Hamilton. Has been all along. An inmate of Mauthausen concentration camp.'

'I see,' Justin Birr said. 'And the price of his continued existence was your cooperation.'

'It wasn't enough,' Canning cried. 'You hear me? Not to excuse what you have done.'

The rage, the anguish in him was personal and obvious to everyone there. His hand came up, clutching his Walther.

'Shoot me then, Hamilton, if you must,' she said in the same flat voice. 'It doesn't matter. Nothing matters any longer. Étienne is as good as dead now.'

It was Finebaum who moved first, getting in front of her and facing Canning, his M1 still slung from his shoulder.

'General, I respect you – I respect you like hell, but this isn't the way, sir, and I can't just stand by and let you do it.'

Canning gazed at him wildly, the Walther shaking in his hand, and then something seemed to die inside him, the light faded; he lowered the pistol.

'Captain Howard.'

'Sir.'

'Lower the drawbridge, then open the gate.'

'I beg your pardon, sir?'

'You heard me.' Canning's voice was flat. 'I don't want her here, you hear me? Let her go. She can't harm us now.'

He brushed past her and went outside.

It was Sorsa, in the observation post the Finns had set up in the trees above the first bend, who noticed the drawbridge descending. Ritter had only just arrived from the village and was still in the field car on the road below.

Sorsa called softly, 'Something going on up there at the gate. They're lowering the drawbridge.'

Ritter scrambled up the bank to join him, and as he did so the judas opened and Claire de Beauville stepped into the light. She started across without hesitation, and the moment she reached the opposite side the drawbridge lifted again behind her. She came on.

'You know who it is?' Sorsa demanded.

'Madame de Beauville, one of the prominenti.' Ritter lowered his night-glasses. 'Now I wonder what friend Strasser will have to say about this rather singular turn of events?'

As the drawbridge started to rise again, Canning went back into the winding-gear room. Finebaum and Hoover were turning the massive wheels by hand, Howard watching them. Hesser and Birr talked together in low voices.

Canning's face was white with fury. 'Okay, that's it.

I've had enough of hanging around and nothing happening. I'm going out there to see what the situation is.'

'Good God, Hamilton, how on earth are you going to do that?' Birr demanded.

'Leave by the water gate. There's an old skiff in the tunnel there. We can cross the moat in that. They'll be heavily occupied with the woman at the moment. They won't expect any move like this.'

Birr shrugged. 'All right, Hamilton. If that's how you want it – I'm your man.'

'No, not you. You're needed here.'

Howard said, 'If you're looking for volunteers, sir.'

'Captain, in my entire career, I never asked anyone under my command to volunteer for anything. If I need a man, I tell him.' He nodded at Hoover and Finebaum. 'I'll take these two. You stay here to back up Colonel Birr. Any questions?'

Birr shrugged helplessly. 'You give the orders, Hamilton You're in command.'

It was damp in the tunnel, and cold. They waited while Schneider got the water gate unlocked and then the sergeant-major and a couple of his men got the skiff into the water.

Hesser said, 'It's in a pretty rotten condition, Herr General. Careful your boot doesn't go through the bottom.'

Howard handed Canning his Thompson. 'Better take this, sir. You could need it.'

'Thanks,' Canning said. 'We'll hit those trees as fast as we can, then work our way through and see if we can make out what's happening round that first bend in the road. In and out again, nice and fast. I'd say we should be back here in thirty minutes.'

'We'll be looking for you,' Birr called softly.

Hoover and Finebaum were already in the skiff.

Canning joined them sitting on the stern rail and Howard gave them a strong push. The skiff glided across the moat, its prow bit into the snow of the other bank and Finebaum was ashore in an instant. He knelt there, covering Hoover and Canning while they pulled the skiff up out of the water a little.

'Okay,' Canning whispered. 'Let's go.'

'Excuse me, General, but I figure we've got something to settle first.'

'What in the hell are you talking about, soldier?'

'You did say this was a reconnaissance mission, General?'

'Yes.'

'Well, that's good because that's what Harry and me and the captain have been kind of specializing in for the past eighteen months, only I always take point, sir. I mean, I lead the way on account of I seem to have a nose for it and we all live longer. Okay, General?'

'Okay,' Canning said. 'Just as long as we get moving.'

'Right. Just keep your mouth shut and follow my ass.'

He was away in an instant, moving very fast, and Canning went after him, Hoover following. They reached the tree line and Finebaum paused to get his bearings. In spite of the darkness, there was a faint luminosity because of the snow.

Finebaum dropped to one knee, his face close to the ground, then he stood up. 'Ski tracks, so those mothers are still around.'

He set off again, going straight up the slope through the trees at a speed which had Canning struggling for breath. Once on top, the ground inclined to the east more gently, through pine trees whose branches were covered with snow.

Finebaum was some yards in advance by now, and suddenly signalled to halt and went forward. He waved them on.

He was crouched beside a snow-covered bush in a small hollow on the ridge above the road. The Finns were encamped below beside the three half-tracks and the field car. The scene was illuminated by a couple of storm lanterns, and in their light it was possible to see Sorsa, Ritter and Claire de Beauville standing by the field car. The Finns squatted around portable field stoves in small groups.

'Hey, this could be a real Turkey shoot,' Finebaum said. 'There must be thirty to thirty-five guys down there. We open up now, we could take half of them out, no trouble.' He caressed the barrel of his M1. 'On the other hand, that would probably mean the lady getting it and you wouldn't like that would you, General?'

'No, I wouldn't like it at all,' Canning said.

Strange how different it seemed, now that they were apart. Standing down there in the lamplight, she might have been a stranger. No anger in him at all now.

'But when she moves out, General?' Finebaum said. 'That would be different.'

'Very different.' Canning eased the Thompson forward.

Finebaum leaned across to Hoover. 'You move ten yards that way on the other side of the bank, Harry. Give us a better field of fire. I'll look after the General.'

'And who'll look after you!' Hoover asked and wriggled away through the snow.

Finebaum took out a couple of German stick grenades and laid them ready in the snow. They were still talking down there by the field car.

Canning said, 'What are you going to do when you get home, Finebaum?'

'Hell, that's easy, General. I'm going to buy something big, like maybe my own hotel up there in Manhattan some place. Fill it with high-class women.'

'And make a fortune out of them or plunge in yourself?'

'That's where I can't make my mind up.' They didn't look at each other, but continued to watch the group below. 'It's a funny old war.'

'Is it?'

'If you don't know, who does, General?'

Claire got into the field car. Ritter climbed in beside her and nodded to Hoffer, who started the engine. 'Beautiful.' Finebaum breathed. 'Just too beautiful. Get ready, General.'

The field car moved into the night, the engine note started to dwindle. And then, as Canning and Finebaum eased forward in the snow to take aim at the men below, there was a sudden whisper in the night like wings beating.

They both turned as a Finn in white winter uniform, the hood of his parka drawn up over his field cap, erupted from the trees and did a perfect stem turn, coming to a dead halt. Finebaum fired from the hip three times very fast, knocking him back among the bushes.

'Watch it, you two,' Hoover yelled. 'Three o'clock high.'

Canning swivelled in the right direction and found another Finn coming down the slope through the trees like a rocket. He started to fire the Thompson, snow dancing in fountains across the face of the slope, and the Finn swerved to one side and disappeared. There was uproar down below as Sorsa shouted commands, ordering his men forward in skirmish order. Someone started to fire from the trees above them, and then below on the road a big Finnish Rottenführer jumped into one of the half-tracks, swung the heavy machine gun and loosed off a burst that cut branches from the trees above Canning's head.

'You wanted action, General, you got it,' Finebaum said, and called to Hoover, 'Hey, Harry, get ready to move out, old buddy. One, two, three, – the old routine. Say if you understand.'

There was no reply. He emptied his rifle into the men and the road below and shoved in another clip. 'Okay, General, let's move it,' he said and crawled through the bushes towards Hoover.

The sergeant was lying on his back, eyes open wide as if surprised that this could happen to him after all this time. There was a large and very ragged hole in his throat where two machine-gun bullets had hit together.

Finebaum turned and started to crawl back to their original position. The Finns were half-way up the slope at the side of the road now. He picked up the first stick grenade and tossed it over. There was a deafening explosion and cries of anguish. He ducked as the Rottenführer in the half-track swung the machine gun in his direction, kicking a wall of snow six feet into the air.

'Good-bye, old buddy!' Finebaum shouted and tossed the second grenade.

It seemed to drift through the night in a kind of slow motion. The Rottenführer ducked, it dropped into the half-track beside him. A second later it exploded, lifting him bodily into the air.

Finebaum yelled, 'Okay, General, let's get to hell out of here,' and he got to his feet and ran up the slope, head down.

Canning lost contact with him almost instantly, but kept on running, clutching the Thompson gun across his chest with both hands, aware of the spotlight over the castle gate in the distance.

There was a whisper of skis somewhere up above him on his right among the trees, and he swung the Thompson and fired. There were two rifle shots in reply and he kept on running, head down.

As he came out of the trees on the final ridge, there was a sudden swish of skis. He was aware of movement on his right, turned too late as the Finn ran straight into him. They went over the edge together, rolling over and over through deep snow, the man's skis tearing free.

Canning didn't relinquish his hold on the Thompson, not for a second, flailing out at the Finn wildly as the man tried to get up, but felt the side of the skull disintegrate under the impact of the steel butt.

He could hardly breathe now, staggering like a drunken man across the final section of open ground, aware of the deadly swish of skis closing behind, but as he fell down the bank of the moat, Finebaum was there, giving them one burst after another.

'Come on, you mothers! Is that the best you can do?'

Canning lurched into the water, thrashing out wildly, the Thompson still in his right hand. He went under once and then someone had him by the collar.

'Easy, General. Easy does it,' Jack Howard was saying.

Canning crouched against the wall, totally exhausted, in real physical pain. Hesser and Birr leaned over him. The German forced the neck of a flask between his teeth. It was brandy.

Canning didn't think anything could ever have tasted quite that good in his life before.

He realized that he was still clutching the Thompson and held it up to Howard. 'I lost your sergeant.'

'Hoover?' Howard said. 'You mean he's dead?'

'As a mackerel. Took two heavy-chopper rounds straight in the throat.' Finebaum squatted beside Canning. 'Anyone got a cigarette? Mine are all wet.'

Hesser gave him one and a light. Howard exploded. 'God dammit, Finebaum, is that all you can say? That's Harry out there.'

'What the hell you expect me to do, recite the prayers for the dead or something?'

Howard walked away along the tunnel. Canning said, 'You saved my skin out there, Finebaum. I won't forget that.'

'You did okay, General. You did as you was told. That's lesson number one in this game.'

'Game?' Canning said. 'Is that how you see it?'

Finebaum inhaled deeply and took his time in replying. 'I don't know about that, General, but I'll tell you one

thing. Sometimes at night, I wake up frightened – scared
half to death, and you know why?'

'No.'

'Because I'm afraid it'll soon be over.'

For the first time since Canning had known him, he
didn't sound as if he was trying to make a joke.

14

Ritter and Claire de Beauville did not exchange a single word during the drive down to the village. When Hoffer finally braked to a halt in front of the Golden Eagle, Claire made no attempt to get out; simply sat there, mute, staring into space, snowflakes clinging to her eyelashes.

'We will go in now, Madame,' Ritter said gently as Hoffer opened the door for them.

He took her hand to help her down and she started to shake. He put an arm about her shoulder. 'Quickly, Erich – inside.'

Hoffer ran ahead to get the door open. Ritter took her up the steps into the bar. Meyer was tending the fire. A look of astonishment appeared on his face when he saw Claire. 'Madame de Beauville – are you all right?'

She was shaking uncontrollably now. Ritter said, 'Where is Herr Strasser?'

'In my office, Sturmbannführer.'

'I'll take her there now. You get Dr Gaillard. I think she's going to need him. Go with him, Erich.'

They both went out quickly. Claire leaned heavily against Ritter and he held her close, afraid that she might fall. He walked her across to the fire and eased her into the large armchair beside it. Then he went to the bar, poured brandy into a glass and returned.

'Come on, just a little. You'll feel better, I promise you.'

She moaned softly, but drank, and then she seemed to choke a little, her fingers tightening on his shoulder as she stared past him.

Strasser said, 'What happened? What went wrong?'

Ritter turned to look at him. 'She is not well, as you can see.'

'This is not your department, so kindly keep out of it,' Strasser told him coldly.

Ritter hesitated then got to his feet and moved a few paces away. Strasser said, 'You were discovered?'

'Yes.'

'Then how do you come to be here?'

'General Canning threw me out.'

Strasser stood there, confronting her, hands clasped behind his back, a slight frown on his face. He nodded slowly. 'Exactly the sort of stupidity he would indulge in.'

'What happens now?'

'To you? A matter of supreme indifference to me, Madame.'

He started to turn away and she caught his sleeve, shaking again now, tears in her eyes. 'Please, Herr Bormann. Étienne – my husband. You promised.'

'Strasser,' he said. 'The name is Strasser, Madame, and in regard to your husband, I promised nothing. I said I would do what I could.'

'But Colonel Rattenhuber –'

'– is dead,' Strasser said. 'And I can't be responsible for the empty promises of a dead man.'

There was horror and incredulity on her face now. 'But I did everything I was asked to do. Betrayed my friends – my country. Don't you understand?'

From the doorway Gaillard said, in shocked tones, 'For God's sake, Claire, what are you saying?'

She turned on him feverishly. 'Oh, yes, it's true. I was the puppet – he pulled the strings. Meet my master, Paul. Reichsleiter Martin Bormann.'

'I really am growing rather weary of that bit,' Strasser said.

'Would you like to know why I did it, Paul? Shall I tell you? It's really very simple. Étienne wasn't killed escaping from SD Headquarters in Paris as we thought. He's alive. A prisoner at Mauthausen concentration camp.'

There was agony on Paul Gaillard's face – an overwhelming pity. He took her hands in his. 'I know, Claire, that Étienne wasn't shot trying to escape from Avénue Foch. I've known for a long time. I also know they took him to Mauthausen.'

'You knew?' she whispered. 'But I don't understand.'

'Mauthausen is an extermination camp. You only go in, you never come out. Étienne died there in the stone quarry two years ago along with forty-seven American, British and French fliers. There seemed no point in causing you needless distress when you already believed him dead.'

'How did they die?'

Gaillard hesitated.

'Please, Paul, I must know.'

'Very well. At one point in the quarry there was a flight of steps, 127 of them. Étienne and the others were made to climb them carrying heavy stones. Seventy, eighty, ninety, even one hundred pounds in weight. If they fell down they were clubbed and kicked until they got up again. By the evening of the first day half of them were dead. The rest died the following morning.'

Canning and Justin Birr had a plan of the castle open across the top of the piano. Claudine Chevalier sat opposite them, playing softly. The door opened and Hesser and Howard entered, the German brushing snowflakes from the fur collar of his greatcoat.

Canning said briskly, 'I've called you together for a final briefing on what the plan must be in case of an all-out assault.'

'You think that's still possible, sir?' Howard asked.

'I've no reason to believe otherwise. One thing is absolutely certain. If it comes at all, it must come soon. I'd say no later than dawn because the one thing Strasser or **Bormann** or whoever he is doesn't have is time. An Allied column could cross this place. However' – he pulled the plan forward – 'let's say they do attack and force the drawbridge. How long can you hold them before they blast that gate. Howard?'

'Not long enough, General. All we have are rifles, Schmeissers and grenades and one machine gun up there. They still have two half-tracks with heavy machine guns and a lot more manpower.'

'Okay – so they force the gates and you have to fall back. What about Big Bertha, Max?'

'She is in position thirty yards from the mouth of the tunnel and overflowing with scrap metal. However, I can't guarantee that she won't blow up in the face of whoever puts light to her.'

'That's my department,' Canning told him. 'I said it, I meant it. If it works, we dispose of the first half-track out of the tunnel and probably every man in it. That should even things up a little.'

'Then what?' Howard demanded.

'We retreat into north tower, get the door shut and stand them off for as long as we can.'

Justin Birr said mildly, 'I hate to mention it, Hamilton, but it really isn't much of a barrier, that door. Not if somebody starts chucking grenades at it.'

'Then we retreat up the stairs,' Canning said. 'Fight them floor-by-floor, or has anybody got a better suggestion?' There was only silence. 'All right, gentlemen, let's get moving. I'll see you on the wall in five minutes.'

They went out. He stood there looking at the plan for a while, then picked up a German-issue parka and pulled it over his head.

'A long wait until dawn, Hamilton,' Claudine Chevalier said. 'You really think they'll come?'

'I'm afraid so.'

'And Paul and Claire? I wonder what will happen to them?'

'I don't know.'

'Or care?'

'About Gaillard – yes.' Canning buckled on his holstered pistol.

'How strange,' she said, still playing, 'that love can turn to hate so quickly – or can it? Perhaps we only delude ourselves.'

'Why don't you go to hell?' Canning suggested bitterly and he walked out, slamming the door.

When Sorsa went into the bar at the Golden Eagle he found Ritter sitting by the fire, a glass in one hand. Sorsa beat the snow from his parka. Ritter didn't say a word, simply stared into the fire. The door from the kitchen opened and Erich Hoffer entered with coffee on a tray. He put it down on the side-table without a word. Ritter ignored him also.

Sorsa glanced at the sergeant-major, then coughed. Ritter's head turned very slowly. He glanced up, a brooding expression in his eyes.

'Yes, what is it?'

'You sent for me, Sturmbannführer.'

Ritter stared up at him for a moment longer, then said, 'How many did you lose up there?'

'Four dead – two seriously wounded. We brought them back here for the doctor to deal with. Three others scratched about a bit. One of the half-tracks is a complete write-off. What happens now?'

'We attack at dawn. Seven o'clock precisely. You and your men are still mine until nine, remember.'

'Yes, Sturmbannführer.'

'I'll take command personally. Full assault. We'll use Panzerfausts on the drawbridge. Hoffer, here, was the best gunner in the battalion. He'll blow those chains for us, won't you, Erich?'

It was delivered as an order, and Hoffer reacted

accordingly, springing to attention, heels clicking. together. '*Zu befehl, Sturmbannführer.*'

Ritter looked up at Sorsa. 'Any questions?'

'Would it make any difference if I had?' Sorsa asked.

'Not really. The same roads lead to hell in the end for all of us.'

'A saying we have in Finland also.'

Ritter nodded. 'Better leave Sergeant-Major Gestrin and four of your best men down here to hold the fort while we're away. You get back to your camp now. I'll be up in a little while.'

'And Herr Strasser?'

'I shouldn't imagine so, not for a moment. Herr Strasser is too important to be risked. You understand me?'

'I think so, Sturmbannführer.'

'Good, because I'm damned if I do.' Ritter got to his feet, walked to the bar and reached for the schnapps bottle. 'I've known a lot of good men during the past five or six years who are no longer with us, and for the first time I'm beginning to wonder why.' There was a kind of desperation on his face. 'Why did they die, Sorsa? What for? Can you tell me?'

'I'm afraid not,' Sorsa said gently. 'You see, I fight for wages. We belong to a different club, you and me. Was there anything else?' Ritter shook his head. 'Then I'll get back to my boys.'

The big Finn gave him a military salute and went out. Ritter moved to the fireplace and stared into the flames. 'Why, Erich?' he whispered. 'What for?'

'What's this, Major Ritter?' Strasser said from the doorway. 'A little late in the day for philosophy, I should have thought.'

Ritter turned, the dark eyes blazing in the pale face. 'No more games, Reichsleiter. We've gone too far for that now, you and I.'

'Have we indeed?' Strasser went behind the bar and poured himself a brandy.

'Is it Bormann in Berlin and Strasser here, or the other way about?' Ritter said. 'On the other hand, does it really matter?'

'Speeches now?'

'I'd say I've earned the right, if only because I had to stand by and watch that sickening spectacle with the de Beauville woman. You left her more degraded than a San Pauli whore. You left her nothing.'

'I did what had to be done.'

'For God, the Führer and the Reich – or have I got that in the wrong order?' Ritter ignored the horror on Hoffer's face. 'Hundreds of thousands of young Germans have died, the cream of our nation, who believed. Who had faith and idealism. Who thought they were taking our country out of the degradation and squalor of the twenties into a new age. I now realize they died for nothing. What they believed in never existed in the first place. You and your kind allowed, for your own ends, a madman to lead the German people down the road to hell, and we followed you with joy in our hearts.'

Strasser said, 'Listen to me, Ritter. This is sentimental nonsense of the worst kind, and from you – a man who has served the Reich as few have done. Do you think we are finished? If so, you are badly mistaken. We go on – only now does the Kamaradenwerk begin, and there is a place for you in this. A place of honour.'

Ritter turned to Hoffer. 'We're leaving now, Erich.'

Hoffer went out. Strasser said, 'What do you intend?'

'I'm attacking at seven o'clock. Full assault. We'll use Panzerfausts to blow the drawbridge chains. It might work, but I can't guarantee it. I'm leaving Sergeant-Major Gestrin and four men to look after things here.'

Hoffer returned and handed him his parka and field cap. Strasser said, 'Let me get my coat. I'll come with you.'

'No!' Ritter said flatly. 'I command and I say you stay here.'

As he buttoned his parka, Strasser said, 'As you so obviously feel as you do, why are you doing this?'

'Most of my friends are dead now,' Ritter told him. 'Why should I get away with it?' and he walked out.

Arnie was sleeping peacefully and the only evidence of the ordeal he had passed through were the dark smudges like purple bruising under each eye. Gaillard placed a hand on the boy's forehead. It was quite cool and the pulse was normal for the first time in twenty-four hours.

He lit a cigarette, went to the window and opened it. It was quite dark except for light spilling out from the kitchen window across the courtyard below. It was snowing and he breathed deeply on the cold bracing air.

There was a knock at the door and Meyer entered with coffee on a tray. The Finnish guard stayed outside. Gaillard could see him sitting on a chair on the other side of the corridor, smoking a cigarette.

'How is he, Herr Doctor?' Meyer asked as he poured coffee.

'Temperature down, pulse normal, fever gone and sleeping peacefully as you can see.' Gaillard drank some of the coffee gratefully. 'And now I must check on Madame de Beauville.'

Meyer said softly. 'They mount a general assault on Schloss Arlberg at seven.'

Gaillard said, 'Are you certain?'

'I overheard Major Ritter and Herr Strasser discussing it in the bar a short time ago. Major Ritter has already left for the castle.'

'And Strasser?'

'There was trouble between them, Strasser wanted to go, but Ritter wouldn't have it. He stays here with five Finns to guard him.'

Gaillard turned and leaned on the window sill, considerably agitated. 'If a general assault is mounted up there they won't stand a chance. We must do something.'

'What can we do, Herr Doctor? It's a hopeless situation.'

'Not if someone could get out with news of what's happening here.' There was a new hope on Gaillard's face. 'There must be many Allied units in the vicinity of Arlberg now. You could go, Johann.' He reached out a hand and gripped Meyer's coat. 'You could slip away.'

'I am sorry, Herr Doctor, I owe you a great deal – possibly even my son's life – but if I go, it would be like leaving the boy to take his chances.' Meyer shook his head. 'In any case, it would be impossible to steal the field car with those Finns out in front, and how far could anyone hope to get on foot?'

'You're right, of course.' Gaillard turned back to the window dejectedly and saw something in the courtyard below that filled him with a sudden fierce hope. A set of skis propped against the wall beside the kitchen window.

He controlled himself with considerable difficulty. 'Pour me another coffee before that sentry decides you've been here long enough, and listen. The skis down there – they are yours?'

'Yes, Herr Doctor.'

'You are right, my friend, you do owe me something and now is your chance to repay. You will take those skis, an anorak, mittens and boots and leave them in the wood store at the top of the yard. That is all I ask. Getting out of here is my problem.'

Meyer still hesitated. 'I'm not sure, Herr Doctor. If they ever found out . . .'

'Not for me or my friends, Johann,' Gaillard said. 'For Arnie. You owe him that much, I think.'

The Finn moved into the room, said something in his own language, and gestured to Meyer, motioning him outside. Meyer picked up the tray.

'I'm counting on you, Johann.'

'I'll try, Herr Doctor.' Meyer looked distinctly unhappy. 'I'll do my best, but I can't promise more than that.'

He went out and the guard made to close the door, but Gaillard shook his head. He picked up his doctor's bag, brushed past him and went down the corridor to the next room. Claire de Beauville was lying down, and when the Finn tried to follow him in, Gaillard shut the door in his face.

She started to get up and Gaillard sat on the edge of the bed. 'No, stay where you are. How do you feel now?'

'A little better.'

'Not if someone comes in, you don't. You feel very ill indeed.'

'The sentry?'

'No, he's been rather more amenable since standing by and watching while I patched up two of his comrades in a room along the corridor. Casualties of some fracas up at the castle.' He opened his bag and took out a stethoscope. 'I haven't got long so listen carefully. This man Strasser or whoever he is. Do you still wish to serve him?'

She shuddered. 'What do you think?'

He glanced at his watch. 'In less than an hour they mount a general assault on Schloss Arlberg. Everything they've got. No holds barred.'

Her eyes widened. 'Claudine, Hamilton and the others – they won't stand a chance.'

'Exactly, so someone must go for help.'

'But how?'

'Meyer is hiding ski-ing equipment for me in the wood store at the back of the inn. Getting out is my own affair. Will you help?'

'Of course.' Her hand tightened on his and she smiled sadly. 'If you want the help of someone like me.'

'My poor Claire. We are all casualties of war to a greater or lesser degree. Who am I to judge you?' There were voices outside. She lay back hurriedly. The door opened and Strasser entered.

'How is she?'

'Not very well,' Gaillard said. 'I'm afraid a total breakdown is quite possible. She has, after all, gone through a lengthy period of intense stress. Add to this the trauma of more recent events. The news of her husband's death.'

'Yes, all very sad,' Strasser said impatiently. 'However, I want to talk to you.'

'It will have to wait. Madame de Beauville needs my full attention at the moment and I would remind you that I have two badly wounded Finns along the corridor.'

'Ten minutes,' Strasser said. 'That's all you can have, then I want you downstairs in the bar.' His voice was cold, incisive. 'You understand me?'

'Of course, Reichsleiter,' Gaillard told him calmly.

Strasser left, leaving the door open, the Finnish guard standing outside. 'That's bad,' Gaillard said. 'It doesn't give us much time.'

'If you don't go now, you won't go at all, isn't that how it stands?' she said.

'Very probably.'

'Well, then, it's now or never.'

She sat up and swung her legs down, somehow managing to knock his bag to the floor. She reached to pick it up, clumsily disgorging most of the contents, instruments, pill bottles and so on, on the carpet.

'Now look what I've done.'

The Finnish guard moved into the room and stood watching. She started to kneel and Gaillard said, 'It doesn't matter. I'll get them.'

Claire turned to the Finn, trying to look as confused and helpless as possible and he responded as she had hoped. He grinned, unslung his rifle, and put it on the bed, then dropped to one knee beside Gaillard.

She didn't hesitate. There was a cut-glass decanter half-full of water beside her bed. She seized it by the neck and struck with all her strength at the base of the skull.

Glass fragmented, bone splintered, the Finn slumped on his face without a sound.

She froze for a few moments, listening, but all was quiet. She said, 'Go, now, Paul.'

'And you?' he asked, standing up.

'Don't worry about me.'

He put his hands on her shoulders, kissed her briefly and hurried out. Claire stood there, looking down at the Finn, surprisingly calm, drained of all emotion and very, very tired. A drink, she thought, that's what I need, and she went out, closing the door behind her.

Gaillard went down the back stairs. As he reached the stone-flagged passage, the door to the courtyard opened and Meyer entered, stamping snow from his boots. He drew back in astonishment at the sight of Gaillard, who grabbed his arm.

'Have you done as I asked?'

'Yes, Herr Doctor,' Meyer stammered. 'I've just come back.'

'Good man,' Gaillard said. 'If Strasser descends on you when I'm gone just play dumb.'

He opened the door, stepped out and closed it. The first pale luminous light of dawn was filtering through the trees. There was a slight ground mist and it was snowing a little. Meyer's tracks were plain and Gaillard followed them quickly across the yard to the wood store. He got the door open and passed inside.

He was excited now, more so than he had been for years, and his hands shook as he took off his shoes and pulled on the woollen socks and heavy ski-ing boots Meyer had provided. The anorak was an old red one which had been patched many times, but the hood was fur-lined, as were the mittens. He pulled it on quickly, picked up the skis and sticks and went back outside.

It was snowing harder now, cold, early-morning mountain snow, strangely exhilarating, and when he paused on the other side of the wall to put on the skis, he was conscious of the old, familiar thrill again. The years fell away and he was in the Vosges, practising for Chamonix. Nineteen twenty-four – the first Winter Games. The greatest moment of his life when he had won that gold medal. Everything after had always savoured a little of anti-climax.

He smiled wryly to himself and knelt to adjust the bindings to his satisfaction. He pressed on the safety catch, locking his boot in position, then repeated the performance with the other ski. So, he was ready. He pulled on his mittens and reached for the sticks.

It was perhaps five minutes later that Strasser, sitting waiting for Gaillard in the bar, heard a cry from outside in the square. He went to the door. Gestrin and the four Finnish soldiers Ritter had left were standing by the field car. One of them was pointing up above the houses to the wooded slope of the mountain behind.

'What is it?' Strasser demanded.

Manni Gestrin lowered his field glasses. 'The Frenchman.'

'Gaillard?' Strasser said incredulously. 'Impossible.'

'See for yourself. Up there on the track.'

He handed the field-glasses over. Strasser hastily adjusted the lenses. He found the woodcutter's track that zig-zagged up through the trees and came upon the skier in the red anorak almost instantly. Gaillard glanced back over his shoulder giving a good view of his face.

Two of the Finns were already taking aim with their Mauser rifles. Gestrin said, 'Shall we fire?'

'No, you fool, I want him back,' Strasser said. 'You understand me?'

'Nothing simpler. In this kind of country on skis, these lads are the best in the business.'

592

He turned away, giving orders in Finnish. They all moved quickly to the field car and started to unload their skis.

'You go with them,' Strasser told Gestrin. 'No excuses, no arguments. Just have him back here within the hour.'

'As you say,' Gestrin answered calmly.

They had their skis on within a few minutes and moved away in single file, rifles slung over their backs, Gestrin in the lead. Strasser looked up the mountain to the last bend in the track which could be seen from the square. There was a flash of red among the green, then nothing.

He hurried into the inn, drawing the Walther from his pocket. He went up the stairs, two at a time, and moved along the corridor. Arnie's door stood open. The boy slept peacefully. Strasser hesitated, then turned to Claire de Beauville's room. The Finnish guard lay where he had fallen, face turned to one side. The back of the skull was soft, matted with blood. There was a trickle from the corner of his mouth. He was quite dead and Strasser went out quickly.

'Meyer, where are you, damn you?' he called as he went downstairs.

Meyer emerged from the kitchen and stood there, fear in his eyes. In the same moment Strasser saw that Claire de Beauville was behind the bar, opening a champagne bottle.

'Ah, there you are, Reichsleiter. Just in time to join me. Krug. An excellent year, too. Not as chilled as I would normally expect, but one can't have everything in this life.'

Strasser ignored her and menaced Meyer with his pistol beside himself with rage. 'You helped him, didn't you? Where else would he obtain skis and winter clothing?'

'Please, Herr Strasser. Don't shoot.' Meyer broke down completely. 'I had nothing to do with this business. You are mistaken if you think otherwise.'

Claire poured herself a glass of champagne, perched

on one of the high stools and sipped it appreciatively. 'Excellent. Really excellent – and he's quite right, by the way. I was the one who helped Paul. I had the greatest of pleasure in crowning that SS man of yours with a cut-glass decanter.'

Strasser glared at her. 'You?' he said. 'He's dead, the man you assaulted, did you know that?'

The smile left her face, but she replied instantly, 'And so is Étienne.'

'You bitch. Do you realize what you've done?'

'Ruined everything for you, I hope. There must be British and American troops all over the area by now. I'm sure Paul will run across one of their columns quite quickly.'

'No chance,' he said. 'Gestrin and four of those Finns of his have just taken off after him. Probably five of the finest skiers in the German Army. You think it will take them long to run down a sixty-year-old man?'

'Who won an Olympic gold medal in 1924. The greatest skier in the world in his day. I would have thought that would still count for something, wouldn't you?' She raised her glass. '*À votre santé*, Reichsleiter – and may you rot in hell.'

He fired several times as the black rage erupted inside him. His first bullet caught her in the right shoulder, knocking her off the stool and turning her round. His second and third shattered her spine, driving her headlong into the wall, the woollen material of her jacket smouldering, then bursting into flame. He moved forward, firing again and again until the gun was empty.

He stood looking down at her and Meyer, his face contorted with horror, backed away quietly, then turned and rushed upstairs. When he reached Arnie's room, the boy was still asleep. He closed the door, bolted it, then dragged a heavy chest of drawers across as an additional barrier.

He went into the dressing room, lifted the carpet in the

corner and removed a loose floorboard. Inside, wrapped in a piece of blanket, was his old sawn-off shotgun from the poaching days of his youth and a box of cartridges, hidden since before the war. He loaded both barrels and went back into the bedroom. He placed a chair in the centre of the room facing the door, sat down with the gun across his knees and waited.

It had been a long time, but some things you never forgot. Gaillard moved out of the trees and started into a flat plateau perhaps two hundred yards across, more trees on the other side. He was using the sliding forward stride much favoured by Scandinavians; a technique he had picked up in his youth and which ate up the miles at a surprising rate.

If you were fit, of course, always that, though at the moment, he felt better than he had for years. Free, yes, but more than that – the knowledge that they'd come to the end of something. That freedom was just around the corner for everyone.

But this was no time for such considerations. He needed a destination and didn't have one. On the other hand, it seemed reasonable to assume that the help he was seeking was more than likely to be found on the main roads, which meant climbing higher, traversing the eastern shoulder of the mountain and then descending.

Something made him glance back, some sixth sense. The Finns were half-way across the plateau, moving in single file, Gestrin leading. He was not afraid, but filled with a fierce delight and started into the trees, moving at a fast, loping rate. He was already a hundred feet up the side of the mountain when the Finns reached the edge of the trees and Gestrin called them to a halt.

'All right,' he said, 'the party's over. He's good this one. Too good to play with. From now on, it's every man for himself, and remember – we want him alive.'

He started up the slope and they moved after him.

Ritter and Sorsa stood beside one of the two remaining half-tracks, drinking coffee and examining the ground plan of Schloss Arlberg which the German had brought from the inn.

'Once we're in they'll fall back to north tower,' Ritter said. 'Nowhere else to go.'

'And what's that going to be like?'

'According to Strasser, a heavy, oaken door opening in two sections. That shouldn't take long. Inside, a hall then a broad stairway that diminishes in size, becoming a spiral at the higher levels. The dining hall, then a maze of passages and rooms right on up to the top.'

'If they take it room-by-room it could be nasty.'

'Not if we keep after them right from the word go. No hesitation, no let-up.'

The Finns were ready and waiting in the half-tracks, half a dozen with the Panzerfausts. Ritter moved closer to examine the ugly-looking anti-tank projectiles. 'Are they good with these things?'

'We've had our successes. On target, one of these can open a T34 like a can of meat.'

'How many have we got?'

'Ten.'

'Then we can't afford to take chances. I'm putting Hoffer in charge. Make that clear to your men. He's the finest gunner I know.'

At that moment Hoffer called from the field car. 'Herr Strasser on the radio for you, Sturmbannführer.'

Ritter leaned into the car. There was no static and Strasser's voice sounded clear and distinct. 'You've not started the assault?'

'Any minute now. Why?'

Strasser told him. When he was finished, Ritter said, 'So we don't have too much time, that's what you're trying to say? You needn't have bothered, Reichsleiter. We've been a little short on that commodity from the beginning. Over and out.'

He replaced the phone and turned to Sorsa. 'Trouble?' the Finn asked.

'Gaillard's managed to escape. He's taken to the mountain on skis. Strasser's sent Gestrin and his boys after him.'

'No problem,' Sorsa said. 'The best in the business. They'll lay him by the heels soon enough.'

'I wouldn't count on it. He was an Olympic gold medallist at Chamonix in 1924. If he runs across a British or American column before Gestrin and his men get to him . . .'

Sorsa looked grave. 'I see what you mean. So what do we do?'

'Get this little affair over with as quickly as possible. We move out now.'

He started towards one of the half-tracks and Sorsa caught his arm. 'A moment, Sturmbannführer. The first half-track through that tunnel is likely to have a hard time. I'd like to be in it.'

'I command here,' Ritter said. 'I thought I made that clear.'

'But these are my boys,' Sorsa persisted. 'We've been together a long time.'

Ritter stared at him, a slight frown on his face, and then nodded. 'I take the point. Very well, for this occasion only, you lead and I follow. Now let's get moving.'

He turned and scrambled up into the second half-track.

15

Claudine Chevalier was sitting at the piano in the dining hall playing 'The Girl with the Flaxen Hair' by Debussy. It was one of her favourite pieces, mainly because the composer himself had tutored her in how to play it when she was twelve years of age.

There was a knock at the door and Finebaum entered. His M1 was slung from his left shoulder, a Schmeisser from his right, and there were three stick grenades in his belt.

She kept on playing. 'Trouble, Mr Finebaum?'

'Well, I'll tell you, ma'am. General Canning, he thought it would be a good idea to have someone look out for you personally. You know what I mean?'

'You?' she said.

'I'm afraid so, ma'am. Mind if I smoke?'

'Not at all – and I couldn't be in better hands. What do we do?'

'I'll take you up to the top of the tower when the time comes – out of the way of things.'

'But not now?'

'No need. They haven't even knocked at the gate yet. Say, my old lady used to play piano. Nothing like that though. I learned the clarinet when she got one cheap, from my Uncle Paul. He was a pawnbroker in Brooklyn.'

'Did you enjoy it?'

'Well, I ain't Benny Goodman but I made front row with Glenn Miller.'

'But that's wonderful. Do you like this piece that I'm playing now?'

'No, ma'am. It makes my stomach feel cold. It worries me, I don't know why, and that ain't good because I've got enough to worry about.'

'Ah, I see. Perhaps you would prefer something like this?'

She started to play 'Night and Day'. Finebaum moved round the piano to look down at the keys. 'Hey – that's great. That's really something. I mean, where did you ever learn to play like that?'

'Oh, one gets around, Mr Finebaum. Isn't that the phrase?'

'I guess so.'

A roar of engines shattered the morning stillness.

'Oh, my God,' she whispered and stopped playing.

As Finebaum ran to the window there was a sudden booming explosion and the rattle of machine-gun fire.

Gaillard, high in the woods now, on the upper slopes of the mountain, heard the echoes of that first outbreak of firing and paused to listen. His lungs were aching as he struggled for breath, leaning heavily on his sticks, and his legs were trembling slightly.

He was too old, of course. Too many years under his belt, and the truth was he simply wasn't fit enough. When it came right down to it, the only thing he really had going for him was technique and the skill born of his natural genius and years of experience.

The Finns, on the other hand, were young men, battle-hardened to endure anything and at the peak of their physical fitness. He really didn't stand a chance – had not done from the beginning.

He langlaufed across the small plateau that tilted gently upwards and paused on the ridge. On the other side the snow slope was almost vertical, dropping into grey mist, no means of knowing what was down there at all.

He turned and saw the first of the Finns appear from the

trees on the other side of the plateau no more than thirty yards away. Gestrin was number three and the big Finn waved his hand to bring the patrol to a halt.

He pushed up his goggles. 'All right, Doctor. You've put up a wonderful show and we admire you for it, but enough of this foolishness. Now we go home.'

There were two more violent explosions somewhere in the mist below. The rattle of small-arms fire persisting. Gaillard thought of his friends; of Claudine Chevalier and of Claire de Beauville and what had happened to her.

He was filled with a fierce, sudden anger and shouted down at the Finns, 'All right, you bastards! Let's see what you're made of.'

He went straight over the edge of that near-vertical drop, crouching, skis nailed together, and plunged into the mist. The Finns, as they reached the edge, followed, one after the other, without hesitation.

Canning, Birr and Hesser were in the tunnel, Howard on the wall, when the engine's roar first shattered the morning calm. A few moments later, the half-tracks emerged into view and took up position. The Finns spilled out and started to deploy. Hoffer and the men under his personal command took up position to the left.

Howard trained his glasses on them, trying to make out what they were doing. In the moment of realization there came a tongue of orange flame; a second later, a violent explosion as the first Panzerfaust projectile struck the wall beside the drawbridge.

Everyone crouched. 'What in the hell was that?' Birr demanded.

'Panzerfaust,' Hesser replied. 'It's an anti-tank weapon rather like your bazooka.'

'So I see,' Canning said grimly, ducking as another violent explosion rocked the drawbridge – a direct hit this time.

'Obviously it's the chains they're after,' Birr said. 'I wonder how long it will take?'

Heavy machine-gun fire raked the top of the wall, bullets ricocheting into space. 'Give them everything we've got,' Canning cried. 'Really pour it on.'

Schneider opened up with the MG34 and the rest of the Germans backed him with their Mauser rifles, sniping from the embrasures in the wall. The Finns took refuge behind the half-tracks, one of which moved position slightly to cover the Panzerfaust group.

The fourth projectile, fired by Hoffer personally, scored a direct hit on the drawbridge just below the chain-mounting on the left-hand side. The woodwork disintegrated, the chain coupling tore free, the drawbridge sagged.

'Strike one,' Howard said. 'Not long now.'

Two more projectiles homed in, a third landing just below the top of the wall above the gate, its shrapnel killing Schneider and the other two men in the machine-gun crew instantly, hurling the MG34 on its side, battered and useless.

Canning crawled across to Howard, blood on his face. 'Not long now.' He turned to Birr and Hesser. 'Justin, you and Howard stay up here as long as you can with half a dozen men. Max, you drop back on the tower.'

'And what about you?' Birr demanded.

'Big Bertha and I have business together. You make things as hot for those bastards as you can on the way in, then get off the wall and join Max in the tower.'

Birr started to argue, but in the same moment there was another frightful explosion just below them. The remaining chain disintegrated, the drawbridge fell down across the moat with a resounding crash.

There was a general cheer from the Finns, and Ritter jumped from the half-track to join Hoffer.

'How many have you left?'

'Two, Sturmbannführer.'

'Make them count, Erich. The gate this time.' He ran to the other half-track and Sorsa leaned down.

'Hoffer is going to blast the gate,' Ritter said. 'You make your move as soon as you like. Smash straight in and we'll cover you. Good luck.'

Sorsa smiled, waved a gloved hand and pulled down his Panzer goggles. He shouted an order in Finnish and a dozen men scrambled over the side and joined him in the half-track. He clapped his driver on the shoulder and, as they started to move forward, took over the machine gun himself.

The first of Hoffer's last two projectiles punched a hole through the massive gate and exploded at the end of the tunnel. The blast knocked Canning, standing beside Big Bertha, clean off his feet, showering him with dirt and tiny fragments of shrapnel.

There was more blood on his face, his own this time, and as he started to get up, Hoffer fired the remaining Panzerfaust. The left-hand side of the gate sagged and fell in.

The lead half-track was half-way there, Sorsa firing the machine gun furiously, his men backing him up, and Ritter followed in the second half-track, spraying the top of the wall with such a volume of fire that it was virtually impossible for the handful of defenders to reply.

Howard tossed a couple of stick grenades over at random as the lead half-track got close and Birr grabbed his arm. 'Let's get out of here!'

Of the German soldiers who had stayed on the wall with them, only three were left on their feet. Howard beckoned to them now, and they all went down the steps on the run and started across the courtyard to where Hesser and seven of his men waited on the steps of the tower entrance.

Canning leaned heavily on the cannon, blood running into his eyes, and Howard swerved towards him. The general sagged to one knee, groping for the length of smouldering fuse he had dropped as Howard joined him.

'Get the hell out of here!' Canning ordered.

But by then it was too late, for, as Howard handed him the fuse, the lead half-track smashed what was left of the gates from their hinges. It emerged from the tunnel, Sorsa firing the machine gun, and Canning touched the end of his fuse to the powder charge.

Big Bertha belched fire and smoke in a thunderous roar, rocking back on her solid wheels, disgorging her improvised charge of assorted metal fragments and chain at point-blank range, killing Sorsa and every man in the half-track instantly, hurling the vehicle over to one side and back against the wall.

Both Canning and Howard were thrown down by the force of the explosion. As the roar of Ritter's half-track filled the tunnel, Howard grabbed the general by the arm, hauled him to his feet and urged him into a stumbling run.

Hesser and his men were firing furiously now, retreating up the steps and back through the door at the foot of north tower, but continuing to give them covering fire. As Howard and Canning made it to the steps, the half-track emerged from the tunnel across the courtyard and its machine gun tracked them across the cobbles.

Hesser's men were already getting the doors closed when, as Howard urged Canning up the steps, the general stumbled and fell. Hesser and Birr ducked out through the narrowing opening and hurried down the steps to help.

Howard and Birr got Canning between them and dragged him up the steps. Behind them, Hesser turned, firing a Schmeisser one-handed across the courtyard, catching a full burst from the machine gun in reply that drove him across the steps, hurling him over the edge into the snow.

A second later, Howard and Birr staggered in through the narrowing gap with Canning and the massive doors closed.

Gaillard's speed was tremendous as he hurtled down into the grey mist, yet he was entirely without fear. What lay ahead it was impossible to say. He could be rushing straight to his death, his only consolation the knowledge that his pursuers would follow him.

And what good would that do? he asked himself, suddenly angry, and moved into a parallel swing, changing course, the right-hand edge of his skis biting into the snow.

The mist was thinning now and he glanced over his shoulder and saw that the lead Finn was perhaps forty yards behind, closely followed by another. Gestrin and the other two were a little further back.

Gaillard came out of an S-turn and went down vertically again, knees together, and suddenly a gust of wind dissolved the remaining shreds of mist in an instant and below was the valley, an awesome sight, the present slope vanishing into infinity fifty yards further on.

Gaillard didn't deviate, but held his course true, skis so close together that they might have been one. At the last possible moment, that edge which meant certain death rushing to meet him, he hurled himself into a left-hand Christie. It came off beautifully and he had a brief impression of the glacier far below as he skirted the ultimate edge.

His pursuers were not so lucky, for behind him the lead Finn went straight over the edge with a terrible cry, his companion following him.

Gaillard, out of the area of immediate danger, started to traverse the lower slope. Above him, Manni Gestrin and his two remaining comrades changed course and went after him.

Canning had a deep cut in his forehead above the right eye of a kind that would require five or six stitches at least. Howard hastily bound a field dressing around it.

'Is he all right?' Birr asked.

'Sure I'm all right,' Canning told him. 'How many of us left?'

'Six Germans and us three. Finebaum upstairs, of course.'

'Not so good.'

He peered out through a spyhole in the door. The remaining half-track had retreated into the tunnel. Nothing moved.

'I'd say they could walk in here any time they choose,' Howard said.

'Then we retreat upstairs, floor-by-floor, like I told you.'

The half-track nosed out of the mouth of the tunnel and stopped. Its heavy machine gun, Hoffer firing, started to spray the door at the rate of 850 rounds per minute. As Canning and the others went down, the door started to shake to pieces above them.

'This is bad,' the general cried. 'No good staying. Better get up those stairs now while we still have a choice.'

He called to the Germans and they all started to drop back.

Gaillard was incredibly tired. His body ached and his knees hurt. The amazing thing was that he hadn't fallen once, but now, as he went into a right-hand Christie to make for the cover of pine trees, he snarled a ski and took a bad tumble.

He slid for some considerable distance before coming to a halt, winded. His skis were still on and apparently undamaged, which was something. No broken bones in evidence. But God, how tired he was. Hardly enough strength to get up. He turned and saw Gestrin and his two comrades traversing the slope above him, terribly close now.

Suddenly, the earth shook, there was a tremendous rumbling like an underground explosion, and above the Finns the snow seemed to boil up in a great cloud.

Avalanche! Not surprising really, fresh snow falling so late in the season. But already Gaillard was on his feet and dropping straight down the slope, taking that vertical line again, for the only way to beat an avalanche was to stay in front of it – one of the first lessons he'd learned as a boy in the Vosges.

And the trees were not too far away, some sort of protection there. He moved to the right in a wide curve that took him into their shelter within seconds. He halted, turning to glance back.

The avalanche had almost overtaken the Finns. The enormous cloud of white smoke rolled over the one in the rear, enveloped him completely, but Gestrin and the remaining man rode the very edge, managing to turn at the last minute, coming to a halt above the line of trees.

The rumble of the avalanche died away, Gestrin pushed up his goggles, searching for Gaillard whose red anorak gave him away instantly. They started down the slope at once and the Frenchman turned and pushed himself forward and through the trees, every bone aching.

From the shattered great window of the upper dining room Finebaum sniped down and across the yard at the half-track.

'What's happening, Mr Finebaum?' Claudine Chevalier, crouched on the floor, asked him.

'Whatever it is, it ain't good, ma'am. I figure it's time maybe you and me made a move upstairs.'

There was a burst of firing and more of the window shattered above their heads, spraying them with glass. Amazingly, she showed no fear.

'Whatever you say, Mr Finebaum.'

'You're something special,' Finebaum said. 'You know that?'

He took her arm and helped her towards the door, and below in the courtyard the half-track surged forward.

For Gaillard, the sight of the road below was like a shot in the arm, and he dropped towards it with renewed hope, although his pursuers were closer than ever now, Gestrin trailing his companion, a young man called Salmi.

Gaillard glanced over his shoulder, aware that this couldn't go on, that he had been existing on will-power alone for too long. There was one final suicidal chance, and he took it, dropping straight down through the trees like a bullet to the embankment at the side of the road below.

As he hit, he dug in his sticks at precisely the right moment, launching himself into space. The road flashed beneath him, he soared across, landing perfectly in soft snow on the other side, sliding broadside on in a spray of snow. At the last moment, the point of his left ski caught a branch hidden beneath the white blanket. As he crashed heavily to the ground, the ski splintered.

He lay there, winded, and Salmi soared through the air across the road, smashing straight into a pine tree with a terrible cry.

Gaillard sat up. There was no sign of Gestrin. He tore at the frozen bindings of his skis and got them off. When he rose to his feet, he was convinced for a moment that his limbs had ceased to function. He took a hesitant step forward and fell headlong over the embankment, sliding down to the road.

He picked himself up and started to walk, putting one foot in front of the other, a roaring in his ears, and Gestrin slid down the embankment about fifteen yards in front of him. He'd taken off his skis and held his rifle.

'No!' Gaillard said. 'No!'

He turned away, and Gestrin shot him in the right shoulder. Gaillard lay on his back, the roaring in his ears louder, then pushed himself up on one elbow. Gestrin stood, holding the rifle across his chest, and now he started to raise it.

The roaring became the sound of an engine and a Cromwell tank came round the bend in the road. Gestrin swung to face it, raising his rifle. A burst of machine-gun fire hurled him back into a snowdrift at the side of the road.

Gaillard lay there, aware of footsteps approaching, his eyes closed, breathing deeply, hanging on to consciousness. He opened his eyes and saw to his astonishment that the officer leaning over him in a tanksuit wore a kepi.

'Oh, my God,' Gaillard said in his own language. 'Can it be true? You are French?'

'But of course, monsieur.' The officer dropped to one knee. 'My name is Dubois. Captain Henri Dubois of the 2nd French Tank Division. We are at present pushing towards Berchtesgaden. But who are you?'

'Never mind that now,' Gaillard said hoarsely. 'You know Arlberg?'

'The next village, two miles along the road from here.'

'Only two miles?' Gaillard said in wonder. 'I must have been running in circles up there.' He pulled himself up and caught hold of Dubois by the front of his uniform. 'Listen to me, my friend, and listen well for lives depend on it.'

When the half-track started across the courtyard Ritter himself was at the wheel, a dozen Finns packed in behind him, Hoffer at the machine gun. The rest followed behind on foot.

In the tower, the defenders had already retreated up the main staircase and taken up position on the first landing, except for Howard who stayed at the shattered door, peering out.

'Here they come!' he cried and started to fire his Thompson furiously.

Ritter gunned the motor, giving the half-track everything, roaring straight up the steps, hitting those shattered doors at full speed. Howard was already half-way up the marble stairs as the doors disintegrated, the half-track smashing through, sliding to a halt, broadside on.

The defenders immediately started to pour it on from the landing, Canning and Birr firing Schmeissers between the pillars of the balustrade, Howard backing them with the Thompson.

The Finns were badly caught, three or four of them going down as they scrambled from the half-track. Hoffer took a bullet in the shoulder that knocked him over the side, and Ritter, without hesitation, stood up and grabbed the handles of the machine gun.

He started to spray the landing expertly, shattering the windows behind the rows of marble statues, an awesome figure crouched behind the gun, his face pale beneath the black cap. Howard loosed off one burst after another, even standing up on occasion, all to no effect, for it was as if the German bore a charmed life.

The landing had become a charnel house, four of the Germans hit, one of them crying out continuously. Birr had taken a bullet through the right hand, and below, in the hall, at least nine of the Finns were down.

The stench of cordite, the smoke, the cries of the dying, the rattle of the machine gun in that confined space, made it a scene from hell. Birr took another bullet, in the chest this time, and went down.

Canning pulled at Howard's sleeve, eyes wild. 'This is no good – we'd better get out of here.'

'Take Birr with you,' Howard said. 'I'll cover you.'

He rammed another clip into the Thompson, and behind him the two surviving Germans got Birr by the shoulders and dragged him along the landing. Ritter stopped firing. He looked down and found Hoffer leaning against the side of the half-track, stuffing a field dressing inside his uniform blouse.

'All right, Erich?'

Hoffer nodded, his face twisted with pain, and from up there in the smoke on the landing, Howard called, 'What's keeping you, Ritter?'

Something flared in Ritter's eyes. He picked up a Schmeisser and vaulted to the floor. He did not say a word, gave no command, simply went up the stairs into the smoke and the Finns went after him.

The curtains were on fire now, the wood panelling on the walls, smoke swirling, billowing along the landing so that it was impossible to see more than a few feet. Howard fired blindly, moving a step or two, then turned and started up the stone staircase.

He paused at the bend, slinging the Thompson over his shoulder, and took two stick grenades from his belt. He could hear voices below, stumbling steps on the stair. He tossed the two grenades down into the murk, one after the other, went round the corner and continued to climb without pause.

There was an explosion below followed by another, cries of pain. He could hardly breathe now, smoke everywhere, choking the landing outside the dining hall. He groped his way round the wall, found the entrance to the upper staircase, and started to climb to the top of the tower.

Had he but known it, the others had got no further than the upper landing, Birr having collapsed completely so that the two Germans had been compelled to drag him into the dining hall.

Canning crouched over him, almost overcome by smoke waiting for the end that seemed inevitable now. He got to his feet, lurched across to the window, and smashed

610

what glass remained in the lower half. The Germans dragged Birr across the floor, choking and coughing.

They all crouched at the window, drawing in deep lungfuls of fresh air. Canning cried, 'The table – get it over.'

They crouched behind it, waiting for the end.

On the landing at the foot of the stairs, Ritter rolled over, pushing a body away from him. There was blood on him, but not his own, and he pulled himself up and leaned against the wall. A hand reached out to steady him – Hoffer.

'Are you all right, Sturmbannführer?'

'Everything in perfect working order, or so it would seem, Erich.' An old, bad joke between them, no longer funny.

A gust of wind blowing in through the shattered doorway, below, cleared the smoke from the landing. It was a butcher's shop, bodies everywhere, blood and brains sprayed across the walls.

There were perhaps a dozen Finns left alive and unwounded, crouched at the head of the stairs. Ritter glanced at his watch. It was almost 8.30.

'All right, damn you. You're still mine for another thirty minutes. Still soldiers of the Waffen-SS. Let's get it done.'

They made no move. It was not that there was fear there. Only emptiness – faces drained of all emotion, all feeling.

'It's no good,' Hoffer said. 'They've had enough.'

As smoke swirled back into place again, the Finns retreated, simply melted away.

'So?' Ritter said, and he leaned down and picked up a Schmeisser.

As he turned, Hoffer caught his arm. 'This is madness. Where are you going?'

'Why, to the top of the tower, old friend.' Ritter smiled and put a hand on his shoulder. 'We've come a long way together, but no more orders. It is over. You understand me?'

Hoffer stared at him, horror on his face. Ritter started upstairs.

When Howard lurched out of the smoke on to the roof, Finebaum almost shot him. Howard fell on his hands and knees and Finebaum crouched beside him.

'Is he all right?' Claudine Chevalier demanded.

Howard answered her, struggling for breath. 'All I need is a little air.' He looked around him. 'Where's the general?'

'No sign of him up here,' Finebaum said. 'What happened below?'

'It was bad,' Howard told him. 'The worst I've ever known.' He got up on his knees. 'I'll have to go back. See what's happened to them.'

Madame Chevalier, who had gone to the parapet to look down, cried, 'There are tanks coming. A whole column.'

Finebaum ran to join her in time to see half a dozen Cromwells, several Bren-gun carriers and trucks, moving towards the castle at full speed. The surviving Finns had just emerged from the entrance. As they started across the courtyard, the first Cromwell emerged from the tunnel and opened up with its machine gun. Two Finns went down, the rest immediately dropped their weapons and put up their hands.

Finebaum turned and found Howard leaning over the parapet beside him. 'Did you ever see a prettier sight?' Finebaum demanded. Howard gazed down blankly, eyes remote, and Finebaum shook him roughly. 'Hey, noble Captain, it's over. We survived.'

'Did we?' Howard said.

And then Claudine Chevalier cried out sharply.

Ritter stood there at the head of the stairs, smoke billowing around him. He wore no cap. There was blood on his face and the blond hair flashed pale fire in the morning light. The black Panzer uniform was covered in dust, but the Knight's Cross with Oak Leaves and Swords still made a brave show at his throat.

'Captain Howard?' he called.

Finebaum turned, unslinging his M1, but Howard knocked it up. 'My affair – stay out of it.'

He was smiling, his eyes full of life again. He leaned down slowly and picked up the Thompson.

Ritter said, 'A first-rate show. My congratulations.'

Howard fired then, a long burst that ripped the Iron Cross First Class from Ritter's tunic, hurling him at the wall. The German rebounded, falling to his knees. He flung up the Schmeisser, arm extended, firing one-handed, driving Howard back against the parapet, killing him instantly. For a moment, the young German hung on to life, on his knees there in the snow, and then he fell forward on his face.

Hoffer emerged from the smoke, a Walther in his good hand, and crouched beside him. Finebaum dropped to one knee by Howard. There was a pause, then the American's M1 came up.

It was Claudine Chevalier who finished it, her voice high on the morning air. 'No!' She screamed. 'Enough! Do you hear me? Enough!'

Finebaum turned to look at her, then back to Hoffer. The German threw down his Walther and sat back on his heels, a hand on Ritter's shoulder. Finebaum, without a word, tossed his M1 out over the parapet to fall through clear air to the courtyard below.

It was on the steps outside the main entrance that Canning met Henri Dubois for the first time. The Frenchman, a pistol in one hand, saluted. 'My respects, *mon Général*. My one regret is that we couldn't get here sooner.'

'That you got here at all is one small miracle, son.'

'We must thank Monsieur Gaillard for that.'

'Paul?' Canning caught him by the arm. 'You've seen him?'

'He escaped from the village this morning and skied across the mountains, hotly pursued by some of these Finnish gentlemen. It was only by the mercy of God that he came across us when he did. He is in the ambulance now, at the rear of the column.'

'Thanks.' Canning started down the steps and paused. 'There was a man called Strasser in the village. He was in charge of this whole damn business. He had Madame Claire de Beauville with him. Did you get them?'

'We came straight through without stopping, *mon Général*. Naturally Schloss Arlberg was our main objective, but if this man Strasser is there, we'll find him.'

'I wouldn't count on it.'

He found Gaillard on a stretcher in the ambulance at the rear of the column as Dubois had indicated. The little Frenchman lay there, a grey army blanket pulled up to his chin, eyes closed, apparently sleeping. A medical orderly sat beside him.

'How is he?' Canning demanded in French.

'He is fine, Hamilton. Never better.' Gaillard's eyes fluttered open. He smiled.

'You did a great job.'

'And the others – they are safe?'

'Claudine is fine. Justin got knocked about a bit, but he'll be all right. I'm afraid the rest makes quite a casualty report. Max is dead and Captain Howard – most of the Finns. Ritter himself. It was quite a shooting match up there.'

'And Strasser?'

'We'll get him – and Claire. Only a question of time now.'

Gaillard's face was twisted with pain, and yet concern showed through. 'Don't leave it, Hamilton. He is capable of anything that one. What he did to that girl was a terrible thing.'

'I know,' Canning said soothingly. 'You get some sleep now. I'll see you later.'

He jumped down from the ambulance and stood there, thinking of Strasser, wanting only to get his hands on his throat. And then there was Claire. Suddenly, he knew that she was by far the most important consideration now.

There was an empty jeep standing nearby. Without the slightest hesitation, he jumped behind the wheel, gunned the motor and drove out through the tunnel and across the drawbridge.

When he braked to a halt outside the Golden Eagle, the square was silent and deserted, everyone staying out of the way. There was an M1 in the rear seat of the jeep. He checked that it was loaded, then jumped out and kicked open the front door.

'Strasser, where are you, you bastard?'

It was very quiet in the bar – too quiet. He saw the bullet holes in the wall, the blood on the floor and the hair lifted on the back of his head. A stair creaked behind him. He turned and found Meyer standing there.

'Where is he?'

'Gone, Herr General. After the Finns left to hunt Herr Gaillard, he moved their field car to the rear courtyard where it was out of sight. When the French soldiers with the tanks came half an hour ago, they passed straight through without stopping. Herr Strasser drove away shortly afterwards in the field car.'

'And Madame de Beauville – he took her with him?'

615

Meyer's face was grey, his voice the merest whisper. when he said, 'No, Herr General. She is still here.'

He stumbled along the hall, opened his office door and stood back. She lay on the floor, covered by a blanket. Canning stood there, staring down, disbelief on his face. He dropped to one knee and pulled back the cover. Her face was unmarked and so pale as to be almost transparent, wiped clean of all pain, all deceit. A child asleep at last.

He covered her again very gently and when he turned to Meyer, his face was terrible to see. 'Do you know where he went?'

'I overheard them speak of it several times, Herr General. There is an abandoned airstrip at Arnheim about ten miles from here. I understand there is an aeroplane waiting.'

'How do I get there?'

'Follow the main road to the top of the hill east of the village. A quarter of a mile on there is a turning to the left which will take you all the way to Arnheim.'

The door banged. A moment later, the engine of the jeep roared into life. Meyer stood there in the quiet, listening to the sound dwindle into the distance.

At Arnheim it was snowing again as the Dakota taxied out of the hangar. Strasser, standing behind Berger in the cockpit, said, 'Any problems with the weather?'

'Nothing to worry about. Dirty enough to be entirely to our advantage, that's all.'

'Good. I'll get out now and see to the Stork. I don't want to leave that kind of evidence lying around. You turn in to position for take-off and I'll join you in a few moments.'

Berger grinned. 'Spain next stop, Reichsleiter.'

Strasser dropped out of the hatch, skirted the port wing and ran towards the entrance to the hangar as the Dakota moved away. He took a stick grenade from his pocket and tossed it through the entrance, ducking to one side. It exploded beneath the Stork, which started to burn fiercely.

He turned away, aware of the Dakota turning in a circle out there at the end of the runway, and then a jeep swung through the entrance from the road and braked to a halt about thirty yards away.

Canning was aware of the Dakota turning into the wind out there, thought for one dreadful moment that he was too late, and then the shock of the Stork's tank exploding turned his eyes to the hangar. He saw Strasser in front, crouching as he pulled a Walther from his pocket.

Canning grabbed for the M1, fired three or four shots, then it jammed. He threw it away from him and ducked as Strasser stood up, firing at him coolly, two rounds punching holes through the windshield.

Canning slammed the stick into gear, revving so furiously that his wheels spun in the snow and the jeep shot forward. Strasser continued to fire, dodging to one side only at the very last minute, and Canning slammed his boot on the brake, sending the jeep into a broadside skid.

He jumped for the German while the vehicle was still in motion and they went over in a tangle of arms and legs. For a moment, Canning had his hands on his throat and started to squeeze, and then Strasser swung the Walther with all his force, slamming it against the side of the general's head.

Canning rolled over in agony, almost losing consciousness, aware of Strasser scrambling to his feet, backing away, the Walther pointing. Canning got to his knees and Strasser took careful aim.

'Good-bye, General,' he said and pulled the trigger. There was an empty click. He threw the Walther at

Canning's head, turned and ran along the runway towards the Dakota.

Canning went after him, forcing himself into a shambling trot, but it was hopeless, of course. Things kept fading, going out of focus, then back again. The one thing he did see clearly, and it was all that mattered, was Strasser scrambling up through the hatch. The Dakota's engine note deepened, and then it was roaring along the runway.

Canning slumped down on to his knees and knelt there in the snow, watching it flee into the grey morning like a departing spirit.

16

It was almost dawn in La Huerta when Canning finished talking. Rain still tapped against the window of the bar, more gently now, but when I got up and looked out the square was quiet and deserted.

Canning threw another log on the fire. 'Well, Mr O'Hagan – what do you think?'

'Such waste,' I said. 'Of good men.'

'I know. They were all that. Not Strasser, of course. He was the devil walking, but Jack Howard, Ritter, Sorsa and those Finns . . .'

'But why?' I asked. 'Why did they persist in going through with it? Why didn't they simply tell Strasser or Bormann or whoever to go to hell?'

'Well, Sorsa and his Finns are possibly the easiest to understand. As he said, they were fighting for wages. They'd taken the gold, if you like to look at it that way, pledged their word and stuck to it – until the final carnage, anyway.'

'And Ritter?'

'He was like a man in deep water, swept along by the current, able to go only one way. He and Jack Howard were a lot alike – opposite sides of the same coin. At the end of things, I believe now that they'd both had enough. After what they'd been through, the things they'd done for their separate countries, the future held nothing. Didn't exist, if you like.'

'You mean they were looking for death, both of them?'

'I'm certain of it.'

'And Strasser, or should I say Bormann?'

'That's the terrible thing – not being sure. Remember Berger, the pilot who brought them out of Berlin? The guy who flew the Dakota out of Arnheim in the end? I found him in Italy fifteen or sixteen years ago. Dying of cancer. He was in the kind of state where a man just doesn't give a damn.'

'And?'

'Oh, he thought Strasser was Bormann all right. Last saw him in Bilbão in June of forty-five. In the ensuing years they gave him plenty of work to do, the Comrades. They looked after him.'

'I'm surprised he didn't get a bullet like the rest.'

'Well, he was something special. A pilot of genius. He could fly anything anywhere. I suppose that had its uses.'

'But all those facts,' I said, 'about what took place in the bunker. Where did they come from?'

'Erich Hoffer,' he said simply. 'He's still alive. Runs a hotel in Bad Harzberg, and when a Russian infantry unit checked out Eichmann's hideout they found one of the assistants still alive, a man called Walter König. He pulled through after hospital treatment and spent twenty years in the Ukraine. When he was finally returned to West Germany he wasn't too strong in the head so they didn't take much notice of his story at his interrogation. I heard about it from a contact in German Intelligence.'

'Did you go to see this König?'

'Tried to, but I was just too late. He committed suicide. Drowned himself in the Elbe. But I managed to get a look at the report. The rest, of course, is intelligent guesswork.'

'So, where does it all leave us?' I asked.

'I don't know. Was it Strasser at Arlberg and Bormann in the bunker or the other way round? That's what's plagued me all these years. Oh, I told it all to the Intelligence people immediately after the events.'

'And what did they say?'

'I think they thought I'd been locked up too long. As far as they were concerned, Bormann was in Berlin right to the bitter end. Strasser was something else again.'

'And what did happen to Bormann then, according to history?'

'He left the bunker at 1.30 a.m. on May 2nd. As far as we know, he didn't attempt to disguise himself. It seems he wore a leather greatcoat over the uniform of a lieutenant-general in the SS. He met his secretary, Frau Kruger, by sheer chance on his way out. He told her there wasn't much sense in any of it now, but that he'd try to get through.'

'And from that moment the myth began?'

'Exactly. Was he killed on the Weidendammer Bridge as Kempka, the Führer's chauffeur, said . . .?'

'Or later, near Lehrter Station, where Axmann said he saw him lying next to Stumpfegger? Those two bodies, as I recall, were buried near the Invelidenstrasse by post-office workers.'

'That's right and in 1972, during building work, they found a skeleton which the German authorities insist is Bormann's.'

'But wasn't that refuted by experts?'

'One of the greatest of them put it perfectly in perspective. He pointed out that Bormann couldn't be in two places at once. Dead in Berlin and alive and well in South America.'

There was a long silence. Rain continued to tap at the window. General Canning said, 'As we know, that bizarre condition is only too possible. I need hardly point out that it would also explain a great many puzzling features of the Bormann affair over the years.'

He went to the bar and poured himself another drink.

'So what now?' I asked him.

'God knows. All of a sudden I feel old. All used up. I thought I was close this time. Thought it would finally be over, but now . . .' He turned on me, a surprisingly fierce expression on his face. 'I never married, did you know that? Never could, you see. Oh, there were women, but I could never really forget her. Strange.' He sighed. 'I think I'll go home to Maryland for a while and sit by the fire.'

'And Strasser – or Bormann?'

'They can go to hell – both of them.'

'It would make a beautiful story,' I said.

He turned on me, that fierce expression on his face again. 'When I'm dead, not before. You understand me?'

It was an order, not a request and I treated it as such. 'Just as you say, General.'

I hadn't heard the car draw up, but there was a quick step in the hall and Rafael entered. 'They have sent the taxi for you from the airstrip, Señor Smith. Your pilot says it would be possible to leave now, but only if you hurry.'

'That's for me.' Canning emptied his glass and placed it on the bar. 'Can I offer you a lift?'

'No thanks,' I said. 'Different places to go.'

He nodded. 'Glad we met, O'Hagan. It passed a lonely night at the tail-end of nowhere.'

'You should have been a writer, General.'

'I should have been a lot of things, son.' He walked to the door, paused and turned. 'Remember what I told you. When I'm gone, you can do what the hell you like with it, but until then . . .'

His steps echoed on the parquet floor of the hall. A moment later, a door slammed and the taxi drove away across the square.

I never saw him again. As the world knows, he was killed flying out of Mexico City three days later when his plane exploded in mid-air. There was some wild talk of sabotage in one or two newspapers, but the Aviation Authority's inspectors turned over the wreckage and soon knocked that little story on the head.

They buried him at Arlington, of course, with full honours, as was only proper for one of his country's

622

greatest sons. They were all there. The President himself, anybody who *was* anybody at the Pentagon. Even the Chinese sent a full general.

I was still in South America when it happened and had a hell of a time arranging flights out, so that I almost missed it, and when I arrived at Arlington, the high and the mighty had departed.

There were one or two gardeners about, no one else, and the grave and the immediate area was covered with flowers and bouquets and wreaths of every description.

It started to rain and I moved forward, turning up the collar of my trenchcoat, examining the sentiment on the temporary headstone they'd put up.

'Well, old man, they all remembered,' I said softly. 'I suppose that should count for a lot.'

I started to turn away and then my eye caught sight of something lying close to the base of the stone and the blood turned to ice-water inside me.

It was a single scarlet rose. What some people would call a winter rose. When I picked it up, the card said simply: *As Promised.*